CUT SO DEEP

a Break So Soft novel

STASIA BLACK

CHAPTER ONE

Bryce Gentry of Bryce Information Technologies doesn't look up from his computer when I enter his huge corner office. Even though I know for a fact his secretary buzzed him to tell him she was sending me in.

Just from his profile I can see he's as good-looking as the online pics I saw last night when I was researching the company. Blond hair, aquiline nose. Long face and squared jaw, like a model. Not that I was paying that much attention last night. Kinda hard when Charlie kept trying to climb into my lap and bang his favorite rubber spoon on my nose. All the while yelling, "Mama! Mama!" to get my attention.

Try telling a two-and-a-half-year old that Mama needs her me-time on the laptop or you're both going to get evicted by the nasty landlord. Yeah. I shudder even thinking about Mr. Jenkins. He doesn't even *try* to pretend he isn't staring at my boobs, no matter if Charlie's with me or not. At least Mr. Jenks-a-lot waited till he caught me alone to tell me to get the rent to him by Friday or come around to some 'alternate forms of payment.' Said while blatantly rubbing at the crotch of his pants.

I stretch my neck and shake out my hands. *Focus Callie*. All that shit just means this interview is more important than ever. Which leads to the mantra I've been whispering over and over to myself all morning: *Don't fuck this up. Don't fuck this up.*

"Mr. Gentry?" I finally venture. Maybe he didn't hear the secretary when she buzzed him or notice when I came in. The wall separating his office from the reception is that cool futuristic glass that can frost and unfrost at the touch of a button. It frosted over as I opened the door. I thought Mr. Gentry had control of it, but maybe I'd been wrong and that had been the secretary as well. Am I an idiot just standing here like a stalker and he doesn't even realize there's anyone in the room with him? "I'm here for the Personal Assistant interview?"

A grunt is all that greets me in return. I stand awkwardly and look down at my shoes. I immediately frown. Shit. I polished them last night but the left one has a giant scuff down the side. They're just crappy knock-off pumps, but I thought they'd at least last the interview process. I've been desperately job-hunting all month ever since the lawyer's fees and rent and student loan repayments have started stacking up too high.

Especially when another custody hearing is looming. My stomach cramps just at the thought, even though it's the last thing I need to be focusing on right now. But God, the money. It's why I'm here. The money has to come from somewhere. Waitressing gigs aren't cutting it, no matter how many hours I work.

And after a month of job hunting, interviewing with no call-backs, turning over every damn rock possible, this is my last shot—and for a job I'm only remotely qualified for. Personal Assistant. I can do that, right? Assist a person. I'm great at thinking on my feet, helping out where needed. And I know computers and robotics. Well, I've taken classes about them anyway...

I look around the pristine room and swallow. The space isn't like the others I've interviewed in. It looks almost like one of those futuristic sets for a movie. Everything is white, glass, or chrome—the floors, the ceiling, the chairs, the desk. It's all so... immaculate. Perfect.

At least I *thought* I was qualified for the job. My hands squeeze into fists but I quickly relax them again. The listing didn't say the PA job was for the freaking *CEO* of the company. And to say that I engaged in a little... *creative truth management* on my resume would be putting it kindly. But doesn't everyone? And if I can actually pull this off... there wasn't a salary listed, it said full details would be offered at inquiry. But damn, who hasn't heard of Gentry Tech? We talked about Gentry Tech products all the time in my classes at Stanford and studied research this man developed. God, this could be the break I've been looking for.

If I don't fuck it up.

Bryce Gentry finally shuts his laptop with a loud clap and looks up at me. For a second I'm startled, just staring at him. He really is attractive, but with a Parisian suave vibe more than an overly muscled All-American football player way. No, he's sleek. The kind of guy you imagine standing in the shadows. Mysterious. Maybe smoking a cigarette. Although the blond hair does throw off the image a little. He's *really* blond, like me. And younger than I would've thought. I'd guess he's in his thirties, but just barely.

"Miss...?" He waves a hand in my direction and I hurry forward, realizing I've just been standing here stupidly instead of introducing myself like a normal human.

Damn it, Cals. Don't fuck this up!

My legs feel wobbly. I've probably only been waiting about five minutes, but it's felt like fifty. God, I hope I don't have obvious sweat stains under my pits already. I put on my extra-strength deodorant this morning, didn't I?

"Miss Cruise. Calliope Cruise." I smile enthusiastically and hold out my hand across his spotless white desk. "Or Callie. You can just call me Callie."

Awesome, way to come across like a bumbling idiot. I just can't believe I'm meeting him. And interviewing in person with him. Although it makes sense, if it's him I'd be working directly with.

Bryce Gentry's eyes finally make their way to me.

But they don't make it all the way up to my face. My excitement deflates. His gaze lands firmly on the real estate that is my chest. Of course. Never my face.

I keep my hundred-watt smile though. It doesn't falter even a few degrees. I don't know why I thought for even a few moments it would be different with this guy. Fortune 500 company or not.

You don't do the beauty pageant circuit without getting accustomed to men ogling you at every turn, even when you're only in the running for Miss *Teen* California. Not when you sprout double D's at fourteen.

He snaps out of it a lot quicker than most, at least. I slide my resume out of my faux leather folder and hand it to him.

I keep that smile plastered as I take a seat in the chair set across his desk from him. Then I jump in head first. "I was very excited when I saw the personal assistant job opening and the chance to work here. Bryce Information Technologies is at the cutting edge of short-range drone technology." Ugh, I want to punch myself. Why am I rambling about shit he already knows about his company?

I pause only to take a breath before refocusing my pitch, "I have extensive experience in public relations and communications. I also have a background in computer science, specifically machine learning and robotics, and I will dedicate myself to this job one hundred and ten percent."

I only realize that I've been slowly leaning further and further over his desk, all but entreating him as I finished my spiel. Shit. Don't look like you're begging, look like you're offering him an opportunity he can't afford to miss.

I pull down the edges of my suit coat and sit up straighter. "In short, I know I can be an asset, both to this company and to you personally."

Mr. Gentry stares at me with an unreadable expression for several moments, his head slightly tilted. Shit. What is he thinking? And does he have to be so handsome? It's worse now that I'm closer. Even his haircut looks expensive, trimmed short at the sides of his head and perfectly edging into the longer hair on top. His face is shaved totally smooth though. The kind that makes you want to run your fingers across to see if the skin is as soft as it looks.

Shit. I'm weirdly staring at his face. And his hair.

I look away even as beads of sweat break out on my brow. Am I smiling? I smile. Shit, that probably looks weird. I just started smiling all the sudden. I drop my lips into a straight line. Dammit. That probably looks even weirder. I wasn't smiling, then I smiled, then I stopped again. What. The. Hell. Am. I. Doing? And what is he thinking?

He finally looks away from me only to glance down briefly at my resume. His mouth twitches. Was that a good mouth twitch or a bad mouth twitch?

"Background in Computer Science, you said? I'm to assume that's from the undergraduate courses you listed, by name." His eyebrows go up.

His deep voice doesn't sound mocking, but I don't see that there's any other way to take it. I sit up straighter in my chair. "Yes." My voice is firm.

"But you never actually finished college." His eyes are brown. They meet mine. I still don't know how to take him or his words. I can't read him. Dammit. Even if he's mocking me, I still have to fight for this.

"I understand that it might not be *conventional* to list an unfinished degree in the educational experience area, but those courses are relevant to the work this company does." I hold my trembling hands together and hide them in my lap. "For example, in my advanced robotics course, we studied the real-time reaction simulation algorithm you and Jackson Vale developed while at MIT. You were only students, but you pushed the state-of-the-art years forward from where it had been." Good. My voice is coming out confident. I sit up even straighter, if that's possible. Fake it till you make it, right?

I continue. "I'm only on a short hiatus from Stanford, with just a semester left. So it's not that I never completed college," I smile a winner's smile, "it's that I'm about to finish and for now I'm just after some real-world experience." He doesn't have to know that with a toddler and a constant need for steady income, the thought of tackling my last twenty-one credit hours of college has been too overwhelming to even consider.

"Real-world experience." This time the lip twitch is definitely a smirk. *Bastard.* It's a struggle to keep my face open and pleasant, but I do it.

He glances back down at my resume. "Such as *The Bridge Bar & Grill?* And *Hooters?* I assume that's where these communication skills you touted were developed?"

Fuuuuuuuuuck. I knew I should've left *Hooters* off. But if I had, I'd have no work history before a year and a half ago. I worked at *Hooters* for three years, from when I turned eighteen till I was twenty-one. I had to hide it from my parents when I was still at home and going to community college for my first couple years before transferring, but it was the only place to earn any real money in our podunk-freakin' town. Plus, I was an assistant manager by the end. That counts for leadership skills.

I feel my cheeks heating up, but when I look at Bryce Gentry, his eyes aren't where I'd have predicted they'd be. He's not looking at my double D's again. He's staring straight at me. In the eye. It's like for the first time in the entire interview, he's looking at *me*.

I don't care if he's being an ass and judging me like everyone else in my life has. I keep my voice confident. "Look, I did what I had to do to get out of the tiny-ass town where I grew up. No one there ever amounted to anything special. That wasn't going to be me."

He doesn't have to know that I've already learned my lesson the hard way that I'm not a special fucking snowflake. I was an idiot with all my big dreams and princess wishes.

All I want now is to be able to pay rent and keep custody of my son, Charlie—and all *this* bastard needs to know is that I want this job and I'll do anything to get it. "I know how to work hard and do whatever it takes to get the job done."

One of his eyebrows lifts and there's challenge in his face. "Will you really, *Callie Cruise?*" Even the way he says my name is clearly mocking. My name has never sounded blonder than it does coming from his lips. "Will you really do *whatever* it takes?"

My jaw thrusts out. I can take what this guy dishes. "Absolutely."

He smiles an easy, carefree smile. "Then open the front of your shirt and take out your tits."

"What?" I choke out.

Some of his easy demeanor drops. A challenging glint enters his eye. "You said you'd do whatever it took. Do you need this job or don't you?"

I— I—

I cannot *believe* this. This is— I can't— how can this be happening in the 21st century? After Harvey Weinstein and Matt Lauer and Me Too? Yeah my assets have gotten me work, and tips, and I know that we live in a shady world where bosses still ogle their employees. But this? This man—so respected in his field, just asking so blatantly for me to... to...

Bryce Gentry waves his hand as if dismissing me. "I really thought you wouldn't be so squeamish considering your work history." He looks completely uninterested now.

I stand up, ready to spit fire at him. "I'm not a fucking prostitute!"

He stands up as well, his interest from a moment ago reappearing in a blaze. His hands are closed fists on the table as he leans over.

"Good," he says, his voice low, brown eyes blazing. "Because I don't want a fucking prostitute. If I wanted a fucking prostitute, I could hit East San Jose any time after dark. I want you, with your big titties, your gorgeous smile, and the fact that you know what a simulation algorithm is. But," he flashes a smile, and I swear it's straight from the devil itself, dimples and all, "I really do need to see the headlights in person."

I can only just stare at him. I don't even know why. This isn't the first time I've been propositioned like this. Well, all right, it's certainly never been exactly like *this*.

This office just looked so classy. Bryce is so handsome. He could have any woman he wants. It doesn't make sense.

He comes around the desk toward me and I take a step back. He holds up his hands and sits on the edge of the desk.

He's got an easy smile back on again, like we're having an everyday conversation. He seems kind of schitzo that way, moving between intensity and a California laid-back vibe. I don't know which one is really him, or if either are. If this guy is showing any of himself at all. This is clearly a game to him, and I don't know the rules.

So much is at stake for me. What am I going to do if I don't get this job? How am I going to afford a lawyer? For half a second, the panic threatens to choke me. I know from the little my ex, David, told me that his (supposedly *ex*) wife is wealthy—yeah, I found out after he broke up with me that he wasn't divorced after all, just separated. Another juicy tidbit in the train wreck that was my relationship with Charlie's dad.

And now I can barely afford an ambulance chaser type lawyer. I can't let them take Charlie. I work two jobs as it is, but it's not enough. Not enough. I look up at Bryce and he's just sitting there on the edge of the desk, staring at me, that easy, expectant expression on his face.

Shit. Shit, shit, *SHIT*. Are my options really to expose myself to Handsome Boss Man or suck off sleazy landlord Mr. Jenks-a-lot? I shudder even thinking about the second option. And that would only get me one month's rent. As opposed to what?

God, Callie, you think showing your tits to Boss Man this once is gonna be the end of it? Don't be stupid. This is just the audition. My mind scrambles for other options when I see Bryce start looking impatient again.

Oh, screw it.

I start opening the buttons on my cheap blouse. I'll figure the rest of it out later. If Bryce tries something I can't handle, I'll just start screaming. His secretary is on the other side of the glass wall, for Christ's sake.

I glance up at Bryce again. The easy smile is gone and the intensity is back. Instead of my chest though, he's watching my face. I look away, behind him at the distant Bay Area skyline. It's a magnificent view. I can even see the Golden Gate Bridge in the background. *Float away, Callie. You remember how this works, don't you? Just float away and let him do whatever he wants to your body.*

I'm at the last button. I let my shirt fall slack.

"Hold it open." Bryce's voice has gone deep.

I keep my gaze firmly on the window as I pull the shirt to the side. It's still tucked into my pants. I have to tug to get it loose enough so that it pulls all the way around the curving edges of my breasts. I look at the floor, but watch Bryce with my periphery vision.

I can always run if he makes a move toward me. But will I?

Shit. I don't know how far I'm willing for this to go. I need this job.

That's the only reason my breath is getting quicker. Right? I'm putting on a performance.

"Pull the cups of your bra down. Sit those fat luscious tits on top of them." There's a rasp to his voice now. Damn. Have I heard a man's voice like that anywhere outside of a movie?

My breath hitches as I push down the left cup and pull my breast out.

"Mmmm, that's right," he says low. "Look at that nipple. So pink and pretty and getting hard just listening to my voice."

Shit. I look down. My nipple is hard, but it's not from what he's saying. It's not. It's just cold in here. That's all. *That's all.*

Right, maybe I could believe that. If I weren't sweating. What is *wrong* with me? After everything? After—

"Look at me, Callie." My name doesn't sound stupid or immature coming from his voice now. "Look at me, in the eye."

And I do. My eyes all but snap up to obey and meet his gaze. He doesn't have his hand on his cock like I expected. His hands are braced on the desk and he's just watching me. Watching my face. Can he see how short of breath I'm getting? Did he see how I just twisted my legs together?

No. Oh my God, this is *not* turning me on. This is all so wrong. I'm disgusted by this. By this whole situation that he's putting me in. I swore I'd never be in a position like this again. *Ever again.*

"Now pull out your right tit," he says in that deep, growling voice of his, so low it's almost like it's mesmerizing me. That's what it is. I'm not doing this entirely consciously. It's some kind of spell he's got me under.

"That's riiiiiight," he says slowly. "Pull out that pretty titty, and then roll the nipple in your fingers. Grab both your breasts and rub them. Grab them like you do when you're touching yourself."

This is the most embarrassing thing I've ever done in my life. But I do it. I grab my breasts in both hands as he watches.

"That's right, twist it." He speaks through his teeth. "Like that, that's right my pretty girl. Massage them. Gently at first. Eyes on me."

I swallow even though my mouth is the driest it's ever been in my life. He slowly moves from the desk. I see it but I don't pull back. He's closer. Just a step away.

"Now I want you to pull a little rougher. Squeeze your nipple between your thumb and forefinger."

I do it.

He's so close I can smell him now. Cologne, aftershave, I don't fucking know what it is or how to describe it. But it smells manly and I can feel the warmth radiating from his hard chest.

And right then and there I decide that *no*, this is not like what happened before. It's my choice to be here. I could leave if I wanted. I could jump off this desk and bolt for the door.

But as I pant even harder—oh God, am I really panting now?—I know that for better or worse, I don't want to go yet. And not just because of needing the money. There's a telltale heat that's started in my stomach. It shoots to the place between my thighs and my panties. My cheap cotton Walmart underwear are wet. I can't— How can—?

Mr. Gentry leans in and I think he's going to touch me. But even though he's so close my hands holding my breasts are near enough to brush his chest, he only runs his nose along my cheek, never actually making contact. Like he's scenting me.

"Are you wet, pretty girl?"

Oh my God. I can feel the heat in my cheeks. He can't smell *that* from all the way up here, can he? My hands freeze on my breasts. Everything freezes. What the hell am I doing? How did I get myself into this situation?

But Bryce Gentry doesn't freeze. He moves again, this time shifting around behind me. His breath is hot in my ear as he reaches around me from behind. His hands cover mine over my breasts. "Yes, you're perfect. A perfect little slut, just for me to take out when I want to play."

At the word *slut*, he pushes my hands gently away and squeezes my nipples.

What the—? *Slut?*

The haze of everything starts to clear. This is fucked up. I came here for an interview. An interview for Christ's sake. What the hell is he talking about? He's calling me a slut and talking about me like I'm a toy. And what, is he thinking he's hiring me, as like his personal sex assistant or something—

But *shit*, that feels *good*. He's started nibbling with teasing bites at my ear while he's still massaging my breasts. God, how long has it been since I've felt this? I haven't been touched in so long. I can't even remember the last time.

It's not just hot between my legs, it's fucking pulsing down there. I need— I mean, God, I need—holy shit—can I come from just this alone? Someone playing with my breasts?

But he's not just playing. I mean, every guy I've known has just been a mauler. They get all excited about my big boobs and just start yanking on them. But this guy is like a virtuoso. I bet sex with him would be insane. Because that's what he wants, right? That's where this is leading? He wants a Personal Assistant he can fuck when he wants?

He'll just keep me up here in his office, push a button, and I'll come in and blow him or he'll fuck me or something? I'd said I'd never get this low, never degrade myself... but if it could feel like this?

I can't help the high-pitched whine that comes out of my throat. Fuck. I'm almost there. And it's been so long. So long...

I can't think. Oh God, if he would just touch me there. Maybe I could touch me there. He'd find that hot, right? And that's what this is about? Sex? What would it feel like if he was sucking on my nipple instead of just playing with his fingers? His face is so smooth-shaven, but even the thought of his tongue—

Another whine comes out of me, and he sucks and bites at the back of my neck.

Holy *shit*, that's hot.

I'm so close. So fucking close. He's gotta know. But he's not doing anything about it. Fuck it. I put my hand down the front of my pants. A girl's gotta get it done sometimes.

"That's right, my dirty girl," he hisses in my ear. "Make yourself a little whore for me."

His words should disgust me. They should *not* be turning me on even more as my fingers find my clit.

"Show me how bad you want this job. Make yourself come." His voice lowers, but the words are intense.

His grip on my breasts continues the same massaging pressure, but he's twisted my body slightly sideways so he can see my face. We're looking eye to eye and all traces of the nice guy fall away as he sneers, "Dirty bitch, I want to see your cum face, you trashy fucking bimbo whore."

The breath is knocked out of me at the nastiness of his words. And in the same instance, I come harder than I ever have before in my life.

CHAPTER TWO

"I'll see you tomorrow morning at 8:30 sharp."

Those were his parting words to me as I stumbled out of his office half an hour ago. My mind still feels like it's in a haze as I ride the light rail back to my apartment south of San Jose.

Did that just all really happen? Maybe I fell asleep in the lobby and had some crazy sex dream?

Or not. Because when I reach in my pocket, the short-term security pass I was issued is still there.

Which means... holy shit. All that really just happened. I exposed myself in front of Bryce Gentry, CEO and billionaire, and he just hired me on to be his—what? Am I just there for sex or will I actually be doing any work? Did I just accept a job as a sex worker? As a prostitute? Because isn't that what accepting money for sex is? Holy shit, holy shit, *holy shit*.

It's getting close to five o' clock and the train is packed. I'm holding onto one of the poles and sweating through my cheap suit. I feel sick. This is what I've fought against my whole life. To be an object to be used by men. To be their whore. I remember his words right at the end. Dirty bitch. Trashy fucking bimbo whore.

It makes other words echo in my ears: *Tell anyone and you'll be sorry.*

No one will believe a whore like you, and I'll get your daddy fired from the bank. Besides, you're just a little slut like always, begging for it.

I squeeze my eyes shut in fury at the humiliation and degradation of those words. I always swore I'd *never* be what Mr. McIntyre claimed all those times when he came into my room. My parents invited dad's boss over twice a month for dinner where they got as drunk as skunks and never noticed Mr. McIntyre didn't leave as soon as they stumbled up to their room. He started touching me when I was sixteen and threatened that he'd get my dad fired if I ever told anyone. It lasted until I left for Stanford at nineteen.

I hated him. *Hated* what he did to me.

So how could I *come* after Bryce said such similar things?

I swallow hard even as tears bite at my eyes. Dammit. I'm almost at my stop. I press angry palms at my eyes for a second to get myself under control. Okay. No way am I breaking my record of not crying for a year and a half, not over *this*.

Then I push my way through the bodies toward the doors as the train rocks to a stop and the bell sounds. I'm almost to the doors when someone grabs my ass and squeezes hard.

"Who did that?" I turn around and yell. "Who just grabbed my ass?"

There are so many people pushing past me—men in business suits and guys in beanie caps, guys with dreadlocks and a few that look like college kids. People pushing in and out. Then the doors are closing.

I jump off the train at the last second. "Damn it!" I yell, stomping my foot like a five-year-old.

But what the hell? What is it about my body that says: 'feel free to grab here?'

That's it. I'm fucking done.

I will not be anyone's whore. I'm NOT going back to that office tomorrow.

I speed walk the six blocks home. It's light out, so I'm safe, but I still keep my eyes peeled. The neighborhood where I live is in the transition area between the good part of San Jose and the bad. On nights I work at the bar and can't catch a ride home, I sleep on the couch in the office and walk home the following morning. Which only works because my sister, Shannon, lives with Charlie and me. Not that Shannon ever believes I'm actually ever just sleeping on a couch at the bar the nights I don't come home. My older sister's favorite pastime has always been judging me.

Of course, getting knocked up by my married—even though I thought he was divorced!—philosophy professor my first year away from home didn't help my case. Yeah, ever lived a cliché and not realized it until afterwards? That was me.

I sigh. Shannon is a Godsend, really. I should be more grateful. When I showed up preggers, my parents cut me off and made it more than clear that I was not welcome on their doorstep. But Shannon stuck by me. She moved in to help with the baby and rent. She works from home doing graphic design work and takes care of Charlie at night while I work. She's great with him. She's super smart and is kind of the definition of a good person...

I really should be more grateful.

I turn my keys and push open the door. All I want to do is grab a bottle of wine and forget everything that happened today, much less what I'm going to do tomorrow. Or where I'm going to get the money to pay for a lawyer better than the shitty one I hired the first time. Let alone rent. God, the next hearing is in a month, and I still owe eight-hundred dollars in back fees to the first crappy lawyer. What the hell am I going to do? Maybe let's skip the wine and go straight to vodka.

Charlie's high-pitched wailing greets my ears when I step inside. The sound makes my stomach clench. I want to hold him to make him feel better at the same time as I wish there was someone else to deal with him so I could sit down for five minutes to decompress from the day. Shame immediately hits as I close the door. Am I that bad a mom?

"Where have you been?" Shannon shouts to be heard over Charlie, a hand on her forehead. She looks exhausted and beyond stressed out. I drop my bag by the front door and hurry over to where Charlie sits in his high chair by the kitchen table. Food is smeared all over his face and he keeps shaking his head back and forth when Shannon tries to spoon in another mouthful. I can tell by his overall demeanor that he's overtired.

"Aw, baby, baby," I croon to him. I go to give him a kiss on the head, but then think better of it when I see how goopy he is.

"Did he not get his afternoon nap?" I ask Shannon as I rinse a washcloth in warm water.

Shannon stares daggers at me as Charlie keeps up his wailing.

"I'm the one who actually knows his schedule." Her shrill voice cuts over Charlie's cries. "I don't just pop in and out of his day whenever I want to."

What the hell? I just walked in the door and she's gonna give me this crap?

I stop and take a deep breath. *She's a Godsend, Callie. You and Charlie really rely on her. Just keep your cool.*

I wipe his face and then the tray free of the baby cereal-chicken combo that Shannon was trying to feed him. This is just an initial wipe down. There's still some in his hair and on his neck. He's going to need a bath, but that's part of the nighttime ritual anyway.

Shannon keeps on going. "Charlie's exhausted. He woke up early from his nap because *somebody* kept ringing the doorbell when I didn't get there fast enough. You know how he hates the doorbell." She flings it like an accusation.

I throw my hands up, exasperated. "How is that my fault? I wasn't even here! I didn't do anything."

"You didn't do anything," she scoffs under her breath. "That's right. You never do."

My shoulders stiffen and it takes every ounce of my limited energy to bite my tongue. *Keep your fucking cool.*

Shannon leaves Charlie wailing in his high chair and grabs a manila envelope from the kitchen table.

Oh shit. My heart sinks to my stomach. I've seen an envelope like this before. Twice. First when Charlie's father requested the paternity test and then six months ago when I got the first notice of an initial child custody hearing.

"You *didn't* make Charlie's father sign away any claim he had on his child when you told him you were pregnant," Shannon says, "That's what you *didn't* do. You *didn't* manage to get a good enough lawyer to keep such a so-called 'father' from getting joint custody even though he told you to," she leans in and whispers the next word, "*abort* our precious baby, but suddenly two and a half years later decides he wants him. And now there's another custody hearing in two months when he's going to try to take our little boy away from us for good." Tears rim her eyes. "What's your excuse going to be then, huh?"

She spins and heads out of the room toward her home office. "I have work to do. Why don't you do something out of the ordinary for once and be a mother?"

My hands curl so tightly into fists that my nails cut my palm. It's only Charlie's continued cries that make me force myself to take a deep breath.

In. Out. In. Out.

I can't let my sister's bitchiness or even that envelope on the table affect my time with my son. I knew it was just a matter of time before this stupid notice arrived.

I couldn't understand it at first, when David's lawyer first contacted me requesting a paternity test. A really stupid part of me hoped it meant David wanted us back. That he'd realized what a huge mistake he'd made. That his family was here waiting for him. Maybe he'd left his wife for real this time.

God, I don't know how I had any naïveté left in me at that point, but seeing David and his lovely wife at the first custody hearing quickly remedied me of any lingering romanticism left in my soul.

They were vicious. They skewered my character, lied and said I'd never told David about the baby and made it clear that while their initial motion was for joint custody since he'd never had any contact with his son before, their intention was to push for full. Their lawyer was polished, well-spoken, presented point after point with utmost precision and made what were several very apparent inside jokes with the judge.

And my lawyer? He had a mustard stain on his shirt, had prepared me *all wrong* for the hearing, and only cared about getting the money in back child support—out of which his fees would come. David was only happy to pay (money I'd later find came from his wife's trust fund). Two and a half years in back-child support should have been a Godsend. Except that the hospital bills for my C-Section and Charlie's two day NICU stay ate up almost all of it. I had just enough left to *mostly* pay off the lawyer and that was that.

I look at my poor baby with his red face and the fat tears rolling down his cheeks. "Oh sweet baby," I coo, my heart breaking. "What a mess." I don't just mean the food that's all over his face and covering the tray in front of him.

God, Shannon doesn't even know about the back-rent that's due. She'd kill me if she knew I hadn't been keeping up on my half of the payments. The little extra I did have I'd been giving Mr. Jenks-a-lot to bribe him not to tell Shannon about it. But he made it clear he won't let me float another month. Dammit. It's not like it would make a difference if Shannon had known all along—she doesn't have the money either.

"It's gonna be okay, baby," I whisper to Charlie, hugging him close. "You need to eat a little more, but it's been a rough day on both of us. How about some applesauce?"

"App-sas," he repeats, his whimpering calming down slightly. "App-sas, app-sas."

Some Mama-attention and sweet treats are always good for the soul. It's a good thing he doesn't know about chocolate yet.

Charlie does well with the applesauce. Bath turns into play time like always and, though there's more whining than usual when he gets out, he falls asleep quickly and without much fuss. That's always been my saving grace with Charlie—he's a great sleeper.

When I close the door behind me and head to the kitchen, I'm less than thrilled to see my sister there making herself a sandwich. I head straight for the wine. I'll be a little classier than straight vodka tonight. Besides, wine and chocolate together are like, a thing, right? In Europe or something? Well, it's gonna be a thing in my kitchen tonight.

I reach up on top of the refrigerator where I keep my chocolate bars. I frown when I pull down just half of a Hershey's. I know for a fact there were two full bars there yesterday. I turn and look accusingly at Shannon. "Did you eat my chocolate?"

She shrugs and turns her back as she spreads mayo on a slice of bread. "It was in the kitchen, I figure it's fair game," is her only response.

"But you know I buy it especially for when I have cravings."

She shrugs again.

I bite my cheek and huff out a breath. It's not worth getting into a fight over. It's not worth getting into a fight over. If I repeat it enough times, I'll start to believe it, right?

I unwrap what's left of the bar and take a giant bite. The chocolate on my tongue makes me feel slightly better. At least until I reach for the bottle of wine. And see that it's only half full.

"What the hell, Shannon?" I all but explode.

She finally turns around to look at me. "What?" She crosses her arms over her chest.

"Stop eating my chocolate and drinking my wine."

"They didn't have your name on them."

It's such a goddamned childish thing to say.

"What are we, nine-year-olds?"

Her jaw locks. "Apparently some of us live as if we were." She nods toward the manila envelope on the table behind me that so far I've managed to avoid thinking about. "You live like a child, as if you don't have any responsibilities."

I step up to her, forefinger pointed at her chest. "You don't know what the hell you're talking about," I all but growl.

She smacks my finger away. "Don't I? I'm the one who's here, living with you and helping you raise your son because you're the naïve idiot who got knocked up by her married professor. You actually thought he'd leave his wife for you?" She shakes her head.

Even after all this time, her words sting. Because I was exactly what she's accusing me of. I was naïve. I was stupid.

I was officially a junior when I took David's class, though it was my first year on a real campus. I transferred to Stanford with credits built up from AP classes and an accredited online college. It was unusual that I got in like that, but apparently my entrance essay won over the board—impoverished, small town beauty pageant girl dreams of studying computer science and becoming a robotics engineer.

Then I took philosophy my first semester and met David. He was so charismatic, so worldly, so wise. It was thrilling when he, a *professor*, wanted to spend time with me outside of class. When he said he wanted to mentor me because I had such a unique mind, unlike any he'd seen in his fifteen years of teaching, I was star-struck.

The night I first kissed him, he pushed me away at first. It seemed like a genuine fight against his conscience before he finally returned my embrace.

My stomach sours now at the memory. He should've taught acting instead of philosophy. He certainly had me fooled. I believed everything. I believed him when he said he'd never met someone like me before. That he'd never even been tempted to start a relationship with a student before me. That I was special to him. When he said words like forever, I swallowed them hook, line, and sinker.

"He said they were divorced—" I defend weakly.

Shannon rolls her eyes. "Sure, sure. I've heard your sob story a hundred times. I stood up to Mom and Dad for you."

"You didn't do it for *me*," I say, calling her on it. We were always at each other's throats growing up. She thought I was spoiled. Our parents' golden child. Until I wasn't. "You did it for Charlie."

"Well, someone had to," she fires back, eyes blazing. "Someone had to take care of that baby. Or do you not remember when I bailed you out of *jail* while you were *pregnant*? It's not Charlie's fault..." She stops herself, but just barely.

"Just say it," I spit at her, my heart pumping wildly. I've always known this was what she secretly thought of me. This is just the first time she's even come close to letting it out.

Her arms lock tighter around her chest and her lips purse. "Say it," I demand, but finally I just say it for her. "It's not his fault *who his parents are.*"

I pull back from her and for a second, I can see myself how she sees me. Really, isn't it the vision I try to fight against every day? That used up, pathetic, broken mess I let David make of me?

We talked so often about a future together. When I was throwing up on Easter Sunday and peed on four sticks to quadruple check it, I felt confident David would welcome the news of our coming baby. When he instead said that this was a sign things have been moving too fast, gone too far and that I needed to get rid of it... I was so shocked I thought it was a nightmare. I kept waiting to come to. I started slapping myself to wake myself up. David said I was crazy and I needed to leave. He said he'd been getting tired of our arrangement anyway and this was the last straw.

I went a little insane.

I don't exactly know what happened then, though the shame of it will follow me until my dying day. I was so weak. So horribly weak. David was my everything, it was all I could see.

I camped outside his door for a week, begging him to tell me what was wrong, to take me back, to do whatever we had to in order to fix it. I would have done anything, been *anything* for him. It literally just wouldn't sink in why he was acting the way he was. I had crazy thoughts, like someone was forcing him to say the things he was, that his ex-wife was blackmailing him, like happened in the books I read— somehow he was being forced to lie to me when in actuality he loved me as much as he'd always said he did.

But none of that was true.

He threatened to call the police if I didn't stop harassing him. Little by little, it finally started sinking in. My beloved David had turned into a stranger and I felt like I was living someone else's life. Even living in someone else's body because of the changes the pregnancy was wreaking on me. It was like being dropped into a parallel universe where no one and nothing was the same. Nothing made sense. Except that I realized David was a liar.

After going days without sleep and having David threaten to call the cops on me, I slid even further down the stupidity ladder. I came back to his house in the middle of the night, bashed in all the windows on his car and then set it on fire. He really loved that stupid car.

The satisfaction at having done it was short-lived, however.

The cops finally came.

Having morning sickness while being in County lockup? Yeah, that's exactly as fun as it sounds. David only agreed not to press charges as long as I promised to leave him alone. That and not report him to the administration. Relationships with students weren't grounds for dismissal—the faculty involved was supposed to report them as soon as they started and David hadn't. Because unofficially, they were frowned upon. It was why he said we had to keep it a secret the whole time we were together. By the end of the whole mess, I would have said anything to be finished with all of it.

Or so I thought. After all that, I never thought about having him sign documents officially giving up paternity of Charlie. Everything settled down and I got counseling at a local women's center. The last thing I ever expected was for David to suddenly decide to fight me for custody two-and-a-half years later.

And win.

Ever since the initial hearing, David's been getting Charlie each Wednesday and every other weekend. I laugh bitterly to myself. Because it's not just David—it's him and his wife who swoop in and take my little boy away from me twice a week. It's her who has the trust fund and whose father is a judge.

Yeah.

I don't know why out of the blue David decided he wanted to be part of Charlie's life, but I suspect it had something to do with the shrew wife. Maybe her biological clock finally started ticking, but it was too late to do anything about it—that thought makes me happy, the idea of David with a dried-up old shrew. But no, from the little he told me, she's a few years younger, only in her late thirties. So, maybe she doesn't want a baby to disturb her perfect figure.

Either way, she found out about my Charlie. Now she's trying to take him for her own.

And if I don't find the money for even a semi-competent lawyer... We're so screwed...

Shannon's eyes fixate on the manila envelope. It's opened and I know she's read through every page. She runs her hands through her hair and then down her face. All of the sudden, the bitchy attitude drops and when she looks back at me, I can see how scared she is.

"What if they take Charlie away from us?"

It's what I've been fighting not to think about. But seeing Shannon, my always untouchable older sister, look afraid puts the fear of God in me.

"They won't." I reach out and grab her hands. "I won't let them."

She scoffs and tries to pull out of my grasp, but I don't let her.

"I swear, Shannon." I move so I'm standing closer to her, forcing her to meet my eyes.

"I got a job today." As soon as it pops out of my mouth, I know it's the only way. I don't even blink as the realization sets in.

I have to keep the job.

Everything was so insane earlier I didn't get the exact salary, but I know from my research before I applied that similar positions in the area can bring in as much as sixty or even seventy thousand dollars a year. I can't turn down that kind of money, not when it means the difference between keeping Charlie or not.

Shannon starts to speak, but I cut her off and squeeze her hands even harder. "Not just another waitressing gig. I'll be making *real* money. Enough to hire a great lawyer."

I can tell she doesn't believe me but I shake her a little. "I swear. I'm not going to fuck up this time. We won't lose Charlie. We *won't*." And as I say the words, I'm making a solemn vow. I *will* do whatever it takes, no matter what.

Which means, tomorrow morning, I'll be heading straight back into the lion's den.

Whatever it takes.

CHAPTER THREE

"Good morning Miss Cruise, I trust you slept well last night?"

I nod and my best pageant smile is back out and in full force. I didn't win Little Miss Siskiyou County for nothing.

For Bryce's part, he's all easy-going charm. If anything, he seems amused by the front I'm putting up.

"Lovely." He waves me forward into his office from where I'm standing by the door. "To get started, I've got a stack of forms from HR. Then we'll begin going over your list of duties. Your office is beside mine."

He gestures at a door I hadn't realized was there before. It's on the side wall, perpendicular to the wall of the door I entered through. With a touch of a button under his desk, the glass unfrosts and a door slides open to the side. I can see every inch of what will be my office through the now-clear glass. My eyes widen.

"I find it most *convenient*," he smirks, "to have my personal assistant close by whenever I may have need of you."

I swallow, stepping toward the door and taking in the room. Like Bryce's office, the three internal walls are made of glass that can be clear or frosted, with the fourth a window to the outside. The offices have a spectacular view of the Bay.

With only the wall between us unfrosted, no one from the rest of the office will be able to see in. I look back at Bryce. He's still just wearing a casual smile, like we're friends out for a beer after work.

My chest feels tight. So... what? We'll be, like, having sex in here while everyone else just goes about their day? How exactly will this work? I hate the not knowing.

"So what are my, um," I stumble over my words, then blink, hating that I'm put in this awkward, bumbling position, "*duties?*"

I lift my chin higher. Screw him. I might have to do this, but I don't have to lose my dignity.

His head quirks to the side. "You're here of your own free will. Remember that, Miss Cruise. If you enter into this—" he tilts his head to the side as if searching for the right word, "—arrangement, I'm not forcing you."

Then the easy charm dissipates and the edge from yesterday comes back into his voice. "But if you agree and sign those forms, you'll not betray my trust. If you ever do, things will go very badly for you."

Chills race down my spine. Not the good kind. This motherfucker's scary. Scary like he was at the end of the 'interview' yesterday when his easy-going-guy façade dropped and I saw the flash of pure meanness. What the hell am I getting myself into?

But then I think of Charlie, nestled so secure in his bed last night. I think of my promise to Shannon. I think of my empty bank account. I can't let David and his wife take Charlie from me.

"I won't disappoint you," I manage to say through my tight throat. "Also, um, we never discussed the actual salary for the position."

"Didn't we?"

"No." I would have remembered. "Is it an hourly wage or yearly salary?"

"Yearly."

That's all the bastard offers, even though it's obvious what I'm trying to get at. It feels like some kind of power play, him making me beg for every scrap.

"And what *is* that yearly salary?" I say, smiling with gritted teeth.

"Ah, of course." He looks down at his desk and searches through some papers there. "Procuring employment is such a mercenary business, isn't it?" he says in the way someone would an off-handed comment. "All about what services or part of our souls we're willing to part with for such and such compensation."

The words sting like a slap. Sure he just described business as a whole, but it was also basically the definition of prostitution.

"Here we are," he holds up a paper with a broad smile on his face. He runs his finger down the page, eyes scanning back and forth. He mumbles under his breath, as if skimming the document, then announces, "Eighty-five."

I stop breathing. Wait. Does he— "What?" I squeak out when I finally manage to gasp a breath.

"Eighty-five," he repeats, looking over the top of the paper at me.

"*Thousand?*" I ask, my voice still unnaturally high. "Eighty-five thousand?"

"Yeeeeeees," he draws out the word. "That's what I said." Both his eyebrows lift until he's staring at me as if I'm especially slow. It's not completely unfounded either. My brain is moving slow. Eighty-five thousand. Holy shit. That's about twenty thousand more than I was really expecting. With that kind of money...

Finally my brain catches up to the moment and I shake my head to clear it.

Once it does, I don't hesitate. "I need an advance on my first paycheck." I keep my eyes firmly on his and manage not even to show my nerves by swallowing like I have the sudden urge to do. "Today."

He doesn't hesitate. "Done. Direct deposit information is part of the packet. Fill out your information and the money will be wired to your account by the end of the business day. Now, I'll give you a couple of hours to get through the forms and set up your email on your computer. You'll also find a cellphone that I expect you to have on you at all times, so set that up as well. Then I have a meeting at eleven that I'd like you to attend and take notes for."

"Oh," I say, trying not to sound too surprised. So I *will* actually be doing real work. Thank God. I smile, and it's the first genuine one since I've walked through the door. "Excellent."

He smiles back and waves me toward the door to my office, then sits down at his desk. He turns to his computer that's gone dark in the time he's been away from it. He leans over, puts his eye to an eye scanner I'm just now noticing is attached to the side of his screen. Then he lays his hand on another small dark rectangular plate that lights up at his touch.

Damn, if I didn't get it that I'm working with some top-secret high-tech shit, it's starting to sink in. This company must deal in big stakes. I know they make drones and just got a big Department of Defense contract from what I read online, but damn.

I pull my purse up on my shoulder and head the way he gestured a moment ago.

"Oh, Callie, one last thing."

I look over my shoulder. "Yes?"

"After you sign the non-disclosure agreement, take off your shirt. You'll work the rest of the morning until the meeting with those fat juicy tits of yours on display. No bra either. I want to see your nipples and remember what it was like having them between my fingers."

Then he goes back to his computer, typing in something on what looks like a password screen. Like nothing unusual just came out of his mouth.

Meanwhile I just stand there for a second, slack-jawed. He can't be serious. What the hell? It's only the hundredth time I've had that thought in the brief time I've spent with this guy.

He's not just some small-time grocery store manager. He has big time government contracts, for fuck's sake. But then it sinks in. Of course. He's a wealthy, powerful man. Used to getting whatever he wants.

And I'm a nobody.

Don't even think of ever telling. No one would believe you, you little bitch. It'd be your word against mine. And who'd ever believe a little nothing bitch like you? I'm the richest man in town. I'll fire your father and then you'll have nothing. Nothing.

I cringe at the memory and then shake my head. This is nothing like that. I'm not a teenage girl anymore. I'm a grown woman with choices.

Choices. Right. I could always choose to walk away, knowing it could mean I lose my son.

Eighty-five thousand dollars a year.

So maybe I don't have that many more choices than I did when I was sixteen after all.

Screw it. Choice is overrated anyway. Besides, it's not like it'll be that much different than working at Hooters. There was just thin fabric separating my boobs from guys staring at them all day when I worked in the restaurant.

And I already decided last night. Bryce just momentarily threw me off guard by being courteous and professional and then it was all *boom* out of left field, 'take off your shirt.' But yeah, I gotta always keep it in mind—as far as Bryce Gentry is concerned, civility is only a slim mask.

I let out a slow breath and walk toward my office. The room is decorated very similarly to Bryce's. It's smaller, but it has the same chrome and white furniture and ultra-modern feel—the kind of place you imagine a Bond villain would use as his lair.

Slapping the paperwork on the desk, I glance down. Naturally, the NDA packet is first. It's not just a single page either. Nope, it goes on for pages and pages. I can only imagine what the actual work contract will be like. Glancing at it below the NDA, I can see it's a giant stapled stack of papers as well. And you better believe I'll go through every page of that damn thing with a fine-toothed comb.

But the NDA I want to just get over with. Bryce was taunting me. He probably thought I'd put off his request. Leave it until the end of the paperwork as some sort of passive rebellion. Screw that. This is what it is.

He's paying for tits, he gets tits.

I read through it quickly. It's long and wordy, with lots of scary legal jargon for all possible infractions regarding the leak of any information I might learn while employed by Gentry Tech. I sign it quickly and then yank off my suit jacket.

If he wants to make this some kind of power play, I get it. He has the power. Hope it makes him feel like a big man.

The childish part of me wants to dramatically throw my jacket and shirt at the window between our rooms. Maybe a shoe while I'm at it. Instead, I calmly walk over to a tall cupboard I notice at the back of the office. My room is smaller than his, but still impressive. All the white is frankly annoying, but it is sleek. When I pull open the door to the cupboard, I not only find hooks to hang up my shirt and jacket, I find *clothes* inside.

In my size. Okay, cause that's not creepy.

Bryce's voice suddenly fills my office. "I'll expect you to take the wardrobe home and dress in appropriate attire from now on."

I spin around. He's still sitting in the chair in his office, not even looking my direction. My gaze goes back to my desk. There's a small, sleek mini triangle tripod thingy I've seen on TV that must be the intercom and maybe even phone system.

But yeah. As if the glass wall didn't give it away, it's clear there's never going to be any privacy. Ever.

"And I believe I said that the bra needs to go as well, Miss Cruise."

Fucker.

I turn my back to him and force myself not to visibly react. He might be putting me in this position but really, it's my circumstances that have me between a rock and a hard place. I smirk. No pun intended. Christ. Maybe it's not so bad after all if I'm still making jokes.

I breathe out a long breath, then take off my bra and hang it along with my shirt and jacket on some empty hangers. I take another quick moment to flip through the rack of clothing. It feels expensive. Silks and fine thread-count wools. All skirts and low-cut blouses. *Shocker.*

At least Bryce's predictable. He thinks he holds the power but apparently all straight males can be moved by the influence of a big rack and a swaying ass. I can use that. I turn around and sit down at my desk without glancing his way. If this is a game to him, I've just been tossed in the deep end. Now I only have to learn how to swim, and fast, or else be swallowed by sharks.

———

At four-thirty, I glance again at the little clock at the bottom of my computer screen. I've almost survived my first day of work. And it's been, well... exceedingly *normal*. Except for the not wearing a shirt for the first half of a day.

But ever since we left for the meeting, Bryce was a perfect gentleman. A charismatic employer.

We greeted several of his research and development team department heads in the conference room and they talked about ongoing projects as Bryce got status updates. It was overwhelming as I tried to follow what the hell was going on and take even semi-competent notes. Yeah, I studied coding and robotics in college, but not even *remotely* at the level of the stuff they were talking about at that meeting. Bryce understood it, or seemed to, though a lot of what he does as the CEO is delegation at this point.

Meanwhile, I realized I'm in over my head, and way more than I thought this morning. Ever since we got back from the meeting, I've been googling note-taking strategies, because I've got to come up with something faster than trying to write down every word. That wasn't cutting it. Writing up the notes was probably supposed to take half an hour but it took me almost two. And I still only caught maybe half of everything that was said. I need to read up more on the Gentry Tech products in general so I can keep afloat of what's going on. They're most famous for their drone research, but they also work in all kinds of surveillance technology. Bryce's famously (or infamously, depending on who you ask) quoted as saying that Gentry Tech products will be the "eyes on the globe." Whether you consider his company big brother or not, he's doing massively ambitious work here.

And shit, am I going to lose this job because I can't do the actual *work* involved? Would that make me feel better or worse than if I lost it because of taking the moral high ground?

"Miss Cruise?" Bryce's voice comes over the intercom.

Double shit. I look over at him. I emailed him the notes document half an hour ago after lunch, but that was probably way after he expected them. He's not looking at me. Is he going to fire me over the intercom?

"Roll your chair over to the window."

Wait. My brain can't follow for a second. What?

"Don't keep me waiting." He sounds impatient, so I do what he says even though it doesn't make any sense. How can I finish working through the emails he sent me to answer if I'm not at my computer? I roll my chair over close to the window anyway.

"Pull your skirt up to your thighs and take off your panties."

I blink.

"Miss Cruise?"

Right. *Sex job*. I follow the instructions, but simultaneously feel like I want to both laugh and cry. I can't believe I got so caught up for the last few hours thinking about this like a real job.

It's just, it *felt* real for a little while there. In front of his colleagues, he treated me like I was a real Personal Assistant. He introduced me as if I was. I let myself forget. Because I'm a stupid girl.

But I won't be. Not anymore. I stiffen my back as I kick off my panties and push up my skirt. It bunches uncomfortably at my waist and I sit back on the chair. The smooth leather feels strange against my ass.

Bryce keeps working without looking up. I just sit there. He still doesn't look up.

"Um," I finally say. "I'm here. In position."

"I know," is all he says.

I can't help the breath of air that huffs out. Bastard. God, what does he want from me? To just sit here like some pornographic statue for the last hour of the day while he finishes up?

He lets me sit there another good long while. Five minutes. Ten.

Finally, he decides to grace me with his attention.

He stands up and pulls his chair to roll with him as he walks over to the glass. He pauses on the other side of the glass right in front of me. He sits down with that charming smile firmly in place.

"Open your legs, Callie." His voice isn't muted at all even though the door between the rooms is still closed. It's coming through the intercom. Handy trick. "Spread them wide. I want to see your cunt."

I sit perfectly straight and do as I'm told. Last night, this is how I determined I'd approach everything he requests of me. Do it without thinking. Be a robot. He wants a monkey on a string, fine. That's what I'll be.

"Wider."

I stretch my legs open wider, eyes focused on the outside wall where I can look out on the city. I'll pretend I'm in one of those cars on the bridge, driving far, far away from here.

"Put your fingers on your pussy lips and open so I can see."

I do.

He makes a tutting noise. "Ah ah ah, Callie, you're being a naughty girl. You aren't even a little bit wet. I want to look at a pretty, juicy, wet cunny. And you're going to give me want I want, aren't you, my pretty little slut?" His voice deepens. "Look at me. Callie." His voice is sharp as he calls my name. "*Calliope*. Eyes on me."

My eyes snap to his. His brown eyes are so dark they seem to bleed into the pupils.

"That's right," he croons. "Eyes on me. Don't you dare take them away. You signed the contracts this morning. You're mine. Stick a finger in your mouth."

My anger flares before I shut it down. *Robot, Cals, you're a robot.*

I pop my forefinger in my mouth and pull it out again, but he's quick to stop me. "Suck on it," he hisses.

Reluctantly, I stick it back in my mouth.

"That's right," he says with a lazy smile. He leans back in his chair. In the bottom of my periphery, I can see his hands are going to his pants. He unbuckles them and pulls his cock out. He's uncut and he pulls the skin back—

I snap my eyes back up to his. Dammit. Why did I let my eyes go there?

"It's okay my pet. I want you to look. Look at my hard cock and suck harder on your finger." And, a second later. "You're not sucking hard enough." The hard edge to his voice. "And look."

I suck, and I look.

His cock is big. Not gigantic or anything, but bigger than the couple I've ever encountered before—and only one of those was a man I actually slept with. Mr. McIntyre never actually went *that* far. Everything else, but not that.

Isn't that the irony?

Here I am. The whore who's only officially slept with one man in her twenty-two years.

Bryce doesn't jerk at it frantically like I've seen other guys do. No, he just rolls his hand lazily, up and down, up and down with a little twist when he reaches the head. A wet drop slips out the slit and then he rubs that all around the head so that it glistens a little in the well-lit room.

I swallow.

Bryce laughs. "Now stick that finger in your cunt. I can see I'm starting to make you wet. That's right, whore, stick it up in there."

A rush of mortification swarms me. I want to turn away from him. But no. This is what I signed up for.

Just do what he says. Be a robot. Be a goddamned robot. I jam my fore-finger up in my vagina, a little harder than necessary. He can get off. That's what this is about. But I don't have to. I can still walk out of here with my dignity.

But it's like the bastard can read my thoughts. "Aw, did I hurt my precious slut's feelings? I'm sorry, baby." His voice is soft. Like he genuinely cares, in spite of calling me a slut. "You need to learn when I say these things, it's because you're *mine*. I like that pretty pussy of yours. You don't have to come today. But you're still going to touch yourself. Put your thumb on your clit and stick two fingers in your pretty pussy. Stretch yourself while you rub and look in my eyes."

I do what he says and look at him. That's the most difficult part, I swear. Because his words are one thing. They're crass. They're dirty. Sometimes they're even mean. But he looks at me with this intensity. A sort of want that borders on *craving*.

And he's touching himself. "That's right. That's riiiiiiight. You know how hard you're making me right now? All I can think about is ramming into that dirty little pussy of yours. Stretching you open so fucking wide." He only breaks gazes with me enough to look down at me touching myself. Unwittingly, I do the same. I look down at him pulling on his cock. He's rougher now. He's still not quick about it, though. Like he's not letting himself rush the experience.

In spite of my determination not to let myself be affected, it's absurdly hot. This attractive, put-together and powerful man, in his suit and tie but with that most intimate part of himself out on display... When I look at his face, I can see his teeth are gritted and his jaw is tensed. And those eyes. They're heated, every ounce of his energy and power directed at me and his pleasure.

His eyes look back down at what I'm doing between my legs. And fuck it, I'm grinding into my hand. My back bows against the leather chair because Christ, it feels good. I've never felt things like this bastard pulls out from me.

Sex with David had been sedate. Some missionary, but more often than not, he just wanted me to suck his cock after he'd had a long day of teaching or office hours. Which worked for me because I rarely if ever came when David and I had sex. That was part of what I liked about being with him. Not cumming during sex made it feel... *cleaner* somehow. Like it meant I was finally different from the girl I used to be. Different from the *little Barbie* Mr. McIntyre liked to play with on those shame-drenched nights in my darkened bedroom.

I glare at Bryce because I can see the satisfaction in his face. He knows what he's doing to me. He can probably see how engorged I'm getting. How wet he's making me.

I arch again in spite of myself. Why? God, why does *this* turn me on? It's wrong. So fucking wrong.

Come on, little Barbie, we'll make each other feel good. It's not wrong if we both feel good.

"You're fucking juicing for me now, aren't you?"

Bryce stands up and presses one hand to the glass, leaning over with his cock in his other hand. I bet it's the same posture as when he's jacking off in the shower.

Because as disgusted as I am with myself, I can't stop the fascination at what I'm seeing. I witnessing something terribly intimate. Yes, I'm touching myself in front of him, but he's doing the same. Just the thought and the sight of him so hard right in front of my face sends another wave of heat between my legs.

Because he's not a dirty old man or some disgusting pageant judge touching himself in front of me. It's Bryce Gentry. He's gorgeous. He's watching and waiting for my pleasure. Oh God, but this is still so *wrong*. My back arches again as the pleasure rises higher inside me.

His cock seems like it's even bigger now, and I don't think it's just because it's closer with him standing near the glass like that. I can't stop staring. It's long, with a thick vein running up along the underside and a pink mushroom head that he squeezes and twists every time he gets to it before pulling back down along the shaft.

"Your cunt is fucking squelching over there, isn't it? Just from looking at my cock. You wish I had you up against this glass, don't you?" He pounds at the glass wall with his hand and I look back up toward his eyes. They're so hot with want. Is he going to open up the door and come around and fuck me? Surely that's what all this has been leading up toward. I keep touching myself, having no idea what I'd do if he did.

"You're creaming yourself just at the sight of me," he says, voice elevated. "Tell me the truth," he slams at the glass again. "Come, you fucking slut! Do it now!" He hammers again at the glass, looking wild as he pumps so hard at his dick it looks almost painful.

Oh Christ, we're losing control together.

I'm panting so hard I can barely breathe and rub at my clit while pumping fingers from my other hand in and out of myself, imagining it's his cock and I come, quick and hard—

A high-pitched squeal that barely has sound eeks out of me as my vision goes white. I feel it to the tips of my fingernails and the furthermost edges of my toes. Quick. Sharp. Like lightning, and then it's gone, leaving a warm haze behind.

When I open my eyes, ready to see the shared experience on Bryce's face, but he's sitting back down in his chair.

Still rubbing his dick back and forth.

He didn't come with me.

Instead, he pulls a cloth out of his suit pocket and lays it on his lap. Then, looking bored as he glances down at something on his phone, he keeps jerking at his cock. A few seconds later, he spews cum onto the cloth. Without another glance my way.

He cleans up his cock with the cloth, then drops it in a bin in one of his cupboards. He whistles while he packs his laptop in a briefcase and saunters toward the door of his office. Before he leaves, his voice comes through the intercom one more time—he must have it wired through his damn phone or Bluetooth or something, because I can't see him pressing anything,

"Oh, and Miss Cruise, tomorrow I'll need you to take out my dry-cleaning." With that, he's gone.

CHAPTER FOUR

I choke back the sob that's trying to come up my throat and spin my chair away from his office. I stand up just enough to yank my skirt back down, sweat mixing with my makeup and running into my eyes until they sting.

It's just from the sweat and the makeup in my eyes. That's all. That's the only reason I'm crying. Not because of *him*. I find the small container of tissues I keep in my purse and tug several free. I swipe angrily at my eyes until I can see again.

God. Is letting myself be humiliated like this worth it? But what the hell else am I going to do? I slink to the ground with my back to the desk and bang my head against it. Then I grab my purse and frantically reach for my phone.

I log into my banking app. Instead of the $44.53 that was my entire balance yesterday, there's now a balance of $6583.76.

I sit up straighter and immediately wipe again at my eyes.

Holy shit. It's real.

I lean back against the desk and breathe out. Holy *shit*. I mean, I believed the bastard when he told me the salary earlier, but seeing the number in my bank account. Sixty-five hundred dollars. Every month.

I let out a little laugh. That's my paycheck *after tax*... holy shit.

The three-thousand-dollar retainer fee for my dream lawyer is suddenly... totally *doable*. As in, I can pay for the attorney *and* make rent. Or well, pay off some back rent, and be current within a couple months.

Oh my God. My chest feels like it's filled with helium. When I laugh this time, it's genuine.

And then I'm just shaking my head, because what the hell? I haven't been wrung through so many emotions in such a short amount of time since... well, since I told David I was pregnant with Charlie.

I take in a deep breath and hold it as I get shakily to my feet.

Buck up, Cals. This is your life. I drag myself off the office floor. Yes, my life might be a string of one fucked up thing after another right now. Yes, I might be getting myself in what I'll just sweep under the rug and refer to once I'm old and wise as 'youthful indiscretions.' But I'll get through this. I'll be able to fight whatever super-attorneys David and his wife throw at me.

One day at a time, one foot in front of another.

I throw my mascara covered tissues in the trash and open up the clothes cabinet at the back of my office. I fix my makeup in the cabinet mirror and smile at my reflection. It looks more like a grimace. I roll my eyes, grab an outfit for tomorrow, and shut the door tight.

————

The rest of the week, nothing happens.

Well, I mean, a lot of things happen. I'm thrown in the deep end as far as figuring out what the hell a personal assistant does.

Some of it is what you see on TV and the movies—getting coffee and the boss's dry cleaning, but the rest of it is just mundane office stuff. Learning how to deal with Bryce's personal and business email correspondence, i.e., copying and pasting similar polite responses with brief personalizations at the start and end, mostly saying thank you for contacting me but I'm very busy, blah, blah, blah. Or fielding requests for meetings, personal appearances, interviews, and managing his very hectic calendar. Along with the emails of the female variety wanting a follow up encounter for a rendezvous. When I ask Bryce about them, he only dismissively rolls his eyes and asks how they got his email in the first place. I very diplomatically do not mention that I can see from the email history that he and whichever woman have emailed back and forth several times—often with him initiating contact after he's met the woman at some social event or other. At his bidding, I write a quick response requesting no further communication and then block their emails. I try to use the nicest language I can. But really, is there a nice way to tell someone you've been intimate with to fuck off and never contact you again? I've been on the other side of that and I know that no, there's not.

But apart from the never-ending task of keeping up with his email, taking notes whenever he has meetings, ordering his schedule, and keeping him in hot, caffeinated beverages, Bryce doesn't request any extras outside the scope of a normal PA's duties. I'm both relieved and on edge every second waiting for the other shoe to drop.

At home each night I've started taking the hottest baths I can stand to loosen the muscles in my back and neck. I'm sore from being so tense all day, just waiting for the next crass demand from my boss.

But other than that first day... nothing. Friday comes and goes, and it's a totally normal workplace situation. I'm baffled. I mean, is Bryce just screwing with me or did he decide I'm not his type? Hell, maybe he's found some lovely woman who's so worth his time he's actually decided not to send her to my inbox for the impersonal email FU.

But I'm to the elevator and free from the office for the weekend without anything else happening. Oh glorious weekend! I get to be the uncomplicated mommy version of me.

Shannon catches up on her graphic design work and Charlie and I do mundane things like shopping and laundry and cleaning the house.

And of course, playing blocks together over and over and over. This is his favorite pastime. It involves stacking blocks.

And then knocking them over.

Stacking them.

Knocking them over.

Over and over and over and on and on for all eternity.

Most of the time it drives me bananas, but this weekend I find the monotonous action soothing. Especially when Charlie giggles every time the blocks fall over like we've just invented the absolute most hilarious thing in the world.

When I finally can't handle the blocks anymore, I put on my favorite upbeat playlist and dance with Charlie all around the apartment. He giggles like crazy every time we do this. No one can stay stressed out or unhappy when he's in full-giggle mode.

He's more than ready when I put him down for his afternoon nap. I collapse on the couch with a pile of laundry that needs folding and push play on a Netflix series I've been meaning to catch up on.

———

It's not the ringing doorbell that jerks me from sleep. It's Charlie's screaming from down the hall. I shoot to my feet, disoriented from the awkward cramped position I must have drifted off in. The doorbell continues its shrill chirping. I glare.

Do I go ream out whoever's pushing it repeatedly in spite of the clearly ducktaped note over it that says 'DO NOT RING' in capital letters, or go soothe Charlie?

"I'll be right there!" I yell as I jog toward Charlie's room, aka, my room.

He won't calm down until the noise stops. I don't know why, but he just starts to screech whenever the damn bell is pushed. And the idiot is out there isn't letting up.

"Stop pressing the bell!" I shout at the door. Charlie screams bloody murder in my ear as I hoist him on my hip and then hurry toward the door. I stub my toe on Thomas the fucking Train and I'm ready for a mommy beat-down when I finally swing the door open.

There stands David. And walking away from the stoop is a tall, slim, and immaculately dressed woman who must be his wife. She's wearing some kind of expensive-looking wrap dress that falls just slightly past her knees. She doesn't give a backward glance before sliding into the driver's seat of their Audi parked at the curb.

Dammit. I must have forgotten this was his weekend. He emailed last week, but I totally spaced it. Usually on his weekends he picks up Charlie on Friday night, but he had some work mixer last night and asked to pick Charlie up this afternoon instead. I blink, still trying to wake up.

"What's wrong with him?" David tries to pull Charlie from my arms.

I step back and glare at him. Is he crazy trying to pull Charlie away from me when he's so upset? He needs his mother.

"What's wrong is someone can't read." I nod toward the sign over the doorbell for emphasis. It's hard to be heard through Charlie's continued crying. He's squirming in my arms and I bounce him. "Shh, it's okay, baby. No more bad noises." I spin around a couple times until I start to feel dizzy.

It does the trick though. His cries turn to giggling squeals. I drop down to the ground. I have to keep distracting him if I really want to win the battle and keep the crying at bay.

"What's this, Charlie?" I rip off a blade of grass from the small square of green space that counts as 'lawn' in this place. It's basically a place for the tenants who have pets to take them to piss and crap. *Most* of the time they're good about bagging it. And when they aren't? Well, there's a reason these patches stay so green.

I run the blade of grass down Charlie's nose, across his cheeks and down underneath his neck until his grin and giggles seem like they're going to stay. Soon he's got a clump of grass in his hand, tugging to try to get it out of the ground. He yanks and yanks, and finally a few pieces come off clutched between his tiny knuckles. He looks delighted and smiles his big drooly smile at me.

"You're so strong, Charlie! But no," I grab the fist that's heading toward his mouth, "grass is *not* for eating." Especially considering what I know about what these patches are used for.

I hear an unfamiliar phone ringtone and look up and around. David pulls his phone out of his pocket. He looks tired today, wearing his forty-two years roughly in the lines on his face.

He straightens and frowns—I can't tell if it's because he caught me watching or because of what's being said on the other end of the conversation.

Either way, when he hangs up, his voice is clipped. "Enough of this. You're delaying me taking my son. I can document this, you know."

My mouth drops open and immediately my eyes shoot to the car and the woman waiting there. Sure enough, she has her phone up like a camera, maybe even like she's taking video of the event.

"What the crap, David?" I whisper to him.

He stubbornly resists meeting my eyes. "You're half an hour late in delivering him to my care. That's another breach of our court custody agreement."

I scoff in disbelief, popping my own phone out of my pocket to look at the time. "It's four-twenty. I didn't spend twenty minutes getting to the door. You were late. Plus, I was cool with you guys picking him up today instead of yesterday like you were supposed to. Then I had to calm Charlie down after you terrorized him with the doorbell!"

Dammit, Cals, get yourself together, he's goading you.

"That's not the way I see it," David says. "Or the way the courts will see it." He looks down when he says it, like he's parroting someone and it's obvious to even him. Two guesses as to who—my eyes shoot to the profile of the woman sitting in the Audi. I bet it was her on the phone telling him to hurry up. She is such a *shrew*.

When I look back, David's scooping Charlie off the ground and up into his arms. I hate what a good picture they make together. Charlie has the same wide, flat nose and dramatic eyebrows as his father. It was a little difficult for me in the beginning—Charlie looking so much like his dad when the abandonment was fresh. Most the time now, though, I see Charlie as his own little person. It's only rare moments like now where I feel that kick in the gut about the resemblance.

David flips Charlie over his shoulder. Charlie squeals and giggles as his dad heads with him toward the car. Away from me.

"Wait!" It's a mixture of pissed off and desperate, and I hate it. I hate being reminded that I ever felt anything for this man. I hate that he has the legal right to just walk off with my son like this. "Just wait a second, okay? I need to wash his hands off."

David looks impatient, but I go jogging into the house anyway. Charlie's health is more important than some stupid feud going on among his parents. I scramble through Charlie's diaper bag, having to all but empty the damn thing before I finally find the baby wipes. I hurry back outside. Of course, David's already almost to his car.

Goddamn. I was only gone a few seconds. "Just wait," I call while David puts Charlie into his car seat and starts to strap him in. I squeeze in between him and the side of the car, no small feat considering the narrow space and my wide hips. David backs away almost immediately as soon as my hip bumps into his. Instead of the tailspin of lust it would have shot me into three years ago, now I just feel the pressing need to make things right with my son.

"*Col*?" Charlie says, his *d*s not very well defined yet.

"Yes, cold." I smile as I wipe down his hands with the wipes that do feel a little chilled compared to the early summer air.

Icy, neatly made-up eyes narrow at me in the rearview mirror. "This is just more time that you're intruding on with our son. We're making a note of every minute over and the judge will hear about it."

For a second I just stare back at her through the mirror. Bitch say *wah*? There's so much in that last statement that is fucked up—

Charlie grabs the wet-wipe from me and starts smacking me in the face with it.

Court. I breathe out. This is why I will hire a good lawyer. We're going to court and everything will get settled there. Opening the driver's door and bitch-slapping her in the presence of my son might feel awesome in the short term, but it won't do me any favors in the long run.

I turn back to Charlie and give him a smile and an extra-smoochy kiss on his forehead. "Nose kisses." He snuggles his nose against mine and my smile turns real. "Momma loves you."

"Wove you."

My grin is wide as I pull back from him and wave. David immediately slams the door shut. I spin on my heel and glare at him.

My voice is a heated whisper. "You try to pull any of that counting minutes BS on me, I'll do the same to you. You were at least fifteen minutes late. I can keep records, too. And you might want to remind your," I grind my teeth together and bite back the adjectives *batshit crazy,* "wife that, while Charlie might be your son by an unfortunate quirk of biology, there is no way in *hell,* that he belongs in any way to that woman." I jab an elbow toward the Shrew in question.

David just rolls his eyes at me and walks away. Just walks away without a word.

My fists ball together until my nails are biting so hard into my palms I'm almost drawing blood. Old me would have chased after the bastard and demanded he listened to me.

But this has always been his super-power, after all.

Leaving when shit gets real.

Their fancy-ass car takes off almost the moment his door closes. With my son inside. And I have no say about it.

It still shocks me, that some stranger who didn't know me or Charlie or anything about any of it could sit down one day and just decide that these people get to take my son twice a week.

What if, someday soon, another stranger decides that David and the Shrew get to drive off with Charlie and never bring him back?

The light-headed feeling swoops in. I sit down on my steps and put my head between my legs. I take a deep breath in. That decides it. I paid off my two month's back rent but was holding off paying this month's until I figured out if the money needed to go toward rent or for the lawyer.

Lawyer it is.

CHAPTER FIVE

"Undo your top two buttons." Bryce eyes my breasts critically.

I'm caught aback. It's week number three that I've been working here, but other than a few emails from afar requesting I work topless while the glass between us was clear, he hasn't directly engaged me other than professionally at meetings. What's changed today?

"Don't make me repeat myself," he all but snaps.

Shit. I forgot how mercurial he can be. I get to the buttons. *Remember what it's all for, Cals.* I have an appointment with my top family law firm pick in a few days. Eyes on the prize, eyes on the prize.

Bryce tilts his head, eyes narrowing. "One more." He makes a gesture of impatience when my fingers hesitate on the buttons, and I quickly comply. *Eyes on the fucking prize.*

Then he looks me up and down. Almost immediately, he starts shaking his head. "No, that skirt won't do."

I look down at myself. I'm wearing a gray pencil skirt. It hugs my curves. I look up in surprise. Almost all the clothes in the closet are replicas of this style in varying colors.

He walks to the cabinet and pulls it open. The next thing I know I hear hangers clanking and the swish of cloth. What the hell? He's a fashion consultant now?

"This one."

He pulls out one of the few dresses. It's very classy and... cute. Not slutty at all. It's an A-line black and gray hounds-tooth dress with a fitted bodice that flares slightly at the bottom. Like something I might buy at Modcloth, but probably of higher quality fabric. My eyes flick up to Mr. Gentry in question. He's smirking at me. Naturally.

"Change." He holds out the dress. And doesn't make a move to turn away.

Right. Back to game playing. I didn't really think he was done with them, did I? No, I just tried to pretend it was over so I'd have enough peace of mind to focus on not fucking up learning all I had to over the past few weeks. But that's probably exactly what he's wanted, me on edge, waiting for whatever twisted shit he has coming next. Sadistic bastard. Always keeping me guessing and off kilter.

Don't give him the satisfaction of rattling you, Cals.

I undress at the same pace as I would do if at home. No faster or slower. I keep my gaze somewhere around the area of his chest.

Is that a cop out? Should I be glaring him in the eyes? Or is that what he wants? Would my defiance make it worse? Dammit. I hate having to second guess every single thing I'm doing. No matter what I do, I'm still probably out of my depth in this stupid chess match.

I finish undressing and put my clothes in the cabinet. I can't help glancing at him as I reach for the dress he's still holding. He pulls it away when I do. I bite back the urge to roll my eyes. What? Are we in grade school?

His smirk gets bigger. *Goddamned* bastard.

"I approve of your undergarment choices." He nods at my black thong. In spite of myself, my cheeks flush.

"I didn't wear it for you."

His eyebrows raise as if in disagreement.

I grit my teeth.

He gives me a winsome smile. "Either way, it does well for our purposes today."

What does that mean? I keep my posture straight. I swear my posture's never been as good as it has been since I've met this man. I always stiffen like it's some kind of armor. Ridiculous. "How so?"

He ignores my question. "Go to the bathroom and bring yourself to orgasm. Make sure to touch yourself *through* the underwear. I want them drenched with your scent."

"Wha—" I start, but break off mid-question. Of course, this fucker would make this kind of request.

His face darkens. "You have," he pulls his phone from his pocket, "approximately eight minutes. If you haven't soaked them sufficiently at that point," he leans in close so that his breath is hot on my ear, "I'll come and give you a helping hand."

I pull back from him and his smile goes wide in what I can only feel is an imitation of a shark—all sharp, white teeth.

I push past him and head to the en-suite bathroom in his office. His easy-going laugh follows me. I don't know what this new game is, but if I have the opportunity to do something without his hands or presence, I'm all for it.

I get in the smaller, bright room—all white, of course, and shut the door with a slam. For a second I lean back against it and just breathe. I see myself in the mirror. Against the backdrop of this oh so stylish bathroom, standing in my black bra, thong and high heels, with my blonde up-do and pristine makeup, I look like I'm some kind of pin-up model. Or a high-paid prostitute. My arms immediately raise to cover myself and I turn away from the mirror.

But who am I kidding? I came in here with the express directions from my boss to get myself off in eight minutes. Shit, probably more like seven now. My arms drop. Or six.

Screw it. There's no time for shame or anything else. I just have to get it *done.* Just push everything else out.

I sit down on the toilet and start touching myself. I'm sure Bryce's threat to do it for me if I don't isn't idle. Bastard.

Then again, how is he going to know if I don't do it? Apart from if the panties aren't wet? I mean, I could just drip some sink water on them. I sit up on the toilet lid and look around the bathroom. Are there cameras in here? Dammit.

I look up at the ceiling and in the corners. I don't see anything. Just smooth white ceiling tiles. There's not much decoration in here, just those abstract Japanese art prints on the wall and the bamboo shoots in a clear vase. I lean closer. Is there a camera hiding in those pebbles at the base? I can't tell.

But Gentry Tech is famous for their surveillance technology. I squeeze my eyes shut. I don't have time for this, anyway. I start rubbing at my clit. No doubt the bastard will smell my damn underwear. He's that tactless. There's no getting around it.

All right. Think sexy thoughts. Channing Tatum. I wince. *Ugh, no.* All of the sudden I just imagine him going "S'up?" like some dumb California surfer dude, and it's a total turn off.

Okay. All right. Think about all the romantic comedies I've seen lately. Prince charming type guys. Kissing scenes. I grind at my clit.

Nothing.

Fine then, there were some hot sex scenes from the romance novels I read. The one where the guy was really sweet when he took that girl's virginity and held her close all night after they made love? I try to recall it as I push my panties up inside myself. But I'm still almost all dry.

Shit. It's less than five minutes now. I have to get this done. I glare at the door. Dammit. I close my eyes.

My fantasies are my own. They don't matter.

I squeeze my eyes shut tighter and ignore the darker places my mind has to go to make myself come. Rough hands. The grip of a stranger. Taking what isn't his. Harsh words. Harsher hands. And God, oh— oh God—

———

I come out of the bathroom, ignoring the fact that I'm sure my cheeks are flushed. Bryce waits right outside the door. Was he listening? If he was, he didn't get any thrills there. I was careful not to make a single sound.

But he knows what I was doing. While he was standing right here. And in spite of myself, I feel it. The shame. He doesn't miss it, what I'm feeling.

He smiles, the shark smile. So maybe that's what it was about, this little trip down mind-fuck lane. He gets off on my humiliation. He holds the dress out to me and it's difficult to keep myself from ripping it out of his grasp.

But I don't. I take it calmly, unzip it and slip it over my head.

"Help with the zipper?"

I don't say a word as I settle the dress on and then turn my back to him. His knuckles graze my spine as he slides the zipper up. If he notices the chill I get, he doesn't say anything.

"I'll be needing that thong now." He says it calmly.

I'm not surprised. At least he let me put the dress on first. He offers me an arm to steady me so I can take the damn thing off. What a gentleman.

I smile at him as I refuse his arm. Look at that, I'm getting my own array of smiles now. This one I'll call my sugar-snake smile—it's all apparent sweetness but with venom underneath. I slip my heels off so I'm not off balance while I pull the thong down my legs as discretely as I can. I ball them up and hand them over to him.

He brings them to his nose and inhales.

I arch an eyebrow at him as I slip my heels back on. "So crass?"

He looks at me with genuine surprise while he sticks the underwear in the inside of his suit coat pocket.

"Watch out for that wicked tongue." He steps close. For a moment I think he's reaching forward as if to adjust something on the front of my dress, but then he grabs my breasts and tweaks at my nipples.

I yelp and pull back but he just keeps plucking at them while he talks as if nothing's amiss.

"There." He looks down at my breasts in satisfaction. "See that your nipples stay like that. I want them puckered when we walk into the restaurant."

I'm breathing hard as he turns away.

Damn him. I want to run forward and kick him with the tip of my pointy high heel. For a second there, a *second*, I felt like I was on an equal footing with him. And then, just like that, he stole it away from me. Put me back in my place.

I follow him but I'm breathing hard, feeling stupidly like I want to cry. But screw that. I bite it back. I'm sure he would get such a kick out of my tears. Humiliation is this guy's high, after all.

"Don't forget your tablet," he calls over his shoulder. "This *is* a business lunch." He says it like I'm a moron who's slacking on the job.

I smooth my hair as I hurry back into my office to grab my tablet and purse. I barely make it to the elevator before it closes. Just as he intended, I'm sure.

———

Bryce doesn't speak to me the entire ride over to the restaurant, which is fine by me. We're in the back of a luxurious town car and he leaves plenty of space between us on the bench. He stares at his phone. I suppose I could be doing the same, trying to keep up on the endless emails that I'm sure are stacking up.

But trying to read in a car makes me nauseous. In addition to the nerves already roiling in my stomach. Dammit. I am not in over my head. I'm *not*. I can do this. I can handle whatever Bryce throws at me. I have to. No matter what's going on inside, I resolve to show nothing. I make my face a perfectly pleasant mask while I watch the busy streets.

It's not a long drive. When the car slows, Bryce only looks up long enough to stare at my chest pointedly. I don't even bother to wonder if he's serious about wanting my nipples perky. I pluck at them myself, even twisting them a little. They're sensitive from his handling of them earlier, and they harden right up.

I don't meet his eyes, and I'm glad when he opens the door. He gestures for me to step out first.

I give him a disingenuous smile as I slide past him to exit. He follows me and then puts a hand on the small of my back. It immediately puts me on alert, but I don't pull away. I won't let him know he's disconcerting me. It would just feed his ego or whatever head-trip controlling me gives him.

"This way," he says in my ear, guiding me forward.

I stiffen under his touch and clutch my purse a little tighter.

"Relax," he laughs. He squeezes my waist. As if that's supposed to help. "This is a meeting with a very old and dear friend. I know you'll be my good girl."

What a condescending assh—

Before I can finish the thought, we're inside and being greeted by a hostess. Bryce has his charismatic smile out, and I can tell the hostess is entirely dazzled by him. She looks like she's still in college, all doe-eyes and impressionable.

"Mr. Gentry," her face lights up. He must be a regular. "We have your private dining room all ready. Just this way!" She beams at him and I don't miss the way she pops her chest out. I inwardly smirk. It's a good move, after all. The dude is a boob man. She sways her hips as she leads us forward into the dark and intimately lit restaurant.

The Bay Area doesn't lack for all kinds of eateries, and I didn't check out the name before I was ushered inside. From the décor and dark wood paneling and aroma, I'm guessing this is some kind of European inspired cuisine. Italian? French? I can't tell.

I follow Bryce, and to my surprise he isn't watching the perky waitress—he's looking at me. Scrutinizing me. Like he's watching me take everything in. It's unnerving and I start moving again, quickly catching up to the hostess where she's waiting ahead at a set of double doors that lead into what I'm assuming is the private dining room she was talking about.

Bryce keeps right beside me, arm at my back.

When we step inside, our other party is already waiting. The man stands up as we enter. And. Holy. Shit.

It's Jackson Vale, the founder and CEO of CubeThink. Everyone knows he's Bryce Gentry's former best friend and collaborator—together they wrote that breakthrough robotics algorithm I studied in college—and though they compete in different markets, their drones now rival one another for technical prestige.

So why the hell are we sitting down to a cozy lunch date with the guy?

"Jackson," Bryce says with a breezy smile. He rounds the table and gives the man that half-hug-slap-on-the-back thing guys do.

"Bryce," Jackson returns. His voice is stiff and it's only when Bryce pulls back that I get a better look at the other man. Jackson is slightly taller than Bryce. Where Bryce is sleek, Jackson is built and muscled.

Bryce has always seemed like the most intimidating man in the room just because of his bearing and charisma.

Until now.

My gaze is caught on Jackson. It's not charisma he exudes. He's not smiling or even outwardly attempting any charm I can see. He's just got... *presence*. Physically because he's such a big man. Brown hair so dark it's almost black. He's smooth-shaven but I can see the outline of his five o'clock shadow even though it's only noon.

And his eyes. They're so dark. Not because they're brown. I think they might even be blue. But there's a darkness there.

I can't help but take the slightest step back when his eyes move from Bryce to me. My heart's suddenly slamming a hundred beats a minute in my chest and my eyes flick to the doors that the hostess shut behind her. Six feet from me to the door.

Fight or flight. Bryce's one thing. Somehow, I've always felt I can handle him. But this man...?

"And this is?" Jackson addresses the question to Bryce, but his eyes don't leave me. My feet seem locked in place. I want to whimper. My palms are sweaty. *You're in a public place, Cals. He can't do anything to you.* Because that's why I'm whimpering, right? Fear... right?

But there's something else happening, too, something even more screwed up. Those nipples Bryce wanted perked up? They're hard right now. And they're pointing like rock-tipped arrows aimed straight at Jackson.

Bryce's arm slips around my waist. "This lovely creature is my new personal assistant, Miss Calliope Cruise. Isn't she just a vision?" He pulls back and stares at me with pure adoration on his face.

I can only gape. The hell? Not once has he ever looked at me with anything like what his expression is now. I try not to let the confusion show on my face and keep my features pleasant.

"Not only that," Bryce turns back to Jackson, "but she's pursuing a degree in advanced robotics from Stanford."

Again, I struggle not to reveal my surprise. When Bryce interviewed me, he made me feel like a college dropout, but now he's putting the best spin on everything. Like he's showing me off.

And suddenly it clicks. He *is* trying to show me off. He's trotting out his prize show pony to impress Jackson.

The possessive hand around my waist suddenly drops and pinches my ass. Right. Time to get with the program and perform. I can wonder about the why later. I smile up at Bryce graciously and try to channel the hostess from earlier, adding a touch of awe in my expression.

"And I can't thank Mr. Gentry enough for giving me the real-world experience of working at such an amazing company," I gush. "I'm learning so many things by getting to see the inner workings of how he develops and grooms new ideas through each stage of production."

"Ah, yes," Jackson says with a mocking tone. "Bryce always was good at taking other people's ideas and pretending they were his own."

I don't miss the tick in Bryce's jaw at the jab.

"Why don't we sit so we can enjoy this delicious lunch I took the liberty of ordering for us?" Bryce holds out his arms to indicate the table.

Jackson continues standing still as a statue except for his eyes. They sit on Bryce for several long seconds, flick to me, then move back to Bryce.

"Drop the shit, Bryce." Jackson's voice is a deep, rumbling base. "You said over the phone you're finally willing to discuss negotiation on the CQ-9 patent. You've never had any use for it and have held it all these years just to spite me. So why on earth would you change your mind now?"

Bryce sits and again waves to the chairs at the table. I glance toward the door one last time, but then take the seat Bryce indicates for me. I try not to stare at Jackson, wondering what his next move will be. Will he stay or go?

Everyone in the tech world knows these men are rivals. I'm curious as hell about Bryce's motives. I can almost taste the tension between them in the air. There are rumors of what happened to set the former friends against each other, but no one really knows.

Was it a woman like some of the online gossip sites have suggested? Or a parting of philosophies like my machine-learning professor thought—Jackson was more interested in commercial ventures while Bryce wanted to pursue government-funded research?

Either way, what would bring them together in this room if they are competitors and enemies? And what the *hell* does Bryce expect my role to be in all this?

"What if I told you I wanted to let bygones be bygones and allow the past to stay where it belongs? In the past."

Jackson's hard stare remains immovable. "I'd say I know you better than that."

Bryce laughs, a big bellowing laugh from his stomach. He shakes his finger at his old friend. "See? Now that's the kind of honesty I miss! Everyone around me these days just tells me what I want to hear. Yes men. *Yes, Mr. Gentry*," he mocks in an obsequious voice, "*of course, Mr. Gentry, whatever you please.*" He shakes his head. "Fucking ludicrous."

Bryce sits up in his chair, the humor replaced by earnestness. "I miss you, Jackson. I miss the machines we used to build, the concepts we dreamed up when we put these two brains together." He gestures back and forth between their heads.

Jackson scoffs and looks like he's about to walk out of the room when Bryce continues, "Have lunch with us. Listen to what I have to say. No matter what, you walk out of here with your father's patent. Give me an hour of your time."

That peaks Jackson's interest. Mine too. How does Bryce have one of Jackson's *father's* patents? What's the story there?

Jackson stares hard at Bryce, like he's trying to figure out his angle. "Just like that?"

"Just like that." Bryce holds up his hands. "I'm a different man from the boy you used to know. Get to know the new me."

Jackson doesn't look like he's buying what Bryce's selling, but he does sit down at the third seat at the table. The private room we're in is large, but this table is almost uncomfortably small. It makes the whole space feel too intimate for two men who may or may not be reconciling rivals. Especially with me here as an uncomfortable third-wheel.

I take a sip of my water in the silence that's quickly grown awkward.

"So, Jackson," Bryce asks, "how're things with you? How's the company? And Miranda?" His voice is cajoling, like one might sound when ribbing a friend. "Still enjoying fucking my former fiancée?"

I choke on my water at the same time as a waitress pushes open the door with appetizers. I grab my napkin to wipe at the water dripping down my chin and glance back and forth between the two men. So it *was* a woman.

Bryce never loses his pleasant, happy-go-lucky smile and Jackson continues to sit there looking formidable and impassive. To be fair, it's the same expression Jackson's had the entire time we've been in the room, so I can't tell if he's reacting at all to Bryce's comment.

The waitress sets down a basket of buttered garlic bread and two trays of small finger appetizers. Mini crab cakes and bruschetta as well as a selection of other antipasti.

My mouth waters just looking at all the delicious food. I get so little time with Charlie that I got caught up playing with him a little bit this morning after he crawled in bed with me. I was late feeding him and when I realized the time, I was a madwoman rushing to get ready. I didn't get time for breakfast myself.

Still, I don't want to be the first one reaching for food. Again, I look back and forth between the two men. They are still locked in a stare-off.

I smile and gesture toward the platter. "Appetizer anyone?"

Jackson's eyes finally break from Bryce's and look to me, as if just remembering he and Bryce aren't alone in the room.

"Of course." Jackson takes one of the small plates and begins to load it with appetizers. His hands look gigantic next to the dainty little portioned food. Bryce and I fill our plates as well, but I can't take my eyes off of Jackson's hands. For a second my mind wanders, thinking about what they say about the size of a man's hands...

Because that is a *completely* appropriate thought to be having right now. God, is this my thing now? Instead of being a nervous eater, I'll start thinking about dick sizes and what his cum face looks like. I steal a look at Jackson's face and my mind starts trying to rearrange the features. What would this man who always seems so controlled look like lost in pleasure? *What the Christ, Cals, you're doing it again!*

"CubeThink is doing very well," Jackson says as if there was no awkward lull in conversation. I take a sip of water and look down at my plate of food, mortified at my own thoughts.

"As I'm sure you well know," I look back up just in time for Jackson to glare in Bryce's direction before continuing, "Our stock prices have never been higher and the same goes for consumer confidence. Our quadcopter was the highest grossing commercial drone in the country last year. As for Miranda," a look of rich amusement cracks Jackson's stoic façade for the first time, "I thought you'd heard through the grapevine that we've tired of each other."

I don't miss the slightest tick in Bryce's coolly-aloof expression. A tell. One he hates himself for giving away, no doubt.

Jackson seems to have seen it, too, because the amused expression on his face settles deeper. I should be disturbed that he's taking satisfaction in digging the knife in his former friend's gut, but I can only stare.

Jackson only looked foreboding and frankly, a little scary, earlier. But the amusement softens his sharp features. The cut jaw and sharply angled eyebrows don't seem quite as menacing now. And, oh help me God, there's a dimple. Just on one side of his face, but still. That's just not fair to the female population. Seriously.

Bryce smirks. "Couldn't keep the faithless bitch in line either, huh?"

The ugly words make me stiffen in my seat.

The softness leaves Jackson's face, dimple disappearing. "Our parting was by mutual agreement after we both enjoyed ourselves, that was all. Maybe if you'd known how to treat a lady, she wouldn't have gone seeking fulfillment elsewhere."

I expect Bryce to explode in fury. Instead, he laughs amiably. He's firmly adopted his charismatic persona for the moment. I breathe out and reach for another crab cake. I've just popped it in my mouth when I feel Bryce's hand on my knee. I struggle not to choke on the bite I've just swallowed as his hand slides up my thigh and toward my pantyless crotch. But surely he's not going to—

I jolt in shock as he does it. He sticks a finger inside me. Right there at the table with Jackson sitting not two feet away from me on my other side. I exhale in shock and look down at my plate. What is Bryce thinking?

It's not as if he's being discreet about this. His left hand is obviously reaching under the goddamned tablecloth. And moving around.

Oh God. Does Jackson know what he's doing right now? Does Bryce *want* him to know? I can't look up at the other man or I'll die. I'll die right here where I'm sitting.

"Well," Bryce says amiably, "good for you and Miranda. I'm glad you both became so enlightened. And yes, I have seen that Cube-Think's stock was on the rise lately. In fact, that's why I wanted to ask you for this meeting. In the past, we've had such... How shall I put it —" Bryce pauses, and as he does, he pushes another finger into me. I can't help squirming against it. It doesn't hurt because I stretched myself as part of my self-love session in Bryce's office bathroom, and I'm even still a little moist. But Christ, why does he have to do this here? Now?

"—fruitful collaborations," Bryce finishes with a smile.

"Collaborations," Jackson says. I dare a peek over at him and see a dangerous and disingenuous smile on his face. As if he can feel me watching, his eyes meet mine.

Then he looks back to Bryce. "Is that what we're calling it when you steal things that are mine and then market them as your own? But then, you always did like putting your mark on things."

I'm still watching him as his eyes drop to where Bryce's arm disappears beneath the tablecloth. I feel the blood drain from my face even as Bryce's fingers work in and out of me more forcefully than before and his thumb starts rolling circles over my clit.

In that moment, I hate him.

I hate him even as my body reacts to his touch. I'm so humiliated and yet I'm also turned on. The fact that Jackson knows—that this other huge, handsome, God of a man knows what's going on not two feet away from him... that my shame is complete... So why God is it so *fucking* hot?

I stop thinking, I just feel. Bryce's hand, where it's not supposed to be. In this room, with these two absolutely powerful men, no one saying anything even though everyone knows exactly what's going on—

The waitress pushes open the door, holding a huge tray of food. Thank God. Surely Bryce will have to pull away now.

But. He. Fucking. Doesn't.

He keeps fingering me the entire time the waitress moves the appetizers out of the way and sets down the main course, pasta with a white sauce, mushrooms, what look like scallops, other herbs and a fancy garnish in the middle. Focusing on the food can't distract me from Bryce's touch for long though. It smells delicious, but there's too much sensory overload going on in my most sensitive of places.

"Would you like some fresh mozzarella?" the waitress asks, holding a shredder and a block of cheese over my pasta—at the same time that Bryce starts rubbing doubletime at my clit. Jackson continues watching all of it with a darkly intensive stare.

Sweat breaks out on my brow. "Um, I— I—" I stutter, squirming my legs to try to pull away from Bryce's hand. He just follows, though, no matter that it only makes his hand under the table that much more obvious.

I feel my cheeks flare and I shake my head vehemently. "No," I manage to choke out. The next second, my back stiffens from an especially sharp jolt of pleasure. "I'm good." My voice comes out much more high-pitched than normal and I want to cry. Stupid, fucking traitorous body.

Bryce starts to talk to Jackson about the robotics industry in Silicon Valley as he rolls pasta on his fork. Somehow he manages it one handed. I don't even know how. He eats lazily, like his other hand isn't so obviously occupied.

I keep my gaze locked firmly on my plate, only daring to look in Jackson's direction out of the periphery of my vision. Enough to tell that he too is staring only at his plate while he eats. I don't know whether it's chivalry or embarrassment for me. I just want all of this to end. Shakily, I pick up my own utensils and try to pick at my food.

Bryce's fingers have slowed down. I'm not right on the precipice anymore. He's torturing me at a low heat, pushing his fingers lazily in and out, in and out. Never letting me forget he's right there but not letting me over the edge so I can be done with it either. I hate him. I hate him *so* much for doing this to me. The sweat prickling at my brow feels like it's going to drip down my temples any second.

I grab my water glass and take a deep swallow instead. I hazard an outright look at Jackson. Still not looking my way. God, is it possible he doesn't know what's going on? Maybe he thinks Bryce is just adjusting his napkin on his lap for a really long time. Please God, let him be oblivious somehow.

It's just a horrible, ugly secret and— Oh, oh God, yeah, right *there*, that spot. Come on, you bastard, just a little more pressure... I struggle against arching in my chair and try to cover my short panting breaths with another drink of water.

Bryce keeps the conversation light and never even approaches talk of either company. But near the end of the meal, or at least when Bryce's plate is almost empty, his tone changes.

"That's not the way I remember it, you know," Bryce says, voice going from light-hearted to more serious. I'm confused for a second, then realize Bryce has abruptly gone back to the remarks made at the very start of the meal.

"The way I remember it, we were best when we shared things." He arches an eyebrow and it seems like there's some innuendo to his words I'm not catching.

But then his thumb begins to press more urgently at my clit again and he inserts a third finger inside me. I readjust myself in my chair so that I can press up against his hand, praying that it's unobtrusive. Dammit, what am I doing? But oh— Oh shit, oh God, oh—

Jackson scoffs. "And yet when we supposedly shared, you were the one who always came off with all the," his eyes narrow, "*prizes* in the end."

I'm trying to pay attention to their conversation, I really am. Every word seems laden with double entendre or some kind of code I'm missing the key to. But the way Bryce is so masterfully playing my body, the edges of my vision are starting to go hazy as heat rushes to my lower core.

Jackson's low rumbling voice isn't helping either. I've never heard a sexier voice. I try to focus on what he's saying. Christ, I have to get myself under control. I'm not going to come right here. I'm *not*.

"I want to collaborate with you again," Bryce says. "I'm developing a new drone that I'd like you to take a look at. I'll have legal draw up papers so everything's clear up front. Any patents developed would have clear fifty-fifty ownership. But out of it could come knowledge and business relationships that would benefit both of us in the long term."

How can he talk logically while so thoroughly finger-fucking me? Christ, I shouldn't have even let myself think that phrase. Finger-fucking. It made it worse. Dirty. Forbidden.

I grit my teeth against the pleasure but I swear I can feel myself getting wetter and wetter. Oh God, did Bryce's fingers just *squelch?* Did Jackson hear it?

But Bryce's still busy talking, thank God. "I have relationships and exclusive contracts with suppliers that I'd be willing to cut you in on if you agree to this partnership. These manufacturing contracts could slash your bottom line by more than twelve percent. Sharing my connections with you won't hurt my bottom line since we don't operate in the same marketplaces."

"And you'd just hand them over?" Jackson's eyes are drawn in cynicism.

Bryce smiles affably as he nods. "Of course, I'll get something out of the collaboration as well. I've been watching the clean energy solutions you've developed and incorporated into your machines with some interest over the years. I've drawn up designs for a new UAV incorporating AXCO plastics, Kuramoto motors, and your energy-saving technology. We'd take over the top performing models in the business and lock in the DOD contracts for the next decade."

Even through my sex haze, I saw the spark of unintentional interest light in Jackson's eyes when Bryce began talking. But it doused at the very end of Bryce's spiel.

"I was never interested in military applications." Jackson shakes his head. "And I stopped playing your games a long time ago, Bryce. You said if I sat through this meal, I'd get CQ-9." He folds his cloth napkin and places it beside his plate. "I'm not in the mood for dessert. I fulfilled my end of the bargain."

Right as Jackson moves to stand. Bryce does something with his hands, the fingers inside pressing up while he hits a certain place on my clit and oh God, yes right *there*. After the entire lunch of teasing, I'm so swollen and ready and Bryce somehow knows the exact way to play my body. A short tremor of pleasure shoots through me.

Oh— oh— yes, don't stop, don't— oh— *oooh*—

It's all white spots and chest-seizing fire for a moment. When I can finally take a full breath again, I realize that I've grabbed at the tablecloth, squeezing it in a death grip between clenched fingers.

Dammit. I probably look like a lunatic. A horny, sex-craved lunatic.

When I open my eyes, Jackson's just staring at me, an unreadable expression on his face. And I've never felt more mortified or shamed in my life. I drop my head and want to curl into myself and my misery. How do I keep letting this happen to me? Why am I so goddamned weak when it comes to Bryce?

I see it now. I'm going to be destroyed by the time this is all over. He's going to crush me because I'm not strong enough for his... What was it Jackson called it?

Bryce's games.

That's all this is to Bryce. A game. He brought me here just for this. He knew what he was going to do ahead of time.

He planned this... this... public shaming. Except to him, it's a game. I'm a plaything to toy with until I'm all worn out, used, and broken. And just like a six-year-old does, he'll toss me in the trash and forget me once he's done with me.

I feel like I'm going to throw up my crab cakes.

Bryce stands and holds a hand out for Jackson to shake. The same hand that was just inside me. Still probably wet from my juices. I have to fight not to hunch even further into myself.

It's not the way I should be playing this. I should be showing Bryce that I am not affected. That I'm strong and can face up to anything he dishes out. I have to. I already paid rent from the money he fronted me for the first month's work and God knows I'm not backing out of my attorney's appointment. Not after how far I've already gone.

This might be a game to Bryce, but I have to keep holding on long enough to keep my family together. A year at least. He might be using me, but I can use him right back. I'm not a victim here. I *won't* be. I straighten my back even as I keep up the internal pep talk. I can *do* this.

"Don't forget I know you," Bryce says. "You rarely make decisions without weighing all the odds. All I'm asking for is collaboration on *one* drone design. The exclusive contracts I can connect you to, with some of the best suppliers in the business, will bring your company a bright future."

Bryce leans in, and I realize this is the hard sell the entire lunch has been leading up to. "You might be number one in the US, but if you want CubeThink to be internationally competitive, you need an edge. I'm offering it to you. Why don't you mull over the opportunity and get back to me?"

Instead of just shaking hands, he pulls Jackson forward and gives him another half-hug pat on the back thing like he did at the beginning of the lunch. And then, to my further mortification, I notice him slip my thong into the pocket of Jackson's jacket.

I cringe and look away. I suppose I played my part in the meeting after all, even if I don't understand it.

When Bryce pulls back, Jackson's face is, as always, unreadable.

"Perhaps after you've had some time for further consideration, I could have Miss Cruise send over more proposal details." I look up sharply at the mention of my name, but Bryce's already moving on. He holds out an arm for me.

I stand and take it, face still to the ground. I can't look up at Jackson. If I never see him again in my life it will be too soon.

I don't even flinch when Bryce guides me by the small of my back out of the room.

It's only once we leave that my stomach settles and I realize how hungry I am. I barely touched any of that delicious looking pasta. Part of me wishes I could be back in that dining room finishing my meal with Jackson instead of leaving with Bryce. Because I wonder if the scarier-looking shark might just be the safer of the two.

CHAPTER SIX

"Mommy! Nose! Nose!" Charlie grabs my nose with his slightly grimy fingers and a delighted smile.

I laugh, pulling away and wiping any dirt from my nose onto the shoulder of my shirt sleeve. Ah, the weekend, when I can wear ratty old t-shirts and jeans. "Yep, nose."

I bop his nose with my forefinger and he giggles, then toddles away from me in a short circle on the grass. I grin at him.

We're at the park where I'm sitting on my favorite picnic blanket. I took him to the small kids play set, but all he wanted to do was run around on the big grassy area. Fine with me. Sitting out in the sunshine on this Saturday paradise? You don't have to twist my arm.

Charlie runs back at me, full toddler speed. I hold my arms out. "Whoa, buddy!"

He slams into me and then grabs a chunk of my hair. "Hair!"

"Yes, hair." I snuggle him close. He smells like baby powder and sunshine. "How'd you get to be so cute?" I ask him. "I didn't think you could get any cuter but then you got to be two-and-a-half and now you're talking and toddling and you're more fun than ever!"

"Fun!" Charlie echoes. Then he starts wriggling to get out of my hold. "Up. Up."

Ah, ain't that the way of it? When he was small, all he wanted was cuddles all day long. Now he's always squirming to get away so he can run around. They always say kids grow up too fast. I let go of him, and he's off again.

"Stay close," I call. I don't have to worry though. He's already stopped and is bending down to inspect something on the ground. Now I just have to keep a close watch to make sure whatever it is doesn't go in his mouth.

"Miss Cruise? Is that you?"

I look around and see a jogger. For a second, I can't place him. He's a runner, that's obvious. A big man. A mountain of a man, really, with powerful thighs and a sweat-soaked chest that's so wide it requires a full swivel of my eyes to take all of him in.

"Miss Cruise?"

And then I blink, because the deep voice is familiar. I put my hand over my eyes to block out the sun that's shining from behind his head.

Finally it clicks and my mouth drops open. It's Mr. Vale. Recognition hits with the force of a taser striking my nervous system. I sit up stiffly, and my head whips around to find Charlie. He's got a stick and pokes at something in the dirt. My precious innocent baby.

All I can think is: *no*. No. My two lives do *not* cross. Charlie's mom and... that other woman do *not* share the same space. Can*not*. I'm on my feet in the next second and backing away from Mr. Vale toward Charlie.

"Come on, honey." I turn toward my son, grabbing the diaper bag to swing it over my shoulder and then yanking the blanket. "Time to go."

"Wait, Miss Cruise—"

I pause only long enough to shoot the coldest glare of my life over my shoulder. It seems to convey everything I can't say in the moment —*step off, get the fuck away from my son*—because Mr. Vale immediately holds up his hands and starts backing away. "Have a nice day."

He resumes his jog along the path, but I don't stop long enough to watch him go.

"Playtime's over."

Predictably, Charlie starts crying. He fights it when I try to wrangle him back in the stroller, but I manage it. We're getting close to naptime so that's not helping matters either. I head in the opposite direction Mr. Vale went and look over my shoulder as I go. It's probably an overreaction to leave, but seeing him *here* of all places...

I grit my teeth together. Fuck that shit. I've compromised myself enough already to make ends meet, but I draw the line at any of it affecting my son. I don't care what Bryce or any of his friends—or enemies—think. I'll move across the goddamned country and change my name before any of this, these so-called *games*, pour over into my personal life.

As I push the stroller back for the long jog to my house, I keep checking over my shoulder. Another reason I chose this park was for the cardio I get from the jog on the way here and back, but now I'm ruing the decision. Maybe a lot of my recent decisions. What if all I've done by trying to solve one problem is bring on even more trouble?

————

Charlie falls asleep in my arms on Sunday as I rock him after his bath. I carry him gently to his crib in my room. He barely stirs as I settle him down. I can't help doing that parent thing where I pause in the doorway and just stare at him for a minute or two with my heart going all gooshy.

He was whinier today than most. My standard silly-dance around the living room trick almost didn't work the last hour before bedtime, and he was fussy during almost every other activity all day. Shannon thinks another tooth is coming in and from the amount of drool pouring out of his mouth onto my shirt and whatever toy he could shove in his mouth all day, I think she's probably right. Poor baby.

He's so beautiful when he sleeps. Precious. Perfect. His mouth moves in a sucking motion like he's dreaming about his sippy cup. I grin and shake my head before slipping out the door.

Shannon's in the living room on the couch with a blanket tucked around her, watching some gruesome forensic TV show. "Is he down?"

I nod and go reheat the spaghetti I made earlier. Feeding Charlie dinner tonight was a feat all on its own, he was so fussy, and I didn't get to my own dinner. At least he's not usually like that. I sit down on the ugly-ass seventies maroon velvet lounge chair beside Shannon. It was a dumpster-dive score I'm especially proud of. A neighbor down the street put it out on one of those rare big-item trash pick-up days, and Shannon and I hauled it home. It's hideous but comfortable as hell and therefore, my favorite place in the whole apartment to hang out.

I go to take a bite of my spaghetti but then catch sight of the blood and guts on the TV screen. As in, literally some dead guy's organs and intestines.

"Oh hell, Shan. Why?" I avert my eyes, but way too late. Why do they always feel the need to go for the autopsy shots in these shows? "Seriously? Can't we watch something else while I'm trying to eat here?"

"Hey, I was watching it first," she shrugs. "You're the one who decided to come in here with your spaghetti."

I grumble and keep my eyes firmly on my food while I eat. I wince a little as a meatball squishes in my mouth. I'd like to say I'm one of those delicate girls who is put off her meal by it all, but nah, I close my eyes, let the queasy moment pass, then get over it and enjoy the hell out of my pasta.

I look back up at the screen only when my plate is empty. Of course, the detectives are past the forensic part and are now storming the bad guy's apartment. I've missed too much of the plot to care about what's happening, but I keep watching anyway. I relax into the chair and let the stress of the day with the fussy kiddo roll off me. Ahh, evenings. God's gift to mothers everywhere.

"So how's the new job?" Shannon asks, eyes still on the screen. After a brief shootout, the cops have the bad guys in cuffs.

I tuck one of my legs up underneath my bum, trying not to let the surprise show on my face. Shannon and I might be sisters, but we've never been buddy-buddy. Well, that's not exactly true. When we were really little, we used to do everything together. She's three years older than me and my earliest memories are of her half-carrying, half-dragging me everywhere. Dressing me up and calling me her dolly. Holding my hand when we went to the park with Mom and sitting behind me with her arms around my waist as we slowly slid down the slide together. She's the one who taught me how to tie my shoes.

I don't know when it changed. Maybe around when I was seven or eight and started doing pageants? But the change was drastic. She began completely ignoring me and hanging around with her older friends. She never had time for me anymore and whenever we did spend time together, we just fought.

"It's...fine," I finally say.

She rolls her eyes. "Just fine?"

Well, it's not like I can tell her what it's actually like. I think of the business lunch with Mr. Vale that Bryce put me through last week. God. Instead, I put on a false smile. "No, I mean good. It's really good."

She nods and it's quiet for a second.

"What about your week?" I ask. If Shannon's trying to connect, I want to encourage the effort. She's so good with Charlie, and it's more than that. She was here supporting me when no one else was. I don't know how I would have made it after Charlie was born without her. I wish we could get along better. "The graphic design stuff?" I don't know a ton about what she actually does. Freelance for advertising firms, from what I understand.

Her body tenses. "I lost another client." She picks up the bottle of wine I didn't notice on her side table and pours herself a glass. From the level of the bottle, I'm guessing it's not her first. When she puts the bottle back down, it lands with a heavy thud. "That fucking Gregory from In-Line Design is undercutting me and poaching my clients." She keeps taking liberal swallows from the glass.

"I'm sorry, Shan. That totally sucks."

Her eyes shoot a glare at me. Crap. Wrong thing to say. I was going for sympathy but from the look on her face, she took it as pity.

"I didn't mean—"

"So tell me more about this job. It's *fine*," she makes air quotes. "What's that mean?"

"I said it was good," I try to clarify again.

"Your boss. The one your personal assisting for?" She smirks, like it's some kind of inside joke, or she's insinuating something by it. What I hate is that she's not that far off the mark.

"He's fine." Without meaning to, it comes out through clenched teeth.

"*Fine* again. Of courssse." The word comes out a little slurred. "I shouldn't have even asked. Nothing's ever good enough for you." She clicks the remote to flip back through the DVR menu.

"What's that supposed to mean?" Why does she have to take every single thing I say the worst way possible?

"Nothing," she mutters, selecting another episode of the same show. Without asking me what I want to watch. Naturally.

I sit up straighter. Why does she have to be such a bitch? What did I ever do to her? "No, I really want to know. What do you mean, nothing's ever good enough for me?"

Her eyes flash my direction. Apparently I have the same effect on her that she does me—we've both gone from zero to pissed in point three seconds. Sisters.

"Oh, *you know*," she says in a voice dripping with condescension. "You had everything growing up. Everything was about you." She scrunches her eyebrows together and talks in a mocking high-pitched voice. Aw, poor little Calliope needs money for her beauty pageant dresses."

Her jaw locks. "You and Mom getting manis and pedis every other week, even though it was the last thing we could afford. Oh, our Callie is a beauty *and* has brains, she's the Valedictorian of her eighth-grade class. And then, oh no," the high-pitched voice returns, "beautiful Callie has quit the pageants, what's going *on*? Is she depressed? Does she have body image issues? Maybe we should get her counseling, even though that would cost us another arm and a leg."

Her face goes hard. She downs the rest of her glass of wine so fast that some sloshes on her face and down the front of her shirt. "No matter that dad's scraping by at the bank, never able to get that promotion he was always working so hard for even though he was always kissing his boss's ass!"

I jerk back like she's slapped me.

"Shut up!" I jump to my feet. "You don't know what the hell you're talking about." I'm conscious to hiss it in a whisper-shout because of Charlie in the next room, but fury pulses through my whole body so hard I can hear my ears ringing. "I'm sorry you had a shit day at work, but you just shut up about shit you don't know anything about."

Shannon's eyes are wide and I can see that she realizes she took it too far. But I can also see that she thinks my reaction is over the top. Because of course she doesn't understand.

Because I never told.

I never told any of them about what dad's boss did to me. And yeah, tonight's not the time for late night confessions. I shake my head at her and walk out of the room.

––––––––

Shannon slept off her night of wine-bitchery and we avoided each other all of Monday. Then today we pretended nothing ever happened. You'd think we were born in the Midwest for our ability to just gloss over any of the bad shit in life and present a happy all-is-peachy façade.

I shake my head and ride the elevator down after another long day of work. I look back up in the direction of the fifteenth floor offices in bewilderment. Both yesterday and today at work, Bryce was all *Miss Cruise this* and *Miss Cruise that*. Like, he treated me with the utmost professional respect. Both in public in the meetings with project managers *and* in private.

What. The. Fuck. If only every day could be like that.

I let out a sigh. As if I, Callie Cruise, would ever get that lucky. My track record would indicate it'll never happen for me. I'll daydream about it anyway. A simple life. One where I just do my job in peace, get a killer paycheck, and go happily along my way. Have a sister like in the movies where we share makeup tips and text back and forth about guys. Kick my ex's ass in the upcoming custody battle. You know, live the American dream.

Speaking of—I slip my phone out of my purse to check the time as I hurry out of the building, and shit, I'm running late. I walk as fast as I can down the sidewalk in my heels. Damn, I should have brought a pair of comfy shoes today to change into. I knew the attorney's office was several blocks away and I wouldn't have a lot of time before my appointment.

Don Maury is a respected attorney, available, and only *somewhat* pricey. Check, check, and *check*. Not only is his law firm at the top of my wish list, he in particular is my number one pick. I've checked out two other lawyers just in case, but I've been holding out for him. I did my research. This guy has tons of reviews on the review sites where clients rate their attorneys. I traced the reviewers to actual cases to make sure they weren't trumped up reviews and they were all real. He's not only gotten great settlements, he didn't waste money in useless billable hours. Exactly what I need.

His office had the longest wait time for an appointment, even for the phone consultation I did with him last week. After facing David and the Shrew's piranha lawyer last time, I know I can't afford to go with second best just because I could get a quicker appointment time.

I keep up my pace no matter that my feet are killing me by the time I get to the office. I end up being only a couple of minutes late and manage not to even limp when I'm led into his office.

"Miss Cruise," Mr. Maury stands up and shakes my hand as I come in and sit down in his office. "How can I help you today?"

He's a middle-aged man, but his suit is sharp. The slightest paunch at his stomach and gray in his hair somehow only adds to a sense of gravitas about him. It's a good look for a lawyer.

Considering how much this guy costs per hour, I don't beat around the bush. We only went over the barest basics over the phone, so I jump right in and explain my situation with David and Charlie in full detail. I don't leave anything out. Even the restraining order and the part where I lit David's car on fire. This is no time to be shy or embarrassed. Their lawyer knows all this stuff, I want mine to be just as equipped.

Mr. Maury taps his pen on the desk where he's been making notes, looking thoughtful.

"And you feel your previous lawyer did not prepare you for the hearing?"

"God, no." I shudder. "Every single thing he'd coached me to do beforehand was wrong. He assured me no judge would take a child away from his mother. That fathers *never* won custody." It sounded wrong and sexist at the time, but all I cared about was keeping Charlie, so I shut up about it.

I shake my head. "He said all I had to do was show a lot of emotion in front of the judge. Like, cry as much as possible. Show passion about my child." Meanwhile, even before the hearing, the fees for billable hours in 'discovery' racked up to insane amounts, at least for me on my paltry waitresses' salaries.

"Then the day of the hearing, when I kept crying and trying to impress on the judge how much I loved my son, the other attorney attacked me and said I was demonstrating what an unstable and unfit mother I was, just like I'd been years ago when I'd stalked their client. When I became visibly upset about this and tried to deny their accusations, the judge himself chastised me. Meanwhile my lawyer just kept scrambling with his papers." I sit back in my chair with a huff that blows my hair out of my face. "Their lawyer tore my character to shreds. By the time he was done, if I didn't know myself, even *I* would have wondered about the wisdom of leaving a child in my care." I shake my head, my hands trembling at reliving the absolute helplessness of that afternoon.

Mr. Maury looks disturbed on my behalf. "Did your lawyer at least seek back child-support? Sometimes that alone is enough of a deterrent to a father seeking custody."

I sigh, leaning back in my chair. "Not to David. His wife is independently wealthy. And the money was gone almost as soon as the check cleared." I explain about the emergency C-Section and the days Charlie spent in the NICU.

I sigh again, this time in defeat. "I thought I was insured when I had the baby." I decide not to tell the drawn-out story about how I never thought to check the 'maternity option' on my college insurance when I signed up for it, so when I got pregnant, none of it was covered.

"But I'm more financially sound now," I hurry to add. "I can pay you, I just got a new job."

He smiles in a reassuring way. "I'm not worried. We do a credit check on all potential clients after the phone consultation and you have a reliable history. That's what we'll start building on for the next hearing. It will be all about proving how stable your life is and what a steady, cool-headed, and reliable person you are now. We'll get affidavits of witness statements on your behalf testifying this. Your excellent credit history will speak to your stability. And employment records." He's speaking out loud, but it seems half to himself as he scribbles notes on a notepad.

He looks back up at me. "Are there any men in your life?"

My mind immediately shoots to Bryce and how he's made me come in front of him twice now. And then again in front of both him and Mr. Vale. I feel my eyes widen slightly, but then I try to cover my first impulse and don't look down or away. "No. I haven't dated anyone since David." Okay, well, that's not a lie.

More scribbles in the notebook.

"All right." He taps his pen against the side of his notebook. He looks over my shoulder at the wall and it's as if I can all but see the gears turning in his head as he thinks. "I think we should take this on a two-pronged approach. On one hand, we present a defense by demonstrating what a stable influence you are, as I already mentioned, and on the other, we attack by pulling apart David's story at the seams."

I sit up straighter in my chair. "Oh? How?"

"Well, first of all, is there anyone else who can attest to the fact that he knew about the baby when you first told him?"

"I don't know," I bite at my lip. "My family knew. And one of my friends at college, but I never told her David's name since I didn't want to get him in trouble. Just that the baby's father didn't want him. I don't know who he told, if anyone. Obviously, he eventually told his wife, not that it helps," I mutter. But then I look up in excitement. "But the police! I told the police all about what happened and they were communicating with David after the fire. When I was in jail I got dehydrated and passed out. In the infirmary, the doctor confirmed I was pregnant. Maybe there was documentation that the police told David about it?"

Mr. Maury nods, taking notes.

"And in the previous hearing, you said he stated that he didn't know about the baby at all until...?"

"Until, I don't know." I shrug, feeling useless. "He never said in court how he supposedly *found out* about Charlie. One day I just got a court-ordered paternity test in the mail."

Mr. Maury's eyes gleam as he nods and makes more notes. "Even more proof he already knew. Then there's the even bigger matter."

"Which is?"

Mr. Maury looks up at me, eyebrows up. "The obvious. The fact that he was your professor. You were his student. He was how much older than you?"

I pick at my finger nails. "Um, at the time?" Duh, obviously. I answer my own question. "Nineteen years older."

Mr. Maury nods. "A man old enough to be your father, *in a position of power*, seduced you, got you pregnant, and then left you with nothing."

Oh. *That* obvious thing. I swallow as Mr. Maury continues.

"Yes, you got upset when he suddenly dropped you to go back to his wife, but he'd emotionally abused you by separating you from friends and family by forcing you to lie to protect his reputation and therefore creating an unhealthy bond." His eyes flash down at his notes before looking back at me, "It was the first time you'd ever left home. While professor/student romances are not officially banned at Stanford, they're discouraged. He was seeking tenure back then and it would have reflected badly on him."

He looks back up at me. "I looked into it after our phone consult. And isn't it interesting that David's only now seeking custody after he's been granted tenure and you're no longer a danger to his career?"

I can't help huffing in a sharp gust of breath. That bastard. He's only willing to try to see his son after he made sure his stupid career was safe. His own *son*.

"Miss Cruise? Are you all right? Miss Cruise?"

I look up, startled to realize Mr. Maury's been repeatedly calling my name and looking at me with concern. That's when I notice my hands are clutched into fists and I've all but half-risen out of my chair.

"Yes," I try to smile. "Fine." I relax my hands and smooth out my skirt. "Just realizing what a bastard my ex is."

Mr. Maury's features turn sympathetic. "Quite. Now, let's see what we can do to keep him from getting custody of your son."

I nod emphatically.

"Good. Let's start with you making a list of everyone you can think of who can testify to your fitness as a stable guardian. Then everyone you can remember talking to at the time of your pregnancy who may have known about your relationship with David. The hearing is in four weeks, so we have to work fast."

We talk and strategize some more and then the hour is over. I swear it felt like I was only in there for ten minutes. He promises he'll get his investigators on discovery. I tense as soon as I hear the word.

"Hold up," I say, body tensing. "I've done my research on your firm and from your reputation, you don't waste client hours. But my last lawyer did and I was charged for a ton of sh-" I pause, "er... stuff I didn't end up needing."

Mr. Maury shakes his head, lips curving down in what I would almost call disgust. "Miss Cruise, I would hardly call that man a lawyer. He's a bottom feeder. My firm is all about transparency. Every associate and paralegal in this firm is aware of the tight spaces our clients are in and we work our hardest not to add to your burdens. But discovery is a necessary part of our work. I can keep you updated via email of everything we're doing so that nothing comes as a surprise. You'll have control over how in depth we go."

I nod, feeling the weight lift at his words. But words are just that—words. Still, I can't afford to get screwed over again. This is a business decision. I smile to soften the blow. "You have my email. I look forward to receiving those reports."

He doesn't look at all offended. "Of course. And call me Don."

"Thanks, Don." I reach out a hand.

He gives my hand a firm shake. "Make sure to make appointments with my assistant before you leave. And Miss Cruise," he says before he turns to go, "you have a strong case."

I nod and give a tight smile in return. I can't quite bring myself to return any platitudes. No matter how well this meeting went, I don't want to jinx anything.

Still, as I finally change from my toe-pinching heels into my sneakers on the steps outside the office, I can't help but feeling hopeful for the first time in forever.

CHAPTER SEVEN

When Bryce calls me in for a meeting with an investor at another private lunch on Wednesday, at the same restaurant we met Mr. Vale at no less, I'm sure I'm about to be put on sexual parade again. But no, I'm only there to do my job. I have to scramble to come up with the numbers and figures from last week's production meeting that Bryce requests on the spot. It's a different sort of performance, I guess, and no less nerve-wracking. But at the end of that meeting, having success-fully met each of his demands, I feel proud of myself, not humiliated and ashamed.

"Good girl," Bryce says with a pat on my ass as we get back to the offices. But that's as far as he took it. Patronizing and sexist sure, but it was praise all the same. It even sounded genuine. Stupidly, it lit me up inside.

Because I'm a fucking idiot and part of me hopes it means that somewhere deep down he's coming to respect me.

Just wait for the other shoe to drop, Cals. Never let your guard down.

Which is my mentality as I go in on Thursday morning. But again, it's all professionalism as Bryce comes in and we go over the next week's agenda. He's traveling to Japan in a few weeks and it's my first-time booking travel plans.

His smile is easy as he thumbs in a name on his phone. A ping resounds on the tablet I'm holding. "I just sent you the booking agent my former PA used. She'll help you arrange the hotel and car service I prefer in Tokyo."

"Great, I'll get right on that." My tone is clipped and professional. It's my go-to when I'm dealing directly with Bryce. I can't tell if he's pretending not to notice how stiff I've gotten around him or if it simply amuses him. While I grow increasingly rigid, his posture only gets more relaxed. I've tried to loosen up. I realize that even my stiffness plays into his control over me—this constant paranoia on my part that keeps me always on edge.

"And you already have the contacts for the meetings I'll be attending?"

"Yes, I've got your itinerary already in your inbox and I'll be calling to confirm each appointment."

If it was anyone else, I'd describe the expression on Bryce's face as *encouraging*. "You're doing great. I know I'm in good hands." There's not even a trace of sarcasm in his voice.

I just stare at him a moment before I realize I haven't responded. He arches an eyebrow. "Right," I finally get out. "Thank you." Then I turn on my heel and high tail it out of there.

But that's it. I'm not called back for a strip tease or anything else.

I spend the morning arranging his flight plans and accommodations and double-checking his itinerary as promised. That turns out to be a good thing because his previous PA who'd initially set up the meetings had him double-booked one morning. It takes an hour of pleading/arguing with two Japanese PAs to get it settled so that one of the appointments can be switched to a lunch meeting. Then I had to make sure I could get a suitable table at an illustrious enough eatery to satisfy Bryce's gastric snobbery.

By the time I email the updated itinerary to Bryce, it's about five minutes till lunch. I glance over at him. Like always, the glass is unfrosted, and like always, he appears completely unaware of my presence.

Goddammit, what is he playing at? My stomach is constantly in knots waiting for whatever he's planning next. Or maybe he doesn't plan. Maybe that's his deal. There's no agenda at all and he just randomly decides to screw with me when he feels like it. Just for kicks. Maybe he genuinely doesn't care what this is doing to my head. God, he probably doesn't give two fucks about me and here I am stewing about what he's going to do next almost every hour of the day that I'm here working.

Impulsively, I click print on the itinerary in front of me and then march over to Bryce's office. The sensor-triggered door between our offices slides open smoothly as I approach.

Bryce looks up as I enter. If he's surprised, it doesn't show on his face. "Yes?" he smiles easily. The way he's been acting, I'd swear he had an evil twin and the nice one switched places this week.

I eye him, looking for... I don't even know what. A flash of the sinister? Christ. Why did I even come in here? I just need something to happen. Or not happen. This not knowing is seriously screwing with my head.

"I finished your itinerary for the Tokyo trip. I emailed it to you but thought you might like a hard copy to look over as well. So, you know..." I flounder, "you could tell me if you'd like to make any changes."

I set the piece of paper on the desk in front of him.

"Very good." He looks at me. After an uncomfortably long beat, he asks, "Is there anything else I can do for you?"

Dammit. How does he always do that, even when he's the nice guy version of himself? Make me feel like I'm constantly on uneven footing with him. "No, well... I—"

"Yes?"

"I was just wondering..." I trail off. Damn it. How do I ask what I want to know? *I was wondering when you plan to start up your games of messing with me again? Would you just tell me why you're doing whatever it is you're doing with me? Why you hired me in the first place?* I sigh internally. Even if I did have the lady balls, he'll just give me some vague non-answer that will put me at even more of a disadvantage because I was stupid and vulnerable enough to ask.

"Miss Cruise?"

I paste on a fake smile. "Nothing. I'm off to lunch now. Can I bring you anything back?"

He nods. "A Philadelphia club on rye from the shop on the corner."

"All right. I'll be back at the end of my lunch hour." With that, I all but scurry from the room. I only feel like I can really breathe again once I'm in the elevator and heading away from Gentry Tech offices. Which is how it usually goes.

Stepping into those offices every morning is like jumping down the rabbit hole. I become some strange Not-Me version of myself for eight hours only to emerge on the other side a bit dazed. Then I try to block out everything that happened until I have to return again.

When I come out onto the sidewalk, I take in a deep breath of air. It's noon and the sun is right on top of the city. I love the way it warms me. Summer in the Bay Area never gets very hot and it's still only mid-June. It feels like a perfect seventy-degree day, balmy with an idyllic breeze coming in off the bay. I pull off my suit jacket so I can feel the sun directly on my skin.

There *I* am.

I'm still here underneath the craziness my life has become. I saunter down the street, not even caring that I'm wasting minutes of my lunch hour. I haven't actually gotten to take my full lunch hour very often since I started working for Bryce. Usually I work straight through it and just grab a granola bar from the vending machine and other times there have been business or working lunches.

But the couple times I've taken the escape like this, it's just pure pleasure getting out of the madhouse. No expectations or anxieties.

I don't have to be Personal Assistant/Sex Toy or even Mommy. I'm just an anonymous face in this big, diverse city. Speaking of diverse— last time I was out on my own, I ate at one of the food trucks. But today I'm looking for something a little more interesting.

I stop at a Korean restaurant because they have tables outside. It's too beautiful a day to shut myself back up indoors yet. A hostess seats me and brings me water while I look over the menu.

I don't recognize most of what I'm looking at. I didn't do a lot of adventurous eating even when I was at Stanford simply because I didn't have the money for any frivolous spending.

A cute young girl, maybe college age, introduces herself as Seo-yeon. It's on her name tag, too. "What can I get for you today?"

I smile up at her. "I have no idea, but I'm pretty game for anything. What do you recommend or what's the special today?"

"Are you vegetarian?"

I shake my head no.

"Then how about the bulgogi beef tacos? They're a favorite."

"Tacos?" I laugh. "I thought this was a Korean place."

She grins. "It's California. Everything comes in a taco. Though shh," she lowers her voice and leans in, "we call it Korean-Mexican *fusion*."

I laugh again and it feels good. "That sounds awesome. The Korean beef taco it is."

I order iced tea with it and soon I'm sipping my iced tea and leaning back with a relaxed smile on my face as I people watch on the busy street. There are people in business attire like me, but blended in are college kids since the U is only a few blocks from here. Plenty of tourists, too. Take for example that sun-burned couple with the fanny pack who can't stop taking selfies with every palm tree they see. Then there's a dad pushing a stroller with two little girls, one a baby and one who looks about a year older than Charlie. The older one is chattering nonstop while they roll past me. I'm still smiling even when a shadow comes up behind me and blocks my sun.

"Miss Cruise."

I almost spill my drink as my whole body stiffens. I look behind me. What. The. Fuck?

"Mr. Vale." I'm halfway up and out of my chair before he holds out a hand as if to calm me down. "Are you stalking me?"

He walks around the table and takes the seat across from me. I still don't know whether to sit down or take off down the street.

"Relax, Miss Cruise. I'm not, as you put it, *stalking* you." The idea sounds ludicrous coming out of his mouth and his next statement calms me even more. "Coming across you and your son the other day in the park was entirely coincidence. And please, call me Jackson."

I sit back down in my chair.

"As for meeting you now, well, I was hoping to catch you at lunch. I did have my driver watching for you. My office isn't far and he reported you were here. I wanted to apologize. It felt like I might have..." he swallows and looks across the street, "made you uncomfortable when I approached you and your son at the park last Saturday."

I blink. So he wasn't stalking me on Saturday at the park, but he *is* today. That's supposed to make me feel better?

"Um... okay?" I eye him warily. He's dressed very similarly to how he was when Bryce and I met him for lunch last week. Sleek, dark gray business wear. White shirt, gray tie. Obviously expensive. Again he's got that sexy five o'clock-shadow-at-noon thing going on. Shit, did I just refer to him as sexy?

I shake my head and am about to look away when I'm caught by his eyes. Ice blue. Focused entirely on me.

I do look away then. This guy is too intense. I've already got one of that kind of man in my life. I definitely don't need another. Especially one that witnessed what Jackson Vale did. My cheeks pink with shame at the memory and I duck my head.

"All right. Apology accepted. The meeting at the park was an accident. Got it." I give an awkward hand wave. "Nice to see you again, Mr. Vale. If you'll excuse me, I'm just going to enjoy my lunch now."

I keep my eyes firmly on my table but I can tell out of my peripheral vision that his hulking body isn't moving to leave.

"I told you, it's Jackson." His voice is a deep baritone, like the air is echoing around in that large-chambered chest of his before it makes it up his throat and out of his mouth.

"I feel like I need to warn you about Bryce Gentry. He's not a good man. Associating with him..." he pauses as if not knowing how to get out what he's trying to say. "I worry— He's just not—"

My eyes flash up at him and I can't help the laugh that comes out of my mouth. "Are you kidding?" I lean over the table. "Look, pal." I meet his dark eyes with mine. I don't bother hiding how pissed I am. "I don't know you. You *really* don't know me." I enunciate each word carefully. "I can take care of myself just fine. I don't need strangers trying to get involved in my business."

Just then Seo-yeon comes back with my food. It looks and smells delicious. As ever, I'm not a girl who loses her appetite when stressful things are happening. I'm the opposite. I stress eat. The longer Mr. Vale sits across from me, the more I want to stuff my face.

Screw it. I just told him I don't care. I grab the taco and take a huge, satisfying bite. And a juicy bite. Did I mention juicy? Because some kind of sauce drips down my chin. I try not to be too obvious about searching for my napkin. Yeah. Tacos, not so great for dining with a companion.

Then again, I never asked for this companion.

"If you don't mind," I say with my mouth still full of food. No need to bother with politeness, after all. "I'm trying to have a nice, relaxing lunch here. *Alone.*"

As I watch, one edge of his mouth quirks up. He reaches over and hands me a napkin.

I snatch the napkin and swipe at my chin. I can't take my eyes off Jackson. Is that a smile I see on the untouchable Mr. Vale's face? It's not like Bryce's smiles either, which always feel fake or manipulative. No, from the little I've known of him, Mr. Vale doesn't seem like the kind of man who bothers with fake smiles. If I've managed to get one out of him, it's genuine. Granted, I did it by being a gross lunch companion, but...

But nothing. I do not want this man around. Frankly, I don't want any men around, and certainly none associated with Bryce. Even if they are enemies. Although, if this guy is Bryce's enemy, doesn't that actually say good things about him?

Shut up, brain. I grab my ice tea and take a big swallow to wash down the too-large bit of taco I just ate. The whole time, he just keeps sitting there, watching me with that steady gaze of his.

I huff out an exasperated breath. "What?" I ask. "Why are you sitting here? What do you want from me?" It feels good to ask the question, the one I didn't dare put to Bryce earlier.

Mr. Vale... *Jackson*... leans back in his chair, his eyes narrowed, scrutinizing me. "I'm trying to understand. Why you?"

"What do you mean?" I genuinely have no idea what he's talking about.

"Why is Bryce dangling you in front of me?"

Wha— I just blink. "Dangling?"

"Why do you think he brought you to that lunch meeting?"

Um. To screw with me?

He looks at me like he's waiting for me to catch up with the program. "You were bait."

"Oh my God, dramatic much?" I drop my head back and look up into the blue sky. Except it's not just blue now. There are gray clouds floating in. "Perfect, just perfect," I mutter to myself.

"What?" Jackson asks. "If you've spent any time with him, you know he likes to play games with people."

I glare back at him. I'm tempted to take another bite of my taco, which is freaking delicious by the way, but I figure this will go faster if I don't have to talk through a mouthful of food.

"Look," I toss my hands up in the air. "This is really none of your business. But even if Bryce's trying to play at something..." I shake my head again. I don't really get what Jackson's even saying Bryce's trying to do, but whatever. "I'm up to my eyeballs trying to handle that guy already, and he's my boss. I don't need you fucking with me, too. If he's trying to mess with you," I gesture between us. "It seems like you being here or seeking me out or whatever is playing right into whatever he wants, right? So just ignore me, go off and do what you do, and I'll do the same. Groovy?"

He's quiet for a long second before responding, "Did you just say... groovy?"

I feel my face color slightly, but before I can say anything else, he continues, "and what do you mean, you're up to your eyeballs trying to handle Bryce? What's he doing that's making you have to *handle* him?" He leans in closer and his voice drops. "Things like what happened at lunch last week?"

How could he ask that? How *dare* he ask that?

Suddenly I can't stand to be sitting here. In spite of how good my lunch looks and tastes, I can't do this. He's ruined it. Ruined it just like the rain drops that start to spatter the sidewalk around me. I reach into my purse blindly and pull out my wallet.

"Miss Cruise," Jackson says, but I ignore him and slap down money for my lunch including a nice tip on the table. It's not Seo-yeon's fault my lunch got ruined.

I swallow hard and only then realize I'm biting back tears. I never cry. I'm *so* not a crier. How dare he bring up that fucking lunch? What a bastard.

I stand and then start walking as fast as I can away from Jackson.

"Wait, please wait," he calls behind me but I don't slow down.

But then as the rain starts to fall harder, he grabs my arm and swings me partially around. His blue eyes are as dark as the clouds above our heads. "All I need to know is if you're his willingly. Are you?"

Of all the— "I'm not *his*," I sputter indignantly. "He doesn't fucking own me."

And for some reason this sets off a flare of intensity and... satisfaction? in Jackson's expression. That's it, I officially give up trying to understand any of this.

But then he leans over and speaks so softly in my ear I can barely hear it above the falling rain. "If you belonged to me, Miss Cruise, you wouldn't look so disgusted. True ownership goes both ways. I would own you, but you'd own me, too. A concept I'm sorry to say Bryce Gentry's never understood."

My breath hitches and I pull back from the intimacy of his voice on my ear, only to get lost in the dark blue of his eyes.

"Let me go," I whisper.

He does and then he turns and is gone into the rain-soaked street, leaving me behind, breathless and confused.

———

I'm drenched down to my skivvies by the time I get back into the office. I'm such an idiot for not checking my weather app before I left. The warm of the afternoon is totally gone. Now I'm a wet, shivering mess.

On the elevator up to the fifteenth floor I shove another huge bite of sandwich in my mouth. I can't believe I had to buy two lunches for myself. I thought my appetite was ruined after the run-in with Jackson. Yeah. That lasted until I got to the sandwich shop to order Bryce's food and was assaulted by the delicious smell of fresh baked bread.

Stupid, *stupid* to let Jackson get to me. I roll my eyes at myself. Not that there would have been much time to enjoy my first lunch anyway. I had to wait in line almost twenty minutes for the sandwiches. Hence stuffing my face on my way back up to work.

I manage one more bite before the elevator pings open.

I try to walk through the lobby toward my office with as much dignity as I can while looking like a cross between a drowned rat and a chipmunk with cheeks stuffed full of sandwich. Maybe no one's looking.

"Mr. Gentry said to go directly to his office when you return," the receptionist says oh so helpfully, looking me up and down. She's blonde and skinny as a rail, one of those model thin chicks.

"I gug gogga," I try to say with my mouth full, gesturing toward my office first, but she shakes her head vehemently.

"Oh no, Mr. Gentry was very clear that you were to go to his office first thing."

I chew hard and try to swallow quickly. "Look, Madison, I'm soaked, I'm just gonna go in my office real quick to change—" but she's already pressed her little intercom button.

"Mr. Gentry," she says in this girlish voice that's higher pitched than the one she was just using with me, "Miss Cruise is back from lunch."

"Why isn't she in my office?" Bryce's voice is annoyed.

"I don't know," says Madison, sounding innocent, "I gave her your message right away, just like you asked, sir."

Seriously? I just stare at her and she smiles at me, one of those petty bitch girl smiles. Oh my God, why am I surrounded by all these people determined to create drama? It makes me just want to go home, put on my rattiest pair of pajamas, and play building blocks with my two-and-a-half-year-old. Stack the blocks. Knock them over. Adorable giggling ensues. An hour playing blocks with Charlie and all the world's problems could be put in perspective and solved, I shit you not.

I breathe out. *Remember the bigger picture, Callie.* All of this BS is so that you can keep having that time with your little boy.

I turn on my heel and walk, dress and hair still dripping, into Bryce's office. He's typing away at his laptop.

"Your lunch." I drop the slightly damp bag onto his desk and turn to go toward my office.

"Stop."

I do and with effort, keep the annoyance and frustration off my face.

"Yes?"

"Did you have a nice lunch?" he asks. For once, he's stopped what he's doing and his face isn't buried in his computer screen while he addresses me. Nope, he's gazing at me like he's trying to ferret some clue out of me. I shift uncomfortably in my heels.

"Not especially," I say slowly, gesturing down at myself. "I was sitting at a café outside and it started raining."

He keeps staring at me.

I raise my eyebrows like I'm waiting for a punch line. "Is there something else you wanted?"

"Yes, actually," he smiles and it reminds me of a suddenly satisfied shark. I shift uncomfortably on my heels. Are we finally getting back to asshole Bryce?

"I had a call while you were out. Only about fifteen minutes ago, actually. Can you guess who it was from?"

"I never was good at twenty questions," I quip. I'm ready to get into a dry change of clothes.

His smile only sharpens at my short reply. Bastard. "It was my old friend Jackson Vale from CubeThink. You remember our dining companion from last week?"

My breath hitches and it doesn't go unnoticed. Bryce's eyes narrow and again I'm reminded of a shark.

"What did he want?"

Bryce sits back in his chair, fingers crossing underneath his chin. "Well, if you can believe it, he was interested in discussing the very collaboration he seemed so against last Thursday. Do you have any idea as to what might have changed his mind?"

"No," I whisper. And really, I don't. I mean, the offer of collaboration Bryce laid out at the lunch sounded like a good deal, but Jackson's distaste for Bryce seemed deeply rooted. Then again, he also came across as a dispassionate man—maybe he can separate personal feelings from business. But no, *dispassionate* is the wrong word.

My cheeks heat at the memory. *If you belonged to me, Miss Cruise...*

"Well, he intimated that for particular... *personal* reasons," Bryce sneers, "he'd rather not work with me on the project. I suggested several of my project managers, but do you know what he said?" He continues scrutinizing me with his head tilted slightly sideways.

I swallow and wish I had grabbed a bottle of water from the sandwich shop. I shake my head.

"He said that he preferred to work with none other than my promising personal assistant. It seems you made quite the impression on him the other day."

I feel my cheeks go even hotter.

"But I— I mean, we barely spoke— And I—" Christ, most of what Jackson saw the other day was Bryce getting me off under the table. Is *that* what Jackson wants me for? Am I being passed around as a sex toy now?

The rest of Jackson's words from earlier come back to me. *True ownership goes both ways. I would own you, but you'd own me, too.*

Was that all just a line of BS? I shake my head internally. *Christ, Cals, of course it was.* Right afterwards, he called your boss to arrange some kind of business swap, for Christ's sake.

"Is everything all right, Miss Cruise?" Bryce's voice jolts me roughly back to the present.

"Yes." I straighten. "Of course."

"Oh, *of course*, is it?" Bryce asks in a voice just short of mocking. "So you feel that you're up to the task? You'll be able to present the drone models we have on contract with the Department of Defense in such a way that Jackson Vale, top of his class, graduate of MIT, and winner of the MacArthur Genius Grant will want to join the project? You'll be able to detail technical specifications to get him to agree to a collaboration that's too attractive to say no to?"

Bryce stands and puts his fists on his desk, leaning over. "Because that's what a good salesperson does when they pitch. They *seduce*," his voice drops. "Do you have what it takes to seduce Jackson Vale, Miss Cruise?"

My mouth goes even more dry and I feel my eyes widen.

"If you do," Bryce's eyes glitter, "then you can move up in this company. You won't be stuck as my personal assistant with all the," his eyes drop to my breasts, "*personal* responsibilities it entails." His gaze returns to mine. "If you succeed at this acquisition, I'll put it in writing that you'll have paid leave while you finish your degree at Stanford and a product management position at any Gentry Tech research lab in the country."

It takes a beat before what he's just said sinks in.

"Seriously?" A completely fresh start. The job of my dreams. Away from him, away from Charlie's father, making money—real money, being able to live quietly and securely. It's all I've ever wanted. I bite my lip. Which means it's too good to be true. *Don't be a goddamned idiot, Callie.*

"Seriously," Bryce smiles. "This acquisition is that important to me, so if you succeed, I'll give you the things that are important to you."

Damn it, he looks so genuine.

"Go get changed and then we'll start discussing your pitch. For the next week, you'll eat, breathe, and sleep Gentry Technologies."

CHAPTER EIGHT

And so I do. Bryce makes no sexual advances or strange requests at all for an entire week. All I do is study. Because everything Gentry Tech does is under government contract, I can't take any of the materials home to study. That means I arrive early and stay late. It's David's weekend with Charlie so I come in on the weekend to work.

I study marketing reports, research grants, and every detail of the defense contracts Gentry Tech won last year. It's crazy impressive. Far more than that, though, I study the specs of every product Gentry Tech has made in the past and the project up for collaboration.

These aren't the kind of long-range drones that are used for bombing—the exact opposite in fact. These are surveillance drones, and they're far more sophisticated than anything on the current market. They'll be able to get into territory that is too dangerous for human scouts to venture into, both to detect targets and to make sure there are no civilians before bombings are green flagged.

But for drones like this to be effective, they have to be fast, durable, and even semi-intelligent. At least intelligent enough to map terrain as they go, to locate possible shelter when there's bad weather, to react to objects in their flight path, and to avoid other nearby projectiles. According to what the material I'll be presenting promises,

Bryce's come up with algorithms that push the boundaries of what AI has ever been able to do before in responding to real time situational obstacles.

Frankly, I'm shocked and impressed by what I'm reading. I had no idea drone technology was this advanced. Bryce might be a bastard, but he's an incredibly intelligent bastard. He's pushing the state-of-the-art to places it's never been before.

I don't have access to all the algorithms themselves, since they are the equivalent of state secrets, but what I'm able to see is still impressive as hell. In spite of myself, I start getting excited about the whole thing. This could be my future, being a part of such cutting-edge tech. When I go home at night, there's a pep in my step as I cook dinner for me and Shannon and spoon mushed peas into Charlie's mouth.

"What's up with you?" Shannon asks on Wednesday night. The night before the big meeting.

"Nothing," I say as I hum to Charlie, zooming the spoon toward his mouth again. He clamps his lips shut right as the spoonful of peas mashes into his closed mouth and spatters down his chin. I scoop up the sloppy peas with the spoon and try again.

"Charlie!" I raise my eyebrows and do a goofy little dance. "Charlie! Lookee here!"

He cracks a smile and I use the opportunity to slip the peas in his open mouth. Only a third of them stay in, but hey, it's all about the little victories when it comes to peas.

"High five, little man," I say when we get through the jar. "It's all about the little victories," I murmur, this time out loud.

And I believe it. I've got to. For all our sakes.

———

The morning of my meeting with Jackson, I take extra time getting ready. Shannon's already taken Charlie out for the morning to get groceries, so for one rare opportunity, I have the apartment entirely to myself. Not that I'm actually enjoying the time relaxing. Ha. Nope, pretty much the exact opposite.

My favorite mantra is back in play as I wet the end of a Q-tip and rub off the eyeliner I've screwed up for the third time in as many tries.

"Don't fuck this up," I whisper into the empty bathroom. I can barely hear myself over Adele's power ballads coming out of the ancient speaker dock my iPod is plugged into. I take a deep breath and then try one more time with the eyeliner pencil. I get it right this time, thank God.

I have to channel Powerful Woman today. Confidence. I've got to land Jackson Vale's business. Bryce made that clear enough. I finally have the chance to show I'm more than just a blonde with air bags for a chest. I pop the lid on my mascara and set my jaw.

I'm determined to make this happen. I stare at myself in the mirror. The face looking back is as attractive as I can make it. Still, I frown at the pretty reflection and then sigh. I might want this to be all about the product, but I'm not naïve. Pretty packaging has proven to help things sell whether I like it or not. And I need every advantage I can get. After I finish with my mascara, I flip through my makeup bag and look at my assortment of lipsticks and pull out three shades.

Well hell. Do I go with a soft pink, a nude, or siren red? What's the message I'm trying to portray? Again, not an idiot here. Each of these colors says something different. My gaze lingers on the red. Yes, it says sexy, but it's also a power color. And I'm not there to be a sweet blushing pink, or to fade into the background like a nude. I pick up the red, decision made.

I've already smoothed my hair back into a sleek chignon. Putting on the fitted dark gray skirt suit, a chic and expensive number from Bryce's collection, only completes the feel. I check one last time to make sure everything's in my bag.

Shit, my shoes. I grab my black pumps and settle them at the top of the bag, then slip on my comfy pair of Toms for the train ride—this time I won't arrive to an important meeting with scuffed shoes. I pull my sleek laptop case over my shoulder in addition to the bag. Bryce let me bring my work laptop home for once since I'm heading straight to CubeThink for the ten a.m. meeting with Jackson. Finally, I'm out the door.

On the light rail, there aren't any seats left. Of course, on the one day I would kill to sit down. That's not going to stop me. I hold on to one of the poles and shuffle through the notecards of handwritten notes I wrote up yesterday, studying the points I need to make sure to hit this morning. I close my eyes and whisper them over and over to myself. I'm sure I'm getting looks from people around me. It's the behavior of a college student jamming for a test but the outfit of a business woman.

I open my eyes again as I whisper under my breath, "modified aerial algorithms to seek and react in ways that outperform both current military and commercial models. For example, the RQ-16 T-Hawk—" I pause when I notice that the guy beside me is not only staring at me, but seems like he's trying to listen in to what I'm saying. I smile awkwardly and shift so that I'm standing with my back to him. Where was I? Right. *The RQ-16 T Hawk...*

I keep reciting talking points to myself all the way to my stop. CubeThink's offices are in a building only a couple of miles from Gentry Tech. Then again, it's Silicon Valley—everything is just a few miles away from everything here. The Google Complex is only four miles further from CubeThink. All these genius brains, cooking here so close together in the northern Cali fog. But there's only one genius mind I need to sway today.

I stride down the steps at the light rail stop, ignoring the homeless that inevitably crowd the station. I'm too focused on my task to pay them any attention. *Don't fuck this up.*

The train stop is about a block away from the CubeThink building. I stop when I'm halfway there and check my makeup with a compact from the outer zipper on my bag where I keep my last-minute makeup supplies. It's not a hot day but I'm sweating. *Real attractive, Callie.* I pull out some oil blotting strips and dab at my face. I smile and see lipstick on my teeth. *God.* I almost walked in there like this. I scrub at my teeth with some spare napkins in my purse until they're nice and shiny white again. I breathe out and sniff myself. Okay. Thank Christ I remembered to put on deodorant at least. I opted not to go for perfume, because that just says I'm trying too hard, right?

I straighten up and walk around the corner and into the Cube-Think offices. I am *not* going to fuck this up. I've studied the hell out of the product I'll be discussing with Jackson. I know the material in and out and upside down, both Bryce's proposal and what products Jackson's company is currently pursuing. What we have to offer and what Jackson has to gain.

I *can* get this deal made. I *will* get this deal made.

I pull open the door and head into the building. I'm let past security and take the elevator up. Whoa. As I step out of the elevator into the CubeThink offices, I'm taken aback at what a different vibe they have from Gentry Tech. From the sumptuous throw rug on the floor to the overstuffed leather couches in the waiting room, this place screams old world elegance.

Even the receptionist, a woman who looks like she's in her fifties, sits behind a heavy cherry mahogany desk. She's dressed smartly, but it's more what I might call cardigan-chic. Cute retro cats eyeglasses frame her shrewd eyes.

"I have an appointment with Mr. Vale," I say, smiling and standing up straight. "Miss Calliope Cruise."

The woman eyes me for a second like she's appraising me and then picks up her telephone to notify Mr. Vale that his ten o'clock is here. She nods at something he says and then sets the phone down.

"You can go on back," she says to me. "Down that hallway," she points behind her. "Last door at the very end."

I smile, my mouth feeling suddenly dry, as I head back. Again, unlike GentryTech's offices, this place isn't laid out on an open floor-plan, but seems very old-school. The hallway is somewhat narrow, with office doors at intervals on either side. But I can see that the hallway ends at Jackson's door. Of course. Corner office.

I knock lightly on the door when I finally make it there.

"Come in."

I take one last deep breath and then step inside.

Jackson stands up and walks around his desk when I enter.

"Oh," I can't help expelling a surprised noise as he approaches, hand out.

"Calliope, so nice to see you again." The furrow between his eyes softens as I enter. Instead of stoic or brusque, he looks almost... agreeable. Maybe even pleased. To see me?

I shove my hand out, thrown a little off my game. And I've only been in his presence less than thirty seconds. *Off to a great start here, Cals.*

I mentally give myself a shake even as I clasp his hand in what I hope is a firm grasp. But not too firm. What is all that crap I've heard about the psychology of a handshake? Be firm and confident? I strengthen my grip but then realize I might be coming off like I'm grasping desperately onto his hand. I loosen my hold. And now that was just weird, so I let go entirely and try not to grimace. If Jackson notices anything strange, at least he has the grace not to let on.

He quickly looks me up and down. One edge of his mouth quirks up, and then he walks back around his desk and takes a seat in his office chair. Again with the old-world luxury—it's a burgundy wing-backed leather affair with brass buttons lining the sides. I can't help staring for a second. Who uses such an overstuffed antique chair for their regular office chair? That thing could double as a throne.

"Nice chair." It just pops out of my mouth. I bite my lip and wish I could recall the words, but it's too late. They're out there and echoing in the lavish room.

Jackson simply stares at me, saying nothing. He's still looking at me like my visit is pleasant, though, so that's... something? A good start, at least.

"I'm a man who enjoys the finer things in life, you'll find, Miss Cruise," is his only response after another half minute of silence.

Why does my stomach swoop when he says that? Maybe because he's staring at me the whole time, eyes so focused. I don't know what to make of it. *Come on Cals, is that really true?* Damn it. If I'm being honest, I know what I'm seeing in his eyes right now is attraction. And it's flattering. He's a handsome, powerful man. But I'm not here for that. It's the *last* thing I need to deal with right now. Especially since I can't be sure if he's actually attracted to *me* or if it's just that he's attracted to the thing he can't have—Bryce's plaything.

That thought's enough to sour any sizzle I might feel at his attention.

I take the seat across from him, drop my heavy purse, keeping the laptop case balancing on my knees. "Shall I begin with the opportunity

Gentry Technologies is proposing?" I slide out the laptop. "I have all the specs here and the proposed collaborative schema—"

Jackson rolls his eyes and waves a hand. "Do we have to dive into work right off the bat? I'd much rather talk about you, Calliope Cruise."

I'm struck dumb for a moment. Dammit. That's not good. Maybe the red lipstick was a bad idea after all. I need to get the focus onto the product and off of me.

I smile demurely. "The best way to get to know me is to see me work, Mr. Vale. Now, why don't I start by showing you our project proposal? Where can I hook up my laptop to a projector?" I look around the office. "Or we could go to a conference room if you'd prefer?"

Jackson just sits back in his throne-like chair and crosses a leg at the ankle in a relaxed posture. "Our systems are being updated." He gestures toward a chair in the corner that's also leather, but has wheels. "Besides, there's no need for such formalities when it's just the two of us. Your laptop looks like it has a large screen. Just grab that chair and come sit beside me."

"Oh." My eyes shoot between the chair he's nodded to and then back to him. Is he lying about the projectors? Really, the whole company is updating their systems the day I happen to be visiting?

I turn and coolly walk to the chair so he can't see my inner freak out on my face. This isn't going at all how I expected. I was going to be calm and collected, dispassionately explaining my slides, preferably in a large conference room setting. Not cozying up beside him in this luxurious office. My eyes flick around all the dark wood, the landscape oil paintings on the walls, the luxurious carpeting and—oh *shit*!

Shit, shit, shit!

I never switched to my heels.

Here I am in my power suit... and my ratty old faded red Toms. Because nothing says classy like kitschy canvas shoes that have a hole near the big toe. Christ. If Jackson didn't notice before, surely he's going to notice now that I'll be sitting beside him for the next half hour.

I grab the chair quickly and get behind it as fast as I can. Maybe it's hiding my feet? God let it be hiding my feet! I can feel the heat in my cheeks.

Stop freaking out, Cal, maybe he's not even looking at you. I glance up at Jackson.

He's looking right at me.

Crap. Did he see my feet? I can't tell.

I shove the chair over the small space between the corner of the office and his desk. "So as I was saying, Gentry Tech is doing really advanced, um...," dammit, brain fart, brain fart, "really advanced things," I finish lamely. I sit down in the chair and hide my feet under the desk even though it makes me sit at an odd angle.

Okay. Time to recover. I try to clear my head. Remember the talking points. Right. Talking points. "Like the government contracts I was talking about." I nod. Yes. Government contracts. Right.

Jackson makes a disgusted face. "Bryce's always been obsessed with getting Defense contract money. It's one of the things we disagreed about early on."

I nod as I open my laptop lid. I'm familiar with the difference in their philosophies. My job is to show him that the gap between them isn't as wide as he thinks. "While you were always more interested in going commercial."

"You've done your homework."

I bring up my initial slides. Good. Getting into the work I've prepared is calming me down and centering me. Yes. I can do this. This is what I've prepped for. I take a deep breath as I bring up an ad for CubeThink's latest top-of-the-line commercial drone on the market. It's for serious enthusiasts and runs in the three-thousand-dollar range.

"Now, take your newest model you released at the beginning of this year." I list off the specifications. "Ten pounds, has a rechargeable electric battery life of thirty minutes—impressive, by the way," I interject, and he gives an acquiescing nod. "It goes at speeds of up to forty miles per hour and takes HD quality film that streams directly to your mobile device."

I look up at Jackson. "All of this is impressive and makes you a competitor in your market." He nods, but he's starting to look impatient.

"If you're going to sit here all morning and tell me what my company's already accomplishing, Miss Cruise—"

"But," I cut him off, narrowing my eyes at his intrusion, "all that makes you only competitive. The DJI Phantom currently holds the international market share in commercial UAVs. What's going to push you ahead in the upcoming decade of drone wars?"

I click through the next few slides, feeling my confidence building. "I'll skip the history lesson. I'm sure you're as familiar with military drones as you are with commercial. You know the RQ-16 T-Hawk was used for almost a decade in Iraq and Afghanistan." I don't bother posing it as a question.

"Naturally."

I click past the slides detailing the specs for the gas-powered scouting drone that soldiers carried in backpacks and then sent ahead for reconnaissance to check an area before entering.

I look up at Jackson before I click to the next slide. His dark eyes seem to miss nothing as he watches me. It almost trips me up, but I push through. It's far easier if I keep my eyes on my laptop. Why does his body have to take up so much *space*? "Gentry Tech is building the next generation of small recon drones."

The specs for Bryce's new design come on screen. "As you can see," I start, "this model is sleeker, much lighter, and is battery instead of gas powered. We hope in our collaboration with CubeThink to change that to electric battery or even solar charged. If you'll look here—"

Jackson reaches over and grabs the laptop, brow furrowed in interest as he zooms in on several parts of the design.

He's even closer now and it's impossible not to...well, inhale him. Pine. He smells like pine and man and for a second I imagine him sitting in that big leather chair of his out in a forest cabin somewhere, just having come in from chopping wood.

"Interesting," he says under his breath and I startle back to the moment. "He decided not to go for a coaxial motor design." Then he huffs through his nose. "And just how does he expect to get the quick lift he needs without the multiple motors?"

He's still got the laptop in hand and I bite my lip. I can't exactly snatch it back, but at the same time, I can't afford to lose control of this meeting now. "If you'll just click through one slide over, you'll see the modular design for a single centralized motor. This way there's less chance for engine failure on one of the limbs that could take down the whole copter."

He does and it's a close up of the internal motor. I start to describe the unique aspects of what Bryce's done, just as I studied, but Jackson's already clicking through several slides ahead.

"Wait, you just skipped—" I start to say, my voice strangled, but he only waves his hand at me like he's brushing away a fly. His focus is entirely engaged in the laptop. He clicks through slide after slide of the specs for Bryce's design and then he comes to the end of the presentation and looks up to me, exasperated.

"Where's the rest of it?" He looks back down at the computer, double-clicking on the presentation and going through it at lightning speed as if this time, he'll find a different conclusion.

"That's all there is."

"What? But where's the code?" He looks up at me like I've just said something ludicrous. Again his eyes make me pause. They're such a dark blue. I've never seen anything like that color before. Not to mention the way he looks at me—with such a direct intensity. "Or at least some pseudo-code that tells me the direction his programming is going to take?"

I swallow and look away from the disturbing force of his gaze. I thought it was strange that Bryce didn't send any code too, but I give him one of the answers Bryce provided when I asked him the same question.

"Aren't you most interested in the hardware side?" I sidestep. "That's what you're getting out of the bargain, isn't it? The contacts with the best parts-makers in Japan and around the world? That's what he's showing you here." I point to the screen.

But Jackson starts shaking his head before I'm even done speaking. "That has nothing to do with what he's proposing we collaborate on. That's just the bait. All that tells me is that he's desperate to get me on board for this project."

Dammit, I'm losing him. I try again with Bryce's second explanation. "This is just the first discussion to start laying our cards on the table to begin the process. Gentry Tech is showing you ours and letting you see what we're working on ahead of anybody else. It's a show of good faith."

Jackson scoffs like that's the biggest steaming pile he's ever heard and sets my laptop none-too-gently down on his desk. "A show of good faith?" He laughs and puts one elbow on the arm of his chair, then leans his chin on it and watches me with narrowed eyes.

"What good is hardware without the software to run it, Miss Cruise?"

I can't help the slight slouch of my shoulders in spite of my determination not to show any sign of weakness. "It's like a human body without a brain. Useless."

His eyebrows rise. "Exactly. So you see now what Bryce has offered me in this *so-called* show of good faith. Nothing. A beautiful car with nothing under the hood. The future of drone technology is how intelligent they are."

I perk up. This is in my talking points. Why didn't I think of it sooner? "But he's discussed that in meetings with our product development team. That's what this new project is all about—developing a drone that's intuitive and can map terrain to find shelter, avoid projectiles and other objects in the air. Didn't you see? There was even a slide about it." I start to open the laptop, but he puts his hand on top of mine to stop me and I look up to find he's leaned close. So close I'm inhaling his scent even more deeply. Pine. Woodsy. God, he smells really good. And his hand is warm. If I closed my eyes, I could imagine us both there in the cabin.

"I'm not interested in his claims. Bryce could always talk a good game." His face is only inches from mine. "Follow-through, however, was always more my strong suit," his voice is low, so low I'd swear I can feel the rumble of it up through my chair and straight to my—

"Oh," I pull away to put more distance. "I'm sure Mr. Gentry wouldn't make claims he couldn't deliver on."

Jackson's eyes narrow and the edges of his mouth dip down. "You have so much faith in him after working with him for what, a month?"

I feel my face flush. Damn my easy blushing cheeks. "I didn't say that. I just meant that anyone of his reputation couldn't just waltz around making false business promises. I mean, he won a Department of Defense contract to build this drone. Besides," I say, a bit confused now, "I know you two don't..." how to put this diplomatically? "see eye to eye, but you've worked together. Surely, you admit he's a genius when it comes to software development."

Jackson says nothing, he's still just staring at me.

"And that's how you see him? Are you attracted to that kind of arrogant, *genius*, as you put it?"

I balk. "It doesn't matter how I see him. His intelligence can't be denied."

"What if it matters to me? How you see him."

His gray eyes are staring me down. He's so focused on me it's like he's looking past any façade I thought I was putting up today—past my attempted professionalism, past my pretend cool and straight into *me*.

Which is not what this meeting is supposed to be about at all.

I breathe out, praying with my last bit of patience that I don't sound as frustrated or confused as I am. "In the end, it doesn't matter what either of us feels about Bryce." My neck feels hot as I look back up at Jackson. "All that matters is that he's a man who can get the job done. Haven't you ever wanted to be part of something that matters?" I'm leaning forward on my chair and slightly into Jackson's space, but I don't care.

"If Bryce delivers on what he's promising, he's building the next generation of reconnaissance drones that are going to protect our soldiers. It means saving the lives of scouts. This new, much lighter and quieter drone will be able to recon areas for a longer range and provide even more assurance so that soldiers aren't walking into traps."

His face which was curious and ever so slightly predatory a moment before goes hard. "And are you so naïve to think that's all they'll be used for? That if Bryce perfects this technology, it won't be used to seek out and kill insurgents?"

I shake my head. It was the first thought that popped into my head, too, when I heard the word *drone*. But surely out of anyone, Jackson should understand. "You know these aren't the big, fast-flying long-range drones that drop bombs. This is the kind that's used for close surveillance. To check for civilians and give a better picture of what's happening on the ground instead of relying on satellite imagery. It can be used to check for civilians so that the kinds of artillery drones you're talking about *don't* take out innocents as collateral damage."

I'm talking so vehemently my arms are involved. Crap. That only happens when I get passionate about a topic. I try to ramp it down a few levels. I take a quick breath and then finish. "Even if I don't respect Bryce as a person, it's a vision I can still find inspiring. Tell me, Mr. Vale," my eyes flick up and lock onto his, "can you say that your commercial products have saved any lives this year?"

I'm prepared for another pithy comeback or for the sparring to continue, but there's only silence. Again, Jackson just watches me. Like he's taking my measure. It's hard not to squirm under the microscope of his gaze. Did my little speech move him? Or is sweat smearing my makeup and he can't believe what a hack Bryce sent to represent his company? I lock my jaw and stiffen my spine.

Finally, when the staring goes on for at least another ninety seconds —I know because I started counting—I raise an eyebrow in challenge.

Not that it seems to affect him. He just continues to stare for a few moments longer before finally speaking. "Accompany me as my plus one to the Red Cross Gala on Friday night."

It's more a statement than a question. And a what-the-fuck of a non-sequitur. We were just talking war and drones and saving lives, and now he's inviting me to a party?

Not just that, but the way he phrased it, it sounded like he assumes I'm going to go. "Isn't that a bit presumptuous? What if I'm busy?"

"You're not."

Well that *definitely* pisses me off. He apparently sees it on my face.

"You're not the only one who did their homework before this meeting, Miss Cruise," he cuts me off before I can go on the warpath. "Obviously I met your son when I accidently ran into you in the park the other day, so I know you have a child. A simple Facebook search told me you were single. You really should update your privacy settings on there, by the way.

"So, a single mother," he shrugs, "maybe you do already have plans lined up for your Friday night," he squints at me. "But with your new— and if I know Bryce," his face darkens, "—very stressful job, I'm betting the last thing you want after a week of putting up with that asshole is to go out and put up with other assholes on the whole dating scene. No," he shakes his head, still eyeing me. "I'm betting you're more of a wine and bubble bath on a Friday night kind of woman. Maybe a good book?"

I glare at him. All right. It's disturbing how well he's guessed my Friday-night routine. Seriously. The books are only sometimes, though. And once I'm out of the bath, it's more classic movies, like *Gone with the Wind* or anything with Jimmy Stewart, Spencer Tracey, or Katharine Hepburn.

I give him a little acidic sweetness with my smile. "Wrong on all counts. This Friday I have an evening full of plans to deep condition my hair and paint my toenails."

He's never once looked away from my eyes in the last nerve-wracking five minutes. He doesn't now either as he does the half smile thing that's charming as hell. "I consider care of one's feet and footwear to be essential to the presentation of one's person. Though I must say, I appreciate quirk as well as quality." He holds out a hand and pulls me to my feet before I even realize what he's doing. His eyes are still on mine as he says, "I was quite beguiled by your own choice in footwear today."

I feel my eyes widen but I can't think of even a stumbling excuse. It's not like pulling out one of my pretty pumps at this point and saying, "No, wait, I was supposed to be wearing these sexy things!" is going to help my embarrassed blush. And damn him, he's managed to get the upper hand on me, right here at the end of the meeting. That's not supposed to be how this goes. He slips my laptop back into its case —shit, did he see the pumps at the top of my purse right beside the laptop case?—and his hand drops to the small of my back.

He walks me to the door and I'm moving with him. Wait, this can't be the end of the meeting. We didn't even come to terms—I have no idea where the proposal stands or if he even—

"My driver will be around to pick you up at 6 pm for the gala,"

Jackson says smoothly when I'm at the threshold of his office. "And I hope it's not too presumptuous, but I have a personal shopper who I haven't used nearly enough this year. She works on commission, you understand. She'll drop by on Thursday with several dress options as well as shoes." There's a definite twinkle in the bastard's eye as he says this. And wait. What? A dress? Shoes? I never even agreed to go to the damn gala!

"Mr. Vale—" I start, but he smiles at me. Not those odd half smiles he's been teasing with all morning either. No, this is a genuine full-teeth affair. And he has such white teeth. And that damn dimple. *A dimple*. In what world is that fair?

I'm, well, dazzled for a moment. And then the door closes.

I just stand there. As I head back down the hall, I can only shake my head, still a bit dazed by that entire interaction and its outcome. What I do know is that I haven't convinced him to collaborate with Gentry Tech yet. I have to salvage the deal somehow and that boils down to the only option left to me.

I guess I'm going to a fucking gala.

CHAPTER NINE

I don't pull any punches when I report back to Bryce about my meeting with Jackson. There's no point in softening the fact that Jackson didn't make any concessions or sound very open to collaboration. I take Bryce through every step of how the meeting went and his jaw grows more and more tight. But then, as soon as I tell him that Jackson invited me to the Red Cross Gala, his entire posture relaxes.

"Good," he says. "You can use that opportunity to get closer to him. I'm sure between your persuasive skills and my innovative designs, we'll sway him to our position in time. Today was only an opening salvo."

"I did want to talk to you about that," I hesitantly start. "Mr. Vale seemed..." I cast around for a diplomatic word, "less than thrilled that our presentation included only the external modeling. Perhaps if we could present some of the internal algorithms, he might be persuaded more quickly —"

Bryce makes a derisive face and waves a hand dismissively. "I'm not giving away industry secrets unless he's willing to commit."

"But how can he commit unless he knows something of what you're bringing to the table?" I ask, a little of my exasperation coming through.

Bryce's sharp glare makes me wish I'd bit my tongue.

"Don't forget your pay grade, *Miss* Cruise. Only a novice would think that showing their hand at this stage in the game was a wise move. In poker, do you give your opponent a glimpse of your Ace?"

This time, I do physically bite my tongue. This isn't fucking poker. He's trying to get Jackson to collaborate with him. *Collaborate.* As in, incentivize him to cooperate. Not outgun him at a freaking duel or, to use his stupid metaphor, win at a poker game. Still, I swallow down my real thoughts and shake my head no.

Bryce smirks at me. "No. You don't. Why don't you go back to clearing up my backloaded correspondence? You know, your *job*. At least until you're needed on Friday. Then you can do your other job. Be arm candy."

He looks down at his computer. I'm already dismissed from his presence even while I still stand there.

I turn and walk to my office. I wish I could say I'm fuming the whole way. But Bryce's words are stuck in my head. *Arm candy.*

Old, veined hands groping me. *Pretty girl. I could just eat you up.*

I cringe and startle at the sudden memory. I press my hands to my face when I sit down at my desk. *Pull it together, Cals.* I take my hands from my face, careful not to muss my makeup, then force them to my desk. I will not go to the restroom and wash them over and over until the skin is rubbed pink. I won't give into the old compulsions that took over every time I thought about that old dirty bastard.

I count to ten, breathe out, and open my email to get back to work.

———

On Friday I'm taking notes at a teleconference with Gentry Tech's Japanese manufacturing partner. Bryce's been having similar conferences with various companies all week. I wonder if these are the very contacts Bryce is dangling in front of Jackson. And why can't Jackson just contact them directly? Bryce did keep saying 'exclusive contracts' in that first meeting with Jackson. Maybe that means Gentry Tech has them hired out only to work for them and no one else for a contracted period of years?

"Miss Cruise," Bryce's voice jolts me. "Repeat back the specifications we've agreed upon so far."

Shit. I sit up in my chair nervously and scroll through the notes on my laptop. My improvised shorthand is all but second nature after six weeks and my fingers have been flying furiously for the last forty-five minutes. Well, except for those few moments when my mind was wandering thinking about Jackson.

I take a quick second to adjust my Bluetooth earpiece and then get talking. "The motor should be made of carbon fiber with fiberglass central and mounting plates." I continue paging up on my laptop. "To deal with high temperatures, the surrounding case should have a finned heatsink design to self-ventilate, able to withstand temperatures up to 240 degrees Celsius. The entire motor should weigh no more than 160 grams, 200 with copper wiring in place. The voltage range should be 16.8 to 34." I continue rattling off statistics from my notes for another five minutes.

When I finish, there's silence on the other end. Mr. Kuramoto finally responds, "I thought we agreed on 12 kHz for the ESC PWM Rate. That's generally accepted as standard."

Bryce rolls his eyes, but his voice is calm and professional as he responds, "With the specs of this motor, it should easily push to 16 kHz, maybe even 20. I'd like to set that as our goal."

There's a murmur of assent on the other end of the line. "Yes. I like the idea that our motor will set the new standard."

"Exactly. Gentry Tech and KDI Industries should be the names that come to mind when people think of the future of robotics, don't you agree?"

"Very true, sir."

"Excellent. I look forward to touring your factories and getting to speak more one-on-one when I visit in two weeks."

"Yes. We will have some initial drawings of what we have discussed today and you can talk with our engineers."

Bryce and Mr. Kuramoto finish with some more closing pleasantries and then Bryce closes the teleconference. I breathe out in relief as I take out my earpiece. We've had several of these teleconferences with different manufacturers this week and each one has made me nervous that I'll miss out on recording some important detail.

I should have known he'd put me on the spot today. All week, Bryce's been occasionally tossing me a question out of nowhere, so I always have to be on point. It's been terrifying, but if I'm honest, also totally thrilling. A few months ago, I could only dream of being involved with work like this, even if just in this peripheral support position.

Bryce leans back in his chair and smiles at me. It appears genuine, not calculating in any way. "You've done a wonderful job this week on these calls, Callie. Not just coordinating their set up and getting everyone connected at the right time. You're fielding every query I've tossed your way. Don't think I haven't been noticing." He nods as if to himself. "You're really proving yourself here."

I feel a ridiculous blush at the praise and stand up, laptop clutched to my chest. "Thank you," I murmur as I turn away. "I'll have the notes from the meeting typed up and to you within the hour."

And then I get the hell out of there, forcing myself not to look back at Bryce. When I get into my office, the window between Bryce's room and mine stays frosted, just like it's been all week. I finally let myself look back in the direction of his office, even though I can't see through the opaque glass.

But seriously. What the hell?

It's like some other boss has body-snatched the Bryce I'd known for the first few weeks I worked here. Again, it feels like the good twin has taken up residence. I dub him Mr. Respectful. As opposed to Mr. Asshole.

Today isn't the first time he's complimented my work. He's been at it after every teleconference and even after the weekly internal head of departments meeting.

Just my work. Not accompanied by any lewd remarks about my body or person. I shake my head. No requests to work topless. Nothing. He must really want this deal with Jackson to go through. As if I didn't already feel enough pressure not to fuck up tonight. I don't know how much shop talk Bryce really expects I can accomplish at a social outing. I rub my temples and then get back to work typing up the notes from the meeting with Mr. Kuramoto.

———

After I send Bryce the meeting notes, he emails back with a one-liner saying I should go home early so I have extra time to get ready for my *event*. So I take off at four o'clock, unsure if I'm grateful or not for the extra time without the distraction of work to obsess about the night ahead.

I get home a little bit faster than I normally do since it's not yet rush hour. There are actually seats available on the light rail too, something that's never true at five when I usually get on. Since it's a little earlier in the day, I don't feel quite as exhausted. Not to mention, in spite of myself, some really stupid little girl Disney Princess part of me that I thought long dead and buried got all excited last night when the three dresses were delivered.

Disney's screwed us all. That's all I'm saying.

Long flowy dresses? A *gala*? Apparently that sounds close enough to a ball to my inner eight-year-old princess's ears.

And the dresses. Let me tell you. That personal shopper that Jackson was talking about? Yeah. She deserves her commission for the year and then some. How am I supposed to choose just one?

I tried on each one and Shannon took pictures. For once, we actually got along. I thought she would give me shit about a bunch of super fancy dresses being delivered—it reeked too much of my beauty pageant days, which had always been a sore subject between us. But when I explained it was for a work function, to my surprise she asked if I wanted help looking through them and choosing what to wear. After our blowup the other night, I'd noticed her making small moves toward reconciliation and maybe this was another one. I wasn't going to hold a grudge.

I agreed and we unzipped each of the three garment bags, assessing each like we were guest judges on Project Runway.

"Well," Shannon said, eyeing each of the three dresses critically.

"They're all pretty and even have good hanger appeal, but you really need to try them on before we can make any real decisions."

I grinned. I hadn't enjoyed dressing up in a very long time. Being poked and prodded and pinned into pageant gowns for a significant portion of my adolescence had killed it for me, but seeing Shannon's enthusiasm made it feel fresh. Enough to even forget that this was supposed to be a working event. I clapped my hands like a little kid.

She rolled her eyes at me, but for once it was a good-natured gesture. "Just get your butt in the blue dress." She held a strapless blue bandage dress that looked like it would hit just below the knees. "I'll go get my camera."

I tried on each dress in turn and Shannon took pictures. Though, saying she *took pictures* is an understatement. She got all into it like she was a budding fashion photographer or something. Actually, thinking about it, didn't she minor in photography in college? I remember thinking it was so strange because it was like, *artistic,* and that was always the last word I would've associated with my dreary, studious sister.

Anyway, she was really into the photoshoot. She had one of those cameras with the giant lenses and everything. It was pretty hilarious, but I didn't dare laugh. Shannon actually seemed like she was having *fun*.

My sister.

Fun.

Yeah, it took a while to compute for me too.

"The lighting is better over here by this lamp," she said, after I changed into a shimmery gold dress. She all but dragged me by the wrist over to a standing lamp near our front curtains. "It has a yellow bulb and the ambient light will really make the gold color pop."

She nodded as I positioned myself in front of the curtain. The dress had a sweetheart neckline with a peplum detail at the waist before dropping dramatically to the floor.

"Mmm, yes," she murmured, "that's much better."

She brought her camera up to her eye and adjusted the big lens on the front several times before clicking away. "Drop your chin. No," she shook her head after I moved my head, "not that much." I re-adjusted. "Better. No, now I can see up your nose. Down some. There. Now don't move."

I barely stopped myself from shaking my head. No wonder Shannon loved this. It was the perfect excuse to order me around.

Finally we finished with the gold one. Then there was the last dress. The red one.

No, *red* was the wrong word. The dress was magenta, a deep, rich *magenta*. Made from an expensive chiffon, the neckline swept down in a V that showed just a hint of cleavage but still kept it classy. The rest of the bodice was fitted, and it kept its shape over the hips but then it flared—or no, again that was the wrong word—the material *floated* as it brushed the ground.

I spun in a circle and the material swirled in a cloud of flowing fabric around me. Shannon's camera was *click, click, clicking* away on some super-fast shutter speed.

I looked up at her and our eyes met across the small expanse of our living room.

"This is the one," I said at exactly the same time as she said, "that's the one."

We both laughed and I couldn't remember the last time we'd had a moment like this between us. I walked over to her, lifting the hem of the dress as I went so I didn't step on it.

Shannon was busy looking at the screen on her camera, clicking to look through the pictures. I lifted a hand to the camera and lowered it.

"What happened to us, Shannon?"

Her eyes briefly flipped up to mine, but then she lowered them again. She lifted the camera and went back to clicking through the pictures. I could see flashes of red and then gold as she ticked through the pictures way too fast to really be seeing anything.

"I don't know what you mean."

I let out a snort. "Oh, come on. I hate how it is between us."

Silence.

I tried again. "Do you realize how much I appreciate all that you've done for me and Charlie?" And then I wondered if I'd told her that.

Well, I knew I'd told her, but it might have only been in the beginning. I thought it in my head all the time. Granted, I thought it because I was trying to remind myself to be nice to her, but still. I didn't say it out loud nearly enough. "Because I do. I really do. I couldn't have made it without you, Shan. I so appreciate you."

She moved her finger to another button and reversed to look through the pictures again. She shrugged, still not looking up at me. "I know you do."

"Do you?"

She shrugged again.

"I want us to be the kind of sisters who can talk to each other. Not just about the bills and Charlie's schedule. About real things."

I could see her body start to shrug again so again, I blocked the camera screen.

She sighed and finally looked up at me. "What do you want me to say, Callie? We can't just magically fix things with one conversation. Of course I wish things were better between us. But it all just got..." Again her shoulders went up and then dropped.

She looked toward the ceiling as if searching for patience or for a word to encapsulate everything she was thinking. "...I don't know. We just lost that kind of connection a long time ago."

My own shoulders sank. So that was it then.

"That doesn't mean it's how it always has to be, though," she knocked me on the shoulder with the hand not holding the camera. "We're adults now. The past doesn't have to define us anymore."

That only made me more confused. Exactly what had I done when we were younger that was so bad she was still so pissed about it? I was her younger sister and all I'd ever wanted was for her to give me the time of day. Mom smothered me with attention during all the pageant crap, but what I really could have used, then and certainly during the much worse situation that followed in high school, was a big sister. If anyone should be still mad about it, it was *me*, not her.

Then she let out a heavy breath. "I admit that I can be one to hold a grudge," she smiled in a self-deprecating way. "I'm sorry for that. I'll try to work on it."

In spite of the part of me that wanted to be upset about the past, I felt a stupid grin start to light up my face. It seemed like my big sister might finally be willing to let bygones be bygones. She rolled her eyes again. "Oh for God's sake, don't think we're going to hug it out or anything."

I put my hands up and took a step back. "Wouldn't dream of it."

She shook her head again, but I didn't miss the smile teasing the edges of her lips. She lifted her camera and started looking through pictures again. "Okay. So the red dress is obviously the winner. Come check you out."

Yeah. So not only did I have this great night with my sister, but the dress also looked amazing on me. For serious.

All day I've been fighting these random terrors that something has happened to it in the twenty-two hours since I first put it on. That Charlie has gotten into it and decided to have funtime with scissors on mommy's new dress. Or the apartment has flooded or suddenly gotten an infestation of mice overnight. Something will have happened. Something always does. This is my life we're talking about, after all.

But when I step in the house and immediately go to the closet, not only is the red dress perfectly fine, but so are the others that the personal shopper texted they'll pick up tomorrow. I breathe out and then lay my forehead against the doorframe. A note says Charlie and Shannon are out for their afternoon park outing. Another rarity, for me to be home before them.

Alrighty. No time to enjoy that I get the apartment to myself. I scurry into the shower and turn it to as hot as I can stand it. Ah, that feels good.

Usually I shower at six-thirty in the morning along with everyone else in the complex. I'm lucky to get tepidly warm water at that time of day.

So I bask in the first truly hot shower I've had in what feels like forever. Which means I stay in longer than I should.

When I finally get out and notice the time, there's a lot more cursing involved. I still have to blow out my hair and figure out some kind of styling to do. Son of a bitch. Because there's that gorgeous magenta dress and I'm supposed to do something with my hair that matches its elegance and... I'm screwed.

I swipe at the steam that's gathered on the mirror and then stare at my hair that's dripping on my towel-covered body. Yeah. No sudden inspiration is hitting me. Dammit. I run out to grab my laptop and google easy updos when the doorbell rings.

I glance at the clock. I'm not running *that* late. The driver can't be here to pick me up already. Can he? My heart starts hammering a thousand beats per minute. What if I got the time wrong? Oh God. This is like one of those dreams where you show up to the final exam and haven't studied any of the material.

How the hell am I going to convince Jackson he needs to collaborate with Gentry Tech? It's so much easier to just focus on the things I can control, like the dress and hair and makeup, but all of that's just window dressing. He's this genius and who am I? Just some lowly—

The doorbell rings again. I suck in a deep breath. Negative self-talk isn't going to help anything. I'll sell Jackson on collaborating because I *have* to. I can do this.

"You can do this," I whisper, looking at myself in the steam-fogged mirror.

I hear knocking at the door. Crap. Time's up. I look down at my towel. Boobs and who-ha covered, check. I hurry to the door and look out the peep-hole. Not a driver. I breathe out like I've just gotten a stay of execution. Thank God. I've got a little more time left. Instead, standing on the stoop is a woman with two suitcases. Is she lost?

I open the door and peek my head out. "Can I... help you?"

She's an attractive brunette in her mid-thirties, stylish in a cute t-shirt dress and ankle boots. She gives me a friendly but professional smile. "Calliope Cruise?"

"Um. Yes?"

"I'm Breanna Monroe, professional stylist."

At my continued look of confusion, she says, "Mr. Vale sent me. I'm here to do your hair and makeup."

"Oh. Cool." And, um, weird, but I don't say that out loud. I mean, I can do my own makeup for God's sake. Does Jackson think I'm that clueless? But I step back when she pushes through the door, dragging her two suitcases behind her.

When she sees the state of me, she nods her head. "Good, you've showered. It's best to start with a blank canvas. Where should we set up?"

"Um." I look around the living room, then glance at the wall and remember that Shannon will be home with Charlie any minute. "How about my bedroom?"

"Lead the way," she says. When I gesture toward my room in the back of the apartment, she confidently charges in front of me. By the time I join her in my room, she's got one of her cases open on the bed and is pulling out supplies.

I pull the old ratty fold-up chair I keep in my bathroom into the room while she sets up two small tray tables she removed from her super-duper suitcases. Seriously, she's like Mary Poppins with those things. She keeps pulling more and more stuff out of them. In the blink of an eye, she's got a couple of double decker makeup cases arranged on one of the small tables, and on the other, an intimidating array of curling irons of various sizes, a straightening iron, and several devices that I don't know the purpose of at all. I sit back in the chair, eyes wide.

Breanna produces an extension cord strip with six outlets that she immediately begins to plug devices into.

"Now," she turns back to me after one satisfied glance at her perfectly-lined-up instruments, like I imagine a doctor might before surgery. "Darling." She smiles toothily at me and I'm only further intimidated. "Which dress did you end up choosing?"

"Magenta," I say, but my voice is all weird and dry and it barely comes out as a whisper.

"*What*, darling?" she says extra loud like you might to your grand-mother at an old folks' home.

I try again, attempting more confidence. If I let myself be run over by the hair and makeup lady, how am I ever gonna make it in the business world? "The magenta one."

This time when she smiles, she meets my eyes and I can see what I can only imagine to be a slightly manic glitter in hers. "Well of course you did. Time to make some *magic*."

And with that, she comes at me, makeup brush in one hand, tweezers in the other.

———

When the doorbell next rings, I've been plucked, brushed, painted, moussed, and spritzed into a glamorous version of myself that I could hardly believe was me when I looked in the mirror.

Breanna just finished up and left about five minutes ago with several last-minute instructions.

"Make sure to double-check your face before you step out of the limo because there's going to be press there. Especially check for lipstick on your teeth. There's nothing worse than showing up on Page Six with a lipstick smile." She shuddered.

"Press?" I squeaked. "And a red carpet? It's not like this is Hollywood."

She just laughed. "But it *is* California and tonight the richest of the richest will be out to play. They all want the red-carpet treatment too and, of course, the press will be there for the society pages. Oh," her eyebrows narrowed in distress, "I wish we had time for me to teach you which angles you photograph at best."

I just stared at her wide-eyed. Great. As if I didn't have enough to worry about already tonight.

The next second she brightened again, obviously missing the trepidation on my face. "If anyone asks who your stylist is, my last name's Monroe. Like Marilyn." She winked at me in the makeup mirror she'd set up. "Breanna Monroe." She leans over and flashes a grin at me. "Can't miss an opportunity to network. Most of my work comes through word of mouth."

I smiled, but it was just an uncomfortable reminder of what the night was really about.

People might pretty it up at an event like this evening, but I lived in a world where no one ever gives something for nothing.

I look down now at the rich colors of the magenta dress I'm wearing. Everyone has an agenda. Even Jackson Vale. Or rather, *especially* him. I'm sure he didn't get to be the CEO of such a powerful and successful company by being nice. That's the question: what does he want?

Then again, I've got my own agenda for the evening: land the CubeThink account. I have to make this happen for my future.

The way to make that happen? According to Breanna, make sure there's no lipstick on my teeth—she repeated that one at least fifteen times. No one wants to kiss a woman with lipstick on her teeth. She ignored me when I said I wasn't planning on kissing anyone tonight.

"I'll get the door!" shouts Shannon and I jerk in my chair. Dammit. The door. Right. I jump to my feet.

Shannon, who has been sneaking glimpses ever since she got home with Charlie an hour ago, is already to the door right as I'm hurrying out of my bedroom, high heels in hand.

"Wait, Shannon, I'm not —"

But before I can finish, she's swung the door wide. I'm expecting it to be Jackson's driver. Instead, it's Jackson himself.

"Good evening, Calliope," he says in his characteristic low, gravelly voice. He's tall and dapper in a tailored black tux, complete with a magenta handkerchief tucked neatly in the pocket of his coat that perfectly matches the color of my dress. With his large, hulking stature, he should be too big to pull off a tux. But no, he makes it work and then some. Which yes, is doubly ludicrous because I need all of my head in the game tonight. Talking points. Competitive market shares. Access to key exclusive manufacturing contracts. Damn, those slacks look *fine* on him.

And... I'm ogling. I yank my gaze back up to his face and that's when I see that he's doing his own perusal of me.

"Um," I mumble stupidly. 'Hi." I suddenly wish I'd had time to put the heels on before stupid Shannon opened the stupid door. I have the ridiculous desire to look perfect for him.

"Mama," Charlie toddles toward me. Shannon snaps him up before he can grab my skirt with his gummy fingers. He squirms to get away from her, pointing at me. He says something that's unintelligible at first. When I finally understand him, I start laughing.

Shannon's brows furrow. "What's he saying?"

"Elsa. Like from *Frozen*." I laugh some more. Looks like Disney is inundating a whole new generation. Charlie's only two-and-a-half, but he's already got the picture. Princesses wear long dresses. Momma's wearing a long dress, therefore, princess. *Obviously*.

I turn back to Jackson. "Sorry, I'll be out in just a minute. It's always a bit of a madhouse in here." I smile apologetically. The quick second with Charlie helped to ground me, thank God.

And reminded me that I do not need to make any more stupid choices when it comes to men.

"I only need to put on my shoes and grab my clutch, if you want to wait in the car."

"That's all right. I'll just wait here." Jackson steps through the door and takes a seat on the arm of my ratty couch. I blink at the incongruous image. Jackson and his multi-thousand-dollar suit against the backdrop of my thrift store couch? Just... No.

But it'll sound stupid if I sit here and argue with him about it. It's quicker to just get my shoes on.

"Elsa! Elsa! Elsa!" Charlie keeps chanting, squirming with his body to get out of Shannon's arms. I throw her a grateful look and sit down on the armchair to quickly secure the strap on my heels. I was extremely grateful when I first saw that the heels were the kind that had a strap across the ankle. The heels of my feet are narrow and tend to slip out of shoes if they aren't strapped on. The last thing I need tonight is to pull a Cinderella moment, losing my shoe—with me inevitably tumbling after. Cinderella meets Humpty Dumpty. Yep, that'd be me. Strapping myself in it is.

I glance over and see Jackson watching me with what appears to be avid interest as I fumble with my straps. Which only makes me all thumbs. God, why couldn't Jackson have just waited in the car? The awkward silence of the adults with Charlie babbling away is killing me. Motherfucking strap, fit in the damn little fancy buckle!

"So, Mr. Vale," Shannon starts, shifting Charlie around on her hip. "Callie hasn't told me much about you. You're a work friend of hers?"

Shannon ignores the death glare and a quick line I draw across my throat at her when Jackson looks away from me. I have to pretend I'm adjusting the straps when Jackson glances my way again. At least I finally get the first shoe strap hooked in. Thank *God*.

"A work *friend*, am I? I've been upgraded to a friend?" I freeze at his words and suddenly can't look away from him when I see that tell-tale lift on the right side of his mouth. "And here I thought when we'd last left things, I was merely the target of your boss's business interests?"

I dip my head to hide my reddening cheeks and focus on my second shoe. "We're heading to the ball tonight, so that makes us acquaintances at least."

"A ball?" There's amusement in his voice.

I wince. Fucking Disney. "*Gala*," I rephrase. "The Red Cross *Gala*. You know what I meant."

There. I finally finished the second latch and stand up, trying out the heels. I manage to not even wobble. Gold star for me. Now if I can just make it through the rest of the night without falling on my ass.

Jackson rises and holds out an arm to me. Deep gulp. I grab the clutch that Breanna filled earlier with what she called my essentials—cell phone, keys, lipstick, eyeliner, a tiny compact, and touchup concealer. All of that barely fits in the tiny clutch. I'm afraid if I open it at any point during the night, I won't be able to fit everything back in again.

I glance nervously around the apartment, wondering if I'm forgetting anything. I want to go look in the mirror again, just to check that I haven't screwed up the makeup.

Still, crap, maybe I should go check it now in the bathroom mirror. But I checked like, seven times already. Surely none will come off between now and the hotel where the Gala is being held, right?

But before I can pull away to go check, Jackson gently urges me forwards toward the door. Damn, he smells *really* good. What if there *is* lipstick on my teeth? And I'm trying to talk to him about why collaborating with Gentry Tech makes both financial sense and could help push CubeThink to new heights of the state of the art but all he can focus on is the fleck of red on the tip of my incisor—

"Wait," I pull my arm away from Jackson's.

But I don't go toward the bathroom to check my teeth. Instead I go toward Charlie, who's starting to whine in Shannon's arms.

"Oh, poor baby, Auntie Shannon will let you go just as soon as Momma is gone." I tickle him at the neck even as I kiss his cheeks.

Then I just kiss him all over his face and tickle his belly. His high-pitched giggles fill the apartment. I snuggle my cheek against his.

All the noise in my head quiets.

Right.

This is what it's all for.

I pull back and I can't help grinning at my beautiful boy. "Momma's gonna be home late tonight, but I'll see you bright and early tomorrow morning. Will you wake me up tomorrow with kisses?"

"Kisses!" he repeats back to me and then makes an approximation of the kissing noise. I laugh with him and give him a few more tickles.

I take one more deep breath of his baby scent and then turn and hurry toward the door, gesturing at Jackson to follow me. Shannon's distracting Charlie by getting him ready for dinner and I catch Jackson watching me, then flicking a curious look back at Charlie.

I frown. I never leave without a little bit of a goodbye ritual and I did it without thinking. But now I really wish Jackson had waited in the car. I don't like that he got to have that part of me. I don't want my life to be like a Venn Diagram where the two circles of home life and office life ever intersect or overlap. They should never touch at all.

I shut the door to my apartment with a little more vehemence than is strictly necessary.

"Calliope?" Jackson's voice surprises me from my thoughts. "Everything all right?"

I smile, even though I'm sure it's obvious how forced it is. "Great."

I hurry forward to the car. Or well, limo. It looks out of place on this street of mid-level income apartments.

Jackson holds out his hand to help me in while the chauffeur stands by the open door. Just like in a movie. Too much, in fact. Because this is real life. And in real life Cinderella doesn't end up with the prince.

Though, when I sit back in the buttery leather seats and arrange the fabric of my gown so that it flows around me, I have to admit, it does bring a little of the storybook feeling back. The gown is so, so gorgeous. For just a night, I could pretend I'm the woman who belongs in such finery.

Isn't that the rub? I don't know whether to be bitter about the make-believe of tonight or if it's better to let myself go with the fantasy even if just for a little while—to pretend that good triumphs over evil and the most unimportant and unluckiest of girls can be not just a princess, but a queen. At least over her own life.

Be the queen.

Win the account.

Live my happily ever after with Charlie in a castle far, far away from anything that could ever threaten us.

CHAPTER TEN

Both Jackson and I are silent as the driver pulls away from the curb, and we head toward the city. Finally, he speaks. "You look lovely tonight."

I glance over at him, and my breath catches. Somehow when I'm not looking at him, I can forget how imposing he is. He sits across the limo from me, but there's a panther-like grace to his large body that makes it almost impossible to look away. Back at the apartment, there were other distractions.

But here? There's nothing but me and him, confined in the box of this limo. Even though the inside of the limo is huge, it suddenly seems far too small.

"Thank you," I belatedly respond to his compliment. Then I add, "You, too. Look good, I mean. Handsome."

Oh God. Did I just say that out loud? Can we go back to not talking now?

"Do you mind if I ask how old your son is?" His head is cocked slightly to the side.

"He's two and a half."

"How old were you when you had him?"

My jaw tenses. What the hell kind of question is that? I'm already looking at my lap after my previous foot-in-mouth statement, and now I avert my eyes to the window at the endless billboards that stretch along the 101.

"Sorry," Jackson's low voice comes from closer than I expect, and then I feel the heavy warm pressure of his hand on mine. "I don't mean to pry."

I turn and meet his gaze. He's leaned forward, closing the gap between the benches so that our knees almost touch. I can smell his cologne. The masculine woodsy scent of pine sweeps over me. The earthy smell is so at odds with the city around us. Again, I envision him belonging in a log cabin, maybe in another century. And his size. He's too large—like he was made to be a lumberjack or out hunting wild boars. Not sit behind a desk writing computer code.

"How did you get into working with computers?" I ask instead of answering his question. Somehow I need to get this conversation onto business, but I also want the evening to play out organically. And I'm frankly just interested.

He tilts his head again in that way that makes me feel like he's trying to puzzle me out, but doesn't move his hand from where it rests over mine. I have to slide it out from under his to pull it back toward my waist. He doesn't react to my withdrawal.

"My foster dad."

The answer is short and he goes quiet after, looking down at his hands.

I think that's all he's going to say but after another long moment, he starts talking again. "It was... I don't know, our thing. I was sort of a," he shrugs and looks out the window, "handful when I came to live with them. So Dad gave me a bunch of old computers to take apart. Then after they were in pieces, we'd put them back together. Anything to keep my hands busy and keep me out of trouble."

Okay. Wow. I really wasn't expecting him to open up like that.

"I didn't know you were in foster care." I feel stupid after I say it, because it kind of implicitly infers that I've researched him or at least run a few Google searches.

He seems to take it in stride, though, because he holds a finger over his lips. "Shh, I've managed to keep it off my Wikipedia page."

But he's telling me? Then I think about all the stories I've heard of children in foster care. As if he reads it on my face, his lips tip on one side. He leans forward again just long enough to pat my knee. The quick contact is like a jolt, but he pulls back on his own this time.

"Oh come on," he says, "don't look at me like that." His eyes narrow at me. "We've all got a sad story. Mine's not any more tragic than most. I was too young to remember my parents when I lost them. Eventually I landed with good foster parents, the Kents, when I was eleven and the rest is history." He settles back into his seat.

I don't miss two key points of that last sentence. *Eventually* and when he was *eleven*. What happened during all the in-between years?

"I thought I read somewhere that you had trouble in school growing up?"

He shrugs, looking slightly uncomfortable but trying to laugh it off. "You let something slip to a reporter *one* time," he shakes his head and flashes a self-deprecating smile that gives me a glimpse of the dimple in his left cheek.

"Sorry," I cringe. Now here *I'm* the one doing the prying.

"No, it's okay." He waves a hand. "I'm not really embarrassed or ashamed about it. It's always just a little weird when people know things about me already when I first meet them."

Double cringe time. "Yeah, sorry again. I googled you before I came to first pitch you." I scrunch up my face and raise my eyebrows apologetically. "Won't do it again, scouts honor."

He grins, dimple coming out in full force. "How about I choose to be flattered by your interest and we'll call it even?"

I let out a relieved breath. Okay, he's taking the non-douchey path at every turn here. Wow. I don't quite know what to make of him. I'm still trying to think of something to say to cover up my faux pas when he continues.

"Yes, I had trouble," his eyes search the ceiling of the town car like he's looking for the way to put it, "...focusing my attentions when I was younger. It's like my mind was moving three times faster than my teachers were talking or anything else that was going on around me. I was slapped with an ADHD diagnosis and put on meds until I was placed with the Kents." His gaze goes back to the window.

"Did you actually have ADHD?" Well damn, there goes my curiosity again. Except, he's the one opening up. I'm not forcing him and suddenly I'm hungry for every tidbit of information he's willing to share.

Oh," he looks back at me, like he was just lost in memory for a moment there. "Dad didn't like how meds were the go-to solution for troublesome kids in the system. He helped me wean off them. Others just saw me as a disruptive kid, but Dad saw something else." His fingers thrum on the seat beside him.

I like the way he talks about his dad. His voice softens and his usually hard features gentle. By that alone I can tell the man is really special to him.

"He saw how I was always fiddling with things. He worked at Lockheed, so he taught me some basic coding. I really took to it. It was good for me. The control of it. When I started coding it was like this thing I'd been needing my whole life."

I scrunch my eyebrows. "How do you mean?"

"Well, computers just made sense. Like math, but more fun. You have a problem and you write an algorithm to fix it. Life's always too chaotic but computers," he shrugged. "It was like for the first time in my life I finally felt in control."

"Oh." It's all I can say, but inside I can't stop thinking about Jackson as a little eleven-year-old boy who'd been labeled a 'problem child' by the system. He'd probably known nothing but chaos for years before coming to live with the Kents. But then Mr. Kent gave him an arena where he could finally reclaim control of at least a little part of that chaos.

Jackson continues as if he didn't just reveal something so personal. "Dad made it fun and he just had a way of working with me to help me funnel my energy. So I'd be using my hands and my brain, you know?" Another one of those fond smiles crosses his face. "Robotics was always the perfect match for me."

"He was an inventor, too?" The patent that Bryce used to bring Jackson to the table in the first place. Bryce said it had belonged to Jackson's father.

Jackson's jaw tenses slightly. He's obviously recalling how I know this bit of information. He nods, a quick, tight jerk of his head. "He helped me build my first robot. We entered it in a battle-bot competition. Ours won."

"Naturally." I smile.

His dimple reappears as his eyes flash to mine. "Naturally."

He looks so young when his face softens like that. It strikes me then that he and Bryce must be around the same age. They were in college together after all. So that would make Jackson, what? Thirty-two? Thirty-three? Ten years older than me, but considering all that he's accomplished, impossibly young.

"I was hooked from then on," he continues. "I built all kinds of things. For a while I was obsessed with making robots that were elaborate machines to do really simple things."

My smile turns into a grin. I know exactly what he's talking about. I can't believe he's trying to play it off so casually. "Ridiculousrobots.com, right? That site is still epic!" I laugh. "My friends at Stanford were always trying to come up with ideas of things to submit to it."

"Ah," he sighs with a pretend cringe. "The legacy of my seventeen-year-old self. Fifteen years later, and that one's still the thing I'm most famous for. More than my actual life's work."

I'm laughing full out now. "Aw, come on," I slap his knee playfully. "It's a great legacy. My favorite was your ten-foot robot/Rube Goldberg machine that sings Mary Had A Little Lamb, all just to flush the toilet. The grad students at Stanford totally built one like it and installed it for a semester in the lab bathroom. It was awesome," I shake my head, "though we all wanted to torch Mary by the time finals rolled around."

The dimple looks like a permanent fixture in Jackson's cheek at this point. He laughs too. "I disabled the music box after a week and a half. I can't believe you guys lasted a whole semester."

"Oh my God, no way! They'll die if I ever run into them again and tell them! The only reason they kept it was because they were so damned dogged about authenticity." But then the smile fades from my face. I was never great friends with any of the people in the computer and robotics lab—I was too wrapped up in David for that. Then, when I had the baby, even the acquaintances I'd had petered off faster than you can say 'diaper change.' I pull my thoughts back to the present.

Jackson's being so relaxed and easy with me. I don't want to lose any part of the moment.

"Are you two still close?" I ask. "You and your dad?"

A pained look crosses Jackson's face. "He passed while I was in college. Heart attack."

"I'm so sorry." Almost involuntarily, my hand seeks his.

He pulls away before I can make contact. My heart cinches and I'm not sure if it's because he pulled away or because I saw the flash of pain in his eyes about his dad's loss.

"We're here." He straightens in his seat and I see that we're pulling up to a well-lit hotel with a line of limos and expensive towncars waiting at the curb.

I want to ask more about his father, but by his posture and the look on his face, I can tell that the subject's closed. Yet he opened up to me so much—me, an almost perfect stranger. Why? And at the same time, all I want is to know more. What happened after things turned around with his new foster family? Did everything change after that? Did he start to fit in at school? What about college? I still never learned about his father's patent and how Bryce came to have it. And obviously it hit Jackson hard when his foster father died—

"Shall we?" Jackson's eyes find mine, and he holds out a hand to me as the door opens. Immediately the noise of excited voices and activity breaks into the sanctuary of the quiet car. I take a deep breath as a sweeping lightheadedness hits at the thought of stepping out into all of that.

In the busyness of getting ready and the overwhelming nature of Jackson's presence in the car, I haven't thought about this moment. Being here. Actually here, in the dress, at Jackson's side. Shit, am I going to be expected to dance? Or use the right fork at dinner? That's not even to mention what I'm *really* supposed to be doing here. I've let myself get all sentimental about Jackson and his dad when I ought to be cutthroat, using whatever emotional ground I've gained to get to the deal. I have to get this done. And not make an absolute fool of myself in the meantime.

Shit, shit, shit, shit, sh—

"Breathe," Jackson whispers into my ear. As if his hot breath on my ear is supposed to freaking help anything. I shiver from the sensual feel of it as he steps out of the car. Then his hand grabs mine and ready or not, he pulls me out after him.

It's not a graceful exit, let's just say that. I end up tripping on some of my dress's fabric and I fall into Jackson's chest.

"Shit." I grab his lapels in a death grip and my cheeks burn hot with embarrassment.

"I've got you," he says, eyes locking with mine as his hands go to my waist, steadying me.

Wow. His eyes are really blue. Like, really, *really* blue. They must be catching some light from how lit up they've got the red carpet, because they're almost iridescent right now. I've never seen any color like that in my life and—

"I've got you," he repeats in a whisper.

"If you just come this way," breaks in a loud-voiced man with a clipboard, alternately speaking to us and then into an earpiece. "Yes, yes, I'm getting the car cleared right now."

The slick-haired man who I guess is a concierge or event-organizer smiles impatiently at us. "If you'd like to enter the venue, then we can get the next car moved up." He gestures toward the red carpet behind us.

"Of course," Jackson says. Unlike me, he isn't watching the concierge. He's still looking at me. Nervous, I slide away from him, carefully pulling my dress out from underneath my shoe and stepping toward the gauntlet that is the red carpet.

This is just a charity function, but I suppose in California, everything gets the Hollywood treatment. There aren't paparazzi per se, but just like Breanna warned, there are lots of camera flashes taking shots for the society pages. Even a few local news crews are out as the Bay Area's wealthy parade in their finest for charity.

Jackson joins me, arm proffered for me to take. Then we start down the red carpet.

It's not very long, but still, it's red and there are cameras flashing. I'm on the arm of a gorgeous man, wearing an incredible dress. This is the most surreal moment of my life. It's hard to keep my eyes open with all the flashes of light in my face, but I do my damnedest.

Jackson Vale is a somebody, and there are often pictures of him on the society page. He was being absurd in the car when he said he was most famous for ridiculousrobots.com. Gentry Tech is more one of those names you've only heard of if you're in the robotics world or if you studied it like I did, but CubeThink hobby drones are all but a household name. Yeah, they make the professional models that Hollywood uses for filming, but they also make more affordable units, like the toy parents were fighting each over for last Black Friday.

So yeah, I don't want to be the idiot beside him wincing away from camera flashes with her eyes shut. I blink quickly when my eyes start to water and make sure to keep them open.

I paste on the biggest smile I can manage. But does that make me look too beauty queen? I dial it down a notch to what I hope comes across as demure. That's what a companion to *the* Jackson Vale should look like. Right?

Before I can overanalyze it too much, we're at the end of the carpet by the awning for the entrance to the hotel where the gala is being held. Another organizer tells us to pose against the Red Cross logo backdrop for more photos. Oh great, even more nerve-racking. I don't have much time to think about my smile before there are even more flashbulbs going off in our faces.

Christ, give a girl a little warning. I've barely just managed to arrange my features into something I think looks like a pleasant expression, and the next second we're being ushered off the carpet and into the hotel.

"Damn, I wish I could have like, practiced that," I whisper to Jackson as we head to the doors. "I swear I've never had such a hard time walking and smiling at the same time before."

He coughs out a startled laugh as we pass the threshold into the ornately decorated hotel lobby. He looks down at me. Both sides of his mouth are actually tilted up at the same time. "You were brilliant."

There's not much time for the praise to sink in before we're led through to what I can only call a ballroom. I know this must just be an event center on any regular day, but it's been absolutely transformed.

White fairy lights hang from the ceiling and everything else is done in whites and golds. Crisp white tablecloths. Gold napkins. Golden swan centerpieces with vases of white tulips.

It all looks like something out of a fairytale, and that's not even taking into consideration the gorgeously-dressed people who've begun filling up the space. Beyond the tables is an open area for mingling or maybe dancing later.

Few people are sitting at the tables though. They're mingling in the open area beyond the seating, on the ballroom floor where servers thread through the crowd with champagne and appetizers held aloft on trays. That's where Jackson guides me with the slightest of pressures on the small of my back. I'd rather he held out his arm for me to take. I could use the stability of his arm. But the touch of his hand to the skin of my back where the dress dips feels... a little too intimate.

The surreal feeling is back. Like this is one of those dreams where I've gotten myself on a reality show. You know, the kind where they set you up on an elaborate prank and then Ashton Kutcher jumps out at you—except that show was for celebrities and aired forever ago and yeah. Besides, with my luck, it's more like the dream would turn into a nightmare where everyone starts laughing at me and there are clowns and it all goes downhill from there—

"So now you know where I come from and how I got into computers. What about you?"

When I look up toward Jackson, his eyes are so intent and piercing I all but lose my breath. Dear God this man should come with a warning label.

"I, um," I stutter, shrugging ridiculously and laughing. "I don't know. Studying computers seemed like a good way to play against my type cast."

His eyebrows furrow like he doesn't get my meaning.

I feel my cheeks heat. "You know, blonde bimbo." I leave out the *big boobs* part and he's gentlemanly enough not to drop his eyes to my cleavage that manages to make even this elegant dress that looked perfectly respectable on the hanger into something Jessica Rabbit would wear.

The crease between his eyebrow only deepens, though. "I've never seen you that way, Calliope."

A part of me wants to challenge him on it. *Then why did you invite me out tonight?* All my naïveté was used up a long time ago. I've accepted the fact that it's what all men see when they look at me.

But what if... *could* a man ever learn to see past it? I've never doubted that there might be good men out there in the world. I just always knew that those weren't the kind of men who would be attracted to *me*.

Jackson's doing it again. The intense staring thing.

And just like the first time, it takes my breath away. It's like he's looking into me. Seeing *me*.

"Jackson," I whisper, my heartbeat suddenly racing.

"Jackson," an older man with silver hair and a southern accent booms out. He grabs Jackson's hand in what looks like a crushing grasp. "So glad to see you here, my boy."

I take a step back and blink, sucking in a large lungful of air. Jesus, what had I even been about to say? I have no idea what my follow up was going to be. Or maybe I'd just needed to say his name out loud. To know the feel of it on my lips.

"Trevor," Jackson says and I almost jolt from shock at the sound of it because it sounds like a stranger's. All the warmth and animation I've been enjoying all night is absolutely gone.

His voice and face are back to that untouchable mask like they were when I first met him, so that I have no idea his thoughts about this Trevor guy. I think it's just Jackson's go-to, though, not a commentary on this man. But Jackson's cracked that hard façade with me. Many times now. What does that mean?

There's no more time to ponder it, though, because Trevor turns his eyes on me. "And who is this lovely creature on your arm tonight?"

"Miss Calliope Cruise, may I introduce Mr. Trevor Henderson." Again, nothing is given away by Jackson's voice. "Trevor, this is my associate, Miss Cruise. She's kindly deigned to spend the evening with me."

"I'm with Lockheed Martin," Trevor holds out his hand to me. "Don't tell me Jackson roped you into playing with his toys when there are so many dynamic companies hiring in the valley?"

As we shake—a grip that's several touches past too firm from his side, if I do say so. I have to all but stop from wringing out my hands afterwards. And Trevor keeps up the smile. It's a salesman's grin. "What's your specialty? Engineering? Advanced mathematics? What university did you graduate from?"

"How about you turn it off for one night, Trevor?" Jackson's face is impassive, almost bored.

"Come on, Jackson, you know how the game is played," the other man continues, still looking at me with that too large smile on his face. "Never lose an opportunity to network. So what university is it?"

"Um, Stanford," I offer, "though I haven't finished my degree yet."

"She's working at Gentry Tech while she's finishing up her last semester," Jackson inserts.

Trevor's eyebrow goes up at this. "Gentry Tech, huh?" He looks back and forth between Jackson and me several times. "And she's here as your guest tonight? How interesting."

"Careful, Trevor. In a moment, you're going to sound as much the gossip as the beautiful Mrs. Henderson."

"Did I hear my name? My ears are burning," An elegant older woman walks up to our small group and puts her hand on Mr. Henderson's shoulder. She plants a small kiss on his cheek. "I do hope it's a juicy rumor someone's started about me, at least."

At this, Jackson gives a genuine smile. "Is there any other kind when it comes to you, Lucy?"

Mrs. Henderson laughs and then pats down her glossy brown hair. She seems like she might be in her mid-fifties like Mr. Henderson, but I suspect she's had some work done on her face. It's not horribly conspicuous though. Her skin is smooth and her hair a glossy brown. She's beautiful and elegant and when Jackson smiles at her, I'm surprised at the small kick of jealousy that hits me. She has to be at least twenty years his senior, if not more.

"Oh how you do spoil me, Jackson." She pulls away from her husband to plant a kiss on Jackson's cheek, lingering a little longer than is strictly necessary in my opinion.

When she pulls back, her eyes are flushed with excitement. "I don't suppose my husband is any more successful in his attempt tonight to sway you to come work for Lockheed?"

"Alas," Mr. Henderson says, "tonight I was trying to tempt his fair companion, Ms. Cruise."

For the first time, Mrs. Henderson seems to take me in. I'm not sure exactly what all is encompassed in the flash of her eyes as she looks me up and down. "Oh? And what is Ms. Cruise's specialty?"

Mr. Henderson casually puts a hand around his wife's waist and his stare comes back to me. "We were just getting to that."

I feel my cheeks heat. The words at the tip of my tongue are to mumble that I'm a nobody, just a personal assistant. Far less than that if I'm being honest, since half the reason I was hired had to do with my chest size.

But no. Screw that.

I force myself to stand up straighter and meet Mr. Henderson's gaze straight on. I can't hang all of my hopes on Bryce's paper-thin promises of a future at his research labs.

I might only be a pawn to Bryce and perhaps a curiosity to Jackson, but if I can leverage my time among these stratospherically powerful men to a higher position in the world once they're done with me, then all of this won't be for nothing. Mr. Henderson said it himself. Never lose an opportunity to network and Lockheed is one of the Gods in advanced machinery, constantly pushing the state-of-the-art in their field.

"I'm interested in specialized algorithmic design in applied machine learning situations, especially robotics."

"What field work have you done?" Trevor asks.

I realize with excitement that I actually have an answer for him. "In my last year at Stanford, I was working on a project to program imitation learning techniques. We were trying to get our robot," I lean in and smile, "—we called her Ginger—to learn behaviors by 'observing' an end- user performing them, without us having to program each action.

"It was our job to program her *how* to learn. That was the point of the project. She was just an arm and a hand hooked up to a small computer brain, but what we were really interested in was how quickly and intuitively we could program her to pick up behaviors."

Mr. Henderson looks impressed. "And how did it turn out?"

I don't let my disappointment show that I never got to see Ginger's full potential. It was a two-semester project that was supposed to span my entire senior year. Of course, I wasn't there for the second semester. I barely managed that first one—I had to arrange to take my fall finals early because Charlie's due date was in mid-December. He ended up coming even earlier, but thankfully I'd just finished my last test.

But I don't let any of that show. Instead, I keep my smile bright and inviting. "I had to leave the project early, but I was involved in coding the initial breakthroughs. When I left, Ginger could mirror me sufficiently to high-five me. It was enough to hook me for life, I'm afraid."

I shake my head again with a laugh. "I'm fascinated by programing that directly interacts with hardware that can have immediate real-world applications." I arch an eyebrow, lean in conspiratorially and shrug in Jackson's direction. "Whether that's with the drone systems that Mr. Gentry and Mr. Vale are cooking up or with the future of other advanced machinery, we'll see."

When I pull back, I keep my stance tall and I think I've finally managed demure. Damn, that feels good.

Trevor's broad grin tells me I pulled off what I wanted to accomplish. Before I can even dip my lips into a return smile, he's pulled a card out of his suit coat and has it in my hand. "As I said, whenever you get tired of playing with toys, give me a call." With that, he winks at me and my fingers close over the card.

I try not to grin too broadly and instead keep my smile coy. "I'll keep that in mind." I take the card and pop open my stuffed clutch to slide the card inside. To my relief, after only a brief wrestling match behind my back, it latches closed again.

"Yes, well, darling," Mrs. Henderson says, looking bored at the conversation, "I'm famished. Let's go find our seats." With a lingering glance at Jackson and a dismissive glare my way, she pulls her husband off toward the tables.

I can't help feeling a small thrill from the whole exchange. I grab a glass of champagne from a passing serving girl and take a large swallow

of the fizzy liquid. It makes my eyes water, but at least I don't choke
or cough.

I do, however, hear a low rumble from beside me. I look over in
surprise when I realize that it's the sound of Jackson chuckling. It's a
nice sound. More than nice. A girl could quickly become addicted to
the sound of it. To all that is Jackson Vale, if I'm being honest.

He's taken his own glass of champagne and he's looking at me over
the rim of it. He's barely smiling, but his eyes are so... *alive* as he
watches me.

"I should have known that a night out with you would be anything
but boring," he comments in that low gravelly voice of his.

His face is all hard lines, his jaw and cheekbones so sharp they
might cut. He looks ferocious in spite of the gentlemanly suit he wears.
Again it seems like he doesn't belong to this era. Like he'd be more at
home in leather and maybe a bear skin or two.

They say the eyes are the window to the soul, so what do I see in
his? I search, back and forth in those blue depths, but I can't read a
damn thing. He doesn't look away, though, and holds my gaze so that
we're just staring at each other. Or into each other. I may not be able
to read him, but damn if I don't feel this... *intensity* burning
between us—

But then a flash of someone's face I recognize catches in the
periphery of my vision from across the room. My head swings that way.
And all the air in my lungs leaves in one shocked exhale.

It's David and the Shrew.

CHAPTER ELEVEN

What are *they* doing here? How did—?

"Calliope? What's wrong?" Jackson's body goes taut, his hand immediately at the small of my back.

For a second I can't say anything at all. David looks both relaxed and stylish in a tailored black tux. Even from across the room I can tell it's far nicer than anything I ever saw him wear when we were together. His wife hangs easily on his arm. Tall and elegant. Perfectly suited to him.

"Calliope." Jackson's voice is a snap in my ear, demanding answers.

"It's just—no one, someone I used to know," the words come out in a flood. When I look up into Jackson's disapproving eyes, I know he knows it's a lie. I don't care. It's all he's getting right now.

There are two circles in my life, and they must never touch.

They must never touch.

I pull away from Jackson's hand. "Did someone say that dinner was about to be served?"

I walk in the direction of the dinner tables. After a moment, Jackson follows. I know he's watching me and I try to keep my gaze straight ahead, but I can't help it. My eyes involuntarily shoot behind me to the ballroom where I just saw them. They're gone and I feel panicky. Where did they go? Shit.

I don't know why I'm so shocked that they're here. The Red Cross isn't a charity that only tech gurus would frequent. God, I'm such an idiot for not seeing this coming. The Shrew's family is loaded. Of course she'd be here.

It'll be fine. Just stop thinking about it. Pretend they're not here. It's good that I've lost sight of them. This is a big enough event. I probably won't even come across them again tonight.

Yeah, that's what I'll do. *Ignore, ignore, ignore.*

Having a plan makes me feel slightly better and meanwhile, Jackson has led me to one of the many long tables that runs the length of the dining room. A name card sits on the table in front of each of our chairs, penned in beautiful calligraphy. I pick up the delicate card and run my finger over my name before looking up at Jackson.

Three chimes sound out over the room and everyone makes their way en masse toward the dining area. I reach for my champagne glass.

But then I startle when I notice people start to sit at the table around us. To be more exact, when I see David and the Shrew take their seats not two feet away from where we're sitting, on the opposite side of the long table.

Fuck my life.

There goes my plan for ignoring they're here. They've seen me. I can tell by the way the Shrew is so obviously *not* looking in my direction. David, too, is doing the pretend-Callie-doesn't-exist thing. I mean, it was *my* plan originally, but that was before we were seated so close together they could sneeze and it would be in my air space. Seriously. David sees me twice a week. We share a freaking child together.

Who he's suing you for full custody of.

Right.

I set the champagne down abruptly. The last thing I need is them claiming they saw me getting drunk in public.

Maybe ignoring each other in public is the thing to do after all. I crane my neck in the opposite direction.

"Are you sure you're all right?"

"Fine." I answer distractedly, giving up and looking forward again so I can observe the Shrew out of my periphery. I've never really seen her this close up. I mean, she was there at the first hearing, but I obviously had a million other things on my mind. Since then, she's always waiting in the van when David comes to pick up Charlie. Well, other than that time with the doorbell, but even then, the bitch was walking away by the time I actually got outside.

I can't help but stare now. I try to do it unobtrusively so it's not too obvious. Where I feel like I'm playing at dress up, she looks like the real deal. Elegant. Refined. Her long dark hair is down with a slight curl in it. It looks so shiny and healthy, like in the shampoo ads. Flawless makeup. Pearls at her ears and neck. She's wearing a black off-the-shoulder gown that hugs her small, toned frame. She's not much younger than David, but she wears her late thirties well and it only adds to her sense of sophistication.

Fine. So what? I've come to terms with the fact that I was just a cheap fling to David. Lots of people have their hearts broken by their first loves. It wasn't real. It was hard seeing him at the first hearing and when he initially started picking Charlie up for his visits. It would have been difficult on anyone in my position. I'm over it now. But being forced to sit here all through dinner with these people who are actively trying to take my son away from me? This is some bullshit.

Christ, it's hot in here. Would it look weird if I took the cloth napkin and dabbed at my forehead like I'm some southern belle? Great, I bet my face is getting red. That always happens when I'm hot. Damn it, do they not have air-conditioning in this place?

"I really can't help but feel like something's bothering you." Jackson says, angling his body toward me.

"I said I was fine." It comes off more snappish than I mean. But damn it, I'm so thirsty and my glass of champagne is just sitting there, taunting me. I'm desperate for a glass of water. There's a water glass at my setting, but naturally, it's empty. Where the hell are the waiters who come around and fill *those* up? I pick up the name card and try fanning myself with it. "Does it feel warm in here to you?"

Jackson shakes his head and eyes me with more than curiosity.

Dammit. What am I doing? I'm blowing it big time, that's what I'm doing. Seeing David's totally thrown me off my game. Tonight's too important to let my stupid ex distract me. Time to get my shit back together.

"So I was talking with Bryce this week and he was explaining more about the algorithmic—design," I pause to swallow because my voice is all croaky. I swear it's like the goddammed Mojave Desert in my mouth. I cough and there's nothing to do but grab the glass of luke-warm champagne and take a sip.

Except that it goes down the wrong pipe, which makes me cough and sputter. Jackson pounds me on my back a couple times. Liquid from the nearly full glass of champagne sloshes over the rim of the glass into my lap.

Christ. I jump out of my chair at the same second Jackson apologizes and reaches for some napkins. And that's when I feel it. I look up, and sure enough, every eye near us is on me. Including David and the Shrew. Who is smirking none too subtly, a glint of smug superiority in her eyes.

"Excuse me," I choke out, turning away from all of them, David, Jackson, the Shrew, and every other prying eye. I hurry away from the table as fast as I can in these goddamned heels. Water. I need some water and a moment to just—I don't know, pull myself to-fucking-gether.

I have no clue where the bathrooms are, but I head in the direction I think they might be. I'm getting out of the ballroom anyway. Sometimes a girl just needs a goddamned minute.

A waiter passes by with another tray of champagne flutes.

"Bathroom?" The desperation must be clear in my face. He expertly balances the tray on one hand and then points to the back corner of the room. "There's one just there, Miss."

I grab a glass of champagne and then hurry off. It's not until I'm through the door of the restroom—well, two doors, it's one of those fancy ones that has a sitting room before you get to the actual room with toilet stalls—that I'm finally able to take in several deep breaths.

I pour the champagne down the sink and then fill the flute up with water. Then I down the glass of cool water in one long swig. Oh my God, has pure, sweet water ever tasted so good?

I refill it and then drink down another glassful before I finally leave the glass on the counter and head into one of the stalls.

It's only then I notice one door is already closed. Eeek, I hope I wasn't huffing like an overworked cow when I stomped in here like I think I was. I always find it awkward sharing bathrooms with strangers, no matter the partitioning stalls that supposedly give privacy.

I sit on the toilet with the lid down, just using it as a chair, and hope the other woman leaves soon. Then I lean my head back and look at the ceiling. I'm being ridiculous. If she leaves, three more people will probably take her place. The ball is packed out there. I should be glad I'm getting as much privacy as I am.

It's quiet in here. I take in a deep breath and let it out slowly. Oh my God, what a shitshow that just was out there. I grab some toilet paper and dab at the wet spot on the front of my dress. It's not too visible against the dark red of the dress. It's not as much as I initially thought, either. I put the toilet paper in the little garbage on the wall and take another couple minutes to gather myself.

All right, I'm going to go back out there and focus, give Jackson my best pitch. I will salvage the night. I will be calm, cool, and collected.

I use the restroom, then step out of the stall to wash my hands, examining my face to see what needs fixing.

I'm astonished that my makeup looks pretty much just like it did when I left the apartment. I thought I'd be a sweaty mess. Then I remember that Breanna did spritz some kind of makeup fixative all over my face when she was done. I was coughing from the fumes at the time, but it has kept everything perfectly in place.

I smile and am gratified to see there's not even any lipstick on my teeth. Breanna would be so proud.

The door opens as I take a towelette to dry my hands.

"Whoring yourself out to another older man, really? You just don't have any imagination, do you?"

I look up in surprise and see her reflection in the mirror. It's the Shrew. All five foot nine, polished head-to-toe inch of her.

"Jackson Vale." She clucks her tongue and her pointy-toed shoes *click, click, click* on the marble floor as she walks toward me. "You sure are moving up in the world." She glances at me out of the side of her eye as she opens up a small clutch bag and pulls out some lipstick. "At least until he realizes what a crazy bitch whore you are."

I step back from her. "Excuse me?"

She starts to casually reapply her lipstick. She smacks her lips together with a pop before turning to look at me. Or I should say, look down her nose at me.

"Look at you." She smirks. "Cheap bottle blonde." She reaches over and tugs at my hair, pulling a chunk out of the pins.

I can only stare at her, shocked. What the hell? Did this bitch actually just do that?

"Flashing those double D's in men's faces so they don't see the *crazy* in your eyes." She smacks at my cleavage with her rectangular silver clutch purse. Hard enough to sting. She rears back to swing again.

"Don't fucking touch me." I shove her. If she thinks she can assault me like that and I'll just take it, she's got another thing coming.

"What's wrong with you?" she shrieks, her voice suddenly different. She topples backwards to the floor even though I didn't push her that hard. "I just wanted to talk to you, woman to woman, about David getting to see his son more," her voice sounds pleading now, as if she's afraid of me.

What the hell's going on? I shuffle forward and she holds her hands up defensively. "Please stop! I won't approach you again, just don't hurt me!"

I throw up my hands. "What the hell are you talking about?"

But before my eyes, she seems to undergo another complete personality change. She's grinning as she gets up off the floor. "Did you get all that, Manny?"

The stall that had been closed when I came in pushes open and a medium-build guy in what looks like a chauffer's uniform steps out holding up a camera phone. "Got it, Mrs. K."

I look back at David's wife, a horrible sort of realization dawning. She's happy enough to fill in any remaining gaps. She's not grinning now. There's only a lethal sort of determination on her face. "You have kept David away from his son long enough. He belongs with his father. With *us*. I knew I could catch your true colors on video."

I want to launch at her and claw her eyes out, but I see that Manny has the camera up and recording again. "This footage is all manipulated," I say into the camera before turning back to the Shrew. "You're the one who assaulted me first."

She shrugs. "That's not what it's going to look like in the edited version."

"He's my son," I grit my teeth, hands fisting at my side.

"He's David's son."

"David sure didn't think so when he told me to abort him," I struggle and fail to hold my temper. "I'm the one," I stab my thumb into my chest, "who's loved Charlie and been there for him for his first words and steps. I'm the one who sacrificed. Who gave up school and postponed the other things I wanted because he's my number one priority. He's everything to me. You'll never take him away." It takes everything in me to keep my rage from boiling over. "I have a lawyer who knows what he's doing this time."

"You don't deserve a baby," she steps up to me, anger flashing in her eyes. "You're a coked- up whore. We have pictures. What do you think the judge will say when he sees that? You think they'll find you a fit mother when they see you snorting the rent money up your nose?"

My insides drop to my feet. How could—? It was just that one time and David brought it. He told me it would be so hot if we both did it and then had sex. I hated the way it made me feel so out of control. And David took pictures? I don't remember that. But then, that night became extremely hazy after the drugs.

I look up and glare at the Shrew, then at the guy who has the camera trained back on me. Or is this bitch just lying to try to get me to say something on camera she can twist around?

"If you want a baby so bad, why don't you just have one of your own?" Then I see it, the flash of pain on her face.

"You can't, can you? That's what all this is about." I take a step back in realization. So my guess was right. She can't have kids. For a second, I feel sorry for her. I can't imagine what it would feel like not to be able to have my Charlie.

Her face hardens. "Don't you dare pity me, you little whore. You think you can sleep with my husband, get knocked up with his bastard, and then pity me?"

I glare at her. Yep, any pity I had is gone now. I could give zero fucks for this lady. "He told me you were divorced." Most of the time we met at his house—a necessity since I was still living in the dorms. Why wouldn't I have believed him about the divorce? "I'm sorry you can't have a baby, but that doesn't mean you can steal mine."

"It's not stealing. It's David's child," she gestures at Manny and turns for the door, but not before pausing for a parting shot over her shoulder. "And our team of lawyers have more than enough ammunition now to gain full custody against whatever paltry little family lawyer you can scrape up enough cash for.

"We have quite a story to tell, after all," she leans closer as the vicious words continue spouting. "Poor little college girl with a habit of seducing older men. It started early, with the executives at her father's bank, whoring herself out to get favors for Daddy dearest. Or maybe because you just like the control it gave you, having him twisted around your little finger."

Her words hit me with as much force as a bat to the stomach.

David told her.

I trusted him with my darkest, most painful secrets. He told *her.* And he's going to use it against me? I— I just— I mean, I know now that he never loved me, but I thought at least—

My knees feel weak.

No, don't let her see she's affecting you, Cals. Don't let her see. You have to be a fortress. You have to be—

But I must fail because her face brightens in triumph. "Didn't think anyone would ever find out about that, huh, Callie? Or should I call you Lolita? You've always sought out men of power, haven't you? Does it validate your existence, is that what you get out of it? First your daddy's boss, then your professor, now Jackson Vale? You pretend to be the wide-eyed victim all the while leaning over in those skimpy trash outfits, rubbing your oversized chest in their faces. Seducing them away from their wives and their morals so they'll fuck you. But that's all you'll ever be to them. A toy to fuck and then toss away. Like the trash you are."

My hands tighten into fists but I give her the opposite reaction to what she's trying to goad out of me.

Oh sure, I want to stab her eyes out with my hair pins. But I lock it all down, deep, deep inside. I've had practice with this. Don't let anyone see. No one can ever know.

Look what happened when I did open up and tell someone. David betrayed me in every way possible.

No—I swallow hard at the new stab of pain—shove it down deep like a lake that freezes over. From the surface, no one can see any movement at all. This bitch wants hot anger and reaction so she can catch it on video. So I give her ice. Indifference.

I yawn. "You done?" I stretch languidly. "I've got a date to get back to."

Her eyes narrow. Oh, she's good and pissed now. I don't let my gratification show on my face. The only vibe I give off is boredom.

The door opens behind the Shrew and three women come in, all chatting together. They pause in surprise when they see Manny.

Just before I can offer the helpful idea that we call security about a man in the women's restroom, the Shrew jerks her head and Manny follows her quickly out the door.

I just stand stock still for a long moment, watching them as they go. After the intensity of that showdown, my thoughts feel sluggish.

Bad. That was all very bad. The things David and the Shrew are going to bring up about me in court... Mr. McIntyre, that bastard my father worked for, saying I *seduced* him, as if I wanted it... a shudder starts deep in my bone and works its way outward.

David was so outraged on my behalf when I eventually told him about it. We were in bed one night and he'd just promised that we'd be together forever. I'd never known happiness like that and I didn't want any secrets between us. I was scared but I told him anyway because I trusted him.

David jumped off the bed, he was so pissed. He said he'd kill him. I had to beg him not to go on the rampage. He made love to me so tenderly afterwards, telling me that he'd protect me from anything bad ever happening to me again.

He made me believe heroes were real.

But it was all a lie. A horrible, devastating lie...

My lip starts to tremble.

I open the door. My knees are even shakier now. I force myself to walk anyway.

But I can't block out the Shrew's words. My stomach roils. If their lies sway the judge, I'll have nothing left. I will *be* nothing. I survived Mr. McIntyre, in part because of David. I survived David's betrayal because of Charlie. But if Charlie's taken away from me?

A numbness starts to steal over my entire body even while somehow I manage to stay upright and continue walking.

No. There's no way I'm letting them take my baby. They can't. We'll go on the run. I'll change my name, change my hair, hide in Mexico, anything, oh God, *anything*—

"Calliope." A hand closes on my arm as I dazedly stumble out of the bathroom. I look up and Jackson's large form fills my entire field of vision. His face is tight with some emotion I can't name.

All I can manage is to stare vacantly at him. I'm supposed to be salvaging the night. It's very important. There's a voice in the back of my mind yelling at me to pull my shit together.

But... Charlie. That horrible woman is trying to steal my place as mother to my Charlie. She doesn't know how I sing to him before bedtime. How we snuggle together in the mornings. That smile he has just for me—

"Enough. Tell me what's wrong, right this moment." Jackson drags me off to an alcove created in the corner by a column.

"I," I start, but then pause because there are genuinely no other words in my mind. I'm just blank. Other than: *Charlie. My baby. Charlie.* "Home," I finally manage to pull out through my mental fog. "Need to go home."

Thank God, I must have gotten out some words that made sense, because Jackson takes my arm and starts to lead me out of the ballroom in long strides I have to hurry to keep up with. Relief hits through the numbing haze. Home. I'll check in on Charlie and then curl up and sleep.

Sleep. Yes, that'll help. Tomorrow I'll figure all this out. Of course I'll figure it all out. I always do. Don't I? I have to.

Except of course for the first court hearing where David won partial custody. And sure, I have a better lawyer now, but is he really going to measure against the team the Shrew's family is paying for? And all the horrible things they're going to accuse me of? *Habit of seducing older men.*

Oh God, I could lose Charlie. I really could. I always said nothing on this earth could separate me from my little boy.

But it's not true.

David, the Shrew, and their team of lawyers might—

My breaths start coming in short, gasping pants. I try to gulp in air, but I barely manage a short wheeze.

My little boy.

He's my life.

They can't take him away—

I barely realize that we've stepped into the cool night air before the limo slides in front of us. Jackson all but pushes me into the back of it.

"Breathe, Calliope. Take a deep breath, you're hyperventilating."

I try. I really try. But every time I open my mouth to gulp in air, the image hits—policeman holding me back while that horrible woman drags a screaming Charlie away from me. Then the air that I desperately need is gone again.

Spots dance in my vision. Oh God, oh God, oh God—

Then, wait, what's going on—?

Everything goes head over ass and not just because I'm light-headed. Jackson's spun me over so that I'm face down against the seat. And wait... Is he...?

He is. He's bent me over his lap.

Ass up.

And now he's hoisting my gown up.

Before I can even fully comprehend what's happening, his hand comes down on my ass. It doesn't hurt, per se, it's more of a slight sting, but the resounding *smack* of it and just the shock of—did he just *spank* me in the back of a moving limo and wait, can we get back to the part where the guy I barely know just *spanked* me?

And then he does it again. The other ass cheek this time.

Jackson's voice is calm as he slaps each cheek twice more with slightly increased force, "Your safe word is red."

CHAPTER TWELVE

"I assume you know what a safe word is?" he continues, "They've become something of a pop-culture reference."

I just lay there, shocked. I mean, certainly enough in my life has shocked me over the past two months, but I think this just might take the cake.

"Answer me, Calliope." His voice is a commanding growl. "Say the safe word."

I take a deep breath in, ready to tell him to go to hell when I realize what I'm doing. I'm breathing again. Not hyperventilating. But right when I realize it, the crippling terror comes rushing back. Charlie. David and his wife threatening to take him away. The very real possibility that I'll lose my baby. Just like that, my lungs constrict again and my whole body begins to shake.

"The safe word," Jackson demands. "Acknowledge it."

"Red," I squeak.

And then it's like opening the floodgates. Both literally and figuratively. Jackson's hand starts coming down on my ass, a sharp percussion that stings at first and then becomes progressively harsher until I'm squirming in his hold.

It hurts but in the part of my mind still capable of thought, I can tell he knows what he's doing. He's holding back and giving only what I can take, not putting his full strength into it to actually hurt me.

My mind seems to detach completely from everything else. My concentration narrows to each slap as it lands. He works up and down my cheeks, down to the curve where my butt meets my thigh and then back up again.

I don't even realize I'm crying until the blows slow and then stop. It's not from the pain. I don't even try to make sense of it. I can't. I don't want to. And in this moment, it feels like I don't have to. I don't have to think at all.

Jackson's hands are gentle now as he caresses the stinging flesh he was smacking moments before. It only makes me cry harder. Me, who *never* cries.

"That's right," he murmurs, "let it out."

And I do. My ass is warm—no, red hot—under his hands. He continues his gentle stroking and when his massage moves lower to between my thighs, I press back against his touch. Needy. Because God, I was too mixed up to realize it even seconds before, but the spanking didn't only make my ass hot.

I'm wet. Drenched. It doesn't make any more sense to me than anything else since I've stepped into this limo tonight, but Jackson's hands are so sure, so decisive. He's so perfectly in control in a moment where I'm anything but.

One long finger slips easily inside me and he hisses out a long breath. "So ready. So perfect. You're so beautifully made."

Perfect? I let out an ugly sobbing scoff. Beautiful? What's wrong with this man?

"That's right, beautiful," he whispers, his deep voice a rumble as his thumb finds my clit. His other hand delivers another sharp *thwack* against my ass.

I yelp even as I writhe on his lap. That's when I feel him hard underneath me. He's not unaffected by all of this. Should I be touching him in return? Is that what he expects? His talented fingers continue their exploration and my back arches in pleasure.

Yes, I should try to give him some of what he's giving me. That's what this is. A kinky fuck in a limo. I move to maneuver a hand between us to grab at him, but he gives my ass another quick smack. Then he holds my hands above my head, pinning them to the smooth leather seat in one of his with a growl. "Keep them there."

I do and then he's back at work, massaging me everywhere. He has the globe of my ass in one hand while plunging the fingers of his other hand in and out of my pussy. My breaths get shorter and shorter, but it's not like before. No, this is all ramping up toward a goal. That pressure between my legs that's building, oh God, *building...*

I writhe against Jackson's hand. I didn't know it could be like— No one's ever touched me like— His fingers thrust masterfully in and out and then in again, hitting a spot that makes light explode behind my eyelids and my stomach swoop crazily.

Oh God, almost there, almost—

I'm teetering on the most glorious edge and part of me doesn't want to drop over. This is such a beautiful, exquisite torture. I want to stay here forever. With him. Drowning in him.

But then Jackson leans over and bites my ear.

"Come for me now," he says through his teeth, at the same moment pushing the tip of this thumb into the tight rosette of my ass.

And I come and I come and I *come.*

I come so hard I feel the vein in my forehead pulse with that moment of blinding whiteness, like all the blood in my body is pushing outward with the force of the orgasm. When I come back into my body, I'm wracked with aftershocks that make my legs shake. What had been a gentle crying before turns into outright sobs.

God. Ooooooo God.

I gasp for breath but can barely manage it. Warmth suffuses my entire body as I slump, spent, over his lap and partially onto the back seat.

I mean, I know what orgasms feel like. Or least I *thought* I did. I touch myself sometimes. And there have been the few terrible times with Gentry but each of those encounters have been quick, sharp, and drenched in shame.

But this... *this...* God, is this what it could really be like?

I'm embarrassed and I should be doing something in return and then there were all the things I was upset about before all this—Charlie, oh God, Charlie—

"Enough," Jackson says, settling the skirt of my dress back down. He lifts me and settles me on the seat beside him.

Right. Of course he's had enough of me. This was supposed to be some hot, kinky thing, but instead I was just crying the whole time? Not what he was probably hoping for when he picked me up tonight. Are we at my house so he can just drop me off and get rid of me yet? I'm hiccupping through the sobs as my breathing gets short again.

I'm so weak when I swore I'd be strong. *Stupid, stupid, weak Calliope.*

But Jackson doesn't put distance between us or look uncomfortable. The limo isn't slowing down either. Instead, Jackson pulls me onto his lap and secures my head against his chest where I can hear the slow and steady beat of his heart.

"You can cry more or you can talk to me about it," he says almost conversationally, "Either's fine. But you're not allowed to keep torturing yourself about whatever is going on in your head." Short pause. "Or I don't care how sore your ass is, we'll go for another round."

Then he begins to stroke my hair, pulling out pins as he goes so he can better work his fingers through it.

This all seems crazy, insane, batshit, what-the-fuck—

I take option number one out of necessity. I cry more.

But only a little while longer, because it turns out being held in Jackson's strong arms while his soothing hands work my scalp is so calming, I sink against him. Even though part of me knows it's dangerous letting myself feel so safe here.

There are no heroes. This is all a delusion, letting myself forget my worries and pretend things are okay. But I'm so tired and Jackson feels solid and strong and gentle and good and...

———

When my eyes blink sleepily open, the world is bouncing. I'm cradled in Jackson's strong arms, my face pressed into his chest, his piney, manly scent invading my senses.

The hell?

"Where are we?" I stiffen against his body.

"Shh. Rest. We're at my house."

Okay, now I'm wide awake. "What? Wait." I struggle a little in his arms. "Let me down." It's dark out. But other than that, mostly all I can see is Jackson's massive chest.

"No."

I sputter. "No?"

"No. We're almost to the door."

I blink more and really take in my surroundings. We're standing outside a huge house. Strike that. *House* is the wrong word. Mansion. We're at the side entrance of a huge mansion. Jackson hefts me in his arms easily, bracing me with one arm while he reaches into his pocket with his other hand to grab his keys.

"Really, just put me down. Or actually, let me get an Uber because I need to get back home."

"I already used your phone to call your sister," he says easily. "She said she'd be delighted to watch over Charlie for as long as needed."

The fuck? I put my hands to my face. Everything comes flooding back. David's horrible wife. Charlie. The way I fell apart in the limo. Not just the sobbing. The orgasm, too. Oh God. Was that really me?

Now it all feels like some strange dream version of myself. And yeah, not exactly the Cinderella dream the night started out with. Pretty sure Disney never covered getting spanked by the prince in the limo after the bitch wife of Cinderella's ex causes her to have a panic attack by bringing up her fucked up past and threatening to take her son. Ugh, even thinking through the recap exhausts me.

"Look," I start to say, but Jackson pops the door open and then we're over the threshold and inside. He kicks the door closed and then carries me over to the couch where he finally lays me down. Several motion-activated lights turned on at our entrance.

He leads me into a wide living room area that's decorated similarly as his office—sumptuous rugs, leather couches that have an almost antique appearance with carved wooden legs and detailing along the backs. It's not like an antique store with lace draped around or the Victorian style of cramming tons of little trinkets everywhere.

It just reeks of comfort and manly elegance. A man lives here, not a boy.

But I can barely take in the luxury of the house because Jackson quickly crowds out everything else.

"Look," I try again, embarrassment heating my neck. "Everything that happened, back there," I gesture lamely toward the door, "that's not who I am. I don't go around crying about things." I leave out the bit about not normally letting almost-strangers spank me in their limos. Hopefully that goes without saying.

Jackson tilts his head to the side, observing me in that way of his that always makes me feel like he's seeing too much. "So if you're not a girl who cries often, it must have been something pretty big to make you do it tonight. Tell me what it was."

I shift in the overly large couch cushions so that I'm sitting up. I feel my cheeks heat and my hair tumbles around my shoulders. The hair he was running his fingers through just a while ago in the limo. The remembered intimacy makes my stomach tingle. I keep my eyes trained on my lap. "It was nothing."

At his disbelieving scoff, my eyes flash back to him.

"Nothing I can't handle," I amend.

"Maybe so," he says, "but you're still going to tell me what it's all about. I saw that woman follow you into the bathroom. Who is she?"

I avert my eyes. I don't want to go into my messy history. The mistakes I've made. Though I can't really even consider them mistakes since they brought me Charlie. Everything in my past is what it is. As is my present. The devil's bargain I've made with Bryce. Whatever the hell it is that's brought me to this moment. I lean my head back against the overstuffed couch and stare at the ceiling.

The only way out is through, isn't that what they say? Charlie and I will get through this. Somehow.

"Calliope," Jackson's voice snaps. He hasn't sat down and as tall as he is, he towers over me. "I'm tired of you dodging my questions. I swear I'll take you over my knee again if that's what it takes to get answers."

My head jerks up at the threat. His face is dark but it's what's in his eyes that makes me capitulate. In spite of his demanding tone, his gaze is full of what looks like... concern. Like he actually cares about what's going on with me. And when was the last time that happened? Other than Shannon, who is somewhat contractually obligated as my sister to care, who else have I had in my life to give a fuck what happens to me?

So I tell him. At least about David. As the words flow out of me—I know it's a cliché, but I do feel like a weight is lifted off of me. The stress compressing my chest like a tightening anvil loosens suddenly with the telling.

"So let me get this straight," Jackson paces in front of me. "This man took advantage of his position of power and was never punished. Even though you were forced to drop out of college a semester short of getting your degree. Then he told you to get an abortion but now suddenly he wants to take your child because his barren wife decided she wants a baby?"

I cringe. "Yep, that's about the sum of it." I sit up straighter. "But they aren't going to take Charlie from me." The more I say it out loud, the more I can believe it, right? I'll just ignore the wavering quality of my voice.

"I don't care how fancy their lawyers are," I continue. And then quieter, but with no less determination: "I'll take Charlie and go on the run if I have to." Shit. I shouldn't have said that out loud. What is it about this guy that makes me confess my every thought?

Jackson's eyes narrow and I hurry to add, "Not that it *will* come to that. Now that I'm working for Bryce, I can afford a great lawyer." Then I frown. Because my position with Bryce is dependent on my ability to sway Jackson and I haven't even broached the subject with him tonight—

"What? What thought just made you frown right then?"

I sigh. I'm not playing this smoothly at all. I could probably try to twist this into some kind of sympathy ploy, but I hate that kind of shit. I'd rather just put it out there straight.

"I need you to agree to collaborate with Bryce. It will secure me a higher position." I meet his clear blue eyes. "But I'm not saying I think it's something you should just do out of some kind of—" I shrug "— pity for me."

Then I feel a blush rise to my cheeks again. "Not that you'd make such an important business decision based on something so dumb, but, um." *For Christ's sake, get your goddamned foot out of your mouth, Cals.* "You'd get to collaborate on what I truly believe is a quality product. What Bryce has created genuinely is the next phase in drone technol—"

"Come work for me," Jackson cuts me off, stare intense. "Give Bryce your resignation and come work for CubeThink."

I laugh out loud. "Oh." My laughter stops abruptly. "You're serious."

His stern face says it all.

I blow out a huff of air and give him the full force of my glare. "And you want me to do the same thing for you that Bryce has me do for him? Be your *Personal* Assistant?"

"No," he all but barks. For the first time all night, Jackson looks like he's about to lose his composure. His jaw isn't just rigid now, his skin starts to look mottled like he's barely keeping his temper in check.

I scoot further down the couch. I really don't know this man very well, and here I am alone with him in this big empty house. It's true, I've never felt unsafe with him, but...

He takes a deep breath as if steadying himself. "No, I would never expect sexual favors from you as part of your position. Bryce is a snake. He begs for scraps from government contractors, cuts corners, and is all about the bottom line, not innovation."

"CubeThink is light years ahead in terms of global application. We can use drones to solve real world problems—ones *without* military applications." The disgust is clear on his face.

Then his eyes meet mine. "Maybe I'm not saving lives, but that doesn't mean I don't do meaningful work. Planting trees, taking stable oceanography video, delivering care packages to refugees, these are the kinds of things I'm interested in. The commercial stuff is just to gain capital for the experimental projects I'm really invested in."

I can only stare at him for a moment. "So why did you ever agree to a meeting with me if you knew you'd never work with him again?"

He shrugs a little too casually, finally sitting down. He sits so close there's only about a foot between us on the couch. When he crosses one leg at the ankle, his knee brushes my thigh. A little jolt rushes through me at the contact.

"Keep your enemies close," he says. "I'm not going to turn down an opportunity to look at his prototypes. And after all these years he wants something from me. Enough to give my father's patent back, which he lorded over me for years."

"What was the patent for?" I ask, swallowing and trying not to let him see how his proximity affects me. "And how did Bryce get it?"

Jackson's jaw hardens, the way it seems to do whenever Bryce is brought up. "I told you my dad was an inventor?"

I nod.

"Come on," he says, getting up. "Let's walk."

He stands and holds out a hand to me. I take it, letting him pull me to my feet. Again I feel a *zing* at the contact. Damn, what is up with that? It's like I'm back in Jr. High when a cute boy I have a crush on looks at me and I get swoony at the stupidest little things. I shake my head at myself.

Jackson leads me through the living room and then flicks the switch to illuminate a large inner courtyard covered in greenery before he opens the glass doors.

When we step out, I'm immediately assaulted by the smell of flowers. The lights illuminate several blooming beds that run along the edge of the house. It's not all flowers, though. There are trees and all kinds of other tall standing bushes.

The lights have made the outdoor garden come to life. Old-timey lampposts dot the garden, their lights glistening off the pond in the center of the courtyard. Jackson walks toward the pond as he starts talking. It's covered with lily pads and other flora. Everything out here is full of life. I bet there are actual fish living in there too.

"Dad never had the capital or even the..." Jackson looks out at the surface of the pond as if trying to find the right word, "... entrepreneurial interest to really try to make a go of any of his inventions. He loved his machines and working with computers, but he and my mom were always more interested in human projects."

"Like you." I smile gently but also feel like crying as I think of Jackson as a vulnerable, misunderstood teenager and the couple that saw in him what no one else could. Damn it, it's like now that I've accessed the emotional watershed inside, I could just burst again at every little thing.

Jackson nods as we walk the path around the small pond. "I wasn't their first foster kid. They were retired and supposed to be done with fostering when one of my dad's contacts called to talk about me. They changed their minds for me."

He swallows hard but he doesn't look away. "Dad gave me everything he had and while my behavior did improve..." He shakes his head with a bitter laugh. "I was far from perfect. I worry sometimes I took years off his life."

"I'm sure that's not true." I look at him closer to see if he's being serious, but I can't tell. Surely, he can't believe that.

He shrugs and gives a self-deprecating smile. "We'll never know. Either way, when he passed, he was working on a project to create an emotionally intelligent computer. Or at least one that could give a realistic enough imitation. He envisioned it as a tool for at-risk teens—to try to give them someone to talk to when they feel like there's no one else."

This time it's me swallowing back emotion. "That's amazing."

"That was Dad." His lips tip up, and it's a smile that conveys so much—sadness, pride, grief. Or maybe that's all in his eyes. I don't know, but I feel it. There've been times where Jackson seems unreadable, but he's opening himself up to me again, just like he did on the limo ride to the Gala.

Why me?

In my Google research, Jackson is rarely if ever pictured with a girl at his side. He's notoriously quiet about his private life when it comes to interviews. So why is he being so open and transparent with me? Isn't he afraid I'll go revealing everything he's telling me to the papers? Sure I want this deal to go through, but I'm Bryce Gentry's employee. Even more reason *not* to trust me.

We've stopped walking and right beside us is an orange tree. Small unripened oranges are bursting everywhere. We just passed some vines with a ton of strawberries a little while back, and I saw cucumbers before that. I think of Jackson picking strawberries from his own garden to eat, of him sitting out here and enjoying the beauty of his courtyard sanctuary.

It's overwhelming to picture him like that so I try to get back to the point of the conversation. "So how did Bryce get the patent?"

After the words are spoken, though, I sort of wish I hadn't because the shutters on Jackson's eyes that were so open moments ago slam closed.

"I took Dad's death hard. I was a sophomore in college and I..." he huffs out a heavy breath and it's like I can feel his back stiffen. "...went off the rails for a little while. Drinking more, sleeping around, that kind of thing."

"Bryce was a freshman, too—" His features go hard the second he mentions Bryce's name, "—and I had a class with him. Then he was at one of the parties I went to and we got to talking. He flattered me, told me he'd heard all about the things I was doing in the lab. He knew the ridiculous robots website, of course."

Jackson's features darken. "I was clueless back then. Couldn't see that he was manipulating me the whole time. Trying to *collect* me. I was swept up by his charisma. He talked so big. He was smart. We started collaborating on some projects. It was exciting. It was the first time since Dad's passing that I'd felt alive." He shakes his head, the sneer of disgust taking over again.

"I saw how he treated other people." Jackson starts walking again. "How he liked to mess with people's heads. Sometimes he'd even draw me in to help. It all seemed harmless enough at the time. Just like pranks. Sometimes I'd tell him if something wasn't cool, and he'd ease off for a while."

Jackson shakes his head. "But he was always pushing the boundaries of what I was comfortable with. We were doing such good work together, though, I downplayed it all. I was stupid and even shared my dad's idea with him. We were working on developing it together."

He stops again and I see a familiar emotion cover his face. Familiar because I see it in the mirror on my own face regularly—*shame.*

"Eventually, I saw him for who he truly is. But not before he dragged me down with him. I did things I'm not proud of. To get out of the bed I'd made with him, I had to sacrifice Dad's patent. You aren't the only one who's made mistakes in the past, Callie. And trust me," again those piercing dark blue eyes hit mine. "My sins are far worse than any you've committed."

He's still got that commanding gaze on me when he says, "Come work for me. Don't stay at Gentry Tech. Bryce Gentry's not just a bad man. He's dangerous, Callie."

I shake my head, feeling like my brain is still full of champagne bubbles. "You say you don't like games. I know I certainly don't. But this feels like one, between you and Bryce. Like I'm a game piece even though I don't even understand how."

Jackson shakes his head in one decisive movement. "It's why I want you. You aren't trying to play. You're genuine. Do you know what a rare quality that is?" He reaches over and cups my face in the light of a lamp. "This world is so ugly, but you're innocent."

I pull back. I can tell he means it as a compliment, but it doesn't feel like one. Not to mention he's dead fucking wrong. "Don't patronize me," I say. "Just because I'm young doesn't mean I haven't been through shit."

Jackson holds up his hands. "I know. I *know*. That's what makes you even more extraordinary. It's not like you've been shielded from life, but still you're..." he pauses, staring at me with something akin to wonder. "You're extraordinary," he repeats.

My heart swells at the words even while at the same time they feel too slick, too perfect. Even though those aren't ideas I'd usually associate with Jackson. He's not the flatterer like Bryce. From everything I've seen in my short association with him, what you see is what you get.

I shift uncomfortably on my heels and then rub my forehead. "I don't understand. You say you're offering something different from Bryce. So what was that in the limo?" My confusion must show on my face.

Jackson's eyes heat at the reference. "Any personal relationship you and I might share—" I can't help the way my eyes pop at the word *relationship*, "—or not share is completely independent of the work you'll be doing at CubeThink. One has nothing to do with the other. We'd put it in writing with the HR department. Complete disclosure. Everything will be transparent and on the up and up. I assure you, as an employer, I'm only interested in your intellectual abilities."

I sit down on a nearby bench that overlooks the pond, my legs suddenly feeling too much like jelly to stand on.

He's interested in me for my intellectual abilities?

"Really?" I hate myself for the fragile hope that is so obvious in the single word. Jackson just nods as if it's self-evident as he sits beside me. He sits close enough that his knee touches mine, and I hate that I notice the heat of his touch, even through our clothes. He's just such a *presence*. Impossible to ignore.

"Of course. Your professionalism, passion, and understanding of the field as well as your almost-finished degree from Stanford make you an attractive candidate for any company. You saw that tonight. The fact that I'd be grabbing you out from under Bryce's nose is just an added bonus." The edge of his lip turns up in a smile.

"Oh." Understanding finally hits. He just went on and on about how he liked me because I don't play games, but here he is, doing exactly that. This isn't about me or my set of skills. This is about sticking it to Bryce. God. I was stupid to think anything else even for a moment.

I shake it off. It doesn't matter. If I can get out from Bryce's thumb and do honest work for good pay, it's fine. It's all fine.

I stand up and straighten the front of my gown.

"Well, if that's all, Mr. Vale, thank you for a..." I'm about to say lovely evening, but obviously that would be a bald-faced lie. "An experience," I finish with a laugh, ready to go.

"Why do I have the feeling you're willfully misunderstanding me again?" Jackson stands as well, grabbing me around the waist and yanking me toward him until we are chest to chest and forehead to forehead.

"I *want* you, in every possible way the word can be understood. Forget about work for a minute. Let's talk about the personal now. Because tonight was just the beginning. You're going to be in my bed, Calliope. On my desk. Against my wall."

His voice is dark and full of promise. It sends thrilling chills zinging up and down my body. He's not finished, either. "You're going to be begging me to come. In fact, you're going to get very familiar with the concept of taking what I give. I'll spank all this refusal to ask for help out of you if it's the last damn thing I do."

Okay, he's just ticking me off now. I'm about to tell him so, too—

But before I can get a word out, lips close on mine. And it's not like earlier in the car. This time I'm not meek or overwhelmed. I'm not a crying mess.

I bite his lip. He makes a surprised noise and yanks away.

But I grab his face and pull him back to my lips for another long, bruising kiss. I press my entire body against him, soft against hard.

He pushes his thigh between my legs and I yank up my dress so I have enough slack to thrust my core where I need him most.

I'm still swollen from my earlier climax and within seconds I'm right there again, hovering at the edge. I groan and all but ride his leg as I pant against his lips.

God, *finally*.

Here's a man who wants me without any weird fucking pretenses. I didn't even know how much I needed this until now. After things being so screwed up with Bryce and God, even David. I always tried to convince myself that David's and my relationship was based on more than sex, but I can see that now for the lie it was. Whenever I tried to talk to him about substantive things or if I was ever upset, he just said he'd make me feel better and then start touching me. I came about half of the time—it wasn't a priority to David so it wasn't to me either.

But tonight. Tonight feels different from every sexual experience I've ever had before. The way Jackson's attention is so focused on me. The way he held me earlier while I cried. Each attentive touch now.

This is a wanting that feels clean and good—my breath hitches as his tongue circles my nipple—which doesn't mean it doesn't feel hot and dirty as hell all the same.

Jackson's hands grasp my waist, lifting me up and into him as he devours me just as hungrily back. After another few seconds, he hikes me up even higher, supporting me with his strong arms underneath my thighs.

I immediately wrap my legs around him and he carries me back toward the house. He barely stops kissing me the entire time and I grow hotter and hotter with each step. The incredible strength of this man. The way he commands with every touch.

When we're inside, he slides the glass door shut and then drives my back up against it, pressing his weight into me in a way that has me squirming against him for more friction. He breaks from my lips and nips at my ear.

"Where do you want it, beautiful girl? On the couch? Up against this glass right here? In my bed? Your first time with me should be just the way you like it."

I'm torn between being moved that he's asking and wanting to tell him to shut up and just fuck me already.

"That depends..." I say, working the buttons on his fancy white dress shirt before meeting his hot, blue gaze. I drop my legs from around his waist and slide down his body. Then, my eyes still locked with his, I reach for the front of his trousers and continue, "...on whether you're a tits or ass man."

He growls and tries to reach around for my ass.

"Ah, ah, ah," I laugh and back away. "I thought I was running this show."

I hurry around to the back of the couch and lean my elbows on it, ass out. I glance over my shoulder at him.

Another low rumble comes out of Jackson's throat as he stalks toward me. He doesn't come quickly. No, it's the slow, sure stride of a hunter coming for his prey.

Prickles spike up and down my arms. My heartbeat races even quicker than it already was and the heat that's pooled in my stomach sinks lower and hotter.

By the time he grabs hold of my hips from behind, I swear I'm all but yowling like a cat in heat. He yanks me back and grinds his hardness against my ass. Then I feel the lightest touch of his fingers at my spine near the top of my dress and hear the quiet *snick* of him unzipping it. The next second, the bodice of my gown which had been hugging my torso is loose.

Where I expect Jackson's touch to be rough, jerking the gown off me, he's instead gentle. He coaxes the fabric off my arms and down my hips. It slips to the floor in a swish of chiffon fabric. Then I'm standing there in only my red bra and panties.

Again, Jackson's hands are soft on my body. Almost reverent as he starts at my shoulder and then traces the curves downward, sliding his hands over my breasts, cresting my nipples with a quick pinch and then dropping further south until he's sliding my underwear down my hips.

My breath comes in stunted gasps as my sex is exposed. Especially when, after my underwear has joined the pool of fabric on the floor, he starts back up my legs.

He bends over and kisses his way up. When he gets to my most private of places, he pushes me down farther over the couch, exposing me completely.

And then his mouth starts to explore.

Oh. My. *God*. Pleasure ripples up and down my entire body.

First he licks around my entrance before diving his tongue inside. My back arches and I cry out as he tongues around my clit. I have to grab onto the couch so I don't lose my balance when he starts sucking on that taut bundle of nerves because, I shit you not, *he makes me weak in the knees* is not just a saying.

Oh God, oh God, it feels— I can't even— If he stops, I swear I'll—

I can't even be embarrassed about the high-pitched keening cry that escapes my throat when he adds a finger inside me as he continues to suck on my clit. His fingers find that perfect place inside while he sucks outside and that does it.

I shake and then my whole body spasms as I come hard.

So hard the world goes white, but it's not just for a moment. It's one pulse, and then another, and another, and—

I can't breathe, and I'm not sure if my heart is beating and my whole body is one long contracting spasm of pleasure, and oh *God*, I've never felt anything like this before in my life.

Finally I gasp in a breath and my vision starts to clear again. I have a death grip on the top of the couch cushions. A moment before I wasn't sure my heart was beating at all but now it's going triple time.

I'm gasping as I glance over my shoulder at Jackson. He looks very self-satisfied as he wipes his mouth on his forearm. He's mostly naked now except for his boxers.

An aftershock quivers through my body at the sight. His shoulders are insanely broad and while he's not overly muscled, it's more muscles than I've ever seen on a man in real life. And to my shock, his arms are covered in tattoos. Pictures of barren, alien landscapes and oddly shaped, monstrous animals.

He sees my eyes taking in the tattoos. "I went through a phase," is all he says.

He tries to kiss me but I pull back, not done looking him over. He's got washboard abs and—my eyes drop down toward his V.

A genuine, sculpted V that leads to...

"Fuck me," I whisper. Then my eyes flick back up to his and I swear, I've heard people talk about a haze of lust, but I've never felt it before now. "Get that cock out and fuck me with it. Now."

He doesn't smile or laugh. But I do see his eyes flare. And when I look in his hand, he's already got a condom out. Good boy.

"Now," I say even more urgently.

He doesn't bother with any more pretty words. He pushes his boxers down and releases what is most definitely a cock that was created for fucking. It's big and thick. Not monstrously so, but pretty goddamned perfect in my book. Long and even and standing at attention for me. For *me*.

I can't help but to lean back and run my hand up and down it. Jackson jerks at my touch and lets out a hiss. He throws his head back as I stroke him, but only for a moment.

"Enough," he bats my hand away. "I have to be inside you."

I nod and then he's putting on the condom. His eyes meet mine and all I see is hot wanting. And hell, I've never wanted anything more than I want him in this moment.

He steps into me and teases me, rubbing his cock along my opening, wetting himself with my juices. I whine at his teasing, but he doesn't make me wait. The next second, he's shoving inside of me.

It's not a gentle probing to ease his way in either. No, he just fucking shoves all the way home, burying himself. I gasp at the sting and stretch as my body accommodates him, but that only adds to the thrill of it.

"*Fuuuuuuck,*" he breathes out from behind me. He leans his chest against my back and wraps one arm around my waist, the soft bristle of his chin nuzzled into the back of my neck. He holds that position for several insanely long moments, buried to the hilt.

He's everywhere—surrounding me, inside me—and I feel, I feel... I swallow and am suddenly blinking back tears again.

Because I've never felt anything like this before. It's overwhelming. So much pleasure, yeah, but also, it's also... like I'm *safe*, like nothing could ever touch me when I'm surrounded like this.

I still feel it even when he eventually pulls back and slips out of my body. Because then he's pushing right back in, claiming my body again and again with each thrust. His large hands hold me with such assurance, like he was born to command my frame.

I've been naked with men before, but never this *naked.* And suddenly, I don't know if I can continue.

It feels good, God, *so* good, but it's so much. Maybe too much too soon. He's a man and every man I've ever known has let me down. Betrayed me. Do I really think Jackson will be different? I'm not that girl. I'm not the girl who believes in fairytales. Not even for a night.

But just when I want to pull away from him and make some lame excuse about how I need to go, Jackson's strong fingers turn my face so I'm looking over my shoulder at him. He shoves in deep again and then he kisses me while he cradles my face.

And I melt.

My brain shuts off.

It's all just sensation.

And *him.*

Jackson. Jackson, oh God, *Jackson.*

In me.

Surrounding me. Just him. *All him.*

He kisses me and the hand cupping my cheek drops down to massage my breast. The pumping rhythm of his hips never lets up. I didn't think it was possible to have three in one night, but when his hand drops even further and starts to circle my clit, that insatiable tide starts to rise *again*.

He plays my body like an instrument he's spent years intimately familiar with. I can't question it. All my energy pours into every cell of my body, and when I burst this time, it's with him gazing into my eyes. I see the taut strain on his face as he lets himself go in the same moment.

Do fucking universes collide? I don't fucking know. I'm sure someone put it that way once and a bunch of other loopy bullshit runs through my sand-blasted brain as Jackson carries my exhausted body to his bedroom.

He lays me down and then his big, warm body is beside mine. I nestle into him because I need a buffer against the chaos of my thoughts. I still don't have the energy to even begin sorting through them.

For once in my life, I won't worry. I won't overanalyze. Instead, I embrace the haze and complete satiation of my body.

I burrow further against Jackson and I sleep.

CHAPTER THIRTEEN

I wake up slowly. I blink a couple times just long enough to see that it's light out and then close my eyes again. Thank God Charlie is giving me just a few more minutes to sleep. He's usually climbing into my bed and jumping on me right after dawn. Maybe he'll start sleeping later now that he's older. Oh God, that would be amaaaaaaazing.

I twist over to burrow into my pillow more. My body sinks into the luxurious mattress and I snuggle the comforter around me. Mmmm, it's so soft, it's like snuggling with clouds.

But—wait, what?

My mattress is total crap. It bows in the middle and there's that spring that pokes me if I shift on it wrong.

My eyes immediately shoot open and I force myself to a sitting position. My eyes skitter all around the lavish room. Like the rest of the house, all the furniture in the room is antique, but I guess there is a mix of modern. There's no heavy brocade or outdated dark wallpaper. No, the walls are a warm, textured coffee color. Slatted wooden window shades hang in the windows.

Then of course, there's the giant four-poster bed that I'm lying smack in the center of. I look over at the indent on the bed beside me and my air catches in my lungs. Tentatively, I run my hand over the spot. Still warm.

Okay, Cals. No more distracting myself from what happened last night by appreciating the man's decorating taste. Me and Jackson Vale... Oh my *God.* I flop backwards on the bed and cover my face with my forearm. My cheeks flame remembering some of the things that happened last night.

In the light of day, I can barely believe any of it was real. Except here I am, in Jackson Vale's giant bed. And when I twist my legs, I feel a soreness there that speaks of a night of... um, well... *athletic* passions is probably the best way to put it.

I press my palms to my heated cheeks. At least Jackson isn't here to witness my morning- after face.

Which brings out a slew of other thoughts. Number one: I never washed off my makeup last night and I must look like a scarecrow-freak at this point. And number two: Jackson isn't here. A glance at the clock beside the bed shows it's seven-forty-five. That's sleeping in for me. Charlie wakes me up at five-thirty or six at the latest.

But Jackson. It's a Saturday and it's not like he had to slip out early for work. So why isn't he here?

Don't be an idiot, I chastise myself as I roll out of the world's most comfortable bed. I see a door off to the left that's slightly open. As I pad over to it, I see that my guess was right—it's an en suite bathroom.

Thank God. I have to piss like a racehorse, in addition to what I'm sure is the *Nightmare on Elm Street* makeup situation.

Last night things might have felt all mixed up because of the emotions and the nice words Jackson was saying. But I know all about the promises men spout to get into a girl's pants. In the morning, their words are as empty as the bed I found myself alone in.

It's fine. It's all fine. I do my business and then turn the faucet to the hottest setting I can stand it. Last night was a pleasant exchange. For both of us. I don't feel short-changed. No one was used. I wanted it as much as Jackson did.

I squirt out some soap from a dispenser and scrub my face a little too hard. I just wish guys would cut out the bullshit. All that talk about saying he really wanted me to work for him because I'm qualified. Or how he intimated he was interested in some kind of *relationship* apart from work.

Ugh. I scrub extra roughly to get off the day-old mascara caked underneath my eyes.

Can't it be enough to say, *Hey, you make me hot, I make you hot. Wanna fuck tonight, just a one off?* instead of all the lies and subterfuge of, *You're so special, I want to take care of all your problems* bullshit?

"Ow, God," I say after I all but stab myself in the eye with my pointer finger. I rinse my face and dry it, but when I look in the mirror, I'm still wincing.

I put some toothpaste I find on my finger and use it like a toothbrush. But my hair looks crazy, like sex-hair meets bed-head meets riding-with-the-top-down-in-a-convertible-at-eighty-miles-an-hour.   I try to finger comb it, but because of all the goop Breanna put in it last night, it's a lost cause.

I glance back out the door to the main room. No movement. Duh. Jackson's obviously long gone even though it's a Saturday and he doesn't have the excuse of work.

I smirk in disgust, though I don't know if it's at him or myself. God, I wonder if he left me a driver or if he expects me to like, cab it back to the city. What a fuckwad.

The appropriate thing to do at this point is to sneak out and do the walk of shame. Find my purse and cell phone and get an Uber.

But you know what? Screw that.

He didn't kick me out last night and he took the coward's way out this morning with his disappearing act. And I'm not walking in my house with sex hair and still with the smell of him on my skin. I close my eyes and fight the sudden fierce urge to run back to the bed and inhale his pillow one last time. I jerk my eyes back open, appalled at myself.

I look around the rest of the bathroom. Everything in here is very modern compared to the rest of the house. The shower looks like it has several rainwater spouts, but also jets of water that come sideways from the walls. I walk closer and inspect the little digital control panel beside the entrance. I only try a couple of buttons without any reaction before backing off.

Genius. I shake my head at myself—that's right, the *shower* is too complicated for little ole' me. I should have known how out of my league I was with this guy as soon as I stepped into that goddamned *limo* last night.

But when I turn the corner of a small half wall, I see a Jacuzzi tub. It has a few buttons too, but I've used one of these before. Okay, so the one I used was only about a third of the size of this one, but still, the principles are probably the same, right?

Last year, Shannon took Charlie and me along to a graphic design conference she went to. We got bumped to this awesome room because of some screw up with the hotel reservations. We stayed at the hotel all day and played in the pool, but what Charlie liked even better than the outdoor pool was the Jacuzzi tub in the room. Unlike a normal Jacuzzi, I could control the temperature of the water so it never got too hot. We put Charlie's floaters on and he freaked *out* squealing and giggling every time we turned on the jets and bubbles.

The memory brings a smile to my face as I turn on the tub. It has four taps and they all start flowing at full force to fill the tub up quickly. I always swore that one day I'd have enough money to get a house with a Jacuzzi tub. It could be the ugliest-ass house ever, but it'll have a top-of-the-line tub for my little boy.

My hand goes to my chest and I realize that for the second day in a row, I'm fighting back tears. Fucking *tears*. What the hell? I can't even blame it on PMS, I just got over my period and for once, I'm not running on five hours of sleep so it's not exhaustion. I don't know what time it is, but I know I slept like the dead on that too-comfortable mattress.

I shake my head like I can physically shake away the feelings. I pick up the bottles that line the side of the tub. Shampoo and body soap, both very expensive looking.

Great. I'll end up smelling like Jackson all day after all. Well Christ, at least I won't have the sex hair. I'm sure I'll get enough grief from Shannon as it is. I was so overwhelmed with everything last night, I just accepted it when Jackson said he called her and told her I'd be staying the night with him. But knowing Shannon, I'm sure while she was perfectly sweet and sugary on the phone, I'll get the earful of judgment as soon as Charlie's out of earshot. Irresponsible Callie showing her true colors again. God, I don't want to think about any of it.

I'm glad when the water reaches the level indicated on the side and I can switch on the jets. I climb the little steps on the side and it feels like heaven when I sink down into the water. My body relaxes into the bubbling, steaming water.

I submerge my head and just stay there for several long moments, the real world and everything about it completely drowned out. Is this what it's like when we're in our mother's womb? So quiet. All alone. No pressure, no expectation, just existing in silent communion with myself. Or maybe in connection with the whole world? That's how the monks think of it, right? I've flirted with the ideas in some yoga I've done. Being connected to the entire world, down through my feet into the ground to the roots of the trees and then up through to the branches and the rain that soaks the leaves, all the way back up into the sky.

I surface and try emptying my mind. I take in several cleansing breaths of the bath-steamed air. Lord knows I could do with some grounding in my life. Underwater jets hit me from all sides, immediately relaxing my sore muscles. I lazily count to ten, releasing more and more tension with each breath.

Finally I stop counting and just keep breathing steadily in and out, closing my eyes and focusing only on the physical sensations of the moment. The two jets of water at my back massage tired muscles, and the swirl of water pulsing between my thighs eases the slight soreness there. My hand wanders down my body and I gently cup myself over my sex.

I wince—not because it hurts, but just because it's so obvious that there was some definite *activity* there last night. After so long going without—ever since David left me before Charlie's birth—what was it about Jackson that made me surrender? And surrender so completely?

Immediately images and memories of last night come flooding back in. His body over mine. His expert fingers. That mouth of his. My own hand, which had been only investigating a moment before, starts to massage. I keep my eyes closed as I bite my lip. Jackson might be done with me, but what's the harm in one last little fantasy while I'm here, in his magnificent bathroom, his scents surrounding me?

I shift a little sideways so that the water jet that was hitting my hip is suddenly squarely directed where I need it most. I bite my lip harder to keep back the moan that's fighting to come out. I'm sure any noise would echo like a motherfucker in this bathroom.

Jackson might be gone, but what if he has, like, a maid or something who hears and comes to inspect? I sink a little deeper in the water, adjusting my body so it's even closer to the jet. No, this will be my own little secret that no one ever needs to know about.

The water pulses and massages at my lower lips while I stroke my clit. *I have to be inside you.* Remembering Jackson's words plus all the stimulation has my back arching. My breasts crest out of the water into the cooler air of the bathroom. I can't help grasping my nipple with the hand not circling my clitoris.

I bite my bottom lip and try to imagine it's Jackson's hand, but the fantasy can only go so far. My palms are small and soft. It's not the same. The high I was riding loses its fervor. My brow creases and I squirm and rub at myself with more urgency, chasing the high.

All I'll ever have of Jackson are the memories. It has to be enough, damn it.

But the more I rub, the more elusive climax seems. Which only makes me more frustrated and determined.

I let my clit rest for a second and grab my breasts with both hands, squeezing and rolling the tips in between my fingers. Come on. I can do it. Just sink back into the pleasure. Come on.

Crash.

What the—? I startle so much I take in a mouthful of water as my eyes pop open.

Only to see Jackson standing in the doorway.

There's a tray of food upturned at his feet where he must have dropped it. A shattered coffee mug's sprayed brown liquid across the marble floor. A mix of eggs, bacon and pancakes lie scattered beside it.

I cough from the water I unintentionally swallowed and press myself to the side of the tub. Though I feel stupid in the next second.

Why? For modesty's sake? *God, Cals, he just found you in his tub* masturbating.

Oh God.

He. Never. Left.

He was making me *breakfast*.

Breakfast in bed, if the tray was any indication.

And then he found me like this—

Even my full-body cringe isn't enough to express the humiliation I feel in this moment. I close my eyes but what I really want to do is sink back under the water and pretend none of this ever happened.

"That's the fucking hottest thing I've ever seen in my life."

The low growl has me looking up in surprise. He's not... mad? And doesn't think I'm like, pathetic or something? The look on his face as he stalks across the bathroom suggests he feels the opposite. He looks hungry, but not for any of the spoiled breakfast scattered all over the ground.

"Why'd you stop?" As always, his voice has the quality of command to it. "Show me how you touch yourself." As he talks, he pulls off the white t-shirt he's wearing. The sight of his wide, muscular chest and the blue-black fire in his eyes is enough to make me forget my momentary humiliation. Without another thought, my hand drops back below the water.

He groans, low and throaty as he strips off his boxers and steps over the edge of the tub. The bright morning light and bulbs all around the well-lit bathroom leave nothing to the imagination, but Jackson doesn't seem the least bit hesitant. I can only stare at his cock. I mean, I saw it last night, but now I have the opportunity to really examine it in the full glory of the morning light.

And damn is it a seriously beautiful cock. It's the width. That's what left me feeling so deliciously sore this morning. He's wide and round and there's a thick vein that runs underneath the shaft to that beautiful, throbbing mushroom tip. I lick my lip and my breath hitches as he finally drops down to sit beside me.

He groans again and grabs my hand, capturing it in his and wrapping it around his cock. With his hand over mine, he guides me to pump it up and down roughly several times underneath the water.

"See what you do to me?"

For the first time all morning, I hazard to lock eyes with his. His gaze sends my stomach crazy somersaulting, especially looking him in the eye while we pump his shaft together. I barely know this man, but this feels so intimate... I look away and try to pull my hand back, but Jackson doesn't let me.

Instead, he reaches over and grabs my waist in both his hands. With what seems like little to no effort, he maneuvers me through the water so that I'm sitting on his lap, facing him, my legs spread on either side of his hips.

I try to look everywhere except at those intense blue eyes of his. It's futile though.

"When was your last check-up?"

What? My startled gaze meets his, and then understanding hits. "I'm on the pill and I'm clean, but—"

"I'm clean, too."

In the next second, he has one arm around my waist, lifting me slightly in the water while his other hand is on his cock.

I feel him nudging at my entrance. Oh Christ. There's no condom. That's why he was asking. There's a moment when I can pull away. Say that I won't do this without a condom. That I'm not ready to trust him like that.

But I don't.

Then he's got me positioned and is guiding my hips so that I sink down onto him and oh... *God*... That feels—

I throw my head back and relish every inch as he pulls me deeper down onto his shaft. I clench around him and wrap my legs around his back once I'm fully seated on him. He's so deep inside me, he's got to be touching my cervix.

Has any man ever been in me like this? David was never that adventurous and when we did fuck, it was pretty much missionary and in ten minutes, wham bam thank you, ma'am.

Jackson lifts me in the swirling water and then coaxes me back down and any and all other thoughts are driven out of my head.

Like last night, it's just *Jackson*. Just this moment.

With how he's got me angled, I rub against him in a way that makes me crazy with every down thrust. But I still want more.

Without even thinking about it, I wrap my arms around his head and press my breasts toward his face. I get one of Jackson's rare grins at that and then he gives into my unspoken demand.

He suckles a nipple into his mouth, teasing at first, and then pulling at it with his teeth. I hiss and my body clenches around him at the sensation. Then his hand plucks and pulls at the other nipple. It feels on the edge of too much, with jolts of amazing mixed with pain. Especially when he starts suckling hard and pinching at the same time.

I squirm on top of him as the arm wrapped around my waist continues moving me up and down. My legs like jello, I do my best to assist his movements. But even though I'm on top, he's the one fully in control of this dance.

I can feel my climax just out of reach. I twist and wriggle on top of him as he continues pumping in and out, never releasing his hold on my nipples.

Until all at once, he does.

Feeling floods back and my climax hits in one heady rush.

A high-pitched scream comes out of my throat and Jackson pumps even more furiously before stilling inside me. He clutches me to him, his head buried in my breasts.

I realize once I come back to myself and am breathing again that I'm holding him just as tight, arms wrapped around him, fingers clutched in his hair.

Oh God, what am I doing?

After the incredible rush, my heart pumps a mile a minute. Jackson is still hard inside my body. All I want to do is hold him closer and beg him to stay there forever. Which has me tensing and wanting to push off of him so that I can fucking flee from his home.

As if sensing my thoughts, Jackson's grip on me tightens. His cock that's still mostly hard inside me jumps as if it too is claiming some hold on me.

"What are you thinking, baby?"

I absolutely melt against him in spite of myself. *Baby.* The endearment sounds incredibly foreign coming from the usually stiff Jackson.

But it also sounded incredibly perfect and right and natural. What's happening to me? I don't go gooey over men. Never. I know better than this. I learned my lesson. Didn't I?

I try to laugh it off. "Nothing."

I shrug and smile as I finally pull away from his grasp. "Just that I'm getting pruney, I've been in here so long."

I hold up my hand to show him the wrinkled skin of my fingers. I slide a little further away and finally his cock slips out of me. There's both relief and a stunning sense of loss at the sensation. Ridiculous. I barely know him, I remind myself. So what if there's some off-the-charts sexual chemistry? That doesn't mean anything. Nothing at all.

Just when I'm about to say I should get going, Jackson reaches for me again. "Have you washed yet?"

I should say yes or that it doesn't matter. I'll shower when I get home. I'll just put my hair in a ponytail. It'll be fine.

Instead, stupidly, I shake my head. And I get another rare Jackson smile. Dimple and all.

He reaches over and grabs one of the fancy bottles on the side of the tub. Moments later, a creamy white shampoo fills his hand. He rubs it between his palms and then positions his body behind me.

When he starts massaging the shampoo into my scalp, I try to hold myself rigid so that my body doesn't touch his. I can't explain, even to myself, but it just feels like... like I've already given away too much of myself to this man between last night and this morning.

It was almost better when I thought he'd gone. He was the asshole. That I understood. He fit into my neat categories of men.

But this?

Jackson isn't having the distance I try to put between us. After initially working the shampoo through my hair, he wraps that inexorable arm around my waist and pulls me so that my back is flush against his chest. Then he goes back to a leisurely massage of my scalp, moving methodically from front to back and then outward to the sides.

He rinses his hands in the bathwater. "Close your eyes now, baby."

My heart does another acrobatic jump at the repeated use of the endearment. I close my eyes even as I'm telling myself not to be stupid. Baby. It's just something guys say. Even Jackson, apparently. It doesn't mean anything.

I hold my breath as Jackson cups water in his large hands and pours it over my head to rinse the shampoo. Over and over again, he rinses and works the shampoo from my hair.

I keep my eyes closed while he starts to wash the rest of my body. I'm keenly conscious of his hands as they start at my neck and work down my shoulders... then around to my breasts. My breath hitches when he goes there. To my surprise, he doesn't linger, even though I feel him hardening underneath me.

He's so gentle with me. It seems impossible for such a giant of a man. Paradoxical. But as his hands swirl over my hips and wash the crease between my legs, I finally give in and lean all my weight back against him, absolute putty in his hands. I can't *not*.

And like he seemed to feel my tension earlier, so too he seems to sense my surrender. One hand stays there and his other moves my wet hair to one side of my neck. And then he's kissing me behind my ear. I can't help trembling underneath his touch.

"You're so beautiful. I don't think you know how beautiful you are. How precious. When I touch you, all I can think is—"

I turn around in his arms and put a finger over his lips. "Stop." I shake my head to reinforce my words. "Stop talking."

A determined glint comes in his eyes and I can tell he wants to argue, so I silence him the best way I know how.

I kiss him. As his lips welcome me, I know it's not just a kiss to silence him. God, this is what I've wanted all along. Ever since I saw him standing in the doorway of the bathroom and realized he didn't leave after all.

He didn't use me and cast me aside. He still might. No, scratch that —he probably will. But for now, for today, he wants me.

So I kiss him. I wrap my arms around his neck and kiss him with every ounce of the confusion and elation and passion that being around him brings out in me. He kisses me back for just a moment before standing up and lifting me out of the tub with him.

I try to pull away so I can stand on my own and not trip him as he walks down the outer stairs of the tub. Like last night, though, he just puts a hand under my thigh and hefts me up.

Does he know how insanely sexy his strength is? I wrap my legs around him and cling even tighter with my arms. My chest hurts because in spite of all the bullshit I'm feeding myself, I know this is what I really want—to be wrapped around him so tight, to just fucking cling to him and never let go. It's terrifying and I want to make him put me down so I can run away, but for some reason I just clutch him tighter.

He doesn't stop kissing me as he steps out of the bath, one hand on the little rail by the wall for balance. As soon as we're on the fluffy bath mat, he carries me back into the bedroom.

The hand underneath my thigh is positioned in such a way that he has access to my most intimate places, and he's stroking me even before we reach the bed. I'm already so swollen there that I can't decide if I'm close to bursting or too stimulated to come again so soon.

Jackson lays me out on the mattress and when his body comes down on top of me, the pulses that start to rock through my lower belly are close to coaxing out yet another climax. God damn this man's wizardry.

Jackson pulls his lips from mine only to kiss his way down my body. I blink furiously against the flurry of sensations assaulting me all at once. Oh God, it's so close.

He lingers at my breasts, sucking on each sore bud in turn until I squirm beneath him. When he makes his way back up and kisses me deep, I expect the pressure of him between my legs. But, while I feel his length full against my thigh, he doesn't seek entrance. I'm riding right at that edge. So close. But not quite there.

He simply keeps kissing me with deep, masterful dips of his tongue. It's driving me crazy. Why has he turned suddenly languorous when I'm hot and needy?

Impatient, I slide my hand down his body and clutch his cock, ready to position him so he can slide inside. But Jackson takes my wrist and lifts it up. He easily captures my other wrist so that both my hands are sprawled above my head. His kisses become even more forceful and the throbbing length at my leg is more insistent. I moan beneath him. Why is he torturing us both?

"Jackson," I whimper between kisses.

His cock jumps and his grip at my wrists tightens. "Say it again," he growls.

At first I'm confused. Sex haze here. What did I even say?

"My name," he says as if hearing my unspoken question. "Say my name."

"Jackson," I say again, rubbing my core up against him and wrapping my legs around his waist. I'm desperate for him and in this moment, not ashamed of it. "Jackson, I need you. Now."

He kisses me so hard for a moment, I can barely breathe, but I'm greedy for it. I kiss him back with just as much hunger.

The pulsing beat at my core is thrumming *riiiiiight* at the tipping point.

Just a little more— If he would just touch *right there*—

But every time I try to position myself against him, even just his thigh, he moves away. He's intentionally denying me, the bastard.

At my whine of frustration, Jackson lets out a low chuckle. Mother *fucking* bastard. I'm about to bite at his tongue in my mouth when he suddenly pulls away. I let out a growl, especially because he still has my wrists pinned in place. He easily holds me still while he reaches into his nightstand.

What, now he's grabbing a condom, even though he came inside me in the bathtub? Ugh, fine, if that's what's been holding him back, let him get the damn rubber on and then get that glorious cock back inside me!

What the—? He's not holding a foil packet.

"What the hell is that?" The question comes out breathless as I take in the slim metallic tube-shaped thing he's pulled from the drawer. It's about an inch in diameter and eight inches long, with a rounded top and a small switch on the opposite end.

Jackson clicks the switch and it starts to vibrate. Aha. Well, that answers one question, although I haven't seen a vibrator like this before. Not that I've actually seen a lot of them. I've had some friends who swear by their battery-operated boyfriends, but I was always too embarrassed to keep one in the house.

"Open," he orders, bringing the long cylindrical object closer to my mouth. The objection dies on my tongue and for some reason, I do what he says. I open and he pushes the rounded tip inside my mouth. My lips close over it until I'm sucking it like a freezer pop. Jackson's eyes flare and my pussy contracts. He plunges the toy in and out of my mouth and I can feel the wetness seeping from between my legs.

Jackson's eyes jump between my eyes and my mouth. God, I can't believe I'm doing this in front of him. I've never done anything so... dirty. But at the same time, I can't deny how crazy hot it is. I'm not quite able to give into my inner porn star and start deep throating the thing or lapping at it like it's my favorite treat. I just take what Jackson gives me, my eyes on him the whole time, watching for cues. But he seems to like what I'm doing already just fine.

"That's right, baby," he says in a low grumble, "that's right, suck it."

So I do. I suck it like I imagine sucking his cock and that makes me even wetter.

Just when I'm getting really into it, he slips the toy out of my mouth. Then, with his hands on my hips, he roughly flips me over so that I'm on my stomach. The next second, he's manhandling me again so I'm up on my hands and knees, ass in the air. He clutches my ass, massaging the cheeks. He's not gentle and oh... wow, that's... fucking magnificent.

I bow my head down into a pillow. He continues to knead my ass like a deep tissue massage. Then he pulls the cheeks apart wide and I feel his head drop down...

There.

I almost jump off the bed in shock when I feel his tongue rimming my back passage. Oh *God*. Little jolts of pleasure zing all through my pelvic region at the touch. I can't believe— I mean no one has ever—

His thumbs dig in and he's holding the area even wider apart. I hear a noise and... Did he just —? I look over my shoulder in shock.

Yep, he just spit on me. Down there. He's rubbing the spit into the hole with his thumbs and using the moisture to invade with one thumb. My eyes widen and I swear I choke a little at the sensation. I don't have a moment to even figure out how I feel about any of it though, because in the next second, Jackson has the long bullet-shaped toy pressing into my pussy.

"That's right, get it nice and creamy for me," he says in a concentrated whisper, eyes locked on that area of my body.

I'm too embarrassed to keep watching him, so I drop my face back into the pillow. I should tell him to stop. Again there's that thought, that this is all... *too much*. It's too intimate, too soon. But the things he's doing to me, God, I've never felt anything like it before—

Jackson drags the cylinder from my drenched sex and the thumb that was probing at my ass slides out. I let out a breath only to suck another one back in when I feel that metallic toy replacing it.

My whole body jerks at the attempted invasion. I should've seen this coming as soon as his thumb started probing there. Of course this is where it was all leading to.

But no way. He wants to shove that thing up my ass? I'm shaking my head and wriggling to get away but Jackson wraps his strong arm around my waist and holds me in place.

"Shhh, baby, trust me. This'll feel so good. Trust me." He nuzzles his face against the back of my hip and continues whispering to me in that low, hypnotic voice. In spite of myself, I start to calm and stop struggling to get away.

"That's right, my beautiful girl." He rubs a palm languidly down the spokes of my spine. His hand rounds my hip and then he cups me between my legs. I feel his warm breath and then he places open mouthed kisses all over my ass. Occasionally his teeth come out and he nips me.

And while I jerk each time, I don't pull away again. When I feel the toy probing at the puckered opening of my backside, I stay still this time.

"That's right, baby. You're doing so good. You've never been more beautiful. You're so strong. Relax for me, baby. Just relax." The arm still wrapped around my waist reaches down and start strumming my clit.

My head presses against the pillow at the confusing mix of sensations. It all feels strange and wonderful and alien and hot. So freaking hot. The rod at my back entrance is insistent, but with Jackson's fingers working me so expertly, my body suddenly loosens and the bullet pushes in past the first ring of muscles.

I gasp as it slides inside and Jackson makes a noise that I can only describe as male triumph.

"Jesus Christ, you're killing my discipline." It sounds like a pained admission.

Good. It's not just me whose barriers are being broken down by this insane attraction.

When I feel Jackson's fist tangle in my hair and he pulls my head back so that I'm forced to look over my shoulder at him, I'm grinning. His face is a contorted mix of lust and disorientation.

It's the first time since I met him that I've felt the smallest measure of control in the situation. I'm not about to lose it. For the moment, he doesn't have my hands pinned down and I use it to my advantage.

I reach down between us, grasp his cock, and roughly guide it inside me.

He lets out a pained groan, but he doesn't pull back this time. No, he presses all the way inside and his body falls forward until he's covering my back. I'm completely surrounded by him and I love it.

Between his cock and the toy that fills up my ass, I've never felt so stuffed.

"You like that, don't you? You like my cock ramming you while I've crammed your ass so full?"

His dirty words send my arousal to another level.

"Yes," I manage. It's a whisper, but apparently that's not enough for him.

"I can't hear you," his voice is almost menacing as he grabs my hip and starts thrusting in with a sharp, almost punishing rhythm. "Do you love having your ass and cunt full at the same time?" The slap of his flesh against mine each time he pumps into me fills the room.

For long seconds, I can only moan in pleasure. My eyes slam shut and the whole universe seems to stop for a moment, Jackson's body over mine, me stuffed to the hilt, so full that there's no room for any other thought, just the feeling that I'm about to burst from sensation.

It's pleasure with a tinge of pain and way, way too many other feelings to even begin cataloging.

But then Jackson pulls out and hovers there, panting, both of us sweating, and I'm pulled back into the present. "I guess you don't love it so I should stop," he growls.

"No!" I whimper. I look over my shoulder so I can meet his eyes. "I love it. I want it. Please." I reach for him, needing him in me again.

A dark smile lights his face and he licks those sinful lips of his.

"What do you love, baby?" He pushes forward so that his cock teases at the lips of my core. I shudder.

"I love being stuffed full," I whisper.

"Louder," he demands.

My face flushes, but in this moment, I'd do anything to get him back inside me. My body squeezes around the toy in my back channel and that alone sends a thrill of sensation racing through me. At the same time, it just makes me feel incredibly empty in the one place I need Jackson.

"I love it when my ass is full and your cock takes my cunt," I say.

His cock jumps against me and the tip slips back inside. "Louder."

I whine and try to move so that I can take more of him inside, but he moves along with me to deny me friction. I glare at him but give in at the same time. "I love you stuffing my ass and cunt!" I shout.

Before the last word is even out of my mouth, Jackson has jammed all the way in. He pulls out, hammers back in, over and over like a bull in heat. I've never been fucked with such an animalistic fervor. The fullness in my ass only adds to it, making Jackson's already thick cock feel twice as wide as he plows me.

And his words. An endless stream. "That's right, baby. You're my beautiful dirty girl. Dirty just for me. So fucking beautiful. I'm going to fuck that beautiful ass one day."

A few extra hard thrusts accompany that one. "So good. So fucking tight."

Then he reaches a hand around to finger my clit and I'm gone.

My climax is explosive since I've been on the edge of it for so long. Jackson won't leave it at just one, though. He keeps rubbing through the first and coaxes me right back up into another. Tears run down my cheeks by the time he pulls out a third, which might just be an extension of the second.

I don't even realize the noise coming out of my mouth until Jackson's shouting joins me. He shouts expletives as he rams even harder than before into me. I'm biting at the pillow and wishing it was his flesh. I want to bite him, to tear into him the way it feels like he's tearing me apart.

When we finally finish and he collapses beside me, he drags my body so that I'm tucked into him. His large bulk surrounds me from behind, his arm slung over my waist. I smile and pick up his hand, entwining our fingers. That's when I see I've left scratch marks all over his hand and up his forearm since it was one of the few parts of him I could reach from the position I was in. Instead of being horrified, a rush of primitive satisfaction hits me at seeing the marks.

Mine. I've marked him.

I kiss his knuckles and his arm tightens around me, then one of his heavy legs slings over mine. Like he's caging me in.

I don't mind. I snuggle my back into him and focus on the warmth of his breath on my shoulder. Within thirty seconds, his breathing evens out and he begins to snore lightly.

I giggle. I can't help it. It's such a *guy* thing to do. He just fucked me ten ways from Sunday and I've still got a dildo in my ass—but he's out for the count in less than two minutes. I shake my head and reach between my legs. It takes some gymnastic stretching, but I manage to get to the toy and slide it out. It comes out with a slick *pop* noise. I'm too worn out to be embarrassed. I deposit it over the side of the bed and then snuggle back into Jackson's arms.

Doesn't seem like he's letting go anytime soon and in this moment, there's no place I'd rather be.

CHAPTER FOURTEEN

"Mama, do one, two, three!" Charlie tugs on my hand. I look over at Shannon and see him reaching for hers as well. She takes it.

I don't care that the pathways are crowded at the zoo, I love hearing Charlie's giggle.

"One, two, three," I count, and then Shannon and I swing Charlie by his arms up into the air, legs arcing high. Charlie's giggles fill the air and I laugh in response. It never fails.

"Again!"

I'm way ahead of him. Right as his feet touch the ground, I'm already counting again. Shannon joins in with me and when I look over, she's grinning. For the first time in forever, she seems relaxed and easygoing.

She didn't even bitch me out about my surprise sleepover when I got home from Jackson's this morning. And when I invited her to come to the zoo with Charlie and me, she didn't cite her ever-pressing piles of work like normal. Yeah, she takes care of Charlie during the day, but she rarely spends time with him and me outside of her regularly-scheduled hours.

We swing Charlie a few more times until my arm gets tired.

"Again!" Charlie demands.

I reach down and tickle his belly. "Sorry, mommy's a wimp. I need a break." I kiss him on the top of his head. "Oh, look at that big turtle."

Distraction: every mother's best friend.

Charlie looks where I'm pointing and his face lights up. "Tortoise!" The word comes out more like "toy-tis." Freaking adorable. I'm still fixated on my child's absolute cuteness when his small body launches in that direction, his little hand almost yanking out of mine in his ferocity. I stumble after him as we weave through the crowd of other children and parents to get closer to the fence between us and the large turtles.

"What a big turtle," I say and Charlie looks at me with the disdain particular to small children's derision for their ignorant parent.

"*Toy-tis*, Mama. Dora says toy-tises is big and walk on the ground. Turtles is in the water."

"Ouch," Shannon says beside me. "I think you just got schooled by your two-and-a-half-year-old."

I jam an elbow lightly into her and she laughs at me. I pretend I'm put off, but really, it's so strange and nice to have her like this.

Charlie's fascinated by the tortoises so we stay there for several minutes.

"It's such a beautiful day," Shannon muses.

I turn to her. "Okay, seriously. What's going on with you?"

"What?"

I narrow my eyebrows and give her a *for real?* look.

"Nothing's going on." Her eyes cut away from me.

Wow, could she be *more* obvious that she's trying to hide something.

"Oh my gosh, is it a guy?" I ask, getting excited. "Did you meet someone?"

"Oh look," Shannon says loudly, "Charlie's bored with the tortoises. Want to go on one of the rides, buddy?"

Charlie starts jumping up and down.

"Don't think I didn't see what you did there," I grumble at Shannon as Charlie starts trying to run ahead of us, yanking on both our arms to get us to hurry.

"All right, all right, bud, wait up for us," I laugh and quicken my steps. And to think I was wondering if we should bring the stroller. Though I know at some point all this excess energy is going to be used up and then we'll have a suddenly overly-tired little boy on our hands, he's having too much fun to overthink it right now.

"Bet you're rethinking the kid leash now," Shannon says and I shoot her a devil glare.

Right as she says it, we see a kid around Charlie's age toddle by strapped into one of the ridiculous things. The three-foot leash is stretched taut as the kid races in front of his harried looking dad who's got the other end of the tether wrapped several times around his wrist.

"Oh my God, no. Just, no." I finally give in and laugh. "I swear, when I first saw one of those things, I was standing behind a counter and I just saw a woman holding a leash. I leaned over to see what kind of dog she had and there was a *kid* attached instead. I was like what the eff?"

"Language," Shannon frowns at me.

I roll my eyes at her. Did she not hear me edit myself? I always turn off my potty mouth around Charlie.

It's too crazy crowded to do much talking on our way to the rides. It's not until we have Charlie strapped in to the ladybug merry-go-round ride that I can corner Shannon again.

We pull back to stand with the other parents. I take out my phone to snap some shots of Charlie vigorously grabbing the little wheel in the ladybug car and bouncing up and down on the seat as the ride starts to slowly whir around and around. His particular peal of laughter fills me with warmth as I get a perfect shot of his grinning face, dark little curls catching the slightest bit of wind.

"So is it a guy?" I ask my sister. I'm not letting her off the hook. "Is that why I get sunshine Shannon today?"

She lets out a huff of air beside me. "If we're talking about men, you should be the one spilling. From the little I saw of the man last night, I liked him. And he was nice on the phone when he called later."

I look over at her to see if she's mocking me, but she actually looks sincere. Still, I ask, "Are you fudging with me?" Yes, *fudging*. Charlie might be safely out of hearing distance while he's on the ride, but there are other kids around.

She narrows her eyes at me. "What? I can't be interested in your love life?"

I raise an eyebrow. "To tell me I'm doing it wrong, sure."

She gives me a head shake. "Don't be so juvenile, Callie. Mr. Vale seemed like a perfectly nice man. Respectable."

An image of him bending me over his lap in the limo flashes through my mind. Yeah, doubt she would say that if she knew the details of last night. I smirk inwardly as she keeps going.

"He has a good job," she continues. "He's a colleague but doesn't work in the same office so you avoid any complications there—"

"He wants me to come work for him," I interrupt.

Her expression instantly morphs. "You have to make everything more complicated, don't you?" She watches Charlie as he goes around and around, *that* look back on her face. The one she usually wears when I'm around. Exasperation tinged with disappointment.

For a second I don't say anything. God, it was stupid to tell her he offered me a job. We were finally getting along for once. Like, being regular sisters. Then I go and ruin it.

But no, that's shitty. I shouldn't have to keep the peace only by keeping secrets. I'm done with bullshit.

"Shannon, can you just stop?" I touch her arm so she looks back at me. "I know I've made mistakes in the past. A lot of mistakes, okay? But regrets don't do any good. I can't go back and do things different. And I wouldn't," I say more firmly. "They brought me Charlie."

"But that doesn't mean you shouldn't be learning from your mistakes and breaking old habits," Shannon says, eyes flashing.

"I know," I meet her eye to eye. "And I am. Even the past couple months. Believe me," I shake my head, thinking about my stupidity in walking into Bryce Gentry's office and accepting the devil's bargain he offered. I truly believed that was my *only* option to get out of my predicament.

Run into a problem that seems unfixable? Let a man use my body— that's my go-to solution. I've just assumed my body is where my only worth lies. It's what I was taught, after all. From a girl growing up in pageants to the abuse I experienced as a teen to my damn college professor preying on my vulnerabilities my first real year of college. Then to Bryce.

Christ, how have I not seen that it's a pattern before now? "I am learning," I say more quietly. "I'm different now." The more I say it, the more I can believe it, right? "It's not like that between Jackson and me."

"Only if you don't let it be. Don't work for him."

I pause before I say anything else. Is she right? I force myself to really consider it. I just told her I'm learning, but how is Jackson different? I myself just realized that I went from one older man with abusive power over me to David to Bryce. Is Jackson really so different? I questioned his motives to his face last night and all his answers seemed genuine, but I'm not the naïve little girl I once was.

Men lie to get what they want.

This morning when I got home just before noon, I showered. But I swear I can still feel Jackson's hand caressing my cheek as he said goodbye on his huge columned porch. He held me back from going to the town car where his driver waited to take me home.

"I want to be there in court on Monday," he said.

My mouth dropped open. The only way he'd known anything about it was because he demanded to see me for lunch on Monday and I'd explained why I couldn't meet him.

"You barely know me," I sputtered. "You can't come to my son's custody hearing!"

His face darkened. "I think we've gotten to know each other *very* well, very quickly." His eyes were heavy-lidded as he pressed his pelvis into mine. Christ, he was already hard again. The man had the stamina of a bull.

Me being me, I just started blushing like crazy. "That's not what I mean."

"No?" An eyebrow raised. "There's a reason they call it *knowing* one's wife in the Bible. I think we've gotten very intimately acquainted in the past twenty-four hours." He leaned in so that his words were a hot whisper in my ear. "And I for one intend on intimately knowing every single inch of your body."

And I mean, what the hell was a girl supposed to say to that? He pulled back then as if sensing I was getting to my holy-shit-this-is-too-intense freak-out point.

Then, right as I finally turned toward the car, he reminded me he'd be sending over a detailed employment packet.

"It's completely separate from what happens between you and me, Callie," he reminded me. "But please seriously consider it. I could really use you there."

I was flattered this morning, but now the words take on a different context. He could really *use me*. And what exactly will be left over after he's done using me up?

But Jackson's not like that, another voice in my head argues.

How do you know? You've known him, what? All of three weeks? Of which, you've spent a total of maybe sixteen hours in his company? Half of which were spent sleeping.

But last night... and then again this morning... He was so tender. So considerate in his love-making. It was explosive and intense and you felt so incredibly connected—

Awesome. So now I'm letting myself be blinded by great sex.

He wanted to be at your son's custody hearing—

As a way to make me more emotionally dependent on him. He's moving way too fast, too soon. Why? Because he's trying to manipulate me just like the rest of them.

The ladybugs slow and the ride comes to a stop.

"I don't know," I finally say, rubbing my temple quickly. "Maybe you're right." I move to go grab Charlie but Shannon puts a hand on my arm.

"Are you serious?"

I shake my arm out of her grasp. "Don't look so surprised. Look, none of it matters right now. We just have to get through the custody hearing on Monday. Everything else can be figured out after that."

She nods and I see her brows pinch together in worry. She walks with me to grab Charlie. "I've started doing guided meditation my doctor suggested for stress," she murmurs. "It's the only way I've been able to manage all week, I'm so freaked out about Monday."

We get to Charlie and there's no more time for talk.

"Hey buddy," I unlatch the little seatbelt and lift a grinning Charlie out of the ladybug car. I prop him on my hip.

"Again!"

I laugh and snuggle my face into his neck. Best smell in the world. Sunlight and my little boy. "We gotta give all the other girls and boys waiting in line a chance to go."

He rubs his eyes and I can tell the afternoon is finally starting to wear on him. I know he's about to object loudly and probably with a fair share of whining, so I interject before he can, "How about some ice cream to cap off this lovely afternoon?"

"Ice cweam!"

Distraction managed.

He starts bouncing up and down on my hip, his strong muscles all but jostling him out of my arms. "Down. Down!"

All right. I guess his energy reserves aren't completely gone yet.

I set him down and Shannon and I both take one of his hands.

The snack station is close to the rides, so soon we're in line for ice cream. Charlie hugs my leg and leans his head against my knee. Gah. Heart explode. How on earth did I create such an amazing little human being? It still blows my mind sometimes that I carried him in my belly and now he's out in the world walking and talking and growing up more and more every day.

I run a hand through his dark silky curls. When I glance up at Shannon, her eyes are soft as she watches me with Charlie. Which makes me soften toward her. She might have said some things that were hard to hear today, but she's not necessarily wrong. No more jumping into things without considering every angle. I'm not letting my past determine my future anymore. I refuse to keep mindlessly repeating the same patterns. I'm not going to be that girl.

"So it's yoga or meditation or whatever that's got you in such a good mood?"

A slight smile tilts Shannon's lips. "Yes, I have discovered the Zen way of life."

I nod, impressed. I've never really managed to be able to sit still for more than five minutes at a time the few attempts I've made at meditating.

"Of course," she leans in, "it helps that Sunil, the guy who leads the guided meditation class at the Zen center I've been going to, asked me out on a date tonight."

It takes a second for her words to register, but then I grin like a fool. "Way to go, Zen master."

"Ha. Far from it." A slight blush rises on her cheeks. "The only reason we got to talking is because I was having so much trouble emptying my mind even during the ten-minute period at the end of the introduction classes. I went up to him after class and explained my doctor basically prescribed meditation to help my stress levels, but I didn't think I had a hope in hell of it working on me."

"You didn't!"

She nods ruefully. "He offered to give me a private session. I thought it was something the center just offered. Nope. He was just taking pity on me."

"Or he saw how great your legs are in yoga pants."

"Shut up!" She smacks me on the shoulder. "That wasn't it at all. He said he could see how stressed out I was. That I had a sickly cloudy blue aura."

I clap a hand over my mouth but still can't stifle my laugh.

Shannon cuffs my shoulder again, with a lot more force this time.

"Ouch. Sorry, sorry," I hold up one hand, grabbing Charlie with the other since he's let go of my leg and is about to make a break for it into the crowd. "What does a cloudy blue aura mean?"

Shannon rolls her eyes a little bit. That's more like her. I don't see her buying into auras or new-agey stuff. She's so logical and numbers-oriented. It's what makes her a good graphic designer. Her designs are complex, structural, and precise.

"Supposedly that I have a fear of the future, and I'm bad at self-expression."

My eyebrows pop up. "Maybe there's something to this after all."

This earns me another smack.

"You're setting a bad example for Charlie. Charlie," I look down at my little half-pint. "Tell Auntie Shannon whether hitting is good or bad."

His whole body tips back, not just his head, as he looks up at us. If Shan and I weren't holding his hand, he'd be on his butt.

"Hitting baaaaaaaaaaaad!" he exclaims.

I look over at my sister with mock chastisement, shaking my head. "From the mouth of babes."

"Anyway," she does the half-eye roll thing again, "supposedly with meditation, positive thinking, and eliminating toxins and extraneous sugars from my diet, I'll feel like a whole new woman."

"Is it working?"

"I'll tell you after I eat this delicious sugary ice cream."

I laugh and move forward. We're finally to the front of the line.

Shannon and Charlie get chocolate ice cream and I get strawberry. We manage to snag an empty bench right as another family leaves. I eat mine so quickly I get a brain freeze, but damn, it's good ice cream. Meanwhile, Charlie ends up a complete chocolatey mess. No matter how many times I run back for extra napkins, more has dripped down his face. It covers his cheeks, is underneath his chin, and of course, some from his hand ends up in his hair.

But he's laughing and enjoying the goopy treat the whole time, so screw it. My face hurts from smiling by the end of the afternoon.

My little chocolatey-faced angel falls asleep in the Uber we splurge on to get home. I'm sandwiched in the middle between the car seat and Shannon. She leans over me to look at Charlie and smiles.

"You did good," she whispers and gives my hand a quick squeeze. Then anxiety draws her eyebrows together. "You're sure you and the lawyer have everything ready for Monday?"

Really, I'm impressed she hasn't been harping on me about it all day. Or all week, for that matter. Maybe there really is something to the meditation stuff after all. "My lawyer's got it covered. I'm meeting with him tomorrow for one last strategy session, but from email and talks we've had over the phone, he's confident we'll win. There's no way David's getting full custody."

Her hand squeezes mine again and she leans her head back against the seat, breathing out in relief. "You're doing good, Callie."

From my sister, this is high praise.

CHAPTER FIFTEEN

"Have you eaten this morning?" Don asks as we walk into the court-house together on Monday morning.

I nod even though it verges on a lie. Really, I just barely managed to get down a cup of Calm & Soothe tea and half a piece of toast. I wasn't very hungry anyway. I stress ate my weight in bagels and pastries yesterday afternoon at the last three-hour strategy session Don and I had at his office.

Don coached me on what to expect and how to react—or rather, *not* react—through all of it. But no matter how nauseous I feel, I'm ready, Goddammit. Even if my body feels as tight as overly-strung guitar strings. I've got to keep it together and manage not to snap, no matter what bullshit David and Regina's lawyers put out there today.

"Don't forget to breathe," Don pats my shoulder, offering what I assume is meant to be a reassuring smile. Even though he's dressed in a fairly sharp suit, with his unruly graying hair, he always reminds me of a sit-com dad. I've seen him put on his attack lawyer-mode before, though, so when he says, "Come on, we're ready. You know they have no case to push for full custody. You're a great mom. Don't let them get in your head and make you second-guess that," I relax.

I release the breath I've been holding. Yes. Of course, he's right.

The courts aren't the boogeyman. I believe in justice, don't I? No
matter how much they pay their attorney, the facts are on my side. I
didn't know what I was doing last time and I let them steamroll me.

I set my jaw. Not today. Besides, I've got my own bulldog lawyer
this time. I nod at Don and he smiles again as he holds open the door
to the courthouse.

The courthouse is a newer building. My heels *clack clack* on the
black and white tiles once we're inside. Don consults with a uniformed
man who points us down one of the hallways branching from the large
open area.

"We'll be meeting in courtroom three," Don says.

I swallow and follow him. Last time it was so informal. We met in
the Judge's chambers around a table. But when we step into the courtroom, the judge is wearing the full robes. The same judge that heard
our case the first time. Dammit. I hate that he already has precon-
ceived notions of me based on my abysmal presentation at the initial
hearing.

No. Don't overthink it. Today is a new day.

I try to focus on other details. The courtroom isn't large. It doesn't
look like one of those rooms where you'd see a trial like on TV. No
beautifully finished bench up front or rows of pews for the public.
Nope, just fluorescent lights overhead and a bunch of desks arranged
in a large rectangle. Then again, Don told me that this isn't a real trial
yet, that family court cases often don't actually make it to trial. Like
less than ten percent of them. This is what's called a *motion*. It's where
cases are argued to a judge and then he makes a decision.

No one's sitting in the desks that make up the long sides of the
rectangle. But at one end, David and his wife are already in their seats.
I hold my shaking hands behind my back. The last thing I want them
to see is how much this gets to me. That any part of me is scared that
they could actually succeed in taking Charlie away.

I internally shake my head no. It'll be a cold day in hell before I let
that happen. I think of him at the park with Shannon. She wanted to
be here, but neither of us liked the idea of Charlie staying with some
unknown babysitter today. No, instead, Shannon planned a day full of
his favorite things. First, they're going to the park. Then they'll head to

the children's museum with the giant foam blocks that Charlie likes to make a life-sized fortress out of, which then gets bull-dozed with their bodies. God, Charlie laughs so hard every time he throws himself into the walls and it all comes down in a soft tumble of blocks. Charlie giggles and—

Don holds his hand out, putting gentle pressure on my arm to urge me forward.

Oh God. My baby. I can't lose him.

I stand up straighter and then walk to our seats beside David and Regina, our lawyers between us. Not before their lawyer looks me up and down with a smirk, though.

It probably won't set a good tone if I flip them all off.

No. *Control, Cals.* This has to be about projecting the perfect aura of total control and calm. I sit down and stamp the most placid expression possible on my face.

The judge sits impassively at the other end of the rectangle from us. Even though he's not sitting behind a bench, the distance between us and his robes make it feel just as imposing.

"The honorable Judge Casey presiding," says the bailiff.

The judge nods and then we're off. The lawyers argue through each affidavit they've prepared. An affidavit is the large document with all the evidence they've previously filed with the judge. I've learned all kinds of lawyer-speak over the past few weeks. Don and I talked through each individual piece of so-called 'evidence'—aka *exhibits*—David's side produced and it takes every ounce of control not to lose my shit when they trot out all the crap they have lined up for today.

"If you'll look at exhibit twenty-three to my affidavit, Judge Casey," David's lawyer says, "you'll see evidence of Miss Cruise's history of drug addiction."

It's only because Don coached me through this yesterday that I don't stand up and start yelling about what a hypocrite David is. Exhibit twenty-three is a picture of me doing a line of coke off David's glass coffee table, my hair all disheveled and makeup smeared. And oh yeah, I'm in my underwear—a leopard print bra and thong set David bought me that barely covers anything. Great first impression for the judge.

It's the next one that really sets my teeth on edge, though.

"Mr. Kinnock also noticed symptoms of drug use while picking up his son for his weekly custody visits." He looks down and reads from a piece of paper. "Dilated pupils. Traces of powder around her nostril. She was agitated and paranoid."

As he reads, I grow more and more incensed. Seeing all of this in their evidence pile yesterday made me feel sick. A small part of me still couldn't believe that David took a picture of me in that moment in the first place... and now was not only planning to use it against me like this, but that he planned to tell even more lies about me. And such *horrible* lies. Saying that I do drugs regularly and get high at all is bad enough, but that I'd do it while I had *Charlie* in the house? I want to reach over the aisle, grab David's too-fine featured face, and smash his nose into the table. I want fucking blood.

"It's on the basis of her continued drug usage," David's attorney goes on, "and fears of child endangerment, that Mr. Kinnock requests full custody. Effective immediately." He sits down.

Thank God I was prepared ahead of time. It's only because I knew all this was coming that I'm able to sit without twitching a single feature as Don stands and objects on my behalf.

"Your honor, that's a picture from three years ago before my client was even pregnant. Whatever bad decisions my client might have made in the past—before the responsibility of motherhood, no less—have no bearing on the current circumstances. As for the word of his client," Don inclines his head toward David and gives the judge a look that conveys, *seriously?* "it's a clear case of he said, she said. My client does not currently use narcotics of any kind whatsoever. Mr. Kinnock's charge of child endangerment is completely unfounded. My client is so adamant about proving this, she's insisted on voluntarily taking a drug test to shut down this line of questioning."

I smile over at David's side of the room. Their lawyer blocks my sight of him and the Shrew but I can only imagine their faces. They never thought I'd actually call their bluff, did they?

As soon as Don showed me their exhibits yesterday, he made it clear how much they were banking on pushing the drug angle. "They are going to try their hardest to make you look like an unstable drug user. They don't have facts, so they'll go hard with this. You saw the picture and your ex-boyfriend's testimony. That, coupled with the other things they're presenting..." he rubbed his temple. We were sitting in a large conference room at his law office, papers spread out all over the long table. "It's all specious, of course."

Specious. That's when you know you have a good lawyer. When they use words you try to remember so you can google them when you get home to find out what the hell they mean. I could guess enough from context here, though. It's all *specious*, i.e. bullshit.

"But?" I pressed, stuffing another bite of muffin into my mouth as I waited anxiously for him to continue.

"But," he continued, looking apologetic and anxious at the same time, "what I worry about is that, in the end, it all comes down to a human element. The judge. He won't unsee what they're presenting. It's the same judge who presided over your case the first time and gave David initial custody. He might not have forgotten how unstable you came off during that first meeting."

I cringed.

"Don't worry, though," Don was quick to assure me. "The facts are on our side. They don't have any real proof. Just an old picture and hearsay from your ex."

I shoved the empty plate of pastries away, crumbs and tiny seeds from the muffins littering it. "You just said the judge can't unsee what they show him." I shook my head, mind spinning. Then I sat up straight in my chair. "Wait, I know. I'll just take a drug test to prove it's all crap."

Don immediately shook his head. "They can't make you take a drug test. I just said they don't have any proof—"

I waved a hand. "No, I mean I'll volunteer for one."

He kept shaking his head. "It's never a good idea to offer something the court isn't forcing you to do."

"But it will show them. The judge can't think I'm a druggie if the results are right there in his face." I got more and more animated as I thought about it. "And it will show what a liar David is too."

Don paused even though he looked like he still wanted to argue back. His eyebrows were drawn, but he huffed out a breath. "I guess if it's what you really want... I could call my friend who's a social worker and she could set it up. We could even make it happen tomorrow at the courthouse so the judge will see we're serious about it, if you really want to make it a statement. And he'll have the results within the week."

I nodded adamantly. "The sooner the better."

Don still looked reluctant but finally agreed. "I'll set it up."

So it's with great satisfaction that I see David's lawyer startle as Don makes his pronouncement.

"Miss Cruise," the judge addresses me directly, stern eyes laser focused, "is it correct that you are volunteering for a drug test?"

I sit up straighter in my chair, feeling like I'm in the principal's office. Though of course, this is way, way more serious and making a good impression has never been more important. Charlie's face flashes across my mind and my gut clenches. "Yes. My lawyer has arranged for it to be done today by a social worker if that's oka— um, acceptable." I swallow and want to kick myself for stumbling over my words like that.

The judge nods and looks back down at his papers. "Next exhibit."

I finally take a breath again. I still can't believe David would stoop so low as to accuse me in the first place. I glance over and see the Shrew whispering in his ear and roll my eyes. Oh right, I forgot. He can't think for himself anymore.

Then I shudder. That woman wants my son, along with David, the cheater, liar, and all-out bastard. These are the people trying to take my sweet Charlie. No. I won't fucking let it happen.

I look back up at the judge as their lawyer brings up the next affidavit about my brief stint in jail and the stalking charges.

My face flames in spite of my determination to stay cool. I hate how persuasively their lawyer paints a picture of me as an unstable woman. Stalking. Deranged and lighting a car on fire. Being locked up before I could do any more harm. The way he talks about me, *I* wouldn't want to leave a child under my care. I have to fight the urge to slink down in my chair. The blatant facts aren't wrong, but—

But what? It's not the whole story. It's true, but I don't know how to argue it.

Don stands after their lawyer sits down again and I swallow hard, trying to gulp down all my fears with it. All right, time for my attorney to earn those hard-earned bucks I'm paying him.

"My colleague has tried to paint a picture of a manipulative drug addict," Don says, "but that's a tall tale stretched from a single Polaroid picture and a couple other cobbled-together stories."

"I'd hardly call police reports mere *stories*," David's lawyer interjects.

The judge stares David's lawyer down with a glare that says what words don't have to, and he shuts up.

"As I was saying," Don continues, shooting his own heavy look in the other lawyer's direction before focusing his attention back on the judge. "Miss Cruise's story can much more easily be explained *not* as that of a troubled girl dependent on alcohol and drugs—proof of which the opposing counsel has no further evidence than a single photograph—but simply that she was a naïve young woman who came to be in the unfortunate circumstances of finding herself with child."

All right. So far so good. We ran out of time last night before he could tell me his whole plan for my defense. Most of the time was spent prepping me for what David's team had in store for us, but he assured me he had this well in hand. I'm anxious to hear it.

"It's a story as old as time," Don continues. "Her parents were unwilling to take her in. And yes, she might have become a little overwrought when the father of her child rejected her." He looks over at me piteously before turning back to the judge. I shift a little in my chair. I know this is part theater, to paint the girl I was in a certain way, but I hate the pity look. Still, I try to keep sitting with as much dignity as I can muster while Don continues.

"But you have to remember, as testimony by Dr. Ruth Newsome explains in exhibit twenty-three, a pregnant woman is producing up to a thousand times her normal estrogen levels by the end of her pregnancy. That plus extra progesterone and other pregnancy hormones can create incredible mood swings that account for Miss Cruise's actions at the time those police reports were filed."

He goes on arguing the point. I blink as I keep listening. His whole argument is based on the idea that I was crazy because I was pregnant.

Wow. This is kind of humiliating. Hormones. Really, that's the extent of my defense?

I watch the judge's face. I can't tell if he's buying it. God, it sounds like the old female hysteria fable. Men trying to man-splain women's actions and calling anything that has to do with us *hysteria*.

In our briefing yesterday, I tried bringing up Jackson's point, which if I thought I remembered Don even saying something about in our first meeting. Even now thinking of Jackson's righteous fury on my behalf, talking about how David had abused his position of power over me, isolating me by forcing me to keep our relationship secret since it could get him in trouble... At the time I would have said no, that I fully knew what I was doing, that I was an adult making adult decisions.

But looking back now, I can see just how naïve I was. For the first time in years, I've started to think that it wasn't entirely my own fault. That I'm not just a stupid girl who always screws everything up and inflated something in my head to be more than it was. David seemed so wise, so confident, like he'd always take care of me and then suddenly he was just...

Gone.

He didn't want me anymore.

It didn't compute.

Sure, hell yeah I was screwed up.

But maybe the truth is that David was just a predator asshole who saw a pretty, vulnerable girl and wanted some hot ass since he was free from his controlling bitch of a wife for the first time in years. And yeah, the fact that I was an abuse victim probably made me more susceptible and affected how I reacted when my supposed savior suddenly dumped me as easily as if I was last week's garbage.

I'm old enough and mature enough to take responsibility for my actions—but allowing myself to see David's part in screwing me over helps to lift the ridiculous weight of shame I've carried for so long. Staring past his attorney and looking at him now, in the shadow of the Shrew, I can see David isn't who I thought he was. I fell in love with a fiction—he was never the strong, loving, caring man I believed him to be. He was always a selfish coward, out for some pleasure and fun, weak-willed and taking the path of least resistance.

"So she can't be held responsible for her actions because her estrogen levels were at an all-time high," my lawyer declares, zooming my attention back into court. "At the same time she was sleep-deprived due to her break-up with Mr. Kinnock and discomfort from being with child. As you'll see in the study by Baker, Garcia, and Hammock, et al., sleep deprivation plus sharp hormonal escalation can lead to the symptoms of impaired judgment my client exhibited during the period in question. Since then, however, once her hormones leveled out after pregnancy, she has been a model citizen and parent."

I try to avoid scrunching my nose in embarrassment. All right. It's not the most flattering portrait of me, but I suppose it might get the job done. And Don and I did talk about other ways to describe that period of time in my life. There weren't many more attractive alternative explanations to make me come off as sympathetic.

Don said David and Regina's lawyers would paint me as a homewrecker who tried to seduce my older, married professor. Apparently there are pictures of me on social media from that time showing I dressed immodestly, exhibiting 'attention-seeking behavior.' It's all infuriating sexist bullshit and a couple of out-of-context pictures from the one party I went to in the early stages with David when I was still trying to make friends outside of him. A girlfriend dressed me up and dragged me to the party.

David had been furious afterward and confronted me with the pics he'd found on one of my then-friend's Instagram accounts—a person who was also, I might note, one of his students. *Hello red flag.* But I didn't see it that way at the time. He was so passionate about me. He couldn't stand for anyone else to see me like that when he couldn't be there, blah, blah, blah. And now he's resurrecting those pictures to try to take Charlie.

My hands form into fists underneath the table. Don was obviously right about where David's lawyers were going to take this. But why aren't we attacking back? Calling David out for his abuse of power?

I remember back to yesterday. Don said we shouldn't resort to petty name-calling and mud-slinging—that it would go over far better with the judge in proving my character if we took the high road. Instead of an overemotional, bitter ex-lover, we wanted to stick to the facts and prove the positive: why I'm a completely stable and productive member of society, as well as a capable and caring mother. I agreed at the time. It all sounded good when Don laid out the not-attacking-David version of the plan, but God, I feel like my character's getting massacred while David just sits there looking like a fucking boy scout.

When Don sits down, David's lawyer is up once again on his feet, like he's spring-loaded and was just waiting for the opportunity to be unleashed. "Would a model parent frequently stay out all night and leave her child in someone else's care? Wouldn't a model parent provide a stable environment instead of moving," he looks down to reference a paper on the table, "*five times* in two and a half years or rely on a family member to raise her child more than she herself does?"

Goddammit. The private detective. I knew from everything we looked through over the weekend that David had hired one. It was bad enough when I saw that he was having me followed in the first place— at least he was two months ago, in March and April when I worked at the bar before I got my new job. Christ, is he still at it?

My fingernails bite into my palms my hands are clenched so hard. Don puts a hand on my forearm. He must sense how taut my entire body has gone. Shit. I better not be showing how pissed I am on my face. I try to adopt a serene expression. Zen. I am a goddamned tree with roots growing deep in the ground and the sun on my face—

"As you'll see in exhibit twenty-six, Calliope Cruise did not come home fourteen nights during the period of March 1st to April 30th of this year. That means 22% of the time, Calliope Cruise is not at home with her little boy. That's roughly one-fourth. Can you imagine?" The lawyer shakes his head as if he can't believe it. "For one-fourth of her child's life, her sister's at home with her baby while she's out God knows where doing God knows what. And that was when she had full custody! You see why my client believes the child's welfare would be better served if he had care full time."

The feet of my chair squeak on the tile as I jolt backwards. Motherfu—

Don't!

I clench my jaw and stop myself just in time. In my head, I'm on my feet. I'm shouting curses at that bastard lawyer. How can they just let these fuckers get up there and spew this toxic crap? For them to spin the numbers this way...

Though isn't it the same way Shannon looked at those nights. Slut. Whore. The words left unsaid but alluded to a thousand ways. Stupid, *stupid* not to think they'd push this angle of me as an immoral woman and horrible mom. I just thought the facts were so obvious: I was a woman and it was a bad part of town. Walking home alone equaled too much danger to risk.

I take a deep breath and keep my ass planted firmly on the hardwood chair. No giving them what they want. I clasp my hands daintily in front of me. *Charlie.* Remember Charlie.

Don's gaze locks on me, like he's sure any second I'm gonna lose it. He didn't grab or try to stop me this time. Maybe he recognized it as a lost cause. If I was going to blow, nothing was going to stop me. But I manage to keep my shit together. I think of Charlie's toothy smile in the morning when he climbs up on my bed and pulls on my nose until I wake up. His echoing giggles when I blow raspberries on his tummy after I change his diaper. The twang of his voice when he tries to say r's and they come out more as w's. Twuck. Twy. Wun.

I take a deep breath and nod to Don. If the vein in my forehead is pulsing at maximum capacity, well, we'll just hope the judge is sitting too far away to notice.

As soon as David's lawyer sits down, Don's on his feet. "Your honor, my client slept in her workplace those nights because she couldn't get a ride home. It's not a good part of town and she was afraid for her safety on public transit. For Mr. Newsom to accuse her of lewd behavior when she was simply a woman fearing for her safety is completely outrageous."

David's lawyer raises his eyebrows. "Can Mr. Maury produce her employer's testimony as to where she slept those nights?"

My heart sinks. Goddammit. No, of course not. Because I never told him since I didn't think he'd like it. I doubt arguing that I lied to my boss about staying over would help my case much.

"You will direct your comments to the court," the judge says, eyebrows heavy with disapproval as he stares down David's attorney. Not that attorney Douchey McDouche looks repentant. He got in his pot shot after all.

"Judge, has my colleague produced any exhibits with testimony that my client was partying or doing anything else of which she has been unjustly accused?" Don argues back. I nod. Yeah, way to go, Don. I feel like high-fiving him or kissing his cheeks. This is what money for a real lawyer gets you.

"It's a big city," David's lawyer says. "There are any number of places Miss Cruise may have gone."

"Which means you have no evidence that she went anywhere at all."

"What's important here is where she *wasn't*. At home with her son."

"Only because she couldn't be without risking her own safety. But she left him with a caregiver who is extremely qualified. At no point was the child neglected or in any danger."

"Enough," the judge says loudly. "I'll remind both of you that all comments are to be directed to the court. If you can't remember that, I have no problem throwing you out of my court room for contempt. Next."

Yikes. I look at Don worriedly, but he gives me a small confident nod. He must have only risked pissing off the judge if he thought it was an important argument not to lose. I nod back. Okay. I think we might have won that point? Especially when Don goes on to point out I don't have that bar job anymore anyway. I work normal, respectable hours.

Even if my work is far from respectable. Oh my God, if I'm still being followed, what if they caught any of it on film...? For a second I'm so paralyzed I can't breathe, but then realization hits. If they had that one incident from Bryce fingering me at the restaurant on video, they'd have opened with it. And Bryce hasn't had me out in public since then.

Dammit. I bite my top lip and my hands wring together under the table.

I'm only twenty-two but I suddenly feel way too old for this shit. I just don't have the energy for it. How did I not see how much I was risking by working for Bryce? If David's lawyers had any inkling of what was really going on at my so-called *respectable* job... I've been such a fool. I've let my past patterns and insecurities dictate my life for way too long. How has it taken me this long to recognize it?

I feel sick to my stomach. Quickly, I open the water bottle in front of me and take a deep swig. The lawyers work through another couple less contentious exhibits and then we break for lunch.

I stand up for the break and when I do, a serious-faced woman with over-sized glasses in a shoddy pantsuit stands beside the bailiff.

"Callie, this is Rita Hawthorne," Don says. "She'll escort you to the restroom and collect your sample."

Oh goody. The pee test. I nod at the woman, feeling awkward, because do you shake your pee tester's hand? That just seems wrong somehow. Luckily, she must agree because she just gives me a tight smile, then turns and heads out of the courtroom. Right. I follow.

When we get there, the lady bailiff waits outside. Again unsure of protocol, I hold the door open for Rita and she gives an awkward nod as she heads inside. Once we're both standing in front of the large mirror with bright fluorescents overhead, she rustles through her bag and pulls out a cup for me to pee into. Then she follows me into the stall.

Yeah. That's really a thing. They watch you while you pee.

I'm just lucky Don kept me supplied with water bottles throughout the morning. Any other time I'd be too pee shy, but I've had to go like a mother for the past hour and a half.

Rita makes a production of putting on plastic gloves before she takes the cup from me and puts the official sticker seal on it. She signs it before we leave the bathroom. She's real CSI about the whole thing, extra vigilant. That's only good for me, though. This way David and the Shrew can't claim I tampered with it or question the results when they come back clean.

David's such an idiot to even try and claim I'm into drugs. Does he really think I kept up with that crap? I hated the way it made me feel the two times he pressured me into doing it with him. Out of control and vulnerable, like anyone could do anything to me and I couldn't stop them... Ugh, I shudder even remembering it. No, it's nothing I would ever do again by choice. He must have just been banking on the accusation itself making me look bad.

To take away my baby. The thought of possibly losing Charlie—it makes me want to turn back for the toilet and throw up whatever little is in my stomach. David is evil. *Evil.* There's no other word for what he's trying to do. The mix of fury and queasiness makes me light-headed on my feet.

Or hell, maybe it's because I haven't eaten anything today. I lean on the wall outside the bathroom, take a deep breath and grab an energy bar out of my bag. I force myself to take several bites even though it's the last thing I feel like doing. My stomach rebels but I keep it down. I can't risk passing out because I haven't eaten anything today.

When I walk back to the courtroom, I'm more determined than ever to stay calm, cool, and collected. Those bastards aren't taking my son and if they're trying to provoke a reaction from me by one of these exhibits they bring up, they're going to be sorely disappointed.

———

I keep to my internal promise and don't react to anything that comes up in the afternoon. Not even the staged video in the bathroom at the gala. Of course, Don objected that it shouldn't be allowed into the record after it was shown, but the judge had already seen it by that point. The judge acknowledged Don's objection and said he would take the video 'for what it was worth,' whatever that means.

I didn't let my serene expression crack once. I didn't turn my head to look at David or his wife. I wouldn't give them the satisfaction. And, well, if I even glanced at them, I worried the façade would crack, and I might leap over our lawyers to scratch David's eyeballs out. So there was that.

Best to pretend they didn't exist. I focused on the notepad in front of me, at first taking notes as the lawyers got into a war of words, technical jargon edition. I tried to follow along, but it was all 'within the context of the statutory obligation to avoid disclosure of information' this and 'consistent with the provisions of Section 3020(a)' that. Yeah, I stopped taking notes after just a few of those mind-numbing phrases.

Instead, I drew blocks. I drew the sand castles Charlie and I made at the beach when we went in mid-June. It was too cold to get in the water more than getting our ankles wet, but we spent the afternoon playing in the sand. Since it was so early in the season, the beach was mostly empty. It was a perfect day. We played until the sun started setting. I doodled the sun going down in the horizon behind the sand castles. I'm not much of an artist, but my pen starts to put little waves in the ocean below the horizon.

Charlie. Charlie. My Charlie. Everything's going to be all right. Mama's going to make it all right.

I repeat it over and over in my head until, without really thinking about it, I think I'm praying. I don't really know what I think about the Great Beyond, but I'm praying. *Please make everything turn out all right. Please let me keep my Charlie. Let this turn out right. Please.*

Then, around three-fifty it all starts wrapping up. Both attorneys have worked through all their material. My heart starts to fire on all pistons.

This is it.

What everything's been leading up to. The part where the judge makes the decision. My stomach's queasier than ever. Damn it. Maybe the chocolate chip energy bar during lunch was a bad idea after all.

I stare at the judge across the room from us. Which way is he leaning? He's just sitting there, shuffling papers. Do those creases in his forehead mean he's disgruntled about something? Like he believes the other lawyer's crap about me being a bad mom?

His expression looks severe, but then, wasn't it that way this morning when we began? I can't tell if it's changed throughout the day.

I squint my eyes and try to look closer. Was that an eye twitch? What the hell does that mean? Was it a get-this-worthless-mother-out-of-my-courtroom eye spasm or an I-can't-believe-this-deadbeat-dad-has-the-gall-to-try-this-crap twitch?

Don taps me on the shoulder and gives me a subtle shake of his head. That's when I realize I'm leaned half over the table staring at the judge. Crap. That's all I need. What if he's about to make a decision in my favor and then he looks over and I seem like a coked-out freak, all but crawling up on the table?

I pull back and try to make my body loose. Calm. Competent. Mature. This is no big deal. Just the future of my very existence and whether or not they're going to rip my soul out of my body by taking my son away.

Right. Not the most helpful thoughts if I'm trying to calm down.

Just when I think I've managed my shit, the judge starts speaking and I jump in my seat like a live wire was just jolted through my body.

He pauses mid-sentence and stares at me a moment before clearing his throat and continuing, "As I was saying, all evidence and affidavits will be taken into consideration in the case of Kinnock verses Cruise. A court-order decision will be sent to you via certified mail within thirty days and will be effective upon the date noted. In general, that will be the first date of the following month. Court dismissed."

With that, the judge stands up and walks out of the room.

I turn to Don, open-mouthed.

"What just happened?" I hiss when I finally manage to find my voice. "I thought he was supposed to make the ruling." I wave impotently toward the bench-like desk the judge was just sitting behind. "*Today*. That was the point. We come here with all the—" I continue waving my hands. Dammit, now I can't think of the word, when they've been saying it all day. I sputter for a second and then remember "—the *affidavits* and exhibits and then he's supposed to make up his mind!"

Don holds up his hands, "I'm sorry. This often happens. I should have warned you. It's only sometimes that the judge rules on the same day." He cracks his knuckles. He shakes his head and puts a hand on my arm. "I'm sorry. But this will all turn out okay. We have a solid case," he assures. "They have no reason to deny you joint custody of your son. Nothing presented today is going to change that."

I close my eyes and take in a deep breath of air. Can I hold on to believing that for a whole *month*?

Yes, goddammit, yes I can. *Whoops.* I wince. *Sorry God. No more taking your name in vain.* I'm turning over a new leaf.

And I *won't* let that bastard David or his horrible wife get in my head. I open my eyes just in time to see the Shrew in question walking by with David, as ever, at her heels. She has her chin up, like she's too precious to even smell the air down here with us regular mortals. Just thinking about the fact that these two get to be in my son's life at all makes me want to hit something.

Instead, I ball my hand into a fist and turn away from them as I get out of my own chair. "I'm going to go home now," I say over my shoulder to Don. "Thanks for everything you did today."

"My pleasure. And please, don't worry. Your son isn't going anywhere."

I nod and then stride for the door, making sure I'm leaving from the opposite exit as David and the Shrew.

That night, I get home and make a beeline for Charlie. I snuggle my baby boy extra tight in my arms as I rock him to sleep.

CHAPTER SIXTEEN

"What will it take for you to say yes to come work for me?" Jackson asks on Friday over noodles at a Thai place that's smack between the CubeThink offices and Gentry Tech. It's five-fifteen and I hurried here right after work finished.

All week Jackson's texted asking to see me, but I've been spending every spare minute I can with Charlie.

I'm only four days into my thirty-day wait and already it's been absolutely torturous. A stupid voice inside me keeps repeating that the judge said he'd notify us *within* thirty days... which means that really, it could come any day. It doesn't have to take the full thirty. And that thought has been driving me batshit.

I'm not the only one. On my eleventh call to Shannon today to see if a letter had come from the courthouse yet, she finally lost her temper with me. She told me she'd call if anything changed and that I was making her even more nervous than she already was. So in my quest to chill the hell out, I decided to accept Jackson's invitation for an early dinner. We've been texting back and forth all week. I had mixed feelings about meeting up ever since my conversation with Shannon at the zoo, but now, seeing him again... it just feels so natural. So easy. Even if he does keep harping on the same subject.

I shake my head at him and smile. "Why is it so important to you that I come work for you? Is it some power trip? Wanting to know where I am at all times? 'Cause that's kinda creepy, buddy." I'm only half joking. I've looked through the employment package he sent over and while it's tempting, I'm trying to be smart for once. I feel like I need to choose either one or the other—a relationship with Jackson or a job at his company.

Then I bite my lip. Not that the situation at Gentry Tech will continue to be copacetic if I'm going to try to balance having a relationship with Jackson. Bryce still hasn't made any more moves this week. I don't imagine he will while he assumes I've got CubeThink's business on the hook.

But once he finds out I don't?

Jackson reaches over the table and takes my hand. "Calliope." My attention shoots back to him, especially with all the tenderness that's in his voice even when he just says my name. "I don't want to control you." His eyes darken and he tilts his head, "Well, not outside the bedroom at least."

A spike of heat shoots down my body at the admission, but he's already moving on.

"I want you working at CubeThink because I think you'll be an asset to the company." Then his mouth flattens. "I know you want complete honesty though, so yes, there is an alternative agenda in asking you to work for me. That doesn't mean I don't think you don't deserve the position. At the same time, what you make of the job is all up to you. There won't be any special favors or advancement because of your relationship or lack of one to me. I'm serious about disclosing our relationship to HR. There won't be any favoritism. You'll succeed or fail on your own merits."

Everything he's saying sounds good. It's everything I might want to hear. But I don't miss how he glossed over the important point. I put down my chop sticks and sit up straighter. "So what's the ulterior motive?"

Jackson's jaw hardens slightly. "I don't want you working for Bryce."

My own back stiffens. "Because of whatever stupid rivalry the two of you have?" He's assured me several times that our relationship, working or otherwise, isn't about their enmity, yet this is what it always seems to circle back to.

"No, not because of a rivalry." His eyes flash and his hand moves through the air in a cutting motion. "Because he's dangerous. I hate that you're under his thumb right now. I hate that he could hurt you to get to me."

I balk. "Hurt me? He's a bastard, sure, but—"

Jackson vehemently shakes his head. "You don't know what I know about him. I told you some of our history. The way he manipulates people—the way he manipulated me. First to get me to spend time and collaborate with him. But then," his jaw flexes, "to draw me into his games. He likes... he likes..." he pauses for a second before meeting my eyes. "Breaking things. People. Especially women. I can't stand the thought of you spending one more day in that office with him."

For a second, I'm speechless. I think of the mind games Bryce likes to play. But they aren't that... serious... are they? My mind flashes to how worthless and stupid I felt after some of his initial stunts. He's let up and I guess it all doesn't seem that bad in retrospect. I'm not sure why I feel that way. Because I came those few times? A wash of deep shame hits me at the memories. That was almost the worst part, hating how I felt like he could play my own body against me. What if he had kept it up, a long campaign of those kinds of games on a person?

My voice trembles a little when I ask. "What do you mean, *break* people?"

Jackson's mouth turns down in disgust and if I'm not mistaken, with a touch of shame. "I don't want to go into details. I don't even want those things in your head. But I worry about you every day that you work there. I want you to quit without even giving two weeks' notice. Once you've decided, don't go back in at all, in fact. Write out your written notice and I'll get it to him."

I scoff out loud. Suddenly all of this seems like overreaction. Jackson's overprotective. It's sweet but unnecessary. "Don't be ridiculous. I don't need you to fight my battles for me." As I say it, I realize how much I mean it. I'm done being the weak little girl who lets the big bad men decide her fate. After my realizations about what I let David do to me, and that right after escaping Mr. McIntyre... I shake my head. I'm done with being that girl. It's time to take the reins and be in control of my own life.

It's what I like about being around Jackson. He makes me feel stronger—but in my own right, not because I'm using him as a crutch. And that's the way I want to keep it.

The lines around Jackson's mouth tighten and he's also shaking his head. "Don't pretend anything about your position there has been professional. He'll just treat you like he does all his—"

He cuts himself off, but the word left unsaid rings in the silence between us.

Whores.

Bryce'll treat me like he does all his whores, was what Jackson meant to say.

The blow is slow to hit me because I'm so shocked. I know how other people have seen me all my life. Just the blonde with the big tits —obviously a slut. But *Jackson?* Oh my God, I'm such a stupid girl.

I stare back at him, bound and determined not to let him know how he just sliced and diced my insides up. Which makes me fucking furious. Because here I just was, telling myself how I'd never let any man have any more control over me. Jackson was the exception because he made me feel stronger in myself. But it was a crock of shit. He's *never* seen me as strong at all. I've only been a victim to him. And believing in him has only given him power to hurt me. After everything, I'm still so stupid.

Well, not any more.

I smile, hating that my façade feels brittle like it could crack and show him my vulnerable underbelly.

"It's good to know how you really feel." I grab my bag and start to head out of the restaurant. I work to get more control over my emotions as I walk, but Jackson puts a hand on my elbow to stop me.

"Wait, Calliope, that's not what I meant."

I stop, but only to glare at the offending hand holding me back. He better not think manhandling me is a good move right now.

He curses and lets go of me.

Good move, pal.

I push through the door and out into the sunny afternoon. Jackson follows, but he doesn't try to physically restrain me again.

"Just hear me out."

I keep walking. I've gotten ahold of myself, at least a little. Anger works miracles. I grab it like a lifeline.

"God, you are such a frustrating woman!" Out of my periphery, I see him run a hand through his hair. It's a strange sight to see from a man who's usually so unruffled. Part of me wants to crack, to give him a chance to explain...

But then I remember he basically thinks of me as Bryce's whore. It's how he'll always see me. I can't even blame him.

It is, after all, true.

I mean, thank God our relationship or whatever the hell is between us never really got very far... God, really, it was just one amazing weekend together... But in such a short time we connected so deeply. My stomach sinks and the Thai noodles feel like they might come back up. I fight to hold onto anger, but it's quickly sinking into something much less steady.

Regret.

Because I wish I could have a redo of the past two-and-a-half months. I wish I had met Jackson first. But then, if Jackson hadn't first seen me with Bryce, would he have even been interested in me?

It will always be between us. He'll never be able to lose his first introductory image of me as his rival's pitiable whore. I'll never be able to trust his motives for wanting to be with me. At one time in my life, it might have even been enough—just the idea that he wanted to save me. Because I genuinely don't believe Jackson wants me just in order to punish Bryce.

But does Jackson have a savior complex? Hell yes, he does. I glance over at him, keeping pace beside me with a determined expression on his face even though he's not saying anything.

He must take my look as encouragement, though, because he starts pleading his case again. "Callie, God, I'm sorry for what I said. I didn't mean it that way. You know I don't look at you like that—"

I have to avert my gaze immediately, it hurts so much. He keeps talking but I tune him out. He just saw me as this wounded thing all along. He wanted to fix me. No, it wasn't about rivalry for him.

But what about... my step stutters as a thought hits me suddenly... but what about on Bryce's side?

Oh my God, was *that* what Bryce was doing all along? Dangling the one thing he knew his old adversary couldn't resist—a vulnerable woman who Jackson would see as needing rescuing?

But why? What does Bryce get out of the whole thing? Did he really want to collaborate with Jackson's company and think this was the only way to get Jackson on the hook? That seems far-fetched and way too convoluted a way to get a business deal accomplished. Besides, Jackson's not taking the contract anyway. So maybe—

I shake my head. God, what do I think I am now, a conspiracy theorist? All of this is ridiculous. It's far more likely that everything is what it appears to be on the surface, and I'm just stuck in a shit situation.

There is no grander plan. I just happened to fall for a guy who will always associate me as the girl who was hired because she'd let her boss diddle her under the table during a business lunch. I cringe but keep from ducking my head in shame. No more of that. I'm owning my past mistakes and moving on from here.

I was just foolish to ever think our Cinderella story could have a happy ending.

I walk faster. I need to get home.

To hold my baby.

To focus on what's really important.

I've been heading toward the closest light rail station but stop when Jackson physically places his body right in front of me.

"I feel like you haven't been listening to a word I've been saying." He sounds exasperated. He's right, of course. He's been talking, but I've been zoned out, my only focus on getting home. Away from him.

When I try to move around him, he again steps in front of me to block my path. Apparently he learned his lesson at the restaurant and doesn't touch me at all. But this new tactic of not letting me pass is just as annoying, maybe even more so because I know he's doing it in a way that's attempting to respect my boundaries.

"Let me drive you home, at least. My car's right there." He nods behind him to where his town car idles on the side of the busy street. God, has the driver been following us as I took off out of the restaurant? "You'll get home much faster than taking public transit."

I waver. I would get home faster, but I'm not sure I can spend any more time in Jackson's presence. Smelling his aftershave. Why does he have to smell so good?

I know my reasoning is solid. That we can't be together. It'll never work after the way we began.

"Please, Calliope. At least give me the peace of mind that I got you home safely." His voice is soft.

Gah! I can't decide if it rankles that Jackson thinks it's his job to take care of me or if it's terribly sweet. I've been the one shouldering all the responsibility for taking care of myself *and* Charlie for so long. The strong and self-reliant thing to do would be to say screw him and take public transit. Right? Or maybe there's a difference between stubborn pride and self-reliance.

I sigh. Lord, I'm so tired. I look at his town car.

Screw it. Rome wasn't built in a day, and I'm still working through the thorny path of making my own way in the world.

After another prolonged moment, I finally nod my head. Jackson's face lights up, but when he reaches over to take my hand, I ignore him and slide into the car through the door the Jackson has open. Jackson follows without a comment.

But then I want to cry. Because even though I shunned his hand, even though my head knows this would never work, there's still that part of me... The part that doesn't care that it's all wrong. The part that wants me to close the gap between our bodies and throw myself into his arms. The part that remembers just how good it felt in the moments after we made love.

The first two times last Saturday we just fucked, no doubt about it. But the third time, the third time it was gentle and slow. The climax was a long time in coming, but when it did, it shook me down to my bones. Jackson held my face in both his hands, eyes locked on mine as he came with me. They say the eyes are the windows to the soul and I could have sworn he stole part of mine in that moment. Part of my soul slipped into him and part of his into me.

But now, here we are, worlds apart even as we sit side by side on the sleek black leather interior of his town car. And God, as if our selected modes of transportation don't symbolize just how wide the gap is between us. The captain of industry who has a driver and the lowly single mother who takes public transit, struggling to get on by any means necessary. Worlds apart we started, and so we'll end.

———

We're quiet on the ride home. I'm glad he doesn't try to fill the time going on about the job or our relationship or any of it. Truth be told, I'm still considering the job. He's said from the beginning it's not contingent on the personal relationship. Maybe it's stupid after everything I've seen in my life, but I actually believe him. It's got to be better than working for Bryce, where I *know* the job description includes sexual favors. It's certain to become unpleasant again as soon as it's clear the deal with CubeThink isn't going through.

But when and if the time comes to resign, I won't rely on Jackson to clear any hurdles for me. I made my own bed and while I don't want to lie in it, I'll be the one to get myself out of the situation. One foot in front of the other, one disaster at a time. My life's mantra, right?

When we pull up to my block, I'm already sliding away from Jackson. I don't want him to think that just because I rode with him, there's going to be a kiss goodbye or anything. I have my eyes averted firmly out the window, so I immediately notice Shannon running toward the car as soon as we pull up.

I shove my car door open, heart suddenly beating double time. "What's wrong?"

"How could you?" she shouts, almost a wail.

"What?" I catch her as she stumbles toward me, hiccupping and eyes red from crying. She starts to swing wildly at me and I put up my arms in defense. She smacks my shoulder and aims again for my head. Before she makes contact, Jackson is out of the car and has her arms restrained behind her back. She bucks against him like a wild-woman.

"How could you?" she screams again. "They took Charlie because of you!"

"What are you talking about?" I'm shaking all over. No, what she's saying can't be right. There's been some horrible misunderstanding.

"I called you," she accuses, standing on her own now. "I called you, over and over. Where were you?" Then she seems to collapse in herself. She stops struggling against Jackson. He loosens his grip and then lets her go. She sinks to the ground, crying. "They took our Charlie."

"Who?" I demand, leaning over so I'm in her face. I grab her shoulders and all but shake her. I don't know what the hell happened to my phone or why I didn't get her calls, but none of this makes any sense. "Tell me what happened. You have to tell me what happened so I can fix it. Who took Charlie?"

Shannon gulps in a deep breath. "They all showed up at once. David and his wife, and they had police with them and a courier from the judge. It was the envelope with the judge's decision." She seems to get another wave of strength as she glares daggers at me. "They awarded him full custody because you failed the drug test."

"*What?*" I look at Jackson in bewilderment. But then I see it in his face, too. He's wondering. Questioning what he thinks he knows about me.

"You think I did it, too," I whisper. It slices deep. So he not only thinks I'm a whore, but a *druggie* whore.

I back away from both of them. Of course the judge didn't even second-guess the results. Why would he? I'm the trash mother who landed in jail while she was pregnant. Who never could manage to get her life together. Who whored herself out to get enough money for a family court attorney, and it turns out not even that was enough. Because a lab screwed up some results somewhere. How do I even fight that?

God, I guess I call my lawyer? And then we start thinking of appeals? But how long will that take? And in the meantime... I look toward my apartment.

That's when it hits me.

Really hits me.

Charlie is gone.

Taken.

I no longer have any rights to see my own son. A sob chokes its way out of me.

Oh God. Oh God oh God oh God oh God oh God oh God oh God.

This can't be happening. Anything but this. Everything I've done has been to keep Charlie and me together and now...

I drop down into the grass beside Shannon. I want to scream as loud as I've ever screamed in my life. And then lay down and die.

"Callie. Callie. Calliope!"

I look up dully into Jackson's eyes, finally realizing he's holding me in a tight embrace. "Baby, we'll do whatever it takes to bring him home. I have lawyers from the best law firm in the city on retainer. We'll make them earn their keep. They'll retest the sample to prove it was a false positive."

My eyes flash up to his. Does that mean he actually believes I'm innocent?

He kisses my forehead hard. He must see it in my eyes because he whispers, "I'm sorry I doubted you for even a second, baby. There are a hundred things that can cause a false positive. Cold medicine. Other over the counter drugs. Lab error. Even things you ate. We'll appeal this and get it thrown out. We'll have your son back in no time."

With every confident word he speaks, the numbness starts to drop away. He talks like we can actually fight this thing. "How long do appeals take?" My voice is barely a whisper.

"I don't know, but let's go call my lawyer and find out." He pulls back, but only far enough to take my hand in his and help me to my feet. He's already got his phone out and is dialing.

Shannon's been watching the whole exchange with fear and confusion. She might not have faith in me like Jackson does—the reminder that he does sends a wave of warmth over me in spite of the horror of the last five minutes—but I'll prove to her I'm a good mother. Goddammit, I'll prove it to them all, no matter how much fight it takes. Charlie belongs with me. I might fuck up a lot in this life, but he's the one thing I'm determined to get right.

"Come on," I tell her, nodding toward the apartment. My voice and legs are still shaky, but I swallow and try to get hold of myself. Seeing Jackson jump immediately into action is helping me get my bearings back.

"Sandoval," Jackson snaps into the phone, "I need an emergency consultancy in a custody hearing situation. Get your best people together. We'll meet in your offices in one hour."

My hand reflexively squeezes Jackson's. He looks over at me and gives me an encouraging nod while he listens to what the person on the other end of the phone says.

My heart cinches in my chest. What if I was wrong earlier? What if Jackson and I can look past how we first met? I think about a life of this—of partnership, bearing one another's burdens, not being alone when the hard stuff hits...

Jackson finishes the call and drops the phone back into his suit coat pocket. He must see something on my face, because he pauses right before the door to my apartment and asks, "What?" His face softens in concern. "Babe, we'll get Charlie back home to you. I promise." He reaches up and caresses my cheek with one of his mammoth hands.

I turn into the touch, breathe him in, and nod. Then, still not able to make sense of everything I'm feeling, I bury my face in his chest and hug him tight. After a moment, his arms wrap around me in return.

"It's going to be okay, babe," he says, rubbing my back. "It's all going to be okay." I can only tighten my hold.

I want to believe him.

God knows I do. And being here with Jackson Vale's arms so strong around me, maybe I can. Maybe I can.

CHAPTER SEVENTEEN

My hands tremble as I take the elevator up to Gentry Tech to give notice the following Monday.

The weekend was hell without Charlie, but Jackson and I met with his lawyers and they put in the paperwork right when the courthouse opened this morning to retest the sample taken by an independent lab.

Jackson continued being wonderful. He didn't try to kiss or make any moves on me. He was just... *there* for me in a way no one's been ever before.

I don't know what that means. Maybe it *is* possible to look past how we started and consider the idea of Jackson and me exploring a future together? I'm still too mixed up about everything with Charlie to think too much about it. Right now, he's just being an amazing friend, and that's enough. No matter what, though, I won't be giving up my newfound determination to take control of my life. No more letting men assume they can decide my fate.

Which is why when Jackson told me that he would take care of giving Bryce my notice, I refused.

I'll walk into Bryce's office and give my notice. I'll take whatever humiliating tirade I'm sure will come with it. Then I'll walk out of here and enjoy a long hot shower to scrub every inch of this place off of me.

The elevator doors open and I scrunch my trembling hands into fists. I can do this. I'm more than just trash, and I won't let anyone treat me like it anymore. Isn't that what Jackson's always reminding me of, in little ways and big? He sees my body and my mind as two completely separate things, and he's attracted to both. Just the memory of all our time together makes me stand up straighter.

I cross the small, chic lobby and enter Bryce's office without knocking, ignoring Madison's protests. Bryce looks up in annoyance at the unexpected entrance. His wall was frosted, after all, which means that everyone is supposed to leave him alone without Madison checking through the intercom with him first. But I'm not going to get through this by submissively waiting my turn. It's time to stand up for what I deserve and stop letting myself be pushed around by Bryce or any other bully.

"I'll talk to you later, Mandeep, something's come up." Bryce laughs but his face looks anything but amused. "I'll do that. Talk to you next week in our teleconference." Bryce pushes a button to disconnect the call and then the full weight of his displeasure turns my way.

"You know you're not to disturb me while I'm on a call. Or ever when the glass isn't clear."

I know what he's doing, trying to put me on the defensive. Normally I'd be stumbling over myself to apologize.

Not today. I continue standing, my chin out slightly.

"I'm here to give my notice." I slip the envelope with my written and signed resignation out of the top of my purse where I kept it for easy access. I slide it on his desk over to him.

"I know that it's traditional to give two weeks' notice," I continue, "but I'm sorry in this case I can't."

I force the next words from between clenched teeth. "Thank you for the opportunity you gave me." After all, without him, I wouldn't have met Jackson. "I'll have all the clothing you provided dry-cleaned and returned by the end of the week."

Hoping for a nice, clean exit, I spin on my heel to leave.

I expect a lot of responses—curses, shouting, even Bryce's low, commanding tone that is enough to make businessmen the world over sit up and pay attention. But I didn't foresee the loud chuckle that comes from behind me. Or the words that make my feet falter right before I can get to the door: "Oh, you think you can leave? Just like that?"

What does he mean by that? I decide it's not worth engaging him any further and continue for his door.

The sound of his palm slapping sharply against his desk jolts me to a stop again. "Have you forgotten the little matter of the contract you signed with me?"

"What do you mean?" I don't turn around. I knew he wasn't going to make this easy, but what does he mean about the contract?

"Look at me, you little conniving slut. You think I didn't foresee this the first day you walked into my office?"

At this, I can't help but to spin back around. I don't understand. Foresee what?

He's standing, both fists planted on his desk. A slow smile grows on his face as he observes my confusion. He has the look of a satisfied hunter, and I feel like an animal who just stepped into a trap that's snapped shut around me. "Didn't anybody ever tell you to read the fine print on things that you sign, Miss Cruise?"

"I did read the fine print," I object. "I read the entire employee contract before I signed it."

After his initial come-on during the interview, I wanted to make sure there weren't any weird required sexual obligations within the contract itself. I would have questioned the legality of such a document, but still—I *specifically* read the tiny print at the bottom of each page.

Bryce pulls out his keys and thumbs through them before finding a small silver one. He unlocks the bottom drawer of his desk. "Ah, here we are."

He pulls out several stapled papers with a flourish and flips through them to the second to last page. Then he begins to read. "You do covenant and agree that, during the term of employment with the company and for five years after the termination thereof, regardless of the reason for the employment termination, you will not," he looks up and smiles, "—and here's the good part," he directs his attention back to the paper, "—directly or indirectly, *anywhere* in the territory, *on behalf of any competitive business,* perform substantially the same job duties or in any other capacity."

Fuck, fuck, *fuck.*

Bryce glances up to make sure I'm paying attention and for Christ's sake, of course I am. How did I miss a non-compete clause? I could have sworn I'd read through every line of that damn contract. *FUCK.*

"If breached, you agree to a legal reimbursement pursued insofar as a factor of ten of the employee's starting salary."

I cough in shock. Does he mean—? He can't be saying—

Bryce smiles in delight. "That's right, at your current contracted salary, you would owe more than three-quarters of a million dollars if you expect to stop working for me and go work for a competitor of mine in any capacity."

"No." It comes out as a horrified whisper. No, no, he's bluffing. I read through the entire employee contract. I swear I did. "Let me see that." I step forward and grab the papers out of his hand.

"By all means," he says, still with that satisfied grin on his face. "I have copies."

My eyes scan the paper, first glancing down to see that my signature is indeed right there. I initialed each page to indicate I'd read it. Then my eyes scan back up to see the line Bryce so helpfully highlighted in bright yellow. I shake my head, about to accuse him of tampering with it when I realize that these pages aren't part of the employee contract at all.

It's the nondisclosure agreement. The highlighted sentence is in the center of a dense paragraph of long-winded legalese glossary definitions, on the second to last page of a thick packet. Just that one sentence about not competing and the consequences if I do.

My stomach suddenly feels like it's been scraped out like a carved pumpkin. Oh my God. I did sign this. My eyes must have just skipped right over this bit. It was just the NDA. It was just about information disclosure—not my actual work contract! It's not supposed to have anything like this in it. So yeah, I read it, but not as closely as I should have.

Bryce didn't hide this noose in the fine print, he put it in plain sight but camouflaged by all the other jargon.

I slam the papers back down on the desk, my chest heaving. My hand goes to my stomach. Oh God, I feel sick. Bryce lets out another low chuckle, and I can only look at him, horrified.

"Why?" I back away from the desk. "What do you want from me?" This guy is one sadistic fuck. Why would he put that in the contract if he didn't want to put me in this exact position? He'd done this from the beginning. How——? I mean, why——? I look over at him, lightheaded with confusion. "Did you hire me just to fuck with my life?"

Bryce holds out his hands magnanimously. "Not at all. I'm a very generous man. I want only the best for my employees. You can understand that for a man in my position it's important that I don't have employees going off and immediately giving my trade secrets away to my competition."

"But I'm just your personal assistant," I protest. "I don't know any trade secrets!" I might have, but he never shared the algorithms or any other proprietary information. The things I do know he already shared openly with Jackson.

"True," Bryce says. "Which is why I'm willing to negotiate with you." The affable smile is still on his face.

My hackles immediately go up. I feel like the mouse that a cat is playing with before it pounces. What the hell is this bastard's game? I could've sworn just a moment ago he was taking glee in the fact that he had maneuvered me into this exact position.

I think back to my random theory from a few days ago, that all of this was somehow Bryce's endgame—from hiring me, to taking me to that lunch with Jackson, to encouraging me to work with Jackson so we'd connect like we have, only now to... what? Is this, whatever this is, what it's all been leading up to?

But no, God, that's ridiculous. It's not like we're puppets and Bryce can know which strings to pull to get us to respond exactly how he expects... I shift on my feet uncomfortably at the thought before shaking my head.

It's ludicrous. And what *is* it he could even hope to get out of all this?

"What do you mean, negotiate?" I ask through clenched teeth.

"Well, you see, I'm arranging a last-minute meeting this morning for some friends and potential investors who happen to be in town. It's for the same project that you just proposed to Mr. Vale. Considering it's he, I assume, who's offering you the job that has you so quick to render your notice to me," Bryce's smile widens at the stiffening of my posture, "we know how good you are at giving a presentation. Plus, a pretty face never goes awry when negotiating deals."

His posture is too genial, too easy going. If the preposterous theory that he's been maneuvering toward this for months is true, then what he's proposing seems too easy and off the cuff. Which just goes to show I was being too paranoid about it. This is only about Bryce being an asshole, wanting to take his pound of flesh out of me for quitting and going to work for Jackson. The question is, will a pound of flesh be enough?

"And then what? I do the presentation at this last meeting and you just let me out of an eight hundred-and-fifty thousand dollar fine?" I scoff.

Bryce shrugs. "I'm not an idiot. That's money I'll never see out of you. You don't own a house or even a car—it will just bankrupt you and I won't see much more than twenty thousand, if that. No," he shakes his head. "Like I said, I can be magnanimous. All I ask of you is to come, give the presentation and provide a certain degree of hospitality to our honored guests."

My entire body goes on alert. "What does hospitality mean?"

For the first time since I came in, I see a glint in Bryce's eyes that makes me suspect I'm seeing the real man. He always was a shark and for a moment he doesn't bother to veil the predator within. It's gone the next second, but it's enough insight to send chills from the top of my spine down to the tips of my toes.

"It's an hour of your time in exchange for getting to walk away scot free, no strings tying you to me or this place." He raises his eyebrows as if he's giving me an obvious gift and I'm a fool for not jumping at the opportunity.

Christ. If he's trying to make it sound so casual, I'm sure it's the opposite. Shit. Fuck. Shit, fuck. What do I do? Eight-hundred-and-fifty thousand dollars. Almost a million. Just thinking about that number gives me hives. Obviously, he's right, I'd never be able to pay even a tiny portion of it. The alternative? Not being able to work in the field in any capacity for *five years*?

I turn away from Bryce and my hand goes to my forehead. I swallow hard. Christ. How did I get myself into this position?

I ball my fists and I want to scream at myself. *Oh yeah, Callie, you were going to be so different*, a voice inside my head mocks. Make a stand. Be strong for a change. And the first time I try to take charge of my life, here's this fucker grinding me back down into the dust.

My shoulders slump. Because he's going to win.

Once again, I'm in an impossible situation. So much worse than when I stepped in this office two months ago. Now I don't even have Charlie. I made myself a pathetic whore and for what? So I could debase myself in front of yet another man, fall into the role of weak submissive, let myself be shit all over emotionally, and still lose what was most important to me in life?

I can feel Bryce's stare on the top of my head and I can just imagine how triumphant he feels. It's what he's always gotten off on— making people cower in his presence.

God, was that what he saw in me at the interview? That I was a girl who'd be so easy to control? That I could be easily bent? Easily broken.

Bryce likes to break people. Jackson's words echo in my head.

Is that why Bryce hired me, out of all the people who interviewed for the job?

Even the idea pisses me off.

I'm so much stronger than any of them think. I might just be realizing my own strength now, but screw that—I didn't survive all I have, support and raise my baby and be fighting to get him back because I was weak-willed.

So fuck Bryce fucking Gentry. I raise my head, widen my stance, and stiffen my back.

I knew there would be consequences when I resigned today. Bryce's a twisted fuck. Whatever his agenda, be it some long-thought-out thing or a spur-of-the-moment fuckery he's come up with, I'll handle it because I have to. Because I'm embracing my inner queen bitch who can handle whatever life throws at me.

I glare at Bryce. Fuck him and every other man who's kept me down all my life. "How many people will be at this business meeting where I'm to make the presentation?"

He leans back in his chair with his fingers steepled under his chin. "Nine."

I let out the breath I was holding, but I try not to show anything on my face. I don't want to give a single inch to the bastard in front of me. No reaction, no response. Internally, though, I'm preparing. Nine people. Okay. Bryce can't do anything too crazy to me with nine respected businesspeople in the room.

I turn my iciest glare on him. "Nothing happens in that room that I don't okay beforehand?"

Bryce holds up his hands. "Of course. This is your decision. Just remember what's at stake if you try to pull out of the deal at the last minute."

I fill my lungs with another deep breath. "All right."

Bryce starts to stand, but I hold out a hand. "Not so fast. I want it in writing that after the conference today, anything I've previously signed is null and void."

He bows his head with a nod of what looks like respect—though it could just be another form of manipulation, it's impossible to tell with him. "Well played, Miss Cruise. I'll send it to your printer within the hour. The meeting is at ten a.m. in Conference Room B. Do be prompt."

I head toward my office for what I hope is the last time. Whatever Bryce throws at me, I'll be prepared. And I vow, this is the last day I'll let myself be in a position like this ever again.

CHAPTER EIGHTEEN

I've never been in this conference room. It's much smaller than Conference Room A where the project managers convene every Tuesday for project updates. Instead of being a more industrial office space like the other conference room, it's a sleek modern design.

The central table surface creates the top of what's essentially a large ornate Z. The ten chairs set all around the table look more comfortable than the normal fair as well, with white overstuffed cushions held together by chrome supports also shaped like Zs. It's always about presentation with Bryce.

I've arrived twenty minutes early. No way I'm going to be accused of tardiness today. I glance nervously around the room. Right. Time to prep. I might have only been at this job a little more than a couple months, but it took just one false start at a conference to learn Bryce's expectations of his personal assistant—not that he gave me a checklist ahead of time.

I've made my own list since then: Get a piping hot travel carafe of high-end brewed coffee from the coffeeshop on the ground floor of the building (God forbid I try to brew it myself, lesson learned from my second conference attempt). Second, get a platter of finger pastries delivered from the boutique pastry shop that Gentry Tech has on contract—*not* from the coffeeshop downstairs, no matter that it might be much more convenient on short notice. Third, arrange notepads and pens at every station just in case, even though everyone uses laptops now. Every once in a while, there could be an older holdout who still expects pen and paper as a matter of course.

I look around me as I get started. God, this conference room better be as equipped as the other one, or I'm gonna have to haul ass down to Conference Room A to get the nice coffee set. But when I open up the small cabinet in the back of the room, I let out a sigh of relief. This coffee set is even fancier than the one I'm used to using. Not that it's silver or anything. No, of course not. Nothing that reeks of the antique or traditional for Gentry Tech. The coffee set is a modern slate matte black.

I pour the coffee from the cardboard travel carafe into the nice serving one and set up the coffee cups. Then I arrange it all nicely on a tray at the back counter. I put everything else together and am just filling up the ice water pitcher when I hear the door open behind me.

I spill a few drops of water as I turn off the filtered tap at the back sink. It takes all my self-control not to swear a blue streak.

I swipe at the small spill with my hand as I swivel to see Bryce holding open the door for several distinguished looking older business-men. I wipe my wet hand on the side of my skirt and plaster on a smile, taking several steps away from the counter. Shit. Do I go and greet them or wait here like a nice little submissive secretary?

I hesitate midstep and then just pause where I am, halfway between the counter and the doorway. I drop my hand by my side, but then that seems dumb so I put them behind my back. Christ, what am I, five years old? I drop them back by my sides.

Meanwhile, Bryce's completely ignoring me and welcoming more and more men into the room. I silently count. Five, six, seven. Okay, almost all of them. *Breathe, Cals, breathe.* My chest is certainly moving up and down. All right. That's good. Except, shit, now I'm getting light-headed. Goddammit. *Breathe slower.*

I try to take slower, deeper breaths. I can do this. I'm a professional.

A professional what, exactly? asks an inner voice.

Yeah. I tell the inner voice to shut the fuck up. Get through this hour, then I'm free.

"Forgive me," Bryce says, "I've been completely neglecting to introduce my associate, Miss Calliope Cruise. She'll be helping me present the next in our proposed product line."

Bryce holds out a hand to me, gesturing me forward. I'm glad to finally have some indication of my role here, but the butterflies in my stomach start swarming as I step forward. Butterflies is probably the wrong word. They bring to mind a nice image. I should say moths. Yes. It's definitely creepy fuzzy closet moths swarming my innards that I feel as I shake the first man's hand.

He's old enough to be my grandfather and then some. There are wrinkles to his wrinkles. I'd have thought his skin would be dry and crackly, but no, his palms are sweaty. "Happy to meet you, little lady." His filmy blue eyes never leave the vicinity of my chest.

"Richard," Bryce claps him on the back, "don't monopolize my lovely associate's time. I'd like her to meet everyone before we get started. Besides, as I told you earlier," a look passes between the two men, "there'll be plenty of time in the question-and-answer portion later."

"Ah," Richard gives my hand one last sweaty squeeze before stepping away.

After that, it's a parade of men. I can tell by the thread count of their suits that they are all very wealthy. None of them are younger than forty. Several have heavy foreign accents, one who sounds English and a couple from Asia.

"It's good to meet you, Miss Cruise," says the last man, a Carl something-or-other from Atlantic Dynamics. His gaze never once trays below my chin. "There's been a lot of chatter about Gentry Tech's new drone line and I'm excited to hear your presentation."

"Thank you," I respond. He seems friendly and genuine. I can't help the paranoia that's been clawing at me ever since Bryce maneuvered me into this meeting, but as I see everyone settling into their chairs at what looks like a very ordinary conference meeting, the winged creatures in my stomach start to settle.

This was all just another one of Bryce's mind games. He was setting this all up like it was going to be something sleazy or bizarre. But it's all above board. I want to laugh at myself for building it up in my head. Well, that, and I want to punch Bryce in the nuts, the bastard, screwing with me like that.

I turn away from Carl feeling much lighter and go to click on the projection screen. I get my laptop out of my bag and glance at Bryce. He gives me a nod and opens the meeting.

"Gentlemen, I'm excited to welcome you to the future of unmanned aerial systems. What I'm going to show you today is a design that's light years ahead of the current technology."

Bryce goes on to detail the idea behind his design and then he nods at me again while simultaneously pressing a remote to dim the lights.

I switch on the projector and begin to go through my presentation. Since I've done it several times at this point, my voice comes out strong and clear. I don't flub a single point.

There are questions throughout the presentation. To my surprise, Bryce lets me field most of them, only jumping in when it's a question that's too technical in nature for me to answer.

I finish the slide that describes the software that will drive the drones—the part that so upset Jackson as incomplete. The men in the room merely look satisfied and, dare I say, impressed. Either they accept Bryce's promises at face value or don't know any better? But these are men in the industry, surely they know the right questions to ask. Maybe it's just because Bryce's reputation precedes him and they trust he can do what he says he will.

Bryce brings the lights in the room back to full power. There's quiet chatter in the room as a few of the men talk amongst themselves. A couple are still jotting notes on tablets. The physical notepads all sit untouched.

Fine with me. I glance down at my own laptop. I can't believe that I got through that with no hiccups. A flare of relief rushes through me. My time at Gentry Tech is all but officially done. I can't help the smile that sneaks across my face. I even managed to do a good job in my last task here. I actually feel proud of myself.

"And now let's settle in for some refreshments since the first half of our business has been concluded."

Or not. The excitement I just felt fizzles, but only slightly. Okay, I can get through refreshment hour. No biggie.

Bryce nods at me without ever looking my way. Way to remind me of the indentured servant that I am. I raise my chin. I only have to make it through this last meeting. I can handle anything for an hour.

"Get our esteemed guests whatever they would like to drink."

"Of course." I try to keep the tightness out of my voice.

I stand up and move toward the back of the room and—

My ass is pinched.

What the—?

I look back at Bryce in astonishment. Did he just pinch my—?

Bryce reaches out and unabashedly gropes my other ass cheek.

"What are you—?" The words barely come out in a gasp, though.

Because this is not happening. This is a public place. These are respectable businessmen. I just delivered a presentation to them as an equal—

"Unbutton your shirt, Miss Cruise." Bryce's voice is as conversational as it's been all throughout the meeting.

I stare at him, balking.

His affable eyes harden the slightest bit. He leans in and whispers so that just I can hear, "Do you want out of the contract or not? You only get out if you fulfill the obligations of this meeting."

Bastard. My heart sinks and I huff out in frustration and humiliation, Still, I hesitate only a second before my hands go to the top button of my blouse. This is more of what I was expecting all along, isn't it? The consequences I knew were coming for quitting?

From the beginning in my office, I decided I could be strong enough to get through this and still walk away with my head held high.

I will *not* let Bryce Gentry get the best of me.

So the bastard wants to put me on display. Fine. It's nothing he hasn't done before. I glare at Bryce the entire time I snap the buttons from their holes. I'm not going to simper or be cowed by him, but it just seems to amuse him more. Fucking cunt bastard.

Bryce holds out an arm toward me while looking at the rest of the table. "I've told you what an asset Miss Cruise is to the company. What I neglected to say is what lovely *assets* she has."

His lame joke gets a hearty chuckle from the room. I don't look around the table, but I'm stunned. Being in a room with these professionals made me feel safe earlier. Bryce is really going to do this in front of all of them? In what world is this acceptable?

"But what about her ass?" This from Richard, the old man. I don't fight the shudder of disgust that wracks my body. He's staring hungrily at my chest.

"Oh, we'll get to that, don't worry," Bryce says, looking me right in the eye. There's some kind of dark promise there.

I have the impulse to run from the room, right now. I tamp it down just in time.

I'll owe over *three-quarters of a million dollars* if I don't put up with this show and tell, or else I can't work where I want for five *years*. I swallow. Although, I'm quickly getting the idea that it's not just going to be a show and tell, but a show and *touch*. Christ.

But I can put up with anything for an hour... can't I?

I don't have another second to think about it, though, before Bryce has pulled the shirt off my back. The next second he unclasps my bra and jerks it from my frame.

There's a noise of masculine reaction throughout the room as my breasts are exposed. Grunts and low groans.

"Up," Bryce demands.

I don't understand at first, but then he grasps my hips and pushes me toward the table. "Up on your knees. Like a dog."

Humiliation colors my face. What the hell? No. No way did I agree to this.

One of the men in the corner with red hair and a slight gut licks his lips and then reaches out, grabbing my breast and squeezing. I yank back even as his eyes flare at the contact.

Bryce smacks at my thigh again, like he's chastising me. I turn on him, furious.

That's it. I'm out.

"I'm not doing this," I hiss at him. My eyes search out the door behind him. It's maybe ten feet away. I knew Bryce was disgusting, but this is pushing it *way* too far. He said I could have an out if I wanted it and I'm taking it.

But Bryce moves far quicker than I expect and his voice is in my ear. "Remember how much you have to lose. All I'm asking is to let them touch you a little. That's all they'll do. I promise. Half an hour and you're free."

I scoff and pull away, hating the feel of his breath on my ear. It feels wrong for him to be so close after what Jackson and I did last weekend.

Shame floods me in spite of my determination to be strong. *Jackson.* I was with Jackson and here I am, naked, letting other men touch me. We never talked about being exclusive and I don't even know if I'm willing to try it with him, but still... This is just so wrong on so many levels. My stomach churns and I want to be sick all over the table. All over the men who are getting off on my humiliation.

"Yeah, right," I whisper through gritted teeth, backing up several inches away from him. "These men are expecting a lot more than just touching."

Bryce puts a hand around my waist to hold me still. I stiffen.

Just as I'm calculating how close it is to the nearest coffee mug and whether or not I can grab it to smash it over Bryce's head, he says. "You're right."

He's close, still way too close as he whispers in my ear. "They're expecting a show. I give them a little live porno of my super-hot personal assistant blowing me, they'll get their rocks off and I make the deals I need."

I struggle against his hold. "I'm *not* giving you a blow job."

He slides his hand more around my waist and presses up against me, nuzzling his face in my hair. "It was always going to come to this, Calliope. You knew that from day one."

My heartbeat picks up until I feel like a small animal caught in a trap. "Fulfill your end of the bargain, and you're free. Walk out of this room and you owe me eight-hundred-and-fifty-thousand dollars if you try to get a job in the tech industry. Otherwise you'll be stuck wait-ressing for the next five years. You think you're really going to be able to win back your little boy by working minimum-wage jobs?"

I wrench away from him. How the hell does he even know about my court troubles?

But he continues, his voice cajoling. "This is such a little thing." He strokes my shoulder and I want to scream and then kick him until his balls are purple. "I'm willing to bargain. Just *fifteen* minutes and then it's over. You never have to see me again."

I squeeze my eyes shut as his words reverberate in my head.

Fifteen minutes.

Damn it. I could be done with Bryce forever. If I don't, he gets to determine how I live the next five *YEARS* of my life.

No. *Fuck no.*

He's toxic and evil and I'll never be the person I want to be if I'm stuck under his sociopathic thumb.

Goddamn him. He's the devil. If I do this, I'm walking into a deal with him with my eyes wide open. My chest squeezes in pain. I swore I was going to be different. That I was going to stop repeating old mistakes.

But damn it, this is not hearts and flowers land. My body is once again the bargaining tool on the table here. Fucking *literally*, if Bryce has his way.

There are no knights in shining armor, I've known that for a while. Jackson wanted to step into the role for a little while and maybe I wanted to let him, but this will kill it. I'm not sure he'll even want me to *work* for him after this.

And that's *fine*. I try to harden myself from the inside out.

Jackson was always a dream never meant to be mine. He's a good man and I'm— I'm—

You're the girl Dad's boss likes to diddle in the dark. You're the girl who climbs up on tables in front of a room of men like a whore.

This is who you are.

Who you always were.

It's not like Bryce is asking for anything I haven't done before. So many, many times before. Powerful men wanting my body. My mouth.

Open up, Little Barbie. You want your Dad to lose his job? Or I could give him that promotion he wants so badly. It's all up to you. I'm only asking for this one little thing.

"Fine," I hiss.

"Good girl." Bryce's voice goes back to all business. "Now. Up on the table on all fours."

No! Everything screams against it.

I swallow back the bile threatening to choke me. Without opening my eyes, I crawl onto the table. I fucking do it and my humiliation is complete.

Hoots and whistles come from every direction. Being humiliated is part of the point, right? It's what these sorts of men get off on. Power.

Bryce slaps me on the back of the thigh like one might a horse to position me closer to one corner of the table. Without a bra, my breasts swing free like low-hanging fruit with each movement. I keep my eyes squeezed shut.

Fifteen minutes.

Just fifteen minutes and then you can leave and never look back.

Never *ever* look back.

I feel movement beside me as Bryce stands up and addresses the table. "Our naughty girl was thinking about running away. What does a naughty girl get?"

Bryce grabs my skirt and with several rough jerks, has it yanked up around my waist. His hand follows, smoothing up the crack of my ass where my thong disappears.

"Tell us, whore, how much you want it."

My jaw clenches, but Bryce grabs my ass and squeezes it hard.

I squeeze my eyes shut even harder and duck my head. But no, fuck that. I will not cower. *You will survive this, Callie Cruise.* In fifteen minutes, I'll walk away from this building with my future in my own motherfucking hands.

"I want it," I say, hating the words as they come from my mouth.

Just think of that sidewalk. I'm already there. I'm already walking away. Look at that blue sky. That blue, blue sky.

"What was that?" Bryce asks. I can imagine the asshole putting a hand up to his ear like a fucking clown does at a circus. I don't open my eyes though as I repeat louder, "I want it."

"And what do you want, whore?"

My eyes do pop open at this. This fucking son of a bitch. What the fuck does he want me to say? It's not like he gave me a script for this.

He's grinning mercilessly at me. "Are you hungry for my cock?"

My teeth grind together so hard I feel the stirrings of a headache. "Yes."

"Ah ah ah," he chides, waving a finger in the air. "I want to hear you say it. Are you hungry for my cock?"

I bite down on my cheek so hard I taste blood. I close my eyes again and try to remember why only moments ago this seemed like the best course of action.

Get through this and then I'm free. *You can put up with anything in the world for just fifteen short minutes, Calliope Marie Cruise.* Then it's blue, blue sky. Blue motherfucking sky.

I choke out the phrase Bryce wants in a stilted, monotone voice. "I'm hungry for your cock."

"That's right," Bryce croons, "you nasty fucking cum bucket. All you can think about is choking on my monster cock."

If I try hard enough, I can just pretend I'm not here, right? There are *not* nine pairs of eyes on my body and I am *not* splayed out like a Christmas ham on the table.

"Richard, would you like to do the honors of initiating play?"

My head whips up at that. The fuck?

I see Richard moving way faster than a man of his age should around the table. He's rubbing his hands together. There's a huge grin on his face and his eyes are glued to my ass. The front of his pants jut out obscenely.

My head swings back to Bryce. "I'm only blowing you," I whisper through gritted teeth. "That's the only way I do this."

I might be a cheap piece of ass but I am *not* a goddamned whore. No matter what Bryce fucking Gentry might think.

Bryce laughs and grabs my chin in between his fingers. For most people, this would be a sweet gesture, but Bryce puts enough strength behind it so that he's forcing my jaw to make my lips open in an O. "So eager, are we?"

"Only you," I growl through his grip on my jaw.

He nods, sobering for just a moment. "Only me."

I breathe out in relief until the old man's nasty damp hand grabs my ass.

"But the others get to touch," Bryce finishes, shoving his thumb in my mouth. He shoves it in so far I cough. He just looks amused before pulling it out and stepping back.

The old man grabs and slaps my ass like I'm some kind of mare. Unlike Jackson's expert spanking in the limo, Richard doesn't seem to know what the hell he's doing. His hits are too hard and land in the same place over and over. Just thinking of this dirty old man and Jackson in the same thought makes a tide of shame swarm me.

"Look at how she's jiggling, she likes it," Richard pants after the eighth slap.

All right, fucker—

But Bryce must see I'm about to turn and lose it on the old bastard because Bryce grabs my wrists like he's constraining me and chuckles at Richard. "Okay, Rich, time to give everyone else a go."

Richard grunts in dissatisfaction, but from how hard he's breathing, it's obvious he couldn't keep it up for much longer anyway. He lands one last hard smack anyway and I yelp in protest. This time when Bryce holds me back, it's not all for show.

He leans over and whispers in my ear, "Act like you're resisting me now, they love it."

"You can't handle a real man putting you in your place," Bryce says louder. Now we're making fucking theater out of it? These rich, twisted fucks. I can't believe I'm going along with this.

"That's the problem these days," he continues with a growl, grabbing my upper arm. His face is fierce but his grip is light. "Uppity bitches who don't know their place. I'm gonna teach you, right here, right now. And you're gonna take it, aren't you bitch? Stupid fucking cunt."

I glance significantly at the clock behind Bryce's head and glare at him.

Fifteen minutes, fucker.

I wait for the slightest nod of acknowledgment before I go along with his gambit. Then I start shaking my head. "No, no, no."

I close my eyes and pretend to struggle against him. "You can't do this. I don't want to do this."

Bryce slams his palm across my mouth, shutting off my cries.

"Carl," he nods his head at the young, handsome businessman I thought seemed so professional when I first met him. "Hold her for me."

Carl moves closer, eyes bright. Wow, glad I'm so good at spotting the good guys from the screwed-up ones. Then again, I should just assume that anybody who is in Bryce's inner circle is fucked up.

Jackson and Bryce used to be friends. Maybe it's a good thing that will never go anywhere. For Christ's sake, Jackson spanked and then finger-fucked me in his limo while I was sobbing.

No more time to think about that now. Carl leans over my back and puts me in some kind of wrestling hold where my elbows are constricted against my body. Though I can still hold myself up on all fours. Considerate lad, I internally roll my eyes.

I'm bent lower toward the table though, and Carl maneuvers me so that my face is near the edge. Where I'm confronted with Bryce undoing his belt buckle.

I swallow and then swallow again. My breaths get short and I force myself not to hyperventilate. Which, of course, is when I want to let out a crazed hyena like cackle. Because last time I was hyperventilating, Jackson spanked me till I was calm. I'm sure someone in this room would be happy to spank me again. Without Jackson, though, it would only have the opposite effect.

And that's when I feel like sobbing.

Oh God, what the fuck am I doing? Seriously, what the *fuck*?

Bryce unzips his pants and shoves his boxers down. There's no fanfare as he pulls out his cock. I've seen it before, of course, when he was masturbating by the windowed wall, but there had been about three feet separating us. Far different from it being right here bobbing in my face.

Open up, Little Barbie.

How did I let it get to this?

One man holding my hands while I'm face down on a table, surrounded by a bunch of businessmen while another shoves his cock in my face?

WHAT THE FUCK AM I DOING?

Fuck the money!

Fuck it if I have to work as a waitress for five years!

Nothing's worth this!!!

I turn away from Bryce's cock, but I barely get anywhere with Carl holding my arms behind my back.

"No," I say firmly.

I start to struggle against his grip on my arms.

"Don't be a cock-tease, you little bitch," Bryce smirks. "You were begging for it just a minute ago."

He shoves himself toward my mouth again but I lock my teeth shut and twist my head away.

"I said *no*. No, I changed my mind. No to the deal. To all of this. Let me go." I wrestle against the hold Carl has on me.

"Let me go!" I shriek when Carl's hold only tightens.

"That's right, baby," Carl says. "I love it when they play hard to get. Inside you're begging for it, aren't you, cunt?" He's all but laying on top of me from behind and I can feel him fully hard on the back of my thigh.

Oh God. I try to breathe but he's crushing me.

They're not—

Why aren't they stopping—

My chest hurts. I need a breath.

I have to make them understand. Do they think this is part of the fucking act? I manage a full breath in.

"No, I'm being serious! I'm not fucking playing!"

Then I remember the word Jackson gave me—the safeword that's widely acknowledged in all circles of kink. Surely someone in this room is familiar with it.

"Red!" I shout. "Stop! *No! RED!*"

For a second everything pauses.

Bryce looks me straight in the eye.

Then he takes my jaw in both hands.

And jams his dick into my mouth. As Carl grabs my hips and thrusts into me from behind at the same time.

CHAPTER NINETEEN

This isn't what I was warned about.

This is supposed to be the terror that hides in the shadows. That thing that happens in dark alleys. When drinks are left unguarded at clubs. On college campuses at frat parties when no one's looking.

Not mid-morning in a conference room at a respectable office building in the Silicon Valley.

This isn't what I was warned about.

That's the stupid thought that keeps running through my head. As man after man uses my body. A train of men. That's what they call it, right? A train.

I should've run when I had the chance earlier. If I ever had a chance. I didn't realize I was being surrounded by predators as they came in one by one, looking so innocuous. Still, I should never have come into this situation without protection.

I was warned about Bryce.

He's dangerous.

My stupid fucking bravado. Thinking I could handle everything on my own. And then not even bringing any protection, not even a fucking knife. Christ, I didn't even turn on my phone to record whatever might happen. I just never thought in a million years...

I close my eyes. Chant over and over in my head.

I'm not here.

This is not my body.

I'm on the moors in England like in one of the stupid historical romances I like to read. It's stormy and loud and I can't hear anything but the wind battering against the rocks. Yes, that's it. It's just the wind yanking at my body. Nothing more. Only the rain and wind howling in my ears, blocking out all other sounds.

Except my mind isn't always that strong and sensations sneak through. Bryce's voice. Always like a king presiding over each encounter. He gagged me after his first use of me. Sometimes an especially sharp pinch or squeeze brings me back to the here and now. I'm aware enough to know they all wear condoms, except for when Bryce came in my mouth. Each man leaves one by one after they've had their fill of me. It must have been Bryce's plan all along. No. Nothing's happening to me. I'm not here. Not here. *Not here.*

Lords and ladies in ballrooms. Silver tea sets. Lace and ruffles and hoop skirts and corsets... clothes ripped off by violent men.

Violating me.

Violating.

Violating.

I come while the third or fourth man pumps into me. It's a small orgasm. But, God, why? Why?

I want to die, the shame is so thick. How could I? How *could* I?

It continues. On and on.

I have my eyes squeezed shut tight, I don't know how much later, when I notice how quiet it is in the room. There are still hands on me, holding me in place. Always Carl and Bryce while the others used me. But I don't hear the usual horrible introductory bullshit as each man was initiated. I won't let myself believe it's over, not until they're all gone. I hazard a glance around. It's just Bryce, Carl, and me left in the room. I put up only the weakest resistance when Carl pries my thighs apart yet again.

A low-pitched whine is all that manages to make its way out of my throat. All my feisty curses dried up hours ago.

I blink again and try to force some backbone into my voice. "Shtawp. Pwease," I say around the gag.

They don't stop.

"I'm taking everything from you, you shit piece of nothing," Bryce hisses in my ear, taking me from behind while Carl fucks me from below. "Wearing out every hole and marking every nasty inch of your ugly useless body."

And in that moment, I see two ways before me. Either I sink back into the nether and am destroyed by this in a way I'll never come back from. *Or* I take the much more difficult path and fight.

Sink or fight?

All I want is to run in the only way available to me—to disappear, disconnect, fly away to the furthest depths inside my head.

But oh God, if I cut loose my soul right here, right now, will I *ever* get it back?

Goddamn mother fucking thieving bastard rapist liar.

No.

No no no no no no no no no nonononononononononononononono NOOOOO.

I will give him *nothing* more than he is already taking.

I grit my teeth. Bryce yanks my head by my hair so that I'm forced to look back at him while he sodomizes me.

Goddamn fucker thinks this is his moment of triumph.

The purest form of hatred rises up and chokes me as they defile my body.

I'll murder him slowly. I'll yank his intestines out while he's still alive and light them on fire in front of his eyes.

He thinks he's winning in this moment, but he'll live to regret this, I swear it. This will be the last day any man ever has any power over me. I swear it on my dying breath.

I want to growl in fury and let my hatred flash in my eyes so Bryce realizes he hasn't broken me.

It takes every last ounce of self-control not to. I want to react like the wounded animal he's made me. To lash out and claw his face off.

But no—he just *thinks* he's made me that.

I am not an animal.

And.

I.

Am.

Not.

Broken.

I cling to logic. First, I have to get myself the fuck out of here. My mind works through everything I know about Bryce.

And, feeling sick, I know what I have to do. Because I was wrong earlier. Bryce isn't a powerful man. He's weak. So fucking weak he has to grasp at power like this. Humiliate and brutalize women to feel like a fucking man.

And that's my ticket out.

To make him think he's won.

Bryce still has hold on my hair so he can see my face. I make my gaze go glossy and sightless. Then I begin swiveling my hips so that they're in sync with Carl and Bryce's.

This time, when I feel the build at my core, I don't hate myself for it. I'm doing what I have to. What that sick, child-molesting fuck McIntyre trained me for. What will make Bryce finish faster.

The ultimate humiliation. When I come against my will.

So fuck him. I'll give him a show. Give him the appearance of getting what he wants so I can get out of here as fast as possible and as much on my terms as this sickening situation allows. But it will really be *me* who's in control, not this fuckhead bastard.

I close my eyes and give my body over to the mechanics of what's happening to it. I find friction for my clitoris. I lean into the sensation that starts to spark back to life.

"Look how the filthy whore bitch loves it!" Bryce exults from behind me.

That's right, you fucking bastard, you just think *you're winning.*

I force my features into one of distressed but agonized desire. I thrash my body in the simulation of pleasure even as I cry out against the tie in my mouth. A sound of absolute devastation. It's not hard to imitate. All the while I keep my hips pumping, with a twisting grind for the most friction possible.

And I come.

I come because my body is trained to respond to stimuli. And more than that, I'm getting off because I'm taking back control. As much as Bryce thinks he's in control of this shit-show, he's fucking *not*.

He's the one who's going to be coming on *my* terms, and it's going to be a helluva lot quicker than if he'd had it his way.

My theatrics seem to have done the trick. Bryce grabs my hips. He ignores Carl and starts absolutely jackhammering away. There's no finesse. No control to it. It hurts like hell but I don't care. I'll care later, but not right now.

All that matters in this moment is that *Bryce* is the animal now. Not me.

I've made him lose control. He thought he'd planned this scenario so perfectly. That he can just manipulate and abuse anyone he wants like a puppet on a cord. Well this is just the beginning of me fucking him back.

And then finally, *finally*, he's done.

I want to scream at him immediately to get the fuck off of me, but it's more important that I keep playing my part. All that matters is escaping this room.

So I have to play at being the very thing I hate—broken.

That's all Bryce's ever wanted. I've finally figured out his game. It's just like Jackson said. Bryce likes to take things that are whole and break them.

I force myself to weep. Not a hard sob, but just that slight body-shaking cry of a person who has nothing left.

"Calliope?" Bryce calls.

I don't respond.

He calls my name again.

When he grips my hair and pulls my face to look at him, I let him drag me around without resistance. I think of the other path I almost took and what I'd be like now if I'd gone down that road. And that's what I give him.

Lifeless eyes.

No expression.

Soulless.

He snaps in front of my face several times.

I stare past him to the wall.

In my periphery, I see him smile in satisfaction. A chill I pray he doesn't notice runs down my spine. He is such an evil fucker even hell would spit him back out.

He gets off me, tossing me down to the table like I'm a used tissue. *Oww.* Christ, I can't think about how battered and bruised my body is right now. I don't try to check or assess the damage. I don't move one inch from where he deposits me, not even to shift into a more comfortable position. I keep my eyes vacant, too.

Bryce waves a hand in front of my face, then laughs loudly when I don't react.

"See, Carl? It just takes one session sometimes to break a bitch. Like a good branding, they're never the same after. Though I put in a couple months prep time with this one. My ultimate gift to my good old pal, Jackson."

"Amazing," the other man says. "Are you sure it's done?"

Bryce laughs again. "Just look at her."

He slaps my sore ass and it takes everything in me not to snarl at him and bite his fingers off. But I'm just praying they're done with me. Please, please, let them be *done.*

"Here, I'll show you," Bryce says.

I steel myself. I just stayed strong through the worst hell imaginable. Whatever this is, I can handle it. They're almost gone, I can feel it.

Bryce's energy is winding down and he's the one running the show. Still, in spite of all my determination, my stomach sinks when Bryce walks back over toward me.

I force myself immobile when he nears. I don't tense my jaw or flinch or even flick my eyes.

He picks up a cold cup of coffee and pours it directly on my face. I keep my cover and barely move.

The pulling out his intestines idea is too human. I should cut off his balls and cock. Dull scissors. Without anesthesia, obviously. But I shouldn't kill him right away.

I don't react even when Bryce spits on me after the coffee runs out.

Bryce and Carl laugh like this is the funniest thing since SNL was invented, and I huddle on the table, doing my best to look traumatized and out of it.

No, Bryce should live a long, long life, locked up with his cock and balls rotting in a jar beside his cell—

Then, I don't know whether to thank God or not since after this afternoon, I'm not sure I can ever believe in him, but Bryce cuffs Carl on the shoulder, drinks are mentioned, and they both leave the room.

As soon as the door clicks behind them, I roll my battered body off the table.

Oww.

Mother of *Christ.* One arm curls over my breasts and my other hand desperately covers my nether region as I crumple to the floor.

It hurts everywhere.

It hurts, it hurts, it *hurts.*

Then there's just blank space in my head. My face is smashed against the rough office carpet, but I don't move. My limbs seem paralyzed even as I can feel myself start to shake from head to toe.

Shock. I'm in shock. That's what this is.

I blink, but it's like suddenly my brain is working in slow motion. I did what I had to in order to get through it, but now, now I— I—

A noise from the corridor beyond the door jerks me back to the present. Fuck. What am I doing? It's not safe yet.

They could come back.

That thought jerks me like an electric cattle prod jolting me into action. I'm up off the floor and reaching for my clothes.

I squeeze my eyes against the memories of Bryce pulling the shirt off my shoulders and roughly jerking the skirt off at another point.

No, no, no. I can't let myself go there. Not if I want to get out of here without going catatonic.

I'm stronger than this.

I didn't let what they did break me while they were doing it. I sure as fuck won't let it now afterwards.

I refuse.

I fucking *refuse.*

And that means I have to get the hell out of here. Maybe Bryce's really gone for the night, maybe that was all a ruse to fuck with my head and let me think it was done before they come back and it starts all over again. I'm not hanging around to find out.

I pull my skirt up and zip it closed. I ignore the numbness of my fingers and force the tiny shirt buttons through their corresponding holes. My feet get shoved in my heels.

One thing and then another. I just have to get out of the building. Left foot. Right foot. Out of the building and away from here. I grab my purse and rush for the door.

My heartbeat ratchets up to a thousand beats per minute in a sudden panic when I grab for the doorknob. What if he locked me in here until he could come back for me later?

But it turns easily. Oh, thank God. Maybe he does exist. Or she. If there's a God, it's definitely a she, maybe that's my takeaway from today.

I bolt down the dimly-lit hallway and into the reception area. It's long past business hours and the whole place is empty. I feel the same fear when I press the elevator button that I did when I went for the doorknob, but again, the button pings and opens with no problems.

With every level the elevator descends, my heart starts to slow. But it's only when I'm breathing the warm, humid Bay Area night air as I scramble away from the Gentry Tech building that it finally sinks in—I made it. I'm away from him.

I'm safe.

I let out a large, body-shaking breath, but I do not cry.

I'm going to be a new version of myself going forward, and the new Calliope Cruise has no more room for tears.

CHAPTER TWENTY

The next week, I alternate between curling in on myself in bed and running to the shower to scour myself until the water runs cold. Then it's back to bed. At least until the memories of *that day* sneak their way past the tripwires I've set up in my mind.

Inevitably they find their way in and I remember every disgusting touch. The rush of degradation and filth swarms me all over again. I can't breathe until I'm scrubbing at my skin under water that's so hot it's all but scalding.

It brings a little relief. Momentary. Fleeting.

But that's how I'm handling life these days.

Minute to minute.

Breath to breath.

Which is a joke because I'm still suffocating most of the time.

At least it got better once Shannon left. I didn't have her on my ass, asking me every other second what I was doing to get Charlie back.

Another knife piercing my lungs.

Because I haven't been able to face Jackson, even enough to call to check in about the family court lawyer. It's just another thing I'm failing at.

I should never have allowed Jackson to be a go-between for his lawyers and me. If he's still offering me the services of his lawyers after everything, then I should have direct access. Jackson can't be involved at all.

And I'll make it clear to him the next time I see him. I *will*.

But, I shudder and pull my comforter tighter around me, I just can't handle that confrontation today.

Tomorrow, I'll do it tomorrow. Although, that's what I've been telling myself all week.

Shannon left to visit our parents yesterday and I breathed a sigh of relief as soon as I heard the locks click behind her as she left.

Finally, I was alone. I didn't have to put on a mask for anyone. I could simply be. Be as empty as I felt inside. No more pretense. No more... anything.

I close my eyes and let myself start to sink again. My limbs become liquid. One with the mattress.

One. Two. Three. Four. I continue the endless counting. When I get to ten, I start over again at one. The numbers and the distraction they provide are eternal. There don't have to be any other words in the world. No other realities except these ten words.

Numbers have shapes. I think I read somewhere once that for some people, numbers have colors. Smells. I like that idea.

And really there are eleven numbers to get to ten.

Zero comes first.

Zero is black. Zero smells like bleach.

I want to bathe in zero.

Zero surrounds me until it's the only number I can say, whispering over and over in my mind until it's my mantra. *Zero, zero, zero.*

It lays out in my mind like my high school track around the football field. Zerooooooooo. Nothing. Endless around and around and around.

If I do it right, I can trick my brain into not thinking at all. A buffer against all thought. Which is a safe harbor when my own mind is full of jagged and bloody places.

But no, no, I can stay safe in the shallows with my focused zero, zero, zero, zero, zero, zero, zeeeeeeeeeero, zero, zero, zero, zzzzzero,

zero, zero, zero, zero, zero, zero, zerrrrrrrrrooo, zzzzzzzeeeer-
rrrrrrrroooooo, zero.

It stretches and flexes in a million permutations. It's perfection.

Zero, zero, zeroooooooooooooooooooooooooooooooooo—

Knock, knock, knock, knock.

I blink, startled at the noise. It was loud and close. Like someone
knocking at my front door. Who's there? Who could it be? My whole
body goes taut for a long moment.

The string of rapid-fire knocking comes again.

I close my eyes and shrink back into the mattress. Probably just
someone selling something. While most of the time I'd eagerly head
toward the door, hoping it was Girl Scout cookies' season, the last
thing I want to see right now is another human being. I pull my
comforter over my head. Zero, zero, zero, zzzzzzzzzer—

"Calliope, open this door," comes a muffled shouting. I shoot to a
sitting position in my bed, the fastest I've moved in days.

Even through the door, I recognize that voice.

Jackson.

"Open the door, or I swear I'll break it down," he shouts. "You
haven't answered your phone in days and I swear you have five seconds
before I'm coming in. Five, four—"

Shit! Motherfucker is probably crazy enough to do it, too. I
scramble out of bed and dash toward the door.

"Three, two—"

My hand is at the deadbolt before I fully realize what I'm doing.
It's flipped and the door is open in the next second.

My chest heaves up and down as the bright midafternoon summer
sunshine fills my entryway. That is, apart from the large shadow that is
Jackson Vale blocking the door. I wince and squint and take a step
back from him.

He's silent and tall and imposing and immediately he reminds me
of everything I've been hiding from all week.

Pain.

It hurts everywhere.

Just seeing him makes it all as raw as the first day, as when
they, they—

"I'm alive." My tone is clipped and pissed and I don't try to hide it. *Get rid of him.*

I have to make him go. I need a shower. My skin is itching with filth. Have to wash it off. Now. Make him go, make him go, any way I can.

"You satisfied? Surely I'm not the first girl ever to not take your calls." I roll my eyes, "or hell, maybe I am, so let me translate. It means I just didn't want to see you. Take a hint."

I try to shut the door in his face, but he puts out a hand, palm up, and easily stops the door from closing.

"What's wrong, Callie? Is it Bryce? Is he somehow forcing you to ignore me?"

I cringe but the knife's already sliced deep. That name. Oh God, even hearing the monster's name... Zero, zero, zero— Bryce's face flashes. Zero, zero, zero, zero— That sadistic grin.

Why isn't it working? I slap a hand to my forehead. It's been working for days and then Jackson Vale shows up and all the sudden the fucking hurricane is about to burst past the levee. No. Fucking *no*!

"Look, I just don't want to see you right now. It's not a discussion." I go again to close the door.

"The hell it's not," Jackson says, and this time he not only keeps me from closing the door, but moves like he's going to shove his way past me into the apartment.

"Don't you dare!" I shout. I don't know if it's my words or the shrillness of my voice that stopped him, but he freezes. I don't fucking care. The fact that he was even about to—the gall of this guy— Of *all* of them.

He's a foot taller than me and I should be intimidated, but I'm not. I get right up in his face.

"You think you have the right to just come into my apartment when I told you no? You think you can just do that because you're a man and stronger than me? That you have the right to do any fucking thing you want? I told you *no*!"

His face blanches and he takes a backward step so that he's clearly on the opposite side of the threshold, outside the door.

Too fucking late, pal. Way too fucking late.

"No," he holds up his hands, "no, Calliope, I would never think that. God, no. I just thought this conversation should be had in private —but of course I'd never—if you're uncomfortable—" he stops talking, as if finally realizing he's just digging a deeper and deeper hole for himself.

"Jesus." He drags a hand through his hair, looking furious at himself. He looks back up at me and his eyes are tired and haunted.

"Forgive me, Calliope. Even though, shit, it's unforgiveable. No is always no, no matter what, no matter where or when." More than haunted, he looks anguished as he says it. "I've just been so worried. You were going to hand in your resignation at Gentry Tech on Monday, but then I never hear from you again. I've been going crazy all week. Please, I just need to know that you're okay."

"I'm fine—"

He's shaking his head already. "Stop bullshitting me! I can tell you're *not* okay."

I grab onto the door handle so hard I think it might shatter. No, it's me. I might shatter.

Why is Jackson doing this to me? I feel the scratching of my throat and I hate it. *Hate it.*

What, I'm going to cry *now*?

Fucking *now*?

After everything else, this is gonna be the thing that breaks me— stupid fucking Jackson Vale and his goddamned compassion?

Because I can fucking feel it. Cracks in the dam I spent the past week fortifying with every ounce of my strength—I took what happened and I sank it deep, deep down and I've sealed up each and every goddamned fucking emotion until my soul is a calm, placid lake on a windless morning.

There is no more storm or tempest and the things that lay buried in the cold, lightless depths of that lagoon need to remain undisturbed forever.

But that can only happen if I remain in control.

Absolute control.

So I do the only thing I can do to make Jackson Vale disappear.

"God, what makes you think you're such an expert on my life? You can *tell I'm not okay?* Because you have known me, what, all of a month? There's this magical thing called listening to the words that come out of someone's mouth. I'm *fine*."

"And even if I wasn't," I enunciate each word pointedly and manage to look Jackson in the eyes, forcing a glare. "What in the hell makes you think I would confide in you? Again, our whole *four weeks* of barely knowing each other?"

I can tell from the stubborn set of his jaw that he's still ready to argue with me about some kind of connection with me so I push even harder. "Or is it just that I let you put your cock in me?" I arch my eyebrow and let the sarcasm drip from every syllable.

"Fun fact, that doesn't mean that you know me or that you suddenly get any say in my life at all. You don't get to barge into my apartment. You don't get to demand that I tell you things. You don't get to stalk me, come to my house, and ask me why I'm not returning your calls. None of this," I wave my hand between him and me over the threshold of my doorway, "is appropriate behavior."

Jackson's frame seems to fold in on itself. The posture looks all wrong on him. He's a confident man, so assured in everything he does. But my words have made him second guess everything.

It punches me in the chest, seeing him like this, but I immediately numb myself to it. It doesn't matter. It doesn't *matter*. He'll get over it. My points are valid anyway. To any outside observer, his behavior could be interpreted as problematic. Or at least it would have been if it was any other man than Jackson.

Because Jackson cares for me. My throat constricts. He was worried. He knew I was walking into Bryce's den. And he was right to be worried, wasn't he?

Hands. Hands on my body. Everywhere. Sweat. More hands. I'm choking, oh God, I can't breathe—

NO. Zero, zero, zero, zero, zero, zero, zero, zero, *zero, zero, zero, zero, zero,* ZERO, ZERO, ZERO, ZERO, ZERO, ZERO, ZERO, ZERO, *ZERO, ZERO, ZERO*—

"Callie? Calliope? Callie, are you all right?" I come back to myself just to see him reaching out to me. He stops himself even as I cringe and yank back. It doesn't go unnoticed.

I watch as his jaw goes taut. He takes two steps back from me and puts his hands out, like someone might do when they're trying to soothe a spooked animal.

Shit, is that how he sees me? Is that what I am?

He looks like he's about to say something, but I know I don't want to hear it. I can't handle any of the questions or observations or anything else from him.

My own voice has no inflection at all when I ask, "Do I still have a position at your company? If I do, where and when should I report?"

"Callie, please talk to me. If it's something Bryce's doing, if he's blackmailing you or hurting you in any way, I swear I'll—"

Well, that's that. I live in Silicon Valley, and I have at least one contact. I just need to track down a number for Mr. Henderson, the guy from Lockheed I met at the charity.

This is what new Callie does. She sees a problem and attacks it. No room for sentimentality.

Jackson doesn't physically halt me from closing the door this time. It's just his voice.

"Stop! Dammit, Calliope. Of course you have a job at CubeThink. I told you that you always would, regardless of whether or not you ever see me socially again."

His voice is firm but no less intimate as he takes a step closer, though he still doesn't cross the doorway. "I always keep my promises. The law firm will also continue handling your custody case pro bono. I don't have to be part of it at all if that's what you want."

"That's what I want." I swallow, my eyes on the floor. "Also, if I could get the information for the lawyer so I can contact him directly going forward."

He nods and doesn't try to disguise how bothered all of this is making him. "I'll email you the lawyer's information."

For a second I think that's it. That he's going to leave it there. But of course, being Jackson, he doesn't.

He maneuvers his face to try to catch my eyes, but I keep my gaze firmly averted. "You never have to worry about any of it falling through —the job or the lawyers. But I do hope that eventually you'll feel like you can open up to me, Callie. Even if it's only ever as a friend. You're an amazing woman and I'm privileged to know you."

Damn him. Damn him to hell.

My whole chest feels warm and hurts at the same time. I'm hollow inside, but with every word he speaks, it's like I can feel the ache of the emptiness, the contour of all that's missing. *Zero.*

I stiffen my back and swallow hard. *I am in control.* I am fucking *in control.* No more zeros. I will count to ten until I've made it to a billion a million times over before I fucking crack, I swear to God.

Jackson's voice is soft as he continues, "You start next Monday. Go to the seventeenth floor and ask for Marissa in HR. She'll get you your security badge and then introduce you to your team. I was going to do that but," he hesitates, "I imagine you would prefer her."

It sounds like one last lifeline he's holding out to me, but I do what I have to. I quash it. My eyes are still on my shoes as I answer. "Yes, I think that would be best."

Even from the corner of my eye, I can see the pained expression that crosses his face. I force myself to ignore it.

"Goodbye, Jackson."

"Goodbye."

I feel his lingering stare but I don't look up again. Moments later the charged air feels empty and I know that he is gone.

EPILOGUE

One Month Later

My self-defense instructor is a bad ass. When she talks, people pay attention.

"Watch closely," Lydia's voice sings out. "Reach behind you, grab the attacker's shoulder— though in real life you can grab anything you can get your hands on, even an ear—then use your hip as a fulcrum to flip them over."

She repeats the move at the front of the class. I watch in awe as she flips a man in full padding almost twice her size with apparent ease flat onto his back to the mat at her feet. The man lets out a small roof of surprise, but he's smiling the next moment as Lydia holds a hand down to help him back to his feet.

I watch Lydia's body as she moves. Her small frame is strong and graceful and packed full of muscle. She's everything I aspire to be.

When I was searching for self-defense classes a few weeks ago, I just wanted one that was taught by a woman. I had no idea I'd find a friend in Lydia.

After my second class which meets at a local gym, I stayed after. I saw a punching bag, started hitting it and then couldn't stop. I just wailed on the damn thing.

I had no idea what the hell I was doing, of course. It just felt so good to finally *hit* something. I'd done what I promised myself I would —I kept my shit under control. I didn't break, even when that horrible afternoon replayed on repeat in twisted nightmares over and over and over.

The nightmares didn't vary much. Always those sweaty hands holding me down on that goddamned table. The stink of men and sweat and sex. Except in the nightmares the afternoons never end. I'm kept there for eternity, chained like a dog as their slave—

So yeah, I was there smacking the hell out of the standing bag that was almost as big as I was until a soft voice stopped me.

"Hey, aren't you in my six-thirty class?"

"What?" I was in such a haze, releasing my fury on the bag it took me a second to register the petite woman with mocha-colored skin and intelligent hazel eyes.

"You know," she said conversationally, "there's a reason that you're supposed to wrap your knuckles up before you start slamming the bag like that."

She nodded in the direction of my hands. I followed her gaze, only then realizing my knuckles were bloody.

Holy shit. How long and hard had I been going at it?

"I... um..." I dropped my hands, only barely fighting the impulse to put them behind my back in a pathetic attempt to hide them.

"Come with me," Lydia said decisively. "I've got a first-aid kit in my locker."

I followed along after her. I was embarrassed, but she seemed assured about what to do and even a quick glance at the mess I'd made of my knuckles told me they'd be hard to patch up on my own.

Shannon was home after the visit to our parents, but we weren't on the best of terms right now. She stayed in the apartment only because it would look better to the courts, she believed, if Charlie had two stable adults to come back to if and when the custody grant was repealed. But Shannon barely spoke to me. No matter how much I swore the drug test was a false positive, she was convinced I was lying and it was my fault Charlie'd been taken. Just the thought of my sister made me want to head back out to the heavy bag, bloody knuckles or not.

"You live around here?" Lydia asked and I was glad for the distraction.

"Campbell." Everyone around here was familiar with the neighborhood just south of San Jose.

She nodded, confirming my thought. "You?" I asked.

"Just moved into Cambrian Park."

"Nice," I smiled. It was the neighborhood just south of Campbell, but much nicer. "I feel like that's where everyone in Campbell wishes they lived. Sometimes half a mile makes all the difference in the Bay Area."

She nods and laughs. "Don't I know it. Me and my roommate just moved from a total shithole in Oakland."

We walked into the locker room. "Head to the sink. I'll grab my bag and be there in a sec."

I did and she was back beside me in a couple minutes.

I put my hands underneath the tap and Lydia helped me washed the blood off. I grimaced when I saw the damage underneath.

"Well that's pretty," Lydia acknowledged.

"Yeah, I'm a real work of art."

Lydia looked at me compassionately but she didn't hold back from liberally pouring the peroxide on both hands. I held my own even though it stung like a bitch.

Lydia made a noise of approval. "Ooo, I do love the strong, silent types," she said with a flirty tilt to her head.

"Oh," I said, suddenly flustered. I hadn't realized she was looking at me *that* way. "Look, I'm into guys. Or well," I look at the floor, "I was. I mean, at the moment I'm not actually into anyone or anything." I shuddered. "None of it. *At all.*" Right, so that came out way too vehemently. Um, and all that shit before it was major foot-in-mouth syndrome too because she probably wasn't coming on to me at all, and even if she was, I just made it all super-fucking awkward.

I looked back up at her. At the beginning of my word vomit her eyes were sparkling, but now her mouth was a flat, unamused line.

Goddammit. The first time someone was nice to me in forever and I went super-freak on them within ten minutes of them talking to me one-on-one. Shit. I was about to grab a paper towel to dry my hands and rush out of there when her voice stopped me.

"Women come to self-defense classes for all kinds of reasons." Her voice was quiet in the busy locker room. Women bustled all around us, but at our little corner sink, she spoke loud enough so only I could hear. "Maybe they've just moved to the city and want to learn how to protect themselves. Or their friends are doing it so they sign up too. Maybe they see some movie or read a book that scares them or inspires them about women empowering themselves this way. But then there's another category of people."

She paused, her eyes briefly meeting mine in the mirror before she squeezed antibiotic cream onto several large Band-Aids, which she then applied carefully to my knuckles.

"Do you want to know about this last category?"

I didn't say anything, barely even dared to breathe.

"It's mostly women," she went on calmly, her eyes on the task of bandaging up my hands, "but not always. This group comes to the class because they're scared. Or angry. They are in pain for sure. They've been hurt in the past. They've been abused, sometimes in the worst ways possible."

My stomach sank and I felt sweat on the back of my neck that had nothing to do with the forty-five-minute session at the bag. God, how did she know? Was what they did written all over my face? Would every stranger know my worst secrets within three minutes of meeting me, without me ever saying a word?

That I'm defiled. Wrong. Filth. Disgusting. I looked beyond Lydia to the shower stalls that line the walls. If she wasn't holding my hands to bandage them, I'd be scratching at my skin. It's there again, that sense of dirt that goes down to my bones.

She finishes applying the last Band-Aid.

"But you want to know something else about these people?"

I didn't nod or shake my head. I didn't meet her eyes in the mirror anymore either.

She grasped my uninjured fingers in her hands and squeezed. "These are the strongest, most resilient and amazing people I've ever met." Her voice was still a whisper, but the strength in it felt like that of a preacher giving a sermon.

"The fact that you are coming to my class, making a stand against your abuser and saying no!" She shouted the last word like she taught us to do in class on the first day—no matter that we were in a locker room with other strangers milling around. She shouted it so loud it echoed off the concrete walls.

For good measure, she shouted again, "No! We say no! To ever being abused again," her voice then went back to a whisper.

"Amen!" called out several women, including an aging elderly woman with sagging breasts, walking around with a towel wrapped only around her waist who raised her fist in solidarity. Okay, that was an image I didn't necessarily need, but yay sisterhood and all that.

My attention re-directed to Lydia when she continued, "That would be difficult enough for normal people. But for people like us?"

That was when I saw it. She didn't look at me and automatically know what I'd been through because it was somehow rubber-stamped on my forehead. No, she saw it because like recognizes like. She'd known abuse firsthand. She'd known powerlessness while animals stole control of her body.

I couldn't even blink, couldn't process what it meant to meet someone like her. Someone like me. To be able to talk to someone else who understood. Not just that, but to meet someone who had obviously survived and was managing it a hell of a lot better than me.

"For people like us, taking a stand like this is like conquering Everest. No," she shook her head. "It's more than that. Climbing a mountain is something that normal people set out to do. That's a goal they set their minds and discipline their bodies for.

"But us?" Her brows scrunched together in pain. "We don't get a choice. Whether we want to or not, we're dragged back to hell on a regular basis, forced to face our demons." She tilted her head down, eyes direct. "Only way out is to jump into the hottest pot of brimstone and burn those fuckers alive, no matter that it burns us up right along with 'em. That's the trick—if you can be reborn stronger through the process. Some make it. Some don't.

She moved her grip from my fingers to my upper arms and kept her eyes locked on mine. "But hon, you will. I see it in you. You will make it through."

Then she hugged me. Here was this woman who was all but a stranger to me, saying the exact words I hadn't known I needed to hear. Emotion churned in the dark lake, and it took several hiccupping breaths to keep the tide back. I couldn't afford it. I wouldn't let it all loose simply because I'd found a kindred spirit. I just couldn't.

When I pulled back from Lydia, head nodding hard, jaw clenched, her smile was compassionate, as if she understood exactly what I was trying to do. If it had been any other person, I think I would've resented it. But she *knew*. It was a knowing I wouldn't wish on my worst enemy. But there it was, something neither of us could change. A tie of battered bodies and spilt blood that made us sisters more than blood ties ever could.

"Callie," Lydia's sharp voice calls me back to the present. "You're up!"

I blink and realize the whole class is looking expectantly at me. Right. I hurry and jog up to the front of the class. The padded 'attacker' is much more intimidating up close than he was when Lydia was so easily tossing him around a moment ago.

Lydia grins at me when I join her side. "You got this."

She sounds so confident.

I stretch my neck and shake out my hands. I got this. I got this. I glance up again at the volunteer. Mike, was that what she said his name was at the start of class?

He's smiling in what I can only assume he feels is a non-threatening manner. But all I can feel is the prickling sensation that he is way the fuck too close to me.

"All right, Callie. What are the steps to take if he grabs you?" Lydia asks.

For a second, my mind is a complete blank. Hands. Men grabbing me. Sweaty hands holding me down. Goddammit. One, two, three, four, five, six—

"Remember the steps," Lydia's voice breaks in.

I take a deep breath in and let it out slowly through my teeth. The steps. Remember the steps. "Vocalize. Disengage. Run."

"Excellent."

We've practiced the moves involved in different attacker holds so many times they're supposed to ingrain themselves in muscle memory. That way if an attack actually happens, my body should take over without thinking. Then again, I've only been at this for three weeks. How much muscle memory can I have really built up in three weeks?

"Are you ready for Mike?"

I take another breath to center myself and then nod. I know in a real-life scenario I wouldn't have time to prepare for an attacker, but Lydia is adamant that class feel like a safe space for every student. The whole idea of this is to prepare us. And that means working at our own pace. Some of the more advanced students allow surprise attacks, but I'm not there yet.

Mike doesn't move until I drop my hand in the prearranged signal.

And even though I know it's coming, God, I'm expecting it, that's the whole point of this—there's still a moment when his arms drop in a hold around my neck that my body just absolutely shuts down.

I'm back there. I'm fucking back there. I can't breathe. Oh God, I can't breathe. *Say you're hungry for my cock.* It's the nightmare, but the nightmare is real. There's a man's body at my back. His heavy arms around my body.

Oh God, no—

No, no, no—

"NO!"

Someone is shouting in my ear. Lydia. It's Lydia. I open my eyes and see my friend. And then my whole class. They're all shouting *no.* Lydia's eyes are on me, eyebrows raised in encouragement.

"NO!" she shouts again and this time I join her.

"NO!" I shriek. When the word rings through my vocal chords and echoes off the walls of the room, I feel the power of it. The attacker has his arm around my neck in what would be a chokehold if he were pressing any harder, but in a sudden rush of adrenaline, I realize I know what to do.

I turn my neck to the side so my throat won't be crushed and I can take full breaths again. Then I raise my elbow and jam it as hard as I can into the attacker's stomach. I hit the soft padding of the safety suit, but I'm too in the zone to care.

Get him off me! Get him off. That's all I can think or care about. Get his fucking hands off my body. I lift my foot and slam it down on his instep. Again, the stupid protective padding stops it from doing any real damage.

So then I go for the move I know this lesson is all about. God, I don't know if I can do it, but I'll try, because I know it will get me free of his hold. I could call stop and the exercise would be over. In this room stop means stop—but damn it, what if this was real life?

Because I know that outside this room, words don't stop anyone. Instead of paralyzing like it normally might, the thought only propels me.

I scream, "NOOOOOOOOOOOOO!" then reach behind me, grab the top of the attacker's safety suit at the collar, lever him at my hip, and flip him over my body.

I barely even register it, but he's spun and on the mat at my feet. Just like that. His weight wasn't even an issue. I don't get how. But it worked. It fucking *worked.*

I start laughing as the class claps. Lydia puts her fingers between her lips and lets out an appreciative whistle like we're at a ballgame or something. I take several steps away from the man groaning on the floor, a little disbelieving. For the first time since all those weeks ago when Lydia grabbed my arms and told me I was going to make it through this stronger than ever, I believe her.

I wrap my arms around myself and laugh. I look to the ceiling and think of my son, of how my lawyers have worked it so tomorrow I go in for a new drug screening. It's a much more accurate follicle test this time which can prove I haven't done drugs over the past ninety days. In addition to retesting the original urine sample at a lab that can discern street drugs from other substances that can cause false positives.

What does all this mean?

I'm going to survive what was done to me.

I'm going to get my son back.

Life is a shit storm. Still, it's one I'm going to make it through. I might come out beaten, battered, and more than a little bit bruised.

But no fucking way am I broken.

EPILOGUE II

JACKSON

I stomp through the parking lot of Callie's apartment building after she tells me to leave, furious, but not at her.

Gentry. Bryce Gentry, that fucking snake. He did something to her. He *hurt* her. Somehow. Some way. What the *fuck* did he do to her?

I'll kill him. I'll fucking *kill* him.

I shouldn't have left him breathing this long. I of all people know exactly what he's capable of.

"Fuck!" I shout and kick the apartment's dumpster as I pass.

Which only gets me a sore foot and makes some kids playing soccer near by shoot me looks like I'm crazy.

Which I am. For her. Everything for her.

And he *hurt* her.

How bad? How bad is it? What did he *do*?

She was afraid of you. The way she jerked back from me when I tried to touch her... Jesus. My stomach drops out at the thought and I swallow back bile. No. Not that.

I walk down the street in the opposite direction from where my car is parked. Toward the park where I first saw her with her son.

I lied to her. I wasn't just *happening* to jog by that day. I live twenty miles from here. I hired a guy to track her movements and he told me where she was.

It was obvious Bryce was up to something with that whole fucked up lunch meeting.

I drop down onto a park bench and drop my head into my hands. It was months ago, but I'll never forget that day. I've run over everything that happened so many times it'll be etched in my memory until the end of time.

I close my eyes and yet again I'm back there, glancing down at my watch while I sit in the back dining room of the Italian restaurant. The first day I met her...

———

What am I doing here? I might be a genius, but taking Bryce Gentry's bait and accepting the invitation to this meeting has left a sour taste in my mouth ever since I agreed to this meeting. I swore a long time ago I'd never let that bastard ever have any influence in my life again.

I can just feel that he's up to his old games.

My jaw tenses.

I could tolerate it if he'd just made a fool of me. But what Bryce Gentry made of me was far, far worse. My whole body tenses at the flood of memories even his name evokes.

That's it.

The Art of War might say to keep your enemies close, but I don't think I can stomach this. Seeing that man face to face... Pretending to exchange pleasantries while he lords my father's patent over me? And that's just the least of the many things he stole from me.

That's why you're going to take him down. Your way, not his.

I was never one for face-to-face conflict like this. I work behind the scenes. Gather data. Construct algorithms. Plan a strategic attack that he'll never see coming. If I try to play his game I'll lose.

What's the saying? A leopard can't change its spots? Well, neither can sociopaths. I have no doubt he's continued using and abusing people like he did me and the others I watched him destroy. And used *me* as a tool to destroy.

Soon Bryce will have to pay for all his many sins.

But not today.

I stand up and drop my napkin on the table, ready to leave as if I was never here.

And then I hear that goddamned voice.

"Jackson!" Even after a decade it still has the ability to curdle my stomach.

I look up and there he is, smiling at me like we're best friends and he didn't set me up for a rape charge.

He rounds the table and embraces me with a slap on the back.

The fucker has the gall to *hug* me.

I'm not a violent man but it's really taking a lot of energy not to grab the steak knife from the table and jam it through his eye socket.

Outwardly though, I just shut down. I go cold. Calculated. In his games, Bryce always watched people's every cue for an in—a way to play and manipulate a person.

I couldn't trust anyone for years after what he did. I have *intimacy issues*, apparently. That's how one of my girlfriends diagnosed me a couple years ago. We broke up about a month later. It was an ugly scene—she was crying loudly and asking me why wouldn't I just open up to her? I could only stare at her without a word and hand her a box to pack up the things she kept at my place. The more she shouted, the quieter I got.

What could I say? That loud people make me nervous and suspicious? She was always so talkative and outgoing.

Just like Bryce.

I didn't even put my finger on the fact that that was the problem until a week later when my apartment was actually silent for long enough that I could finally pinch out a shit again.

I'd been constipated throughout our whole relationship.

Should've been a red flag right there.

My bowels tighten right back up again at Bryce's embrace.

"Bryce," I acknowledge stiffly, looking down at him. I was always taller than him, but over the years, I've filled out as well. I tower over him not only in inches, but in sheer size. He's a slim man, nothing to the brawler strength I've built up working out my various...aggressions. Certain places have been my sanctuary. The gym and the club in particular.

Bryce has always loomed as such a large figure in my mind.

In reality he's small.

A small, pathetic little fuck-head who wanted to play God with other people's lives.

Not anymore.

It's on the tail edge of that thought that I see movement beside him. There's someone with him. A woman.

A very beautiful woman.

Who looks scared shitless for some reason. What am I thinking? She's with Bryce. Of course she's scared.

"And this is?" I ask Bryce, but don't look away from her.

Her eyes widen in surprise and when she swallows hard, I can see her fluttering pulse.

Bryce always surrounded himself with beautiful girls, but this one seems different. She's not throwing herself at him. She doesn't seem dazzled by his looks and charm. In fact, she looks like she doesn't want to be here at all. Smart girl.

So why is she?

Bryce's arm slips around her waist. "This lovely creature is my new personal assistant, Miss Calliope Cruise. Isn't she just a vision?" Bryce pulls back and stares at her with a look of pure adoration on his face.

I narrow my eyes.

Meanwhile the woman just looks confused for a moment but then she pastes on a smile. This is obviously some sort of show. I can only guess that I'm meant to be the audience?

Why? What the *hell* kind of game is Bryce trying to run on me this time? And why after all these years? Does he know I've been investigating him, is that it? I hired the best of the best and they've assured me he's not onto them.

"Not only that," Bryce turns back to me, "but Callie's pursuing a degree in advanced robotics from Stanford."

Callie seems to struggle to catch up to the program until her whole body jerks with surprise. A quick glance shows Bryce's hand rising from her backside. Did he really just slap her ass?

But like a good little puppet, she starts gushing on command: "And I can't thank Mr. Gentry enough for giving me the real-world experience of working at such an amazing company. I'm learning so many things by getting to see the inner workings of how he develops and grooms new ideas through each stage of production."

"Ah, yes," I respond, not bothering to hide my cynicism. "Bryce always was good at taking other people's ideas and pretending they were his own."

I don't miss the tick in Bryce's jaw at the jab.

"Why don't we sit so we can enjoy this delicious lunch I took the liberty of ordering for us?" Bryce holds out his arms to indicate the table.

I stare at him. I want so badly to punch him in his smug face and then get the fuck out of here. But then I glance back at the woman. How is she twisted up in this? I'm not sure I'd feel right just leaving her here with him. Sure, she's still got a pasted-on smile, but I didn't miss the way she flinched when Bryce pinched or slapped her butt earlier.

Bryce destroys everything he touches. This woman, whoever she is, still has plenty of life left in her eyes. He hasn't broken her yet.

Yet.

Goddammit.

I don't play games. It's not my style, it never was. It's why I couldn't see what Bryce was until it was too late.

Time to get what information I can and then get the hell out of here.

This woman isn't my problem.

"Drop the shit, Bryce. You said over the phone you're finally willing to discuss negotiation on the CQ-9 patent. You've never had any use for it and have held it all these years just to spite me. So why on earth would you change your mind now?"

Bryce sits and again waves to the chairs at the table. I note Callie glancing toward the door one last time, like she too is thinking about bolting.

Would it make it better or worse if I told her to run and never look back?

She takes a deep breath and then sits down at the table.

Double goddammit.

I take my seat as well.

"What if I told you I wanted to let bygones be bygones and allow the past to stay where it belongs?" Bryce says. "In the past."

I stare at him like he's fucking insane. "I'd say I know you better than that."

Bryce laughs, a big bellowing laugh from his stomach. He shakes his finger at me. "See? Now that's the kind of honesty I miss! Everyone around me these days just tells me what I want to hear. Yes men. *Yes, Mr. Gentry,*" he mocks in an obsequious voice, "*of course, Mr. Gentry, whatever you please.*" He shakes his head. "Fucking ludicrous."

Bryce sits up in his chair, the humor replaced by earnestness. "I miss you, Jackson. I miss the machines we used to build, the concepts we dreamed up when we put these two brains together." He gestures back and forth between our heads.

This bastard is setting my teeth on edge. I scoff and again have to fight the impulse to get up and leave because I can't stand a second more of this bullshit when he hurries to continue. "Have lunch with us. Listen to what I have to say. No matter what, you walk out of here with your father's patent. Give me an hour of your time."

I breathe out and try to hold my temper. Is this just more bullshit? Would he actually give up Dad's patent? What's the catch? There's always a catch with him. "Just like that?"

"Just like that." Bryce holds up his hands. "I'm a different man from the boy you used to know. Get to know the new me."

I roll my neck to try to loosen the stiffness. It's a lost cause. I look around. The private room we're in is large, but still too damn small. I hate to breathe the same air as him.

Callie takes a sip of her water in the silence. Her arm is long and elegant as she sets the glass down. Her tongue peeks out to catch a drop of water on her lip. Then her cheeks redden as if she feels my gaze on her.

Who is this woman? Where did she come from? Who is she to Bryce?

"So, Jackson," Bryce asks, "how're things with you? How's the company? And Miranda?" His voice is cajoling, like one might sound when ribbing a friend. "Still enjoying fucking my former fiancée?"

My fists tighten underneath the table. Callie chokes on her water and the waitress opens the door, appetizers in hand.

Yes, this is much more the Bryce I remember. My hands relax as I look placidly at my nemesis. I can feel Callie's gaze ping-ponging between the two of us.

She's the only unknown entity at the table. Probably precisely why Bryce brought her. He always did like keeping his opponents off kilter.

The waitress sets down a basket of buttered garlic bread and other appetizers. If she notices the tension in the room, she doesn't show it.

Callie, on the other hand, fidgets and gestures toward the platter. "Appetizer anyone?"

I finally shift my eyes toward her fully.

She really is startlingly pretty. Beautiful even. Large eyes. Lush lips. Big breasts that are impossible to miss. She manages to pull off innocent and seductive at the same time. Like she doesn't quite realize her allure.

Maybe it's all an act.

Maybe Bryce found someone equally as manipulative as he is to bring along for whatever charade this is.

Then again, it's far more like him to surround himself with people he can use. Not fellow masters of his art.

Her cheeks pinken again under my long perusal.

"Of course." I finally say and begin to load one of the small plates with appetizers. Crab cakes and antipasti.

I've let my attention be distracted by the beautiful woman sitting to my right for too long. Maybe that alone is why Bryce brought her along. Like a magician, I'll be distracted by the lovely assistant and not be thinking clearly enough to recognize his machinations for what they are?

I'd hope I'm old enough not to be that sidetracked by a pretty face.

I pick up the conversation again and make bullshit small talk about my company for a minute. The barest minimum for civility's sake. More than Bryce deserves. "As for Miranda..." Ah, Miranda. I allow a smile. We were a good thing while we lasted. But that ran its course long ago. "I thought you'd heard through the grapevine that we've tired of each other."

There's just the slightest tick in Bryce's coolly-aloof expression. It's gratifying, I can't lie.

Bryce smirks. "Couldn't keep the faithless bitch in line either, huh?"

I feel Callie stiffen beside me and if I were willing to give Bryce anything, my body would be tensing similarly.

Miranda and I met because the tech world runs in small circles. She's in hardware. It's only by very strategic and intentional preparation by my personal assistant that I haven't seen Bryce face to face before today. Everyone knows I refuse to be in the same room as him or attend the same parties or events. Miranda had naturally heard the gossip and sought me out because of it, about a year after she and Bryce split. She told me stories that curled my stomach. While never out and out abusive, from the way she told it, Bryce was a cruel lover. I needed no convincing to know it was true.

She was the one who introduced me to club life, actually. She'd gotten addicted to the pain, you see. Bryce was the one who'd taught her to crave it.

True Doms at the club helped her see there could be control in submission. Sanity. It was a gift she imparted to me at a time when I sorely lacking it. Even though Miranda and I eventually parted, I'll owe her forever for that.

And to hear Bryce now speak so disrespectfully of her... it's difficult, but I keep my tone neutral. "Our parting was by mutual agreement after we both enjoyed ourselves, that was all. Maybe if you'd known how to treat a lady, she wouldn't have gone seeking fulfillment elsewhere."

Bryce laughs amiably. He can come off charismatic and personable when he wants to. If you look at him straight on, you'd see nothing of the sociopath lying underneath. I've learned to recognize it—just *barely*, that slight shimmer his eyes. That edge and manic shine that first came out when the policemen's backs were turned as they dragged me out of my dorm room in handcuffs all those years ago. The sly satisfaction of destroying a life.

Callie doesn't see it.

She relaxes and reaches for a crab cake.

And then all of the sudden her body stiffens again and her eyes shoot to the tablecloth. Where Bryce's hand has also disappeared underneath the fabric's edge.

Her eyes jerk back to her plate and Bryce's arm moves in her direction.

It's so obvious what he's doing but my head still wants to deny it.

Not even Bryce would—

He's not really going to—

"Well," Bryce says amiably, "good for you and Miranda. I'm glad you both became so enlightened. And yes, I have seen that Cube-Think's stock was on the rise lately. In fact, that's why I wanted to ask you for this meeting. In the past, we've had such... How shall I put it —" Bryce pauses, and Callie squirms in her chair as Bryce's hand moves ever so slightly.

"—fruitful collaborations," he finishes with a smile.

He is. The fucker is fingering her right in front of me.

And her? Is she being forced or is she into this kind of thing?

God knows I've seen all kinds of kinks play out at the club and I'm not one to judge. But what the fuck? What's going on here?

"Collaborations?" I echo.

I look at Callie. Her eyes are wide and stunned when she glances up and sees me watching her. I glance back at Bryce. "Is that what we're calling it when you steal things that are mine and then market them as your own? But then, you always did like putting your mark on things."

I look back down at his forearm, the muscles flexing rhythmically underneath his suitcoat. Whereas Callie's cheeks were flush before, all the blood seems to drain out of them as her eyes flick toward me and then down at her plate where she determinately stares at her food.

No, not stares. Glares.

She looks furious.

And in the next second, her mouth drops open just the tiniest bit. Her fingers clench around her fork.

I have no idea what she thinks about what Bryce is doing to her—if she wanted it or not, if this was some sick game they prearranged—but she's certainly getting off on it now.

She swallows hard and blinks her eyes, but it's like she has a hard time focusing.

I can't remember the last time I saw a look of such raw, lost, pleasure on a woman's face.

I date, sure, but when I'm out socially, it seems impossible for women to forget who I am. How much money I have.

And at the club, most of the submissives are, well...too submissive. I'm not looking for a total power exchange. God, that's too much responsibility. I have enough of that at work.

I just want a place to exercise my needs and then leave it behind. But every time I play with a submissive it's like they're performing, trying out for the role of permanent slave. It never feels truly authentic.

It's the same with women I date, except they want the part of Mrs. Vale.

No thank you.

But this woman I've just met, I suspect without meaning to, is giving me a glimpse into her most vulnerable self—the one we usually keep hidden away, tucked under the covers in the dark.

When the waitress pushes open the door holding a huge tray of food, Callie's eyes flash up in relief. Like it will mean some kind of reprieve.

Which confuses me all the more.

Does she want Bryce to stop?

Because God knows I'll rip the fucker's hand off if she gives the slightest indication that—

But her mouth only drops open again before she shuts it and then bites on her bottom lip, her large bosom arching ever so slightly forward against the table.

Godfuckingdammit.

My cock hardens in my pants.

This gorgeous woman is coming apart not a foot and a half away from me. I'd have to be made of steel not to respond to her.

But then I look over at the puppeteer behind this whole shit show. He smiles at the waitress like nothing at all is the matter and I feel hatred swell red hot inside my chest.

Is this what he brought me here for?

To mock me with this... this, this, live porn show? Why after a decade call me up just for this? What the hell is this supposed to *be*?

The waitress moves the appetizers out of the way and sets down the main course, pasta with a white sauce, mushrooms, what look like scallops, other herbs and a fancy garnish in the middle.

"Would you like some fresh mozzarella?" the waitress asks, holding a shredder and a block of cheese over Callie's pasta.

Callie's mouth opens and closes as her eyes dance back and forth between me and the waitress.

"Um, I— I—" she stutters, squirming in her chair like she's trying to get away from Bryce's hand. He slides a little awkwardly to the side, making it more than obvious to me and the waitress what he's doing. The waitress takes a step back from the table after glancing down and clearly noting what's happening.

"No," Callie chokes out and then her back stiffens like she was just jolted through with pleasure. "I'm good." The last words come out as a high-pitched squeak. Little beads of sweat dot her brow.

Bryce starts talking some bullshit about the robotics industry in Silicon Valley as he rolls pasta on his fork. Somehow he manages it one handed. He eats lazily, like his other hand isn't so obviously occupied. I barely listen. I'm too focused on Callie, though I only look directly at her every so often.

Because what if this isn't about me at all? Oh, I've no doubt Bryce wanted to fuck with me. But I get the feeling that this is also about screwing with Callie's head more than mine.

She looks alternately freaked out, turned on, humiliated, and completely bowled over by pleasure.

In other words, she doesn't look like she knows what the hell is going on either.

Bryce's playing her too.

He's running another one of his games.

And I of all people know just how far his cruelty can go. Just how damaging the fallout can be.

What the hell is going to happen to this woman?

So gorgeous, fresh and young and vulnerable.

Bryce's going to eat her alive.

She picks at her food, then takes a long drink of water. I'm watching only from my periphery, but I note every movement. So I see when she glances nervously over at me.

Our eyes lock for a moment, then she looks quickly away.

What does she think of *me?*

I probably didn't make a good first impression. Large and dour and imposing. Bryce is the charming one. I feel my mouth settle in a tight line.

Which no doubt makes me only look more approachable. Dumb ass. But it's not as if the situation calls for smiling.

Callie's breath gets shallow again and she takes another swallow of water.

Maybe I'm reading into things that aren't there and this is all perfectly normal between her and Bryce.

She's obviously into this enough to be getting off. She wriggles in her chair again and looks briefly toward the ceiling. Praying?

"That's not the way I remember it, you know," Bryce's voice interrupts my thoughts, his tone changing on a dime from polite bullshit to cutting.

I look over at him, my attention diverted from Callie for the first time in fifteen minutes of him droning on while we all ate. "The way I remember it," he continues, "we were best when we shared things." He arches an eyebrow and it seems like there's some innuendo to his words.

To my side, Callie readjusts herself in her chair, licks her lips, and swallows hard. I want to stare at her.

Actually, I want to yank her away from Bryce, ask her what the hell she's doing with him in the first place, bend her over my lap and after

I've turned her ass pink, order her to finish herself off while I watch. That's what I really want to fucking do.

Instead, internally, I make myself winter.

Snow. Ice. Freeze. Nothingness. Bryce seems like he might finally be getting down to the point for this whole charade. Let's see where all this has been leading up to.

I scoff, picking up the bait he's laid down. "And yet when we supposedly shared, you were the one who always came off with all the," I narrow my eyes, "*prizes* in the end."

"I want to collaborate with you again," Bryce says. "I'm developing a new drone that I'd like you to take a look at. I'll have legal draw up papers so everything's clear up front. Any patents developed would have clear fifty-fifty ownership. But out of it could come knowledge and business relationships that would benefit both of us in the long term."

Aha, so now we've finally come to it.

And yet, when I need to be focusing on what he's trying to get from me, goddammit, his distraction is working.

Callie's edging near climax. I can see it in the features on her face— her half-mast eyes, flaring nostrils, pink cheeks, slightly opened mouth —in her sweet little gasped breaths and heaving breasts, her peaked nipples pointing straight at me through the thin fabric of her shirt—

And then I hear it—the wet noise of fingers sliding in and out of what must be her soaking sex. She's *that* wet— Godfuckingdammit—

Bryce goes on about relationships with contractors and manufacturing plants and how he wants to share his connections with me.

Even distracted as I am, my bullshit detector goes off. "And you'd just hand them over?"

Bryce smiles affably as he nods and then he spits some more bullshit that's too good to be true.

Even if it wasn't, nothing on *earth* could ever make me get into bed with this bastard again.

Enough.

I've seen what he wanted, sat through his bizarre show, now it's time to get out of here. As alluring as she is, the woman is *not* my problem.

"I was never interested in military applications." I shake my head. "And I stopped playing your games a long time ago, Bryce. You said if I sat through this meal, I'd get CQ-9." I fold my cloth napkin and place it beside my plate. "I'm not in the mood for dessert. I fulfilled my end of the bargain." By focusing just on Bryce and not letting myself look at Callie, I've even managed to tame my hard-on.

Right as I move to stand, though, Callie stiffens and lets out a small cry. She grabs the tablecloth and I can't help staring as her whole face transforms in unbridled ecstasy.

I'm immediately rock hard again.

It's not just a flash in the pan either. It goes on and on, shudders wracking her body as her back arches up off her chair.

When it finally ends, she takes a huge gulp of air and her eyes open.

And then she looks utterly mortified.

Her eyes and mouth both pop open wide, not in pleasure, but total horror at knowing that I obviously just saw her climax and knew what was happening all along.

Then her eyes flash to Bryce and her face absolutely crumbles. Her eyebrows drop and her mouth closes. Her shoulders fall and I've never seen anyone look more defeated. I'd swear I just watched her realize something, and whatever it was, it was soul-crushing.

It's not just a guess anymore.

Bryce is up to his mind-fuck mastery as always, and this woman is his latest victim.

Bryce comes over and holds out a hand for me to shake. I don't miss the fact that it's the hand that was just inside her. I take it and grasp his hand in a finger-crushing grip.

His smile never wavers.

"Don't forget I know you," Bryce says. He leans in. "You might be number one in the US, but if you want CubeThink to be internationally competitive, you need an edge. I'm offering it to you. Why don't you mull over the opportunity and get back to me?"

He pulls me forward and gives me another hard pat on the back. Then the fucking bastard slips a thong in the front pocket of my jacket.

By the way Callie cringes and turns away, her face coloring with humiliation, I have no doubt it's hers.

"Perhaps after you've had some time for further consideration, I could have Miss Cruise send over more proposal details."

Bryce holds out an arm for Callie. She takes it, shoulders still hunched, face to the ground. She doesn't look back at me.

When the fucker puts his hand on the small of her back to guide her out of the room, it's almost too much. The image of a wolf leading a lamb to the slaughter stays ingrained in my mind long after they leave.

Thirty minutes later, I was still sitting there, my food long gone cold.

The waitress finally came back and apologetically explained that she needed to clear the table for another party.

As I strode out of the restaurant, I'd already made up my mind. I touched the screen on my phone and call the lead private investigator I've got looking into Bryce.

"Get me everything you can on a woman named Calliope Cruise. ASAP."

I may not have been able to save that girl so long ago. God, because of Bryce, I was even the main participant in her destruction.

But God help me, I'll save this one.

———

Famous fucking last words.

Because here I am, all these months later. I don't know what happened. I don't know what that evil bastard motherfucker *did* to her.

That you didn't stop *him from doing to her.*

I look around the park. Parents playing with their children. It hurts seeing it. I wanted that with her. Wanted it all. Marriage. Kids. She was my forever.

No. Not *was. IS.*

She is my forever.

If she'll have me. If I can ever atone for my sins.

I'm not good enough for her. I've known that all along. But after everything, I'm a selfish motherfucker, and if she'll have me, I'll worship her till the day I die.

I shoot up off of the park bench. Sitting here wallowing isn't doing anybody any good. Action. It's what I've always been best at.

Because before we can have our happily ever after, we have to cut the head off a snake.

———

The epic conclusion to Callie, Jackson, and Bryce's story can be found in BREAK SO SOFT, *available now.*

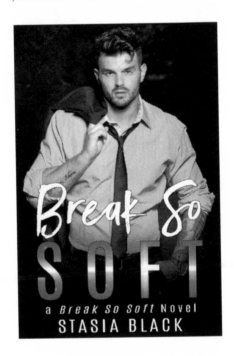

Please consider leaving a few words in review at the retailer where you purchased this book. It helps an author out SO much as we try to get promos with certain advertising sites and gain visibility within the stores themselves.

Want to read an EXCLUSIVE, FREE NOVEL, Daddy's Sweet Girl, a dark stepfamily love story that is available only to my newsletter subscribers, along with news about upcoming releases, sales, exclusive giveaways, and more?

Get it here:
BookHip.com/MGTKPK

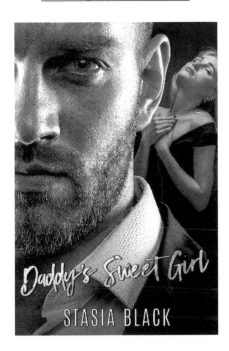

ALSO BY STASIA BLACK

ACKNOWLEDGMENTS

First and foremost, I have to thank my amazing husband, probably in every book I'll ever write. You give me the support and love and cheerleading that keeps me going. Love you, babe.

My Minnesota writer's group gals helped this book get off the ground. Thanks so much, I miss you fabulous ladies! Then I had a group of tremendous beta readers for this book that gave me amazing feedback: Karina (love that you've read all my books, past and present, hugs babe!), Belinda Donaldson (your quick feedback was SO amazing!), Amanda (the very first person to read Crush Me, thank you so much!), Lindsay Johnston (gah, your feedback was so super duper wicked helpful!) and last but not least, Kristin Leigh Jones (you always kick my butt in the best way!).

Thank you to Nicki at Swish Design and Editing for her proofreading pass.

And thank you, beautiful readers! Without you literally none of this would be possible. Thanks for taking a chance on a new author :) If you want to continue discovering sexy romantic stories that ride the motherf#@ing edge, I've got several more books coming out in the coming months.

ABOUT THE AUTHOR

Stasia grew up in Texas, recently spent a freezing five-year stint in Minnesota, and now is happily planted in sunny California, which she will never, ever leave.

She loves writing, reading, listening to podcasts, and has recently taken up biking after a twenty-year sabbatical (and has the bumps and bruises to prove it). She lives with her own personal cheerleader, aka, her handsome husband, and their teenage son. Wow. Typing that makes her feel old. And writing about herself in the third person makes her feel a little like a nutjob, but ahem! Where were we?

Stasia's drawn to romantic stories that don't take the easy way out. She wants to see beneath people's veneer and poke into their dark places, their twisted motives, and their deepest desires. Basically, she wants to create characters that make readers alternately laugh, cry ugly tears, want to toss their kindles across the room, and then declare they have a new FBB (forever book boyfriend).

Made in the USA
Coppell, TX
25 April 2020